Love and Terror

ALAN JOLIS

Love and Terror

Atlantic Monthly Press

NEW YORK

Published simultaneously in Canada
Printed in the United States of America

FIRST EDITION

Library of Congress Cataloging-in-Publication Data

Jolis, Alan.
    Love and terror / Alan Jolis.
        p.   cm.
    ISBN 0-87113-715-1
    1. France—History—Revolution, 1789–1799—Fiction.   2. Fouché,
Joseph, duc d'Otrante, 1759–1820—Fiction.   I. Title.
PS3560.043L6   1998
813'.54—dc21   98-14734
                                                            CIP

Design by Laura Hammond Hough

The Atlantic Monthly Press
841 Broadway
New York, NY 10003

98 99 00 01   10 9 8 7 6 5 4 3 2 1

FOR MY BROTHERS

Paul, Jack, and James

Contents

I.

22 Vendémiaire, Year II
Sunday, October 13, 1793

Those who imagine that one can govern men with pompous formulas and abstract principles know nothing of the human heart, nor the source of power.

—Joseph Fouché in a letter to Wellington, 1815

The Information

I shouldn't be bringing this news. If what I fear is true, I'm a dead man; I know that. If the orders are wrong and we shouldn't have released her, then we'll both be dead, him and me. But even if the orders are right—and I have such grave doubts that I ran all the way from the prison breathless to tell him—he'll want to know why we released her. Why we didn't wait and check with him. I know better than to go through with this. One mistake and they kill you. No mistake at all, and they can still kill you. Only the pregnant avoid shaking the hot hand, and even so it's only delayed until after the woman gives birth, and then she has to go up and shake the hand all the same.

Jesus, what should I do? Escape and flee to the hinterland? Even there, odds are they'll find me. I'll never get through this line, this crowd of lowlifes and no-accounts. One patriot is here to denounce her baker for hoarding flour. Another wants to inform on a nun in hiding. A third heard a soldier cuss that he had not been paid enough and was given worthless paper money.

On this dead Sunday in the dead of fall, as mist curls at the base of Paris buildings and along the wet cobblestones of the rue de l'Ancienne Comédie, the air is heavy. Sounds are muted. Except for a few souls rushing to get out of the October drizzle, the sidewalks are empty.

Suddenly a flow of patriots bursts onto the street singing *La Marseillaise*. Full of wine, drumrolls, and tricolored cockades, the sans-culottes demand price controls with their patriotism, tobacco at no more than twenty sous the pouch, a pound of salt for two sous, soap for twenty-five sous, and the guillotine for émigrés, hoarding merchants, and royalist sympathizers. They rush along in their red liberty bonnets and red-striped pants, dancing the Carmagnole and chanting *Hang all the aristocrats to a lamppost!*

Once they pass, the street is quiet again, and a deathlike silence falls over the city. Rue de l'Ancienne Comédie is narrow and gray. Running parallel to it, the passage du Cour-du-Commerce is even narrower, and the back entrance to the Procope at number 13 of that streetlet has streaked and dirty windows. Here a crowd of informers waits to gain entrance.

What's he doing inside? What is taking him so long? Informers ratting on their neighbors, settling old scores—I've got to push my way in there, or I'll never get through to see him by the end of the day. Every minute I delay will only make this worse. I never knew there were so many old crones denouncing their neighbors.

Louis Larivière, a guard at the Conciergerie, elbows his way through the line of old women and crab-faced men. Soldiers stand at the back entrance with bayonets fixed, barring the way and from time to time administering a beating to those who show too much enthusiasm to get inside. All one sees through the dripping steamed-up windows are waiters preparing tables, washing glasses, mopping the floors.

Larivière imagines the proconsul seated in this rear room, facing the fireplace, his back to the wall. That is why there is so much empty space around him.

I've come here before, usually to give background information and monthly updates, but never with news that is so burning.

⤣

Inside, where only the ticking of a clock punctuates the silence, a man reaches for a roast chestnut, cracks and peels it. Time on this Sunday afternoon is slow, slow as a snail. His boots and black

4

cape drying before the fireplace, his feet warm now, Commissioner Fouché molds a bread ball with thumb and forefinger and remolds it. He has traveled a long way, this *représentant-en-mission*, and he is tired. He feels a need to stretch himself, to bathe and scrub off the weariness. His fingers are stiff.

On the wall facing him is the Declaration of the Rights of Man, decorated with a ubiquitous triangular eye and the words LIBERTY EQUALITY FRATERNITY. Another print shows a woman in a toga, the Republic, holding up a balance, while Industry, represented by a beehive, spills its fruits on the ground. On the other wall hangs a painting of Francesco Procopio del Coltelli dated 1685, the man who started this café as a coffee shop for students. His grandson Marcello sold Le Procope to Dubuisson in 1753, who sold it to Sieur Cusin, who sold it to its current owner, Zoppi.

Mordu, the commissioner's manservant, approaches, escorting a new visitor in from the street to see him. The informer bows his head, waits for permission to speak, then leans forward and whispers: *Citizen, I have seen this. Citizen, I have seen that.*

Fouché usually knows what they are going to say as soon as they open their mouths, but he gives everyone, even the dim-witted, a minimum of ten seconds.

He runs his information gathering in an easily accessible public place. To hide in a back office could lead to accusations of secret intrigue and the greater risk of a crackpot slipping him the knife. He must be careful, though. Since the murder of Marat, Mordu has started frisking and body-searching everyone, even his most trusted agents.

No one stays long. After they are done, they are shown to the back door, and Mordu escorts in a new informer. They advance, stand with their back to the fire, and, with steam rising from their arms and shoulders of wet wool, they spill their guts. Then, hat in hand, eyes wide, they wait while the offender's name is jotted down.

Mordu keeps strict records and pays informers not in paper script but in gold. The price for information on a wanted man or a conspiracy is higher than that for religious ornaments hidden in a basement, but everything has its price. And Fouché trusts Mordu with large sums of walk-around money. The universal solvent, as he calls it, is indispensable in this line of work. Most leave without even counting their coins. A few reckless souls wait for a second raised finger to indicate to Mordu to pay more, but it has to be a good story, one that Fouché has not heard before.

In the street, they jostle and elbow each other to be the next one through the door, but Mordu awaits the sign. The proconsul's hand must go up.

Waiters in white aprons are careful not to come too close. The kitchen has a laboratory where, amid churning gassifiers and bubbling cauldrons, distillation coils *drip-drip* into funnels. The Procope makes its own liqueurs. Recipes for its elixirs of fruit and spice water are codified in *Le Distillateur Français,* and these give the Procope an edge over traditional taverns and wine bars. Zoppi's success with food as with drink lies in his exotic spices: coriander, cumin, musk, cinnamon, coconut. The fare here is for those with refined palates who want to forget that the country is on the verge of a famine. At the Procope, you find the best Burgundy snails, but also *crème bonne amie, oeufs en allumettes, raie au beurre noire,* and the house special, pigeon boiled in syrup of red poppy.

Joseph Fouché does not smoke, play cards, or drink, but he now sips Populo, a liqueur of gray aniseed flavored with amber and musk that leaves a tart licorice taste on the tongue. At his right are the remains of a late lunch, *chou surprise*—a cabbage stuffed with chestnuts, onions, and sausages.

Nenette, the entire nation's sewage, mounds of it, flows through the city and comes to rest at my table, and my prosaic job is to decide what part of the sewage to filter and save for future use. My task is to know who is buggering whom, who is cheating whom, and to what end, for there is no such thing as a private act anymore. If a single young Liberty Tree dies, I have to know whether it is due to human mutilation. Knowledge is power. My eyes and ears have to be everywhere. Plots, counterplots, semiplots, grand designs, intrigues, petty intentions, half-truths, and lies are at my fingertips.

If I do not know something before it happens, why it happens, and for whose benefit, it is not worth knowing.

—A letter, quickly, Mordu!

Fouché was using a brand-new Conté pencil on a small notebook, but now Mordu clears the table and sets out a sheet of writing paper and, from his carrying case, a quill, an inkstand, and some drying sand.

—The minute the Queen is found guilty and dispatched, Mordu, we head back to finish our task in Nevers.

—I'll make arrangements, citizen.

Joseph Fouché, thirty-four, a Breton ex-seminarian, tonsured subdeacon, Catholic priest who never took his final vows, still hears the voices. Today he recalls his father confessor and spiritual guide, Father Merault de Moissy, making him repeat: *The only means of conquering man's inveterate original sin, and indeed the sole path to salvation, is devotion to Christ, whose grace alone redeems human nature.*

Fouché smiles. He is looking inside now. The memory is overwhelming; even his eyes turn inward, recalling the spiritual uplift, the feeling of devotion, ineffable goodness. And cocooned with these rich kitchen smells, a roaring fireplace, and roasting chestnuts, he recalls Father Merault's favorite sayings: *The darker the shadow, the brighter the dawn.* And, *each moment is imbued with a breath of eternity.*

Louis Larivière has made it up to the window, and he can look around into the rear of the restaurant. Against the back wall, he sees Fouché seated with a quill, thinking. Larivière can't believe this.

I am sitting here with news that could send us all to the guillotine, news that will change the course of the revolution and of France, and he is writing down how many candlestick makers and bakers were sent to the guillotine for uttering some unpatriotic oath down in the Bourgogne armpit region of France? I'm so agitated and nervous, my heart is about to leap out of my chest, and this bureaucrat is making us all wait because he is writing another meaningless directive?

Fouché was a priest, and for ten years he wore a cassock and taught physics, math, and logic, but in 1788 his Oratorian Order sent him to Arras, where he met Robespierre and became his close friend. Now a deputy in the National Assembly, proconsul, and *représentant-en-mission,* Fouché reports not only to the Committee of Public Safety but, more importantly, as chief of Robespierre's secret police directly to Robespierre himself (which helps the Incorruptible One bypass the committee.)

Fouché drafts his report to the National Convention:

> In the center heartland of France (the departments of La Nièvre and l'Allier; the towns of Nevers, Clamecy, Moulins, Gannat, Montluçon, Decize, La Charité, Bercy), I can assure my fellow deputies that Christianity is extinct and the cult of the goddess of Reason has taken firm root:
>
> 147 churches have been closed, disaffected, or burned to the ground, and 352 chapels.
>
> All publicly displayed calvaries, statues of saints, crosses, crucifixes, and other sacred images have been destroyed. Chasubles and sacerdotal cloth, stripped of gold and jewels, have been sent to hospitals and old-age homes to provide for the poor.
>
> All clerics have been given thirty days to marry or adopt a child and swear allegiance to the revolution.
>
> The bishop of Moulins, François Laurent, gave up his miter and cross and abjured in the public square, followed by thirty priests.
>
> In Nevers, we led through the streets a donkey covered in priestly garments, with a bishop's miter on its head, and a bible

tied to its tail. The donkey drank out of sacred chalices. Then we burned books, bibles, and nuns' wimples, and the populace danced around the bonfire.

In thirty-five major public squares, we burned a mannequin of the Pope.

The amount of gold melted down and sent this day to the Treasury in Paris amounts to 1,000 marks (250 kilos). This is our fourth such shipment. In addition, I have sent seventeen trunks filled with jeweled crosses, ducal crowns, scepters, candelabras, and silverware.

Let us trample the idols of the monarchy in the dust.

Fouché was born on May 21, 1759, in La Martanière, a tiny village of twenty-three houses near Le Pellerin, close to Nantes. There, on the banks of the great Loire, he grew up with no more than a hundred neighbors, so he knows the provinces well, their closed-in secretive world, their slowness, their deep resistance to change and to directives from the capital. He knows how difficult it is to effect lasting change there. He reviews the documents that Mordu has placed on the table, articles that Zoppi has collected for him in his absence.

September 29—Chaumette, leader of the Paris Commune, reported: Citizen Fouché has operated miracles. He honors the old, succors the infirm, raises the downtrodden, destroys fanaticism, arrests suspects, punishes hoarders. Fouché has done more good in a few weeks than I myself have achieved in a lifetime.

October 2—Deputy Dijannière's report to the convention: What Fouché is doing is for the great good of all humanity.

October 7—Deputy Legendre's report to the convention: The public spirit is finally pronouncing itself in the Nièvre and the Allier. There, thanks to Fouché, republicanism is defeating aristocracy, religious superstition, and federalism.

Fouché now writes to his wife, the daughter of the president of the Administration of the District of Nantes, a man who keeps Fouché's constituents—moderates, landowners, and shopkeepers—under control. They married on September 16, just over a year ago, the week after he was elected to the National Convention. Jeanne has red hair, freckles, and a pale complexion; he has left her behind in Nevers with their two-month-old sickly daughter:

Chère Jeanne,
I am worried about the baby. Let me know how she is doing? And forgive me, I cannot send you any money. I am myself quite strapped.

Joseph

He stops and raises his hands to the fire. A waiter lights a candle in the front room, another sweeps the floor. Fouché loves the orderly silence of men working: setting tables, washing dishes, polishing, burnishing silver, wiping off sideboards, drying. He prefers the Procope in its off hours to when it fills up with loud and inebriated patriots, all wanting to make speeches and bellow their witticisms.

A commotion breaks out at the back of the restaurant, which gives out onto Cour du Commerce. Fouché's handpicked men close ranks to prevent this queue jumper from forcing his way in. His direct-action boys are big, brawny well-paid men, soldiers of public safety, of mustache and muscles, heavy with bandoleers across the chest, and high leather boots; they do not appreciate public disorder.

The queue jumper shouts, *Let me in, let me in!* A gob of spit lands on the ground. *I must see the commissaire, I must see him immediately!*

Mordu, who knows the boss hates interruptions, wades in:

—Who are you?

—He knows me.

—Who are you?

—Tell him Larivière is here, Keeper of the Keys at the Conciergerie, and I do not need to speak to the likes of you.

—Have you any identification?

—Yes, my face.

—Show your travel papers.

—I'm not traveling.

—Guards, frisk him.

—Let me through, don't you recognize me?

—No.

—This is of the utmost importance.

—What is so important?

—Let me through, I must talk to the commissaire in person and to no one else.

At the table by the fire, Fouché checks the time: 5:49 P.M. With a small key, he rewinds his watch, reads the inscription on the back, *To the Master of Complications with love from Nenette.* His watch has never needed repairs. It is a perfect and loyal companion, a simple enamel-faced Breguet in a gold case, bearing number 434.

She will be waiting for me. Nenette spends most of her days waiting for me; I should go to her now, I've had enough. He glances up.

—What is all that shouting, what is going on? He motions to Mordu to bring the man forward.

—Let him through, says Mordu.

The soldiers slowly unclench their hands and let the man go. Mordu checks the man's pockets.

—Your pistol will be returned when you leave.

Larivière straightens his prison guard's uniform. Pushes his bad breath and brown tooth past them. *This is not a good way to start, I shouldn't have come. But it's too late now, I have to go through with it. This is a mistake.*

—Citizen commissaire, I must speak to you in confidence.

Fouché does not want to be pulled out of his reverie. If your love of simple things dies, a part of you dies. He examines his man. Keeper of the Keys Larivière smells of wine and needs a shave. His eyes are small and red. There is nothing trustworthy about an informer, even one worthy of trust, and this one looks like he would not give you the steam off his piss. Larivière has sweat on his upper lip.

The soldiers lean into the room to pick up the conversation.

—I need to speak in great confidence, commissaire.

—Mordu, clear everyone out. Out.

The Gascon hollers for a general retreat, informers first, soldiers second. His elbows and hands fly as he shoves them out. Soon, Mordu shuts the door behind him and stands on the doorstep facing the street to prevent peeping Toms.

Under the table Fouché cocks the trigger and holds his pistol ready. Meetings in private often end badly. At 7 P.M., on July 13, Marat trusted Charlotte Corday, but she had a five-inch kitchen knife hidden in her dress, and it was the last rumor Marat ever heard.

Dealing with thieves, cheats, liars, and turncoats rubs off on us, Nenette. And life too quickly becomes a demonic slut who fills the till with false promises. What we need is more beauty in the world, Nenette.

Larivière puts a hand to his inside breast pocket and extracts a document.

—Citizen commissaire, I thought I should apprise you immediately, that being the arrangement between you and me—uh, concerning the Queen. So I came at once. This order has the signature of Saint-Just for the Committee of Public Safety, and the countersignatures of Fouquier-Tinville, the public accuser, and—

—It has signatures, so what? Get to the point, man!

Larivière flattens the document and, with eyes mad inside his head, approaches a candelabra. The flickering candles cast shadows and play tricks on one's eyesight.

—Citizen, this order came only an hour ago.

Larivière leans forward, warm, damp, and too close. Fouché's left palm glides across the oak table as if to clean it.

Nenette will be wondering where I am and why I haven't come to her sooner or sent word. I must train Mordu to screen my informers and agents better. I should not be wasting my time with housekeeping matters. This prison guard is probably here to complain about his ration card, and I am already late as it is.

—Citizen commissaire, you may not know it, but Marie-Antoinette was summoned yesterday for a preliminary court hearing.

—I know, I know. She was summoned by the prosecutor. So bloody what?

—But today, citizen, it was not the court. Today it was—

The yellowish light shows a patchwork of tiny red capillaries and deltas spreading across Larivière's cheeks. It's the face of a man who would report on his own mother. Fouché reads the document, and a silence descends.

Concerning Marie-Antoinette, the widow Capet, now detained at the Conciergerie: On this 22 Vendémiaire Year II (October 13, 1793), said prisoner is to be taken immediately upon presentation of this order to the office of citoyen Saint-Just. Signed on behalf of the Committee of Public Safety by—

Seven signatures, which may have been forged, follow. Fouché gags.

—You let her go?

—Well, that is what I have been trying to tell you, citizen. This order was presented to us today, and we carried it out to the letter.

Fouché smiles and examines the signatures.

This is a joke, a test, right? But not on the day before her trial starts, that is not likely!

A spark shoots out from the fire as Fouché looks up at the keeper of the keys.

—Concierge Bault followed orders, commissaire, but just to be on the safe side, out of an excess zeal, because that is our arrangement ever since we have had the queen in house—well, I came to inform you.

Fouché is familiar with schoolboy pranks. As soon as he left the Collège des Oratoriens in Nantes, he entered the Seminary of Jesus on rue Saint-Honoré in Paris. With a weak voice, weak chest, and delicate constitution, he studied for the priesthood until he was twenty-three; then his Oratorian Order posted him all over: In 1783 until October, he had a class of twelve-year-olds in Niort; then, until October 1784, fourteen-year-olds in Saumur; until September 1787, sixteen-year-olds at the Royal Military School in Vendôme; and until April 1788, at the Oratorian College in Juilly just outside Paris, he trained a teaching elite. For the next two and a half years, he taught in Arras at the Petit Séminaire. In December of 1790, he became the principal of the Oratorian College in Nantes, until the order was disbanded in May of 1792. So he is used to sawed-off chair legs that collapse as soon as touched, blackboards placed on the edge of a dais that fall off at the slightest pressure of a teacher trying to write with a piece of chalk, glue on chair seats, and so forth. Now he looks around for a trouble-maker or prankster, but this is not school. This is life.

—Correct me if I am wrong, Larivière, but the signatures look genuine enough to you, so you took it upon yourself to let her go?

—Citizen, I only witnessed the transaction. Concierge Bault authorized the prisoner to be taken under guard to Saint-Just's. Bault is the supreme authority at the Conciergerie; he's the governor of the prison, not me.

Fouché rechecks his watch: It is 5:54 P.M. He searches for his boots, his cloak. The room is spinning. A chair leg scrapes the tiled floor.

I can smell Zoppi's expensive meats roasting and his elixirs bubbling. I smell the soldiers in the street and a gallery of spinsters, vagrants, valets, neighbors, spurned lovers, money leeches—all of them straining at the door to overhear. What is he saying? What is so important? I smell the end of day, I smell the guillotine, the odor of despair, boys playing hide-and-seek in dusty attics, and women folding washed linens.

—When did the Queen leave?

—Half an hour ago, commissaire. Not more.

The commissioner's gun barrel glints gray. Larivière had not noticed it before, but it has appeared out of nowhere and is now aimed at his heart.

—Is something wrong, commissaire?

Fouché's eyes fix the silence in narrow slits.

—No, nothing is wrong.

Take yourself in hand, man. Stop grimacing. Act as if this is some simple oversight, a mistake to be corrected. The real devil is vanity; if you worship yourself, you will be dead long before you die.

Fouché dips a quill in ink, scribbles a search-and-arrest order, and dries it with sprinkled sand; then a letter to Saint-Just, which he knows will be undelivered because Saint-Just has just left for the army of the Rhine, after reviewing military strategy with the Incorruptible One. In any case, Saint-Just would not interfere with republican justice; his time is for enemy battalions, not imprisoned widows.

I have to clear this up myself, quickly and quietly.

—Mordu, Mordu!

The back door opens.

—You called, chief?

—Get Lieutenant Pasquier in here immediately.

Larivière jumps up.

—Citizen commissaire, out of a too-great love for the revolution, I wanted to check with you, that is all. Should I not have come here first? Is something wrong? Shall I inform the City Council, the Committee of Public Safety?

Fouché leans over the table, grabs the keeper of the keys' lapels, grabs his sweaty throat. A big man, but Larivière bends at the knees. Fouché presses the barrel of the gun to the man's temple. Dishes clatter; a spoon falls to the floor and skips across the black-and-white lozenge-shaped tiles.

—If you speak a word of this to anyone, you are dead.

Larivière is held too tight to nod.

—Commissaire, my loyalty has never been called into question. Ask anyone who knows me. I have no sympathy whatsoever for Louis Capet's widow. In prison I never showed the Queen leniency of any kind. The Committee of Public Safety knows me for my vigilance and dedication.

The pistol comes down. The trigger is uncocked.

—Larivière, you keep your trap shut. Say nothing. Assume nothing, not even the birthdays of your children.

The big man mumbles.

—Citizen, I do my job at the prison with utmost rigor. That is why I came to report to you straightaway, because I knew it was important.

Another spark shoots out from the open fire. Larivière jumps, but not Fouché.

Pasquier, lieutenant of the Third Mounted Regiment of Civil Guard, enters, salutes, tucks his plumed hat under his arm, receives the order to take a detachment to Saint-Just's office.

—If the Queen is there report back to me. And lieutenant?

—Yes, commissaire.

—Check his home too; if you find Saint-Just, this is for his eyes only. Otherwise I want the letter back.

—Yes, commissaire.

—Mordu, that is enough for one Sunday; clear everyone out.

Mordu motions for the guards in the street to push the queue away from the door.

—Go home, we are done, finished for today, everyone out! Some protest.

—We've waited for hours, my story is crucial.

—Come back tomorrow.

—Tell him I have to see him right now!

—Clear out or you'll speak to my fist.

Footsteps echo on the cobblestones, old muddy wooden clogs, civilian watchdog clogs, riding boots, dainty stylish women's shoes; they grow faint and vanish. Fouché puts a new log on the fire.

Eighty-five hundred soldiers in the city and triple shifts of guards in the Conciergerie, and she escapes? I do not believe this; I do not believe this! The first real policeman was Doubting Thomas. To govern one needs to know, and to know one needs to doubt, to touch everything and gather as many facts as possible.

In the corner of the room, Zoppi's old dog keeps sleeping, jaw tucked between its paws. Through the window, Fouché notices a break in the clouds and a red sun above the rooftops. The sound of horses' hooves fills the air as Pasquier leads a detachment of riders to Saint-Just's office.

So the she-wolf, harpy, crowned monster who drinks French blood has escaped? That libidinous Marie-Antoinette, Queen of Greed and Treachery, the Autri-chienne, is about to make a laughingstock of me?

Fouché sits down, as new flames leap up and wood starts crackling.

—Return to your post, Larivière. I shall bring you the prisoner in thirty minutes.

—The widow Capet, you know where she is? Larivière tries to smile, but it does not quite form; his smiles seldom do.

—Of course. It is my job to know.

Fouché glances at the well-known black-and-white tiles on the floor and the table legs. *I have to tell Zoppi the fleur-de-lys design of this table base is too ornate, too rococo, too ancien régime. There is no such thing as an innocent symbol anymore. Old symbols kill.*

—Larivière, clear the prison courtyard and empty all cells that have a view on the entrance. I do not want any busybodies seeing me enter with the Queen. I want no questions asked. Now get out of my sight.

The keeper of the keys nods and disappears.

Fouché pulls on his boots. His legs are sore, his body sore from the long carriage ride from Burgundy. He is dressed all in black except for a thin red-white-and-blue sash at the waist worn by every proconsul of the National Assembly. But today he is acting on special assignment for Robespierre.

The Incorruptible One charged me with the safety of Marie-Antoinette, to keep her alive until her execution, and the day before her trial she does this to me? She flies the coop! The time on this wet Sunday evening is 6:11 P.M., and the trial starts at 8 A.M., so I have just over thirteen hours left to find the Queen.

Mordu drapes the commissaire's long black cape over his shoulders. He brushes his master's hat and its tricolor cockade then helps him buckle on his sword belt.

I am the heartbeat of the new order and also its cloaca. I can hear the Republic pumping through me, full of life's primal force and energy for change. But am I the only one listening?

His lightweight officer's sword has an elaborate polished bronze hilt and a single-band hand guard across the knuckles. Fouché had the old handle replaced by an ivory one with braided brass wire down the spiral to give it more grip.

I need a bath.

He stands at the mirror and runs his fingers over his stubble. His lips are thin, nose prominent, eyebrows high, somewhat supercilious, but the whole face is bony, tight, and constrained like a small fist.

I need a rest and a shave. I am too thin, the circles under my eyes too black. Nothing attractive or noble is left on a face like this. Police work changes you. It has made my face hard as stone. At thirty-four I am weathered and sallow like an old man.

He uncups his coffee, black and bitter.

—Mordu, get my carriage ready. I will be down in a minute.

He discovers a long blond hair on his shirt sleeve, pulls it off, lifts it up to the light, examines it, then lets it drop to the floor.

—Chief, this came to you for immediate action from Robespierre.

Fouché unfolds a petition signed by three provincial executioners, informing the Committee of Public Safety that hanging is better and safer than the guillotine and requesting a change in national policy. Their arguments are straightforward: First, the blade of the guillotine dulls from overuse. Second, riffraff to be decapitated do not show the same composure as gentlemen. Third, with a heavy caseload unfortunate mishaps occur, especially with unskilled executioners not used to the four-meter height of the uprights. (The power of this instrument is so great that sometimes the blade sinks up to the hilt in the wooden support or causes the head to leap half a meter from the torso, right off the scaffold.) Fourth, the blood flow is so great, one hour's work ruins our clothes, and we cannot wear our shirts or pants a second time.

Fouché jots down his answer at the bottom:

But a noose is not the legitimate self-expression of a sovereign people. The guillotine is.

Joseph Fouché

He hands the petition back to Mordu and climbs the spiral staircase, narrow and dark, where kitchen smells from the restaurant below mix with the vapors of cat urine. On the second-floor landing of 13 Passage du Cour-du-Commerce, in front of room number three, he stops and catches his breath.

Nenette

The revolutionary guard in front of the door salutes Fouché and moves out of the way. Fouché knocks.

No answer.

Another lone knock.

Nothing.

Fouché feels the grain of the rosewood door, soft and smelling of lavender wax. *She is not opening. Good.*

He knocks again, this time three slow and two fast. Then he hears the creaking of the parquet floor inside and her footstep. The bolt slides back, and the door opens.

Her face is so pure and soft, it doesn't need any light but blooms ethereal and blond in the darkened doorway. Her lips are pale and full, and her expectant half-smile waits for him to speak. Nenette is wearing a diaphanous dress of ivory-colored muslin gathered below the breast and fastened loosely with a yellow ribbon. Over her arms and back hangs a simple black scarf. She has a yellow chrysanthemum in her hair but no elaborate coiffure, no stays, hoops, or petticoats.

The flower in your hair makes you look like a freshly harvested luscious fruit, and just glancing at you for a second puts me in a good mood, Nenette.

He enters and closes the door behind him. Her bosom smells of rose hips, she even has blue ribbons on her shoes, as if ready to attend a ball. The whole room smells of her. The bed is rumpled, strewn with books and her sewing.

—I dressed just for you. Don't you like it? She touches the three overlapping ruffled lace collars of her blouse.

—Yes, but we have to leave.

—And I poured your bath the way you like it, Joseph.

—I know, ma belle, but it will have to wait until later.

He glances at the hot water steaming in the tub. The Marseille soap and the bath oils in a blue Limoges dish, the small mirror, the hairbrush—every detail is known to him.

—Nenette, come on, put on your cloak.

—What has happened, Joseph?

—Nothing.

He drapes her dark cape over her shoulders. Her blond hair falls in curlicues to her shoulders, and her whole appearance is pale and ripe. She is not young but her face is cherubic, as though posing for one of those doe-eyed portraits by Elisabeth Vigée-Lebrun, a face made for domestic happiness.

—I will tell you everything later.

She touches his wrist, leaves her fingers there.

—What is wrong, mon ami?

—Nenette, there is no time for long explanations. Hurry, please.

—You work much too hard, Joseph.

—He hates it when Nenette asks female questions or raises objections that have no rational basis.

On the wall an allegorical print, entitled *The Nation*, shows Minerva armed with the pike and hat of liberty, stretching her hand over the flame of the Constitution. *I too must push my hand into the fire and hold it there; that is what tonight is about, strength and fortitude.* Another print shows the hydra-headed dragon of federalism being slain by Virtue. *I chose these safe Jacobin prints to replace your decadent art. The first rule, Nenette, is always to assume spies. And the best protection is to let them see nothing that calls attention to itself.*

—Look at me, Joseph, talk to me!

—You wanted to meet with the Queen one last time and have a chance to say farewell? Well then, hurry Nenette. This is your last chance.

He lifts the hood of the cape over her head.

—Do not let anyone see you.

She smiles and lifts his hand to her lips.

—Can we not go visit Marie-Antoinette a little later, my friend?

—There will be no later. It must be now or never.

—I've never seen you like this. What is it?

Fouché does not give her the chance to confront him, to look into his soul. He opens the door, makes sure that her high heels and rustling muslin follow, then rushes down the stairs and catches up with Mordu.

In the street, where the evening sky is closing in over the mansard rooftops, pink on one side, dark as slate on the other, twenty red-and-blue-uniformed men stand at attention, holding their Le Creusot rifles in tight salute. This is la Garde Nationale. Their bandoleers are scuffed and their Charleville uniforms dirty, but for Fouché these men would go anywhere at any hour of the night, tie up any suspect, remove any aristocrat's assets, distribute them to any poor citizen.

Mordu unfolds the carriage steps and opens the door, and Joseph Fouché and Nenette take a seat on the damask cushions, where all is dark and quiet.

The horses stamp the cobblestones and flick their bridles, as clouds of steam shoot from their nostrils. Riders pull on the reins and yank their horses' mouths up to prevent them from drinking the curbside water.

—La Conciergerie, Mordu, and fast.

Mordu looks bitten, his face askew, as if he wore shoes three sizes too small, but already he has climbed onto the coachman's box and is whipping the horses. The carriage moves past Tobias

Schmidt, maker of pianos, harpsichords, and a wooden apparatus for breathing and working underwater. Schmidt shouts in a thick German accent:

—Citizen, one word with you, if you please.

—Later, Tobias. I haven't time now!

Fouché waves him away, back toward his workmen and carpenters.

Schmidt's was the lowest bid, 304 livres, against a high of 825, so the National Assembly awarded him an exclusive contract to build the invention of Dr. Guillotin, according to the specifications of Dr. Louis. Here at number 9 passage du Cour-du-Commerce, Schmidt's men assembled the first head-losing machine. It took a week to build, and Schmidt tested a prototype, first on three living sheep, then, in the courtyard of the Bicêtre hospital, on corpses taken from the hospital morgue, the bodies of two prisoners and a madwoman.

A soft breeze on the neck is all they will feel, Dr. Guillotin told his fellow deputies in the National Assembly. Less cruel than the wheel or being quartered, burned at the stake, hanged, or axed, and for the first time we will have nationwide standardization. A great advance, he assured them.

Schmidt has a monopoly, and demand has been high. First he built one for each of the eighty-three new national departments, then smaller ones, bigger ones, skinny ones, fat ones, even some on wheels so they could travel from village to village as needed.

The carriage moves past number 8 Cour-du-Commerce, the printing shop where Marat published his newspaper, *l'Ami du Peuple,* and turns left onto rue Saint-André des Arts. Fouché raises the window and smells the lilac varnish on the wood panels.

Nenette's warm fingers, patient and trusting, hold his hand. For a while, he does all he can to ignore her soft lips, parted and waiting.

I always believed I could control you, make you go away. I always told myself that in the midst of so much killing and fear, I could make you disappear whenever I wanted, and as soon as necessary.

He glances at her, catches her silent stare. She wears the lightest touch of powder on her cheeks and gloss on her lips, but no rouge, earrings, or necklace, for Fouché despises ostentation.

Fouché, you assume you can forget Nenette, just go on living and be done with her. You think you can just put her aside from one day to the next, wipe this slate clean and go on with your life as if she had never existed. But at the end she will join you in your grave just as quick as your shadow. She will jump in, no questions asked, because she is your light half, Fouché, your better half. She is not you, but she trusts you completely. That is far worse.

Nenette de Mondoubleau (alias Nenette Prévost) is a pawn passed on to him by Saint-Just.

—Here, this queenly look-alike may help you in your work, Fouché.

You are just another soul in need of protection, Nenette. Without me you are dead, to be tossed away when used. A hundred terrified, desperate prisoners stand at my desk every week, ready to do anything. But Nenette, only you are my last thought at night, my first thought in the morning. I am your dark twin, Nenette, the other side of the mirror, your diable.

At the Carrefour de Buci, where the cobblestones grow uneven, the carriage slows to a crawl. They slip past the first military enrollment center for volunteers to fight the war, past the spot where, last September 2, the sans-culottes dragged four priests from a police carriage and tore them limb from limb, and turn right onto rue de Thionville. It is almost dusk.

—Come on, Mordu, hurry up.

He touches her white muslin dress, the gold tresses down to her shoulders.

On the surface you are the Queen's look-alike, but underneath you are my maze, my truth, what Mordu, who is no mathematician but no fool either, calls the zero hour.

Crowd noises engulf the carriage; groups of men are singing with voices like gravel. Municipals, federals, and sans-culottes wearing liberty bonnets press on both sides of the carriage. This mob in ill-fitting jackets and red-striped pants, their unscabbarded swords belted with rope, crowd into a bakery shouting *Death to traitors, Death to hoarders!*

Before, only the nobility had colors; now everyone does. And new also is the combination of colors—the colors of Paris, red and blue, with white (a concession to the crown) sandwiched in between.

—Take me somewhere where we can be alone, please, Joseph.

—Nenette, how can I do that?

—I do not want to stay in Paris without you. You are a *représentant-en-mission*. Take me with you wherever they send you next.

—Nenette, you don't understand the situation.

—Oh, I do, I do. After the Queen's trial, I will be of no use to you. That much I understand. And the trial is tomorrow, isn't it?

Joseph Fouché, close friend of the Incorruptible One, who helped Robespierre overcome a slight lisp, helped him write speeches, helped him get elected to the first Constituent Assembly, stays calm, but he makes his words precise as knives.

—Nenette, it is not just our heads we can lose tonight. I tell you the whole revolution is in jeopardy.

—That is nothing new, my friend.

She laughs; that is her role, to be insouciant and to lift the affairs of state from his shoulders. This was her role as mistress of the Marquis de Persan and later as confidante of the castrato opera singer Tenducci. And when Fouché gets this pinched hard look on his face, skin stretched back, eyelids pale, lips thin and chapped, when he has worked too long and hard, she knows he needs what they all need but cannot admit needing, for he is no different from other men. Even thinking he is different makes this ex-priest like other men.

The carriage moves past a ragpicker, who wears an old brown overcoat and stands barefoot, leaning up against the side of a building.

—What if that were you, Fouché, says Nenette. and what if you had just climbed the highest mountain, swum the deepest ocean, raced across two continents, all so you could find me and hold me in your arms, and now in the night you would come to me breathless and anxious, open your hand very slowly one finger after another, and give me back what it is you removed from my heart?

—Nenette, our fate is on the line tonight. I need you to be a decoy for just a few hours. Can you do that for me?

She smiles at his answer.

—I can be Marie-Antoinette, I can play any role you want, my friend, but if you put my life at risk, it will cost you.

—This is the last thing I will ever ask of you, Nenette, the last. I promise.

—On one condition.

She raises a finger to his lips, a finger too clean, too soft for him to argue with. A finger he kisses.

—What is it?

—That afterward, when you leave Paris, you take me with you.

In the dark carriage, your open-mouthed smile and heavy-lidded eyes give you an air of a maintained actress, the kind of sexual property that I loathe and avoid, Nenette.

—You promise, Joseph?

He nods ever so slightly and looks out at the street. Fouché has no bourgeois appetites, no obvious sins. He admits only to self-control and zeal in a job well done. Being an apostle of public virtue helping France to be reborn as a republic of friends requires order and vigilance.

—Look, I know where you are taking me, but do you have to be so cold about it? I mean, are you not just a little bit worried that we may never see each other again?

Fouché does not answer, and she did not expect him to.

—What it is that I give you, Fouché—she says this to the street as much as to him.

He knows she wants him to answer, *I take from you a songbird, a key, a seed that will grow into something significant, as big and bright as life itself,* but he would never say anything remotely like that even if he meant it.

In the middle of the loud and crowded city, this carriage interior is an intimate safe haven. It is Fouché's rolling office, dining room, boudoir, interrogation cell—his home away from home, where they have eaten, slept, lived, made love—and no secrets are possible here for long.

—Joseph, I know you are scared out of your wits, but how do you think I feel right now? She pauses. In her voice tonight there is a threat and a promise, an intelligence that he envies and fears.

—Just tell me, tell me!

—Tell you what, Nenette?

—Tell me you love me. Tell me anything!

He carefully closes the window blinds and turns to her. The queenly head is thrown back to receive him and is less queenly now. Cobblestones bump them together, and he kisses her on the neck, on the cheeks, mouth, and forehead. He has told her, Do not fall in love with me, it will destroy you, girl. I am only using you. The minute I do not need you anymore, I will get rid of you. So have no illusions.

Don't do this, man, don't give in to her; this is what Nenette wants, and what you must not do if you want to survive. Keep your hands still or you are lost.

Fouché buries himself in her neck, lingering there, inhaling her smells. Her fingers enter his hair, make their way to his ear, trace his lips.

I am not this weak. I can ignore you if I choose to.

Her fingers pull at his scalp, massage his temples. He kneels before her in the carriage and buries his face in her lap, her muslin folds and rose-hip smells. His pants bulge with tumefaction.

Fouché, you dog, she will be your perdition.

Playfully at first, toying, she pulls back his head.

—Behave yourself, Joseph.

Then, more determined, she yanks on him to stop.

—Don't you dare!

Enter her, Fouché. Give her a quick lesson. Give her your past, your future. Once a priest, always a priest, and for you her hips are a kind of church; you can find yourself there. Do you think you can treat her as a lover, then discard her, and all will be easy, simple, and straightforward? In her confessional, do you think she will listen to you, understand you, forgive you, and say, It's all right, Fouché, my love, I am with you no matter how much you hurt me; no matter what, I absolve you?

—Joseph!

She covers his mouth, and he bites into her wet fingers.

The carriage has stopped; voices of patriots approach outside.

—Cheri, she whispers, let's go back to my room.

His blood is still boiling. He is shaking, but he wipes his mouth, composes himself, and sits back next to her, then lifts the blind to glance out. The red round sun is now resting on the Pont Neuf, and reflections of pink and gold stretch over the Seine, where men fish off the quays. Fires are starting at street corners and hands are being warmed over the flames, but inside Nenette arranges her skirts.

—Have you eaten wolf? What has gotten into you?

A cavalry detachment passes; then the carriage lurches forward. He drops the blind, and she runs her fingers through his thin hair, to straighten it.

—Joseph, the moment you get me out of Paris, somewhere far away and safe, we can begin to live normal lives and we can be fully human again.

—You will be the death of me, Nenette.

—My friend, I do nothing to egg you on. It is all you.

—Yes, that is why you are so dangerous. You will kill me.

—Don't be ashamed for this, be ashamed for that guard you post at my door!

Fouché studies her expression in the carriage darkness.

—I am doing all I can, Nenette. I cannot do more for you.

Nenette belongs to another life, another sensitivity. In spite of all the danger, she speaks of another era, as if she were not living through a revolution at all but were still in the Petit Trianon, dallying there with a parasol by a burbling brook with liveried servants and stone and plaster cherubs on pedestals. She is so otherworldly; that is what Fouché loves about her. She makes no compromise with the real world, so she is something he has never had.

—Joseph, I am your lover because I want to be, not because I am your prisoner. Don't you understand that after all these months? I can disappear, melt into the street crowds anytime I want to, but I have chosen you, so you do not need to put a guard at my door. I am not going to run away. I love you.

—You are too recognizable, Nenette. The moment you run, they will catch you.

—My poor Joseph, one day when it is too late and you have lost me, you will wish you had treated me better.

—Without my protection, the sans-culottes would kill you on sight. Your charm and your manners won't help you; on the contrary, they will betray you.

She gives a lethargic old-world smile and wipes condensation from the window. The blind is drawn, so it is an empty gesture, but to Fouché that is Nenette, wiping off the steam in order to better see the blind.

Her smile turns serious.

—But tonight the tables are turned; tonight the commissaire will be protected by his favorite prisoner, won't he?

Fouché peeks out from behind the blind. They are reaching the river. At this hour, he loves the dark-green waters which ripple with glints of sunset and dark bridge shadows.

Your smell is all over me, Nenette, in my hair, in my mouth, my eyes too, essence of lady-in-waiting.

—Does that bother you, that your fate is suddenly in my hands? Maybe you are in a panic because for once I control things and you do not?

—Nenette, you have as little control of the situation as anyone. You are a useful temporary decoy, that is all.

On Ile de la Cité, the crowd noises thicken. They pass the smell of horse dung and open sewers and the cry of loud voices. From the carriage wall, Fouché takes a pistol and readies it to keep away those who may be too curious.

—Nenette, the Queen has aged in the last month; we have to work on you.

He takes a vial of wig powder from his pocket and sprinkles it on her hair.

—Be careful, you are spilling it everywhere!

She sneezes.

—And Joseph, where shall I play this charade?

The *clip-clop, clip-clop* of horseshoes on the pavement has slowed down.

—In the Queen's cell inside the Conciergerie.

—Are you mad?

At a police barricade, Mordu halts the team. While guards are checking identification and travel permits, Nenette whispers to Fouché insistently.

—Has Marie-Antoinette escaped, or have you killed her already?

He does not answer. Through a spy hole, she watches the horses pull at their bits, smoke rises from their damp coats, bridles glint. A guard waves for their carriage to proceed. Daylight is sinking fast, but now they are inside the prison courtyard and torches appear.

—The Queen is ten years older than I am. It is only at a distance that they paraded me around Versailles. No one up close was ever duped.

Once inside the Conciergerie, a prisoner disappears like numberless others, the way a delicate flower growing between two cobblestones gets ripped up for no reason, merely because it is in the way. Give up all hope, ye who enter here!

—You will be fine, Nenette. Few of those pigs have seen the Queen up close.

—But I am wearing a dress that is the latest fashion, whereas she is probably in rags. There is no resemblance. You want them to kill me, don't you?

—Once in her cell, change into one of her mourning dresses.

—This is not going to work, Joseph. Why are you doing this?

—Mordu, bring me a candle here, quick!

Fouché extracts a piece of graphite from his pocket.

—You think I can trick the Queen's own servants? And her children? Do you think they are blind or stupid?

—Her children and her servants are still in the Temple prison. She is completely alone here. It's nighttime. Just stay at a distance from the guards.

—Oh, yes, right! Nenette forces a laugh.

A candle is passed in to him, and, lighting her face, Fouché examines her features with the attention and care of a master jeweler. *An excuse to rediscover you and your white teeth.* Nenette smiles, for never in all the months of hurried meetings has his examination of her been so deliberate, so careful, so detached. She likes how he traces the lines on her forehead, around her eyes and mouth, as if drawing her outline or taking a rubbing, darkening her personality, deepening who she is, and, in an odd way, making her more real. Being rediscovered like this is so intimate. She holds her breath and stares into his eyes, grateful for the silence and for this moment alone with him.

—Not too much, you will turn me into a hag.

—No, you are far too pretty, too vulnerable.

—I assume that is a compliment?

—You are the most beautiful woman in France, Nenette. He traces her arched eyebrows and sensual mouth.

—You may be an ex-priest, Joseph, but you are the biggest liar I've ever met.

—No, I am serious. You have never looked prettier than tonight.

She feels the way she did at the Petit Trianon, when she read Rousseau's *La Nouvelle Héloïse* to the Queen. How they both wept when the heroine spoke of loving *as one must love, with excess, madness, rapture, and despair.* This evening, Nenette is Héloïse, not as young or innocent, but the sentiments are the same; she too needs the excess cornucopia of love, the ultimate overwhelming certainty, the limitless strength of passion. She too does not want to die unloved. She feels drunk with love-sadness and despair; the only difference is, this is not a book, this is her life. But she knows Fouché would despise it if she attempted such sentimental talk.

—For getting you out of a disaster, Joseph, what will I earn?

—My eternal gratitude.

She laughs in order to make herself sound innocent.

—But what more?

—I cannot bargain with you, Nenette. We have no choice, you and I. Precious time is slipping by even as we speak.

—So where is the Queen?

—I don't know.

—No, come on, Joseph, tell me now. I want to know.

—I swear to you, I do not know.

Nenette's face suddenly turns serious. She grabs his arm, all gaiety gone.

—You have killed her. And now you mean for them to kill me, is that it?

—No, the Queen has escaped. I shall find her and bring her back, don't worry. But until I do, you will have to be her.

—If you don't find her, will you delay the start of the trial tomorrow?

—Talk to no one.

He kisses her lips. *My royal bonbon, my pale goddess, how I desire you. How I want you barefoot in my bedroom tonight, calling my name, holding me, warming me, telling me everything will be all right, giving me your lips as you would the last flower from a mountaintop.*

—If I have to speak, it will never work. Joseph, they will have witnesses in court who are not fools or dupes. The Queen and I don't have the same voice.

—I will be back before the trial starts.

—But what if you are not?

The sun has gone down and the courtyard archways are in shadows, lit by torches, but the sky is still light in the west.

—What if you do not find the Queen in time?

Fouché dons his bicorne hat with cockade and opens the carriage door.

—Joseph, you don't love me. If you really loved me, you would never put me in such risk as this!

—I have no choice.

—Everyone has a choice in life.

He checks her face one last time, wets his thumb, and wipes off her temple.

—I love you.

—Yes, maybe in your own way you do, but this could be my death. Are you aware of that?

—Mine too.

Guards approach. The sergeant stands at attention. Nenette, with her black hood up, follows Fouché out of the carriage into the Cour du Mai.

He leads the way through the council chamber, into the women's prison. The glare of burning torches turns Nenette's stomach. Guards rush to stand at attention; their weapons click at the rustle of muslin. On the ground floor, Fouché orders the third door on the left to be opened. It is chilly and damp, and guards are whispering. *The widow Capet is back.* She enters the royal cell.

Relief is written on Concierge Bault's face, then shock.

—Commissaire, I thought you were in Nevers. What are you doing back in Paris? I've just been reading your latest anticlerical edict, and all the good work you are doing there.

In the hallway, Fouché backs the newest prison governor to the wall and hisses into his eyes.

—I have ultimate responsibility for uncovering any plot concerning the Queen. The Incorruptible One gave it to me personally in this very room. Remember?

Bault, sweating, nods his big walrus mustache, but it is a small uncertain nod.

—When I say ultimate responsibility, anything that happens or does not happen to her is my concern. Was my signature on the order to release her?

—Citizen commissaire, I thought you had left the capital.

—And who exactly gave you the document?

—I don't know. It was on my desk when I returned.

—Because of incompetents like you, Bault, I cannot turn my back even for a minute. What would have happened if I were not here?

—We followed written signed orders, citizen. Is something wrong?

The prison chief, smelling of sweat and mold, buttons his jacket with a trembling hand and adjusts his belt buckle, on which is inscribed, LIBERTY OR DEATH. His guards move back to avoid contagion.

—Commissaire, while she was gone, the widow Capet changed into a white robe with ruffles and ribbons. This is a breach of our rules. We have numbered every item of clothing belonging to her, and—

—Be quiet, Bault. You have committed enough errors for one day. So listen carefully: Tonight you don't question the Queen, you don't disturb her.

—Yes, commissaire. But the order I received today clearly stated—

—I will be back in a few hours. If I hear you have let anyone set even one foot inside her cell, or if you go in there to her yourself, I will have you charged with treason!

Fouché enters the royal cell. He closes the door, faces the prisoner, and motions to the guards posted on the other side of the metal screen to leave. After they exit, with saber rattle and creaking leather, he turns back to Nenette.

The two of them stand by the tiny barred window on the ground floor and look out at the women's courtyard, with its small stone washing fountain set against the wall on the left. The woman in white whispers:

—Do not do this to me. Do not leave me here. I cannot go through with this.

Fouché, close enough to smell her, fights the urge to touch her arm. He whispers also.

—Nenette, change into the widow's common housedress.

—You have been using me, haven't you? What a fool I was to think you had a heart. You never loved me. Everyone warned me you were cold, heartless, a butcher with ice water in your veins. What a fool I was to fall for your charms.

With his eyes, he touches her, caresses her, kisses her. With his eyes only, he makes love to her, more intensely than ever. *The first guard who dares approach or who interrupts us is dead.*

Still staring out of the window, she whispers:

—Where is the Queen?

—Nenette, I will explain everything tomorrow.

—I need to know right now, this minute.

The judas hole in the door opens; two eyes peer in, then move away.

—If I play along with your charade, Joseph, if I risk my life, I need to know.

I will come and fetch you before morning, I swear it; that is all you need to know.

He glances at his watch, 6:47 P.M. Her fear is so palpable he can smell it.

—Joseph, you and I know I am not going to get out of here alive. So please do not treat me like an idiot, not today.

—You are not going to die, Nenette. I will not let it happen.

She turns from the window and looks at him, eyelids heavy. Behind his back, new eyes are at the judas window.

—You can ask me anything, Joseph, but if this is the last time I shall see you, at least be honest; that is all I ask of you. Tell me the truth.

—This is only for a few hours, he whispers without moving; trust me.

—I am not as strong as you are, Joseph. What if I crack up, what if I speak?

—They will think you helped the Queen escape. You will be finished.

He examines her teeth, her pale lips, the curve of her cheeks, her almost transparent skin. The moment lingers between them pungent with silence and with her vulnerability.

—Even uglified and aged for this role, you remain grand, Nenette.

—You think I am a fool, don't you? You think if they discover me, I will not talk; I will submit like a lamb to the sacrifice and will not give you away!

He speaks to her almost as in prayer.

—Everything you feel for me, Nenette, I feel for you, only more so. You are the best part of me and always will be.

Unable to stand this anymore and feeling that eyes are upon him, Fouché turns and retires to Bault's office.

Three candles illuminate what was once a cell. Fouché sits and puts his jaw in his hands. *One wrong move and everything is finished.*

—Mordu, quick. Get me some reinforcements, a squadron of the best men available. Not Municipals. Not the useless gendarmerie.

He rubs his face.

—Republican guards?

—No, a detachment of Santerre's National Guards and fresh horses. On the double. And bring me the day's register, as well as everyone who saw the widow Capet today. I want them to report to me on the double.

A candle drips white wax onto his extended index finger, but he does not move his hand. Heavy steps rush down the hallway. Suddenly Bault enters the room with gasping, halting breath.

—Commissaire, forgive me, but Fouquier-Tinville is not in his room. I have tried to locate him, but—

—Who summoned you?

The prison chief shifts uneasily.

—I thought I should inform the chief prosecutor that the widow Capet was—

—You are not here to think, Bault. You are here to follow orders and to guard prisoners. Police investigations are my responsibility. Now disappear.

Bault does as he is told.

The problem is, no one knows whose orders to follow anymore: the Committee of Public Safety, the Commune of Paris, the Sections.

Ever since I left on mission in the provinces, Fouquier-Tinville, chief public prosecutor, has moved into the Conciergerie and lives in a wing of the prison, la tour César, which gives him constant access to the prisoners and jailers. Fouquier-Tinville's assessor, Herman, is president of the revolutionary court inside the prison. So it is natural for Bault to assume these two are in charge. In a sense they are, for they answer only to the City Council and the Committee of Public Safety.

How fitting that a double should be my lodestone, my anchor to windward, and my only reality a fake. I offered you protection and guaranteed your family's safety in exchange for cooperation. You were employed by the Queen at the Petit Trianon, and Saint-Just passed you on to me for safekeeping. Your family was in danger, and you needed protection; that is what this is about. In the big scheme of things, what other role do you have? And who are you anyway, Nenette?

Do not get excited, Fouché, do not thrash about; you will only dig yourself in deeper. You are in quicksand, and the harder you try to get out, the deeper you will sink.

According to the ancient Greeks, absolute love strikes its victim as a disease, but I know it is also a vocation.

La Conciergerie

Lieutenant Pasquier enters the room and reports.

—There is no one at Saint-Just's office or in his apartment. They are both locked tight, commissaire.

—Of course.

Fouché takes back the letter he had written to Saint-Just, bends over the fireplace, lights it, and watches it burn.

—Pasquier, send one of your men to the Temple prison. Make certain the royal children are secure, especially the Dauphin.

Lieutenant Pasquier has been with Fouché at the head of 250 men in the west, the Loire-Inférieure and the Mayenne, recruiting 300,000 conscripts; and in the center, the Aube and Burgundy (Troyes, Dijon, and Nevers), imposing Fouché's revolutionary tax on the rich. He has seen Fouché aim cannon into crowds and fire at point-blank range. He has seen priests taken on boats and drowned, so he knows what this job entails; Fouché, answerable only to the Incorruptible One, is overseeing Marie-Antoinette's safety and ultimate disposal.

—And have your men ready, Pasquier. I will be done in fifteen minutes; then we will turn this city upside down.

While in the cold damp hallway Mordu assembles all possible witnesses, Fouché starts a list of suspects. Who would want to save the Queen now? He draws up two lists, one of royalist sympathizers who would be mad enough to try and save her, the other of deputies who would profit from helping her escape.

Ten weeks ago, on August 2, Marie-Antoinette was moved from the Temple prison to the Conciergerie. The last known escape attempt was on August 10, when a certain Chevalier de Rougeville bribed his way into her cell with Michionis, then superintendent of prisons, and while the guards were not looking, he dropped a red carnation in which, after their departure, she discovered a secret message. As the Queen was denied ink or a quill, she pricked her answer on a piece of paper with a needle and handed it to Gilbert, a guard she thought she could count on. Gilbert kept the answer for a few days, got cold feet, and turned her in. The Queen had destroyed Rougeville's message, but her answer to him has survived and says, *I am under constant surveillance. I cannot speak or write. I trust you, I will come.*

On September 11, Michionis and Gilbert were imprisoned, as was Concierge Richard, then governor of the Conciergerie and his wife, and their servant, Madame Harel. Richard was replaced by Concierge Bault. Security was tripled, and they took away the Queen's last possessions, everything—her rings, the bracelet her mother had given her before she left Austria. Even a locket in which she kept tresses of her children's hair was impounded, and she was forbidden the use of candles when night fell. Now the Queen has nothing, only a single change of clothes, rags to stanch her bleeding, a small dish of face powder, a hairbrush, and a bottle of water for her teeth. Two men guard her cell around the clock. They sit on the other side of a rough metal screen, with orders to watch her every move, even when she uses her chamber pot.

—Mordu, get Larivière. Tell him I want an exact sketch of the carriage that took the Queen away and of the faces of the men who escorted her out.

—Yes, chief.

Fouché opens a silver vial of liver pills, takes one, and swallows it. His first interview with Nenette took place here. Saint-Just plucked her from the holding pen just beyond that door, and during the lineup she stood in the registrar's office, holding her elbows, head down but eyes alive.

—Are you a patriot, citoyenne?

—I am a follower of Rousseau, she answered, and he knew exactly what she meant.

Rousseau is a code word for honesty, simplicity, and love of truth and nature, but Fouché is supremely skeptical of such altruism.

Truth I equate with lies, simplicity with money (the Queen dressing as a shepherdess), innocence with sin, and love of nature with the leisured classes. As for Rousseau's claim to moral purity, the man by his own admission abandoned his children, was addicted to masturbation, and lived in a ménage à trois. What moral purity is that?

Fouché never finished Rousseau's *Confessions;* the book was an insult to common sense. Yes, breathtaking candor is the order of the day, and Rousseau is a lay saint. But is it enough that a philosopher lay down his many sexual and moral failings on the printed page for the world to deify him?

Nenette, when you said, I am a follower of Rousseau, in an instant I knew that you had a feeling heart. You preferred emotion to reason, nature to culture, innocence to experience, soul to intellect. In an instant I knew we had little or nothing in common. You believed that childhood spontaneity could sustain adult virtue. And from the start I knew you were the opposite of everything I am and need to be as head of the Incorruptible One's secret police. In an instant I foresaw what could happen between us.

Fouché pulls out the locket Nenette gave him, which contains her portrait. Embarrassed at first, he vowed to destroy this cameo as a sign of hyperbole, moral bankruptcy, and weakness, but in the past few months he examines it whenever he is alone and cannot be seen.

Mordu knocks at the door.

—I am ready with the witnesses, chief.

—Bring me the girl first.

Mordu returns with Rosalie Lamorlière, the kitchen maid of Concierge Bault, a simple country girl who has been detailed to bring the Queen her food every day. Rosalie replaced Madame Harel, who was more intelligent and more precise in her reports, but after the red carnation plot Harel is herself in jail. Louis Larivière's wife also served the Queen a few times, but she was too old, too slow, and good for nothing.

Rosalie stands, waist cinched, head bowed, in a white bonnet. Her cheeks and eyes are red from a full day's work.

—Anything to report today?

—No.

She wraps her black shawl around herself to keep out the damp.

—Where is the Queen?

—She arrived back a few minutes ago, citizen. But I have not gone to her yet.

Fouché has checked the girl's past, of course. Young Rosalie is a native of Breteuil and served as chambermaid to Madame de Beaulieu, an actress. Rosalie is pink-cheeked and goodhearted. For an unmarried young woman, prison life cannot be too easy. Only her extreme innocence protects her.

—I know you like to be at the Queen's side as often as possible, but tonight do not help her undress, Rosalie. Leave her alone. Do not go into her cell.

—Yes, commissaire.

—Where did the widow Capet go this afternoon?

Shyness and a shrug of the shoulders. She twists her fingers.

—Who took the Queen away at five P.M.?

—Your men, I suppose. They were dressed like your men. Her voice is squeaky.

—Tell me her routine today.

Rosalie sniffles and wipes her nose, for she has a cold.

—Well, the Queen awoke at six A.M. I helped dress her, combed her hair, and she had a cup of hot chocolate. I cut her a slice of bread, but she left it untouched. She read from seven to eight A.M. Then Concierge Bault checked on her. From nine to eleven A.M. she read and did a bit of sewing. After lunch, which was just some lentil soup and boiled cabbage, she lay down to rest. In the afternoon more reading, and the Queen had various visits. One from Larivière. Another from the court registrar. Then her two lawyers came and helped her draft a letter.

Her lawyers are terrified court hacks. Their main concern is to avoid the fate of the lawyers who defended the King with too much energy. If the Queen does not appear in court tomorrow, they will be the first to be blamed and also the first to be executed. I don't worry about her lawyers.

—At four P.M., Nurse Guyot entered for her daily checkup and provided medical assistance. She's—

Rosalie stops.

—Speak without fear, my child.

—For several days now the Queen has been bleeding.

—What kind of bleeding do you mean?

Rosalie looks uncomfortable.

—Menstrual irregularity . . . due to her sorrows, the bad air, the lack of exercise.

Fouché knows that Rosalie secretly cut up some linen from her own chemise and gave those strips to the Queen for her bleeding. He also knows that Rosalie prolongs her housekeeping to shorten the Queen's time alone in the dark, doing such chores as ironing her cap strings, washing her underwear, cleaning the mold off her shoes.

—And when did Nurse Guyot leave?

—At four-thirty P.M.

—Then what?

—Then at five P.M. National guards took the Queen away, and she came back just now.

—Did the Queen say anything to you out of the usual today or yesterday?

—No.

—Think.

Silence. Fouché waits while Rosalie blows her nose into a handkerchief.

—Anything at all?

—Yes, she did say something.

Fouché checks his watch.

—What did she say?

—She has a hospice card that she holds as a prize possession. And she said, *They will take care of me when the time comes.*

Fouché smells cabbage soup and pig fat as dinner is carried down the hall in a large vat to the guardroom. Rosalie's eyes study the floor.

—That is all the Queen said?

—Yes.

—No communication from any other person outside the prison?

—No.

A finger goes up. Mordu enters, and without a word he shows Rosalie out.

Fouché sips some water and loosens his collar.

This night is an existential excruciating mal-au-cul, no glory for anyone on a night like this. If I find the Queen, no one will congratulate me; no one should even know. If I don't find her, Nenette will have to die, and once the Queen is safely abroad, the revolution will be undone, and the world's tyrants will cover us with taunts and infamy. This night will give you hemorrhoids, Fouché.

He hears one of the guards singing, to the air of the *Marseillaise:*

> O heavenly guillotine,
> you cut short kings and queens.
> Through your celestial might
> we have reconquered all our rights.

May you, o proud device,
exist for ever more.

The next witness Mordu escorts in is the sergeant of the guard, Delbrel. At forty, he has a full head of frizzy hair, a crunched-up unshaved face, eyes a-twinkle, and a hat on the back of his head. You can guess his southern accent almost before he speaks.

—What's happened to the widow Capet in the last twenty-four hours?

Delbrel pulls out his pipe.

—Oh, nothing special. Tronson and Chauveau-Lagarde, her court-appointed lawyers, came today for the first time.

—Did she say anything to you?

—Yes, she has one wish, and that is to be buried next to her husband.

—Capet is buried in a common grave, but assure her I will do all in my power to help her. What else? Any compromising communications?

Delbrel knocks his pipe empty.

—No. I was in the cell all during the meeting with the lawyers. All she did was write a letter asking the court to delay her trial for three days to allow her lawyers time to prepare a defense.

Delbrel is a gay blade, a champagne Charlie; he obviously loves the attention, the notoriety, of being close to the Queen.

—Anything else?

—Oh, wait; yes, she asked me if a doctor was coming to visit.

—What did she say exactly?

—She said, *Is Nurse Guyot coming from the hospice? I need her.*

Fouché's eyebrows rise.

—Mordu, quick!

—Yes, commissaire?

—Where is Nurse Guyot? The Queen asked about her twice today before she came. What hospice is Guyot from?

This is too easy, too elementary. The Capets are inbred, dumb and hopeless, so one polices them with less intelligence, but the Hapsburgs have brains. The Queen speaks five languages. Her defense lawyers may be ciphers, but her regular daily nurse? There is someone she has had time to charm and collude with.

—Delbrel, when was the last time the Queen ate?

—At lunch.

—Who served her?

—Rosalie. She's the only one who attends her.

The finger rises again. Mordu leads Delbrel out and returns with Froissard, another guard.

Fouché admires brevity.

Talk should be taxed. Verbiage cheapens the message, negates thought, reduces meaning. On the other hand, rare words gain value. I would ration the populace to five or ten words a day, let us say a hundred a month, so if anyone had anything to say of any significance they would really say it well, say it only once, and everyone would listen.

Fouché is serious. Too much is blabbed today, cried from the rooftops, spat in your face, and not enough is heard. The freedom to speak your mind means you speak into the wind. No one listens, everyone vomits opinions, clichés, non sequiturs, and wastes time braying like donkeys. But if lives are being foreshortened, and bodies, why not the manner of speech as well? Who has time for long sentences? Life is brief, truth is at a premium. All is cut short.

Froissard reports:

—We watch her day and night, commissaire. We check her cell, her clothes, her books, every twelve hours. The Autri-chienne can't even do her morning toilette alone. Even when she eats or sleeps, we watch from behind the metal screen.

—Tell me about today's medical visit.

—The usual, nothing special. It lasted about twenty minutes.

—Froissard, the mission I have given you is to get cozy with the widow Capet, I know, but be careful. Divided loyalties are dangerous.

The raised finger. Mordu appears, and it is the usual ballet again: *Les Pas Perdus*, the lost steps. Commissaire and servant function like the synchronized parts of a Swiss watch.

I protect the revolution, save it from its enemies, but the revolution is like watching the waves roll in on the beach. Every seventh wave is so large and huge it throws all the rest into chaos. The revolution is not brittle and breakable; the revolution is an invertebrate, an amoeba. It changes every day and goes every which way with no one to control it, so it's surprising that a demonized, demoralized abstraction like Marie-Antoinette can be a danger to us. How could something as pervasive and shapeless as the new order be vulnerable to one single woman, let alone a gray-haired Austrian crone?

As a priest and teacher of logic, Fouché knows that the power of a symbol is in inverse proportion to its lack of power; just look at the crucifixion or the nativity. Weakness can be power, and impotence a triumph.

Now the nation is in danger; the Prussians have crossed the Rhine, the British have taken Toulon. News from the front lines—internal and external—is not good. The English, the Prussians, the Austrians are all closing in.

Fouché is building up the killer instinct. Every mission needs a hunting dog going for the jugular. And tonight the prey is the decadent oppressor of the lower classes. She must be put to death; it is the whole purpose and meaning of the revolution. End the old, start the new.

Marie-Antoinette's reason for living is over; the snake is writhing in the grass. I must make the garden safe for the future of humanity. If I see a snake, I chase it and behead it or we are doomed, for no matter how harmless that snake seems, it can have babies, supporters, followers. The snake is nothing; snakehood is everything.

—Bring back Rosalie Lamorlière.

Now the servant girl again stands nervous before him:

—Rosalie, we know you are passing information back and forth to the Queen.

—Citizen, I do not speak to her.

—We have catalogued your every move. You speak with the widow Capet by a method of complex signs. The fork to the left means yes, the fork to the right means no. The glass upside down means danger. We know all this.

—Citizen, you give my poor brain too much credit.

—Yes, maybe so.

Fouché is aware that Concierge Bault confiscated the white ribbon that the Queen gave Rosalie. He knows Rosalie has given the Queen a paper box to keep her things in and lent her a small hand mirror bought on the quays for twenty-five sous in script; its frame is red, and there are Chinese figures painted on the side. *I know all this, but what I don't know is more important than what I do know.*

—Did Marie-Antoinette speak with anyone today other than Nurse Guyot and the lawyers? Anyone from the outside?

—No.

—But she twice referred to the hospice and the nurse?

—Yes.

Rosalie keeps her eyes downcast, a black shawl around her arms.

—Did Nurse Guyot speak to her?

—Almost nothing. And I was present the entire time of the visit.

Fouché hints at a smile. Rosalie must know that Nenette is the un-Queen, she must smell the counterfeit, or is the widow so smart as to have planned her escape without divulging it to her only prison ally?

—For the money I pay you, Rosalie, you had better be telling the truth.

—I am, citizen.

A finger rises.

When the room is empty, Fouché approaches the fire. No wonder the Queen has a bronchial condition and irregular menstrual bleeding, living in such coldness and dampness. Outside he can hear them singing the *Carmagnole*. What if the Queen only asked after the nurse because of her bleeding?

The air here is fetid. A prisoner screams as they rip off a bandage to see if it hides a secret message. A guard calls out the names of the winners of the day's very saintly guillotine lottery; no prisoner voices the least protest. To tame humanity, there is nothing quite like one meal a day.

A polite cough behind Fouché makes him swivel.

—Mordu?

—Yes, chief.

—Tell Pasquier to ready his men. We will leave right away.

He hands Mordu the lists he has drawn up. The first includes royalists—the Baron de Batz (who has tried to save the Queen twice), the Duc de Coigny (the King's equerry, an early lover of hers), Axel von Fersen (who masterminded the King's flight to Varennes), the Baron de Goguelat (her ex-secretary, often used by the Queen as a private courier), General Jarjayes (who tried to rescue her from the Temple).

—We are too lenient, too patient, not decisive enough, Mordu. I would decapitate every single one of their family members and friends. We must give object lessons—throw their cadavers in the river so everyone will understand what it means to ignore the public will!

Fouché looks down the list of names.

—Add anyone who has ever uttered a word in the Queen's defense. I am not about to allow these bluebloods, privilege hawkers, and peasant beaters to cheat the nation and mock us. But, Mordu, put Nurse Guyot at the top of the list. What do we know about her? Whom does she associate with, what views does she hold?

He points to the second list.

We will follow twin tracks, Mordu. Here are names of corrupt officials who have had their fingers in the sticky pot. I am going to root out corruption and evil from the body politic of this nation, even if I have to break down every door in France and strangle every single national deputy, property owner, moneybag, and grandee to do it. They think they have seen the Terror? Well, now they will see Fouché at work. Let them compare haircuts when their necks spit into the bag.

You may think you have suffered, but then you meet Fouché.

Stop crying, everything will be fine now. It's me, I am here. We are finally together, my love, finally alone.

Ssshhh.

You and I have not been happy very often. The more rare something is, the more valuable it becomes.

Stop crying and sleep. You will need all your strength tomorrow.

A Squeezing of the Heart

The rain has stopped, but it is cold and damp. Fouché sits on his hands to warm them up. There is no time to order a cup of hot verbena. He glances out; hundreds of black chimneys, some short and stout, others thin and crooked, trail filaments of pale smoke into the sky.

He leaves Bault's office, makes his way to the registrar's office and, alone there, he considers whether to excise from the big black registry book any mention of the Queen having been let out or re-admitted today, but he decides against it. Then Fouché heads for the Cour des Dames, stops in the ground-floor hallway, and gazes at Nenette through the small Judas hole. One can escape from prison, but nobles seldom try; they do not want to dress as the enemy, dress as sans-culottes, so mostly it is the poor who attempt to escape.

Given more time, Nenette, you would find a way; you are a survivor.

Her back is turned, and she is looking out into the small Cour des Dames. He sees her neck, her hands, the small of her back, and something like despair, a wave of tenderness, or both rises unstoppable from his guts and flows through him.

I want to rush in, grab you, put my arms around you, warm you up (for you must be frozen), protect you, reassure you, take you out of here, and get you away to safety right now. I cannot stand seeing you there, so vulnerable, so alone.

I used to make love in the dark, quickly, ashamed, guilty; now I need a candle burning so I can see your pale lips, white skin, the skin that you, Nenette, say is too white, too pale. For me your head on the pillow is a sign of purity, of everything that is honest and true in the world.

He watches Nenette hold herself and hears her cry softly into her chest. He does nothing, gives no orders to Bault or to the two soldiers seated beyond the metal screen; he takes his time.

To leave is to send you to oblivion, to kill you.

He recalls the first time they met. It was in a prison lineup here at the Conciergerie. Picking out victims in the main holding pen, Saint-Just said, *I have someone here for you, Citizen commissaire, someone perhaps you can use.*

Across the crowded prison hall, across a sea of countesses, courtesans, and ladies of good standing, Fouché saw Nenette for the first time. What he noticed first was her height, her broad bones, her open face, and that certain roundness that angular men admire, but more important than anything she said or did was her lost-sheep look. In that stone-vault darkness, the anxiety with which she searched his face for a smile, or for any fingerhold she could find, went right to his heart.

When we were alone for the first time, you waited, eyes downcast, facing me as if offering yourself. I expected you to break down and say something, but you didn't; the silence grew heavier. I wanted to see how strong you were, how long you could stand there before me without saying a word, but finally I spoke because I did not want to lose the opportunity.

—Your resemblance to the Queen, citoyenne, is remarkable.

—It's nothing, it can happen to anyone. *You muttered at the floor.*

—But it has not happened to anyone, it has happened to you.

—Yes.

—Do you know who I am?

—No.

—I am Joseph Fouché, deputy to the National Convention, elected from the Loire-Inférieure last fall. The government sends me on short notice wherever I am needed, and the missions are always dangerous and difficult. Would you work for me?

—It depends on what you offer in exchange, citizen.

—I would offer you advantages.

—My life? *You blurted the words out too fast.*

—Your life? Yes, for a time.

I stood at a distance. Staring up at me with such an open face, you made me tense. I felt I was the one being interrogated, not you. Even a Master of the Underworld is aware of beauty, and if I had seen anything in any way corrupt or stained in you, I would have let them kill you on the spot. It was your purity, your simplicity, that saved you, because you were different from all the others. Your purity was more extreme. When I recognized this, it was suddenly not your life I had to save, but mine.

—Citizen, all I want is my life.

—I am afraid you will have to take what I give you, citoyenne.

—Yes, I am afraid of that too.

—What can you do? Have you any talents?

—I can sing, citizen. *You smiled.* I can play the piano, speak bad German; I can sew, keep house, take care of children, cook.

I walked away and for a moment forced myself not to look at you.

—You and I are not free agents, citoyenne.

—I know.

—The door into this prison is small, narrow and tight. But the door out is even smaller, almost impossible to find.

—Before, when I said I didn't know you, citizen, that was a lie. I know you are one of the most powerful men in France, Commissioner Fouché. You can make anything happen.

—*You broke into another smile, a bigger one this time.*

I turned and went to inform Saint-Just, in as disinterested a voice as possible: Maybe I can use her as bait to catch royalists; you never know. Then I signed the register, taking custody of the prisoner Baroness of Mondoubleau, not betraying any sentiment whatsoever.

⌒

Bault appears with two men that Fouché has been expecting, the Queen's defense lawyers, Tronson-Doucoudray and Chauveau-Lagarde, the latter of whom became notorious for defending Charlotte Corday.

—Tell them their client is tired and does not want to see them.

Fouché turns to leave, but the lawyers rush after him. Tronson-Doucoudray says:

—We respectfully protest; this indictment was only given to us today, it is a chaos of miscellany, and we have not seen the list of witnesses who will be called.

—You would do well to sit still and limit yourself to a plea of mercy, says Bault.

—We need more time to prepare her defense, says Tronson-Doucoudray; we have so petitioned the National Assembly.

—Hey, you two wanna avoid your client's fate, says Mordu; I'll give you a fat lip and a legal irregularity to munch on, my friend.

Chauveau-Lagarde takes Fouché aside and whispers.

—The case is a travesty. It accuses the Queen of being a foreigner; well, she is guilty of that. It also says she caused civil war and passed military secrets to Austria; that she prompted the orgy of a Flemish regiment at Versailles by leaving bottles under her bed, as if soldiers needed any such encouragement. It says she bit open the cartridges of the Swiss guards so they need not waste time in murdering patriots; that she forced the King to veto anticlerical legislation, embezzled government funds, organized the flight to Varennes, and corrupted her son.

Tronson-Doucoudray adds:

—Fouquier is even charging the Queen of spreading malicious pornography against herself in order to discredit the revolution!

—If it is all so absurd, citizens, you will have no trouble clearing her.

Fouché takes the indictment papers out of the lawyers' hands, brings the pages to his nose as if to smell them, to his ear, then nods.

—Seems appropriate to me.

He lets the pages flutter to the floor.

The lawyers scramble to collect their work.

☙

Good. Now, Mordu, down to business. Three identification checks, a register to sign, and you are still not sure where Nurse Guyot is tonight!

—We'll find her, boss.

—If we do not find her, Mordu, lives will terminate. And even if we do find her, I promise you there will be big changes all around.

—Chief, she must be at the hospice de l'Archevêché. It's right close by.

—Good, Mordu. When an animal wants to hide, it does not move. Come on, hurry!

Shh, shhh, don't be anxious, I am here, my love. And we are safe. No one knows where we are. The bolt on that door is sturdy, and we will spend the night here. I'll watch over you.

Close your eyes and sleep.

The Suspects

An escape plot takes a huge amount of organization and money; it has to be planned weeks ahead of time. The Austrians could be bankrolling this. Marie-Antoinette's two brothers, Joseph II and Leopold II, did not lift a finger to save her when they were emperors, but maybe Francis II, her nephew, is different? Maybe an assemblage of uncles and aunts, fueled by guilt, has pumped money into France somehow? Or it could be a one-man daredevil mission by one of her lovers.

Von Fersen, the Swedish count, timed the flight to Varennes brilliantly. Paris had 40,000 soldiers at the time, but at midnight on Monday, June 21, two years ago, von Fersen got the entire royal family into a berline and drove straight out of the Tuileries and out of Paris. He would have succeeded except the King wanted to be saved by someone other than his wife's lover—even cuckolds have a sense of honor. So the next morning, halfway to the border, at the village of Bondy, the King made von Fersen leave. That afternoon the carriage broke down and had to be repaired for an hour, and that evening the royal family was arrested just sixteen miles shy of the border.

—Mordu, what have you found on von Fersen?

—He is still Sweden's envoy to the Austrian Lowlands and lives in Brussels. He has been trying to get the allied commander, the Duke of Coburg, to attack Paris. He makes frequent trips to Vienna and the émigré army at Coblenz.

*It is a full moon and chilly. The Committee of Public Safety has many en-
emies—any one of them could be behind this.*

—Danton could be involved, Mordu. The fat pig would do
anything for money, pretend to save the King's life, inflate army
contracts. Danton is against prosecuting the Queen. He has
argued vehemently in favor of selling her to the Austrians for
ransom. And remember that letter we intercepted back in July to
Deputy Courtois, where Danton said:

> The Commune will roar, but everyone will be on our side if
> we succeed; it will be the opposite if we fail; we shall have to
> defend ourselves and God knows what will happen. Be pre-
> pared for anything.

Danton's first plan fell through when the Queen refused to flee
without her son, and the second was foiled by her transfer to the
Conciergerie. When Fouché uncovered what Danton had attempted, Robespierre judged it too sensitive to publicize, but he
proposed a law that anyone negotiating with the enemy for peace
would be deemed a traitor and would be put to death.

—I am hungry, Mordu.

Fouché sits in the back of his carriage with a woolen blanket
over his knees. The tight springs squeal as the carriage careens from
bump to pothole. The horses snort and strain. Saddle-bouncing
leather-sore Nationals, with bridles clicking, lead the way to the
hospice de l'Archevêché.

8:16 P.M.

The Musings of Mordu

I make the mistake of glancing at my diary:

Sept. 16: In the Nièvre, Fouché makes illegal the wearing of ecclesiastical robes.

Sept. 19: Fouché expropriates the rich to give to the poor.

Sept. 22: Fouché leads the feast of Brutus: he places a dagger on the altar of the church of Saint-Cyr in Nevers to commemorate the murder of the tyrant Julius Caesar.

Sept. 25: Fouché gives priests thirty days to marry or adopt children.

Sept. 26: Fouché destroys all religious icons in Moulins.

Oct. 2: The Committee of Public Safety writes: *We rely on your vigilance, Fouché, to destroy all plots of those who would murder liberty!*

Oct. 5: The new revolutionary calendar takes effect. Year II starts September 22, 1793–don't forget!

Oct. 7: New standard weights and measures are adopted. Also a new currency: the gold franc and the silver republican.

Oct. 13: Fouché brings to the National Treasury in Paris 100,000 marks of gold and seventeen trunks of gold and silver spoils with this message: Let us trample the idols of the monarchy in the dust!

Every time I read my diary I feel exhausted, as if a tiring journey is about to get longer.

Tonight I was supposed to rush to the Jacobin Club meeting— held in the disused church of the Jacobin convent on rue Saint-Honoré. The last time I went I heard an hour-long speech of Robespierre's in which he said, *The monsters must be unmasked, exterminated, or I must perish.* Hurrahs on all sides; the galleries were packed. You have to go early to get tickets, and every evening there are new accusations and counteraccusations, so a moment's inattention and you are lost. In political clubs, men of all sorts rub shoulders. You find foreigners bent on witnessing history in the making, gossips chatting and sipping brandy, idiots with nothing to do who want to be entertained, paid supporters who have come to cheer a speaker or boo a faction. The public gallery is an exhausting place: Acquaintances send each other messages, ladies eat fresh fruit and ices. Women visitors are tolerated, but the Jacobins have no women members.

Poor me, poor Mordu. There is too much work for just one man. Over at the Committee of Public Safety in the Tuileries, Robespierre has 140 secretaries working for him around the clock, so no wonder he can handle five hundred matters a day. Here it is only me. The chief does not realize how much he puts on my shoulders. I mean, I never pry, I assume he is writing down search-and-arrest orders, a political tract, or something important. But this morning I open his daybook, just out of passing curiosity, and never was I so terrified in all my life. The words blinded me. I closed the book, shaking; I thought I was dreaming. I swear, I will never sneak a read again, not if I can help it. Is it some sort of trap or an attempt at comedy? He had written, *Along with Pascal and Jansenius, we are nothing but brothers, equal before Christ. We live by, in, and through our savior. What does the Lord require of you but to do justice and walk humbly with your God?*

It was in his handwriting, and if anyone else reads that we are dead. But then it became clear. This was not Fouché the proconsul, not the *représentant-en-mission*, this is Fouché the father of a sick child, and realizing that I calmed down, took a deep breath, and went about my business.

From the very start he was a doting father: He should have been a stay-at home giddy-up horsie, a piggy back daddy dandling fat happy babies expecting nothing, being fed by a clean and honest wife. On August 10, the date of his daughter's birth, he tells me, *I want all the bells to be rung loud and clear!* Well, on August 5 he had ordered every church bell in the Center region to be melted down for cannon. So what could I do? There was no carillon for his newborn.

But he had something else in mind. We are staying at l'hôtel de la Nation in Nevers, and the chief tells me, *I shall organize the first republican baptism in France.* He has me call out the National Guard and all the village leaders. The notaries, the mayor, the town aldermen and department heads, they all gather. And Fouché appears on the first-floor landing of the hôtel de la Nation with his one-day-old baby in a white cotton outfit with a lace bib. The marching band strikes up the *Marseillaise,* and he carries her at the head of the procession to the central marketplace.

He wanted it to be political theater that would strike a blow against religion, but instead everyone there saw a proud thirty-four year-old father having himself an old-fashioned celebration for his firstborn child. He had me prepare not a religious altar but an Altar of the Nation. And instead of godparents, he chose two sponsors—he pointed into the crowd to show that we are all brothers and that any citizen will do—and he picked Citoyenne Damour for female sponsor and Citoyen Champrobert for male sponsor, and he had them swear an oath to help raise the child in good republican virtues. It was really touching. And it was the first time the public saw the fatherly side of Fouché.

Then he made a speech, and being a priest he knows how to give an occasion solemnity. Our Apostle of Freedom said that by not marrying and not having babies, priests were hurting the nation.

To avoid a Christian name, he baptized her Nièvre, that being the department she was born in. Then he marched around town at the head of the military band, and with all the officials in tow, he returned her to her mother.

How is Nièvre? Since that day, no one knows what he means anymore. Does he mean his daughter, or does he mean the region of France that he has been sent to pacify? The land is bleeding, and his two-month-old daughter is not doing well either. The doctors say she is suffering from consumption. She is an ugly pale child, always feverish, and I don't think she will live long. But the chief treats her as if she were the most perfect of man's creations, and he insists she is fine. In one of his letters to his sister I read, *Dear Louise, cry with us!* But in public he does not let on about these problems.

⌒

The Fouché I first met and hired on with in 1790 still smelled of La Martanière, a cluster of twenty households along the Loire River, where he was born. His father, a merchant marine captain, would go on long trips to the Caribbean, and he supposedly owned a small plantation in Santo Domingo, but he died at sea and left the family destitute. Fouché was just sixteen then. He grew up, thin and bony, without friends, avoiding exercise, avoiding fresh air. The only time he went on his father's boat he was seasick and wretched. He was a stoop-shouldered weakling, whose massive brain worked all the time giving him no respite.

He never speaks about his youth, but I learn about it from what he writes to his sister, Louise Broband. Louise is three years older, married and living in Nantes, and he adores her. Their mother died when he was twenty-six. An older brother died in infancy, and his younger brother died at sea following in their father's footsteps. So that leaves only Joseph and Louise. She is the only one he ever opens up to. He wrote to her once, *At school in Nantes, I refused to mix with wealthy boys who were less intelligent than I was. Even now, I still resent the humiliations they put me through.*

I started working for Fouché when he was the principal of the College in Nantes, and even then Father Fouché preferred to read Latin than to visit a tavern or play cards. He had met Robespierre when he was seeking funds to build up the school laboratory in Arras. He wanted a Montgolfier balloon, gases, and chemicals to conduct experiments, and the city of Arras turned him down. The only official who came to see his lab was Robespierre, the man who had defended and won the famous lightning-rod case of 1783.

Back then Fouché was a bookworm who disdained his students, a priest who smelled of failure, a skinny frame that became so thin he almost disappeared, but recent success has transformed him. Being elected to the National Assembly last fall, having direct access to Robespierre, being given the tasks that no one else wants, has made him taller, handsomer, more authoritative, more confident. He is a late bloomer, so much so that sometimes even I can't believe this is the same provincial educator I hired on with. His body has become more imposing, his face less bony, less hungry-looking. Even the look in his eyes has become stronger.

The Committee of Public Safety is neither public nor does it provide much safety, but it is the chief executive power in the land, so it can call itself anything it wants. And Robespierre, head of the committee, acts now through his chief concealer, chief bloodhound, and first spy, Joseph Fouché. The chief has become the finger that identifies danger, that points out traitors and makes the people's vengeance swift and sure. Whenever Robespierre needs a strong arm, a sure hand for a hard job, to quell the uprising in the Vendée, to raise an army, to impose a tax, to uncover the secret movement of émigré funds, one name keeps returning, one above all the others. Now Fouché is a public figure.

Every now and then you shake and start to whimper, and I calm you with a caress or a hug, like a father calms his child.

I see now that the objectivity I have always strived for is blind. Even enlightenment and sympathy are at best one-eyed. Only love knows. Only love knows without words.

That is why you and I have been able to survive the last four years, separated by guns, spies, guillotines, traitors.

Love knows everything.

The Hospice de l'Archevêché

The hospice de l'Archevêché is right next to Notre Dame, contiguous, but its gates are black as the gates of hell. A sleepy silence reigns over the place. No torches are lit, no warning bell is rung.

—Pasquier, gag the watchman, gag his wife and every guard. Cover the rear and every exit. We have come to end treason.

Fouché watches his men enter like preening peacocks, swords drawn and pistols cocked, red-and-blue uniforms in the torchlight.

A *who-goes-there?* is quickly stifled.

Stepping out of the carriage, Fouché's boots crunch on pebbles as the first window is shattered and his men spread throughout the building.

Torches now light every wing. A *poissarde,* one of those herring women, races down the central staircase, her gown held tight and wrapped around her shoulders. The Archevêché echoes with oaths, and wooden clogs slam down the stone steps, trailing screams. Startled patriots appear, swearing and ready to storm the barricades.

—Everyone out of their rooms, orders Fouché, quick, quick!

The senior poissarde, with a plumed hat and a blood-red riding coat, bullies her way up to Fouché.

—Citizen, what the hell is going on here? Her Serene Cipher says.

—Mordu, search the kitchen. Find me a piece of roast meat and some bread.

The chief poissarde waves her pistol.

—I am in charge here, citizen. I was elected from the Section Bonne-Nouvelle. I demand to know what this is all about.

—Be quiet, you sow, before I concuss you and feed you to the dogs.

Other amazons crowd around—women armed with cudgels, sticks, knives, muskets—tobacco-stained fishwives and their foul mouths. These patriots would tear the Queen limb from limb if they got half a chance, but maybe she has been hidden here under their very noses.

I did not expect poissardes tonight, but these Faubourg Antoine (once Saint-Antoine) street brigades are everywhere these days, pushing their dirty noses and bony arses into things that are of no concern to them. Hags from hell.

Robespierre used these sans-culottes gutter fighters to seize power and cow the Society of Republican Women, who demand that women be obliged to enter the National Guard and to wear the tricolor cockade. The poissardes entered the homes of the feminists and beat them up for holding salons of patronage. All that is good, but in order to govern, the poissardes must also be tamed. And that is not easy. Smelling of wet breadcloth and old herring, they wave kitchen knives and clubs and sit astride plundered cannon.

Phallus straddlers! Nenette, what has happened to the wife-mother ideal of patriotic nurturing womanhood? Somewhere France does have beautiful women with generous republican virtues flowing in their maternal milk.

—Arrest everyone, Pasquier, including this old sack-of-teeth mother superior.

Jeers and ridicule erupt as the herring women are pushed to one side. Shouts of, *Don't touch me, salaud!* and, *Watch out, saloperiedemerdebordelletention!*

Rifle butts and boots herd the personnel into a corner. Some are dragged, others kicked and pummeled.

A print on the wall showing the King as a cuckold goat with horns and the Queen as a plumed hyena, both joined at the rear end, is entitled *One and the Same Hybrid Monster.* Another print shows the Queen as a winged harpy with sharp talons, two parallel tails curved back ready to strike like a scorpion's tail, and the Rights of Man bunched in her claws.

—Bring me the head nurse.

—You mean Guyot?

Fouché, relieved:

—Yes, bring her here at once.

Thank you, Father!

In the search for Guyot and the escaped Queen, every room is ransacked. Patients are thrown from their beds, and cell after cell is stripped of bedding and clothing. Bayonets pierce pillows and mattresses.

Once the official residence of the Bishop of Paris, the Archevêché recently became a hospice, part hospital and part prison. Just this month, the Ministry of the Interior filled it with furniture taken from the houses of émigrés. So amid the squalor and filth one finds fancy plundered beds, antique barometers, Louis XIII tables, finely upholstered Louis XIV chairs.

Fouché recalls something Nenette once said:

At the Trianon, the Queen ordered me to bring in market women so that she and her favorites could learn to pronounce *poissard.* They laughed at the assault on grammar, the tough and threatening slang, and they mimicked it in the plays that were put on stage.

Nenette, only the rich have nostalgie de la boue. When one has lived in mud, grown up in mud, eaten mud, every cell in one's body rejects it and loathes it. Believe me, I know.

—Pasquier, leave no stone unturned. Search the coal bins again. Also the storage rooms, the cellars, the attic. The stables, the drainage ditches, the outhouses.

—We have, commissaire.

—Check again, Pasquier, more thoroughly.

Now the doctors appear: Théry, Naury, and Bayard. The first two are *enragés*, but Fouché talks only to Bayard, the one patriot he semitrusts in this unhealthy trio:

—Does nurse Guyot harbor royalist sentiments?

The chief poissarde answers.

—Yes! She is far too ready and willing to help the sick prisoners get better. And she—

Bayard cuts her off.

—That is our duty; we are medical personnel.

The head poissarde spits on the floor.

—Nurse Guyot shows too much love of duty. I never trusted her.

Mordu returns with a dish of roast fowl. Gravy down his fingers, Fouché enjoys the steaming delicacy; the inside is tender, its skin brown and crisp.

If Guyot is part of this plot, she is just a small cog in a huge mechanism of the escape. I should not waste time on her, but she is the only lead we have so far.

—You herring women eat much too well.

The chief poissarde eyes him sideways.

—Yeah? Well, I seen Marie-Antoinette eat. Every year, that harpy received a deputation of us so-called honest folk for the feast of Saint-Louis. My arse. Every August 25, we's came to the castle in ceremonial white, cleansed of market smells, to present flowers and a token of our affectations.

I do not believe in Christian superstition, but that does not mean I kneel at the altar of vulgarity. I am an ex-Oratorian, but you poissardes are worthless dung.

—Commissaire, quickly!

—What is it?

—Quick, quick, in a cell overlooking the river!

They race through the old sacristy, now the hospice operating room and mortuary, then through the renamed Room of the Republic, the Room of Equality, the Room of the Mountain, the Room of the Seven-Year Itch, and they stop in a room reserved for women suffering of vapors.

—Commissaire, over here!

The window overlooks the river. Fouché sees nothing: Reflections on the water are indistinguishable from the darkness, and tree outlines are barely imaginable. All up and down the river a play of shadows—black trees, black barges, black on black.

—Citizen, we found this rope hanging out the window.

—Was the room prepared for a patient?

No. Yes. The herring women trade accusations.

—Nurse Guyot didn't bring any new patient.

—Yes, she did, I was on duty. I saw her register.

—No, you didn't.

—You bitch, what do you know? You were drunk!

—Ah, shut your beak, you old hen. Madame R was too weak to register, you signed her in yourself.

—No, I didn't.

—Yes, I saw you.

The poissarde mother superior hollers for quiet and slams her riding crop into the faces of those who would keep talking. When a sort of silence is achieved, she says:

—Madame R who arrived today has gone to meet her maker.

Fouché turns pale. What if someone poisoned the widow Capet? *We cannot execute a corpse!* The people will demand a live Queen on the scaffold. What if she has committed suicide? His stomach tightens, thinking of Nenette waiting in the royal cell.

Fouché is frozen by the image of Abraham placing his son on his back for the sacrifice, and Isaac trusting his father, obediently doing his father's bidding, not suspecting that he is about to have his throat slit. He sees Nenette, waiting with that same innocence, completely at his mercy. For the new order, a look-alike would do just as well.

Why resist, Fouché? Justice is an approximate science. The Queen is in her cell; calm down, you have a backup. And your Nenette is worm food just like the rest of us.

—Where is Madame R buried?

—In the cemetery out back. The chief poissarde gestures.

—Mordu, have the guards disinter any freshly dug grave.

In the police, we do not get ulcers, we give them, but tonight everything is upside down. Tonight I must save the Queen so she can be tried and executed properly.

The first reports back from his spies are not encouraging: de Batz is still untraceable, Coigny has joined Condé's émigré army, Fersen is still in Brussels, Goguelat has emigrated, Jarjayes also. The suspects are accounted for; their alibis check out. There has been nothing suspicious all evening; no movement of men, no forcing of the barriers at the city gates, no—

—Chief, they say Nurse Guyot has not been seen since morning.

—Where is she?

—No one knows.

Nenette, you are replaceable, you are a mere distraction. Women like you come my way every day, and I pay no attention to them. I am a family man, a loving father; I have no time for anything frivolous. To give in to passion goes against my nature. Whenever I sleep with you, I tell myself you are an aberration. My real mistress is the revolution, an idea, a concept of justice. Each time we are together, I tell myself I can do without you. Sometimes I think it three or four times a day. But is it really true?

—Pasquier, find me Danton; concentrate on him and widen the circle of suspects. Find out what his friends are up to: Courtois, Desmoulins, Rolland. We have to check all the indulgents, all the softies who want to cut a deal with the Austrians, and any royalist sympathizer or Catholic crackpot. Orléans, the misnamed Philippe-Égalité, is in prison, but have him questioned. And Malesherbes may be seventy-two, but the old goat offered to defend the Queen in court; he has a daughter living in London.

—Boss, Malesherbes is in his chateau in Pithiviers, down in the Loiret. There's no time to bring him in tonight.

Fouché looks at his Brequet watch and finds himself jotting down lists of names, some names that he crosses out, others he repeats. He glances at the hospice's leather-bound visitors' book.

—Mordu, check out any patient who arrived or left within the last three hours.

Fouché sees Mordu winking at a poissarde and pumping his fist at the ground to indicate copulation, and he jerks his head back to his notes.

The lower classes are crude, and they are lower. That is their fate. They cannot be otherwise. My village was full of Mordus, and I could have ended up a Mordu myself, but education saved me. Of course, aristocrats are crude, too, but in different ways.

Pasquier now approaches with a report found hidden under a floor tile in Guyot's room. It is said to be in her handwriting:

Medications are being watered down or not given; this is causing gangrene and frequent unnecessary deaths. The ten nurses hired at this hospice de l'Archevêché are drunks, bloodsuckers, thieves, stonemasons, and waiters as well as poissardes; not one of them has any knowledge of health or hygiene. Naury, the health officer, does not bother visiting the sick; he considers bandages a waste of resources. As for Théry, the chief doctor, the best possible cure one can have from him is that he not care for you.

Fouché tucks the report away for further use.

—We have been through all the rooms, says Pasquier; there is nothing there.

Suddenly a rush of men is heard in the courtyard, and a gathering of torches surrounds a carriage. Mordu, excited, with vaporous breath leaping from his mouth, runs up.

—We found it behind the stables, chief! This carriage matches Larivière's drawing of the one that took the Queen away today.

Mordu throws his head back, lets out a silent scream, and clenches his fist.

Fouché is more guarded. He circles the carriage and compares it to Larivière's ink sketch. The big heavy covered berline is pulled by four horses, with space for a coachman seated on top and a footman at the back.

—Mordu, who used this last?

—They say it came here about three hours ago carrying a gray-haired old woman, a patient who hemorrhaged on the back seat.

—Who owns it?

—The Duchess of Tours.

Like doubting Thomas, Fouché extends his hand and touches the blood on the rear banquette.

I love this magical surge in the soul, this elation that makes police drudgery worthwhile, that little tingle when you first sense that an insect cannot untangle itself. They feign, they try to evade, but eventually all get caught in my invisible web. And the more they struggle, the faster they give up.

It is obvious why the plotters ditched this carriage, because it is slow and conspicuous. They will have jumped to a faster, lighter cabriolet or two-horse hackney, which they did not want anyone at the Conciergerie to see. But why did they come here to the Archevêché, a nest of angry poissardes?

—Pasquier, send a detail to check downriver. They may have ditched the carriage, climbed out of that window and into a waiting boat.

Fouché stalks the dark hospice corridors, flagstones worn smooth over centuries, echo with boots. Moths flit at the windows and around the torches. Fouché does not believe in a river escape; it is too obvious. Perhaps the whole reason for leaving the carriage here is to get him racing down the Seine, and yet he cannot afford not to follow up on this trail.

What do I want on my tombstone? HE SURVIVED, HE GOT BY. *No, my sole wish, call it a rage, is not to let this night erase all I have sacrificed, all I have strived for.*

Outside the hospice walls, near the quay, Fouché examines the spot where the rope would have landed; then he examines the river. He smells mulchy tree roots, moss on old stones, the black lapping of waters, and the smell of wood fires burning.

It is impossible to found a new society without completely annihilating the old. The ancien régime will live on as long as its principal symbol lives. To those who say we are priests at a cult of human sacrifice, so be it! The Queen's blood will be our regeneration. To desecrate her is to sacralize the nation. If, as they claim, she is an enchanted, magical figure, we will disenchant her and so enchant the realm. Our point is to make a point. This will not be murder but social progress.

There are no boats, but he stops because an image catches his eye: A barefoot boy, age seven or eight, is standing perfectly still, peeing into the river. He pees so clean and straight, it is almost as if the river were shooting up into the boy, and Fouché stares at him.

—Petit, have you been here all evening?

The boy nods. Fouché hands him a coin.

—Have you seen anyone climb down from that window?

The urchin bites the coin to make certain it is real and stares back.

—Well, have you? Talk, fool!

The boy shakes his head.

—Noticed anyone getting into a boat to cross over the river here?

Again a shake of the head.

The entire revolution, everything Fouché does from morning to night, is for this boy whose feet are muddy and bare and blue with cold, but the boy is not asking for anything, he is just standing there like a dumb animal, waiting, not certain if he will be allowed to go on living, killed, thanked or what. And Fouché has no time to explain any of this to him.

Mordu reports back.

—Chief, we've dug up the one fresh grave there is, but the body is not the Queen's.

—All right, we have wasted enough time here. Let's go. Hurry, Mordu.

He half runs back to his carriage.

I do not want a black stain of shame on my tombstone: You lost the Queen, you were incompetent, you failed, you lacked the requisite tenacity for the job. I do not want to be a refugee in my own life.

—Let us go visit this Duchess of Tours fast, Mordu.

Fouché settles inside his carriage, and on a sheet of paper he draws a large wheel, with the axis being the empty Conciergerie prison cell. The Queen is somewhere on the circumference of the circle, where he has written names of suspects. Clockwise from the top they are Danton, Nurse Guyot, the Duchess of Tours, and so on.

In an ordinary investigation, he would start from the most likely suspect and work his way down, but tonight he must hunt them all at the same time, even the least likely one.

Forget Nenette, Fouché, let her go. No one will suspect a thing. Now is the time to retreat into your persona; dispose of Nenette. Do it now, be true to yourself. The more you give to the public good, the more you receive.

Eight-thirty P.M. Nenette has been in that cold cell watched by Bault, Larivière, and the others for two whole hours. Fouché closes his eyes. It is Breguet time again: Nurse Guyot arrives at the Conciergerie at 4 P.M., leaves around 4:30 P.M. The order with forged signatures is given to Larivière at 5 P.M. Soldiers escort Marie-Antoinette out of prison at 5:10 P.M. The duchess's carriage deposits her at the hospice. In their rush, they forget to hide the carriage, or do they plant it there to send Fouché on a wild goose chase downriver? No, while everyone is searching for a slow berline, they switch the Queen to a fast, lean carriage and hurry her to a safe house.

I must get more sleep, eat better, keep normal hours. My bones are beginning to stick out. I look like a scarecrow. I feel like one too. I need rest.

There were many times when I thought if I were to lose you I would lose everything.

So why did I come?

Out of despair. It was all going at a snail's pace, and all their preparations were such a waste of time. I could not stand it any longer, the waiting and the not knowing, the being without you.

Shhh, now lie still and sleep.

I do not believe as others do, I do not live as they do, I do not love as they do. Every time I tried to tell anyone what I feel for you, or even when I tried to write it down, words limited and constrained the absolute nature of my feelings. I could not stand having my passion denied by my attempt to express it, so eventually I said nothing of what I really feel to anyone. Even to my sister Sophie, I gave only the bare outlines.

The Duchess of Tours

Garbage is being collected, night stalls are closing, and shutters are fastened tight. A city is going to bed. Heads are settling on pillows, excited about tomorrow's show—the trial all of Paris has been expecting for months.

With King Louis, the sixteenth of that name, it was different: He was tried by a vote of the national deputies. Fouché and many others elected as moderates swore they would protect the King's honor, but when the street broke into the National Convention and started chanting and roughing them, they voted for death. It was a matter of survival, fast political education, and thinking on your feet; 254 centrists, Fouché among them, learned that murder in defense of virtue is not a vice. Some deputies made long speeches; Fouché, who the night before told his closest allies he would vote to spare the King's life, appeared at the rostrum pale as a ghost and said only two words, *La mort*. Five of his seven fellow deputies from Nantes voted to acquit. Fouché told his pregnant wife he was scared for her life, and that his vote would not count for much. But it was also the beginning of a new vocation for Fouché, a new path. Since that January 16 nine months ago, he has been one of Robespierre's closest allies.

Now, after a long delay, much bribery and intrigue, and constant popular pressure from extremists, on October 3 the National

Assembly voted to try the Queen. She will be tried by a revolutionary court like any common traitor, and many Parisians tonight have left orders to be woken early so as not to miss a minute of the historic proceedings.

⁂

De Tours lives in a small ground-floor apartment, with two windows that give out onto a private garden. Fouché questions a few neighbors, then orders the soldiers to break down the duchess's door.

It appears as if a whole palace has been squeezed and shoved into two rooms, so there is hardly any space left to stand. Books are stacked two and three rows deep on the shelves, piles of dusty papers and folders fill the shadows, thick with airless old-woman smells. Oil paintings hang all the way up to the ceiling.

A Pekinese lies cozy on the bed, stretched among pillows, in a cacophony of colors. On the floor is a dish of food for the cat, but the kitty is hiding. The duchess in her bathrobe, eighty-eight years old, white as parchment, sits on the bed, waiting. She tries to smile.

—Every day the doctor bleeds me. That is why I could not open my door fast enough for your men.

—You are hiding someone, says Fouché.

She smiles wanly.

—A useless old woman such as myself, who would I hide?

—Citoyenne, we found your carriage at the hospice de l'Archevêché. It was used to enter the Conciergerie illegally this afternoon at five P.M.

—My poor fellow, that carriage was stolen. I have not seen it in over a year.

—That is odd. One of your neighbors, a member of the Fraternal Society of Help to the Jacobins, swears your carriage left here at four P.M. and that the coachman spoke to you in a foreign language.

—Your friends would swear anything.

The duchess touches the hair at the back of her head and stays that way, staring at the floor as if she has forgotten his presence in front of her.

—Do you know where the widow is?

—Which widow? France is suddenly nothing but widows.

—L'Autri-chienne.

— With his boot, he nudges the duchess out of her reverie.

—The Queen of France? Monsieur, the Versailles gossips were jealous of her. They could not stand her independence, her charm. It is not the street rabble that spread lies about her, it was us, monsieur, the court nobility; we were her worst enemy! We are to blame for all this! De Tours raises a handkerchief to her mouth.

She is right; what courtiers would try to save a woman they so reviled?

—Monsieur, at thirty-eight, Marie-Antoinette has the wisdom of one twice her age; seldom before has France had a queen so polished.

On the walls, Fouché sees Greuze paintings of ladies in farthingales and hoopskirts, basket dresses and piled hairdos. Clerks of the devil, Robespierre calls them, she-monkeys all, women in flounces, ribbons, majestic fans, and heelless mules, ornamental pretties designed to catch the male. Even the duchess in her eighties, in her bathrobe, decrepit, white as whalebone, doddering, has a coquettish aristocratic smile. She is falling apart, with no amplitude in her bosom, but she still has that studied smile.

—Mordu, search everywhere.

—Marie-Antoinette is nothing you can imprison, monsieur. Do not even try; you will fail. She is the spirit of an age—brilliant, witty, delicate, but courageous.

I should kill this old bag, throttle her by her frail chicken neck, and hand her to the dogs. No one would care or even notice.

—Commissaire, you are not from Paris?

The duchess addresses him as if they were at a dinner party, oblivious to the men rifling through her drawers.

—Is that why you look so anxious, so breathless tonight—this city does not agree with you?

Do I spare her because in an odd way she reminds me of you, Nenette? Have I become that sentimental and sloppy? Or do I let her live because the best way to break a case is the slow accumulation of fact, like a good story full of detail, and I need this old hag to make a mistake and divulge who was driving her carriage?

On the wall, Diana the huntress bares her breasts and carries a hunting bow. From the ceiling hangs a chandelier in the shape of a Montgolfier balloon with twelve candles and countless crystal pendants. Fouché is glad these balloons are impossible to steer, so there is no likelihood the Queen is airborne, on her way to the border or for instance to Danton's country house at Arcis-sur-Aube.

—Duchess, you are a flea on the body social; you live off the blood of the people. You have never worked, never baked bread or composed a sonnet, or even tightened your own corsets. The most you ever managed is to laugh, play tarot, and talk of nothing.

—And you, monsieur, are you any better? You go around snooping, spying, breaking down doors. At least I have never hurt anyone. Her eyes flicker in her white face, albino-like.

—I defend France.

—You defend your own neck, monsieur.

—I defend the revolution from its enemies, internal and external.

Fouché, just hand her over to Mordu; he will extract the information you need.

—My friend, it is your neck that concerns you most.

—Citoyenne, I have dispatched older and frailer women than you.

—Go ahead, parade my head around on the end of a pike like they did to the Queen's friend, poor Madame de Lamballe.

Fouché, smother this worthless courtesan, this insult to humanity, this human pustule. Do not waste your time talking, kill her.

With supreme self-control, he smiles at her indulgently. Nothing in this apartment is straight, nothing symmetrical; there are no sharp angles. The furniture, the brass fixtures, even the wall hangings are feminine, coquettish, pretty—so too the delicate canopy over the bed, carved upholstered panels, deep cushioned armchairs. The room is so ornamented, veneered, lacquered, and decorated that Fouché can barely breathe. He loathes it, yet he can well imagine Nenette thriving among all this rococo, and that is what arrests him.

—Mordu, turn this place upside down.

The duchess picks up her little dog and walks into her tiny half garden. Behind her, rough hands tear through her things. In front of her, washed sheets hang drying in the unaristocratic air.

Fouché is cold and tired. Despairing, he fights doubt.

You need Nenette, Fouché. You need the very kind of caring and tenderness you say you do not need. So the later the hour, the more panic builds. And it gives you hives to think of Nenette belonging to this decrepitude, this moral swamp, but this is her camp. Nenette is a baroness. When you had nothing to eat, Fouché, she was lounging with courtesans like the whores in these paintings. Forget her, kill her, wipe her from your mind. Single-mindedness is all that can save you now.

Fouché examines a shelf of books. He finds titles by the libertine La Mettrie, a treatise on asthma, another on dysentery. Rousseau's *Confessions* and his *Reveries of a Solitary Ambler* are here, but also books on sewing and needlepoint as well as *The Transoceanic Voyages of Captain Ceola* and Marivaux's *Harlequin Polished by Love*, Beaumarchais's *Barber of Seville*, Bernardin de Saint-Pierre's *Paul et Virginie*, Condillac's *Treatise on Physical Sensations*, two volumes of Diderot's *Encyclopedia*, Voltaire's *Zaire*, Restif de la Bretonne's *The*

Perverted Peasant, and Abbé Prévost's *Manon Lescaut.* He opens one volume, Rousseau's *Fifth Promenade,* and reads:

> What is it that one so enjoys in this situation? It is nothing external to one; it is nothing but oneself. While the mood lasts one is entirely self-sufficient, like God.

Disgusted, he returns the book to the shelf. *Torch it all. Conceit and banality, burn it all down. Who needs culture? Whose interest does it serve?*

—What do you know of a Nurse Guyot?

The Duchess of Tours smiles, and it strikes Fouché that the old thing is lonely and receives no visits. All her friends are in jail, dead, or have emigrated, and she does not mind this visit. In fact she likes the intrusion, the talk. And the destruction of her apartment means little to her because she has long ago ceased feeling any attachment to the things of this world.

—What I know, monsieur, is that your revolution does not value beauty. You allow nothing sensual, that is why you are bound to disappear, unloved and—

—Where is the Queen?

—You have no delicacy, no sentiment, monsieur.

—Answer me! Fouché slaps her hard with the back of his hand.

The duchess is so weak, she falls backward into her bedroom. Broken and pathetic, she lies sprawled out among her papers. Her frozen dreamy birchbark face smiles at the bookshelves. Her Pekinese barks and retreats under the bed.

—Have you paid off Danton?

Fouché shakes the old woman.

—Who have you bribed? Who got the Queen her travel papers? Speak!

—You are the one in danger, Monsieur Fouché. Her smile is now skewed and off-kilter.—You are the one who will end up with his neck in the national razor.

Fouché motions for the men to sit her up, and Mordu wipes the blood forming at the corner of her lips. With a trembling hand, the broken duchess reaches for the medications kept in her bodice, and Mordu helps her to swallow a vial of corrosive sublimate and another of crushed rhubarb. Fouché kneels as if in prayer and whispers in her ear:

—We have your son, citoyenne, and we can make his death difficult for him.

—Egremont?

In a gesture of panic, her hand rises to her neck as if to protect the thin filigree gold chain there.

—No, he is in Switzerland.

—We captured him at the border. If you want him to live, help us.

The pale duchess pales further.

—You did not, you are only trying to scare me; that is your technique. But I am too old to frighten.

—I shall send you your son's finger as proof.

Still kneeling at her side, Fouché prays for the truth.

White-haired duchess, you could be my father confessor. It is the same intimacy here as in a confessional. I can smell your labored breath. I kneel before your female pity, fecundity, and love. Sacrifice has an absolute infinite quality, I know this, and your human frailty permits your human strength. You are an angel, but you have no wings, no magic, no miracles, and you are devoted to the altar of privilege. But you are frail like everyone else. May our nation be born from your tears, and from the blood you will shed for us.

Slowly, he pulls her right hand from the thin gold chain at her neck and finds a signet ring hanging there. He examines its seal. The words are backward, but he can read them: *Tutto a te me guida.* She tries to protect it.

—What is it?

—Nothing, a trinket.

With a swift pull, he rips the filigree chain, pockets the gold ring, and stands up. Whatever they prize you take. The difficulty with one as ancient as de Tours is that there is almost nothing she prizes—certainly not her life.

A framed nude has been staring at Fouché since he arrived, and he has been actively ignoring her, but he refuses to be cowed by her anymore: He stares up at *The Toilette of Venus* by Boucher. With the exception of Jacques-Louis David, painters under the ancien régime were agents of privilege and decadence. Why this obsession with studying every nook and cranny of the female anatomy? And why did each pose have to be an invitation to abandon? Painters became pornographers. They lowered the times by idealizing golden silken curls and feet that have never known wooden clogs.

Rococo makes my skin crawl, Nenette. I despise those paintings' come-hither smiles, the innocent naked plump sleep among libidinous satyrs. Aphrodite and Diana are whores, just sitting around, wasting time. To all those who grow up poor and hungry, I say, Eat the rich, eat an aristocrat, teach them a lesson.

The soldiers ripping apart the rooms have broken a small vial of perfume, and the too-sweet stench invades his throat. Fouché covers his mouth and nose with a handkerchief to block out the thick gluey smell but continues to examine the paintings.

—Boucher's patron, the late Louis XV, enjoyed girls of only eight. He says this almost to himself.

—Oh I forgot—virtue is the order of the day.

The duchess gets up.

—Poor Monsieur Fouché, the price you puritans will have to pay will be the life you lead. That will be your penalty, missing out on life. I too was a prude, and too late I learned that all we have left at the end is love and pleasure.

—You know what your problem is? You aristocrats have no sense of shame.

The soldiers now search the attic and the basement.

—Monsieur Fouché, shall I tell you? You want a New Man, you want perfection, but perfection does not exist. Perfection is found only in death.

—No, the revolution is life. It brings new energy to the nation. From now on France will be ruled by merit, not decadence.

She is still bleeding, but her voice is uncowed, persistent:

—If you eradicate all that is bad in man, you will end up by killing man himself.

He recalls the signet ring, *Tutto a te me guida.* Everything leads me to you.

Nenette, it is the motto I would like us to have.

—Why have you not killed me yet, Monsieur Fouché? You seem to hesitate; maybe you are not as inhuman as you pretend to be.

—I am giving you a chance to save your son. Do not make the mistake of doubting me. If you do not help us, madame, we will torture and kill him.

She smiles slowly and looks into the middle distance:

—Maybe you too have a vice, monsieur, a guilty pleasure that dares not speak its name, a hidden flower?

In a sudden rage, or mock rage:

—Madame, we know your carriage was used today for the getaway; that makes you an enemy of the people. The question is, Who are you working with, and where is the Queen?

—Do you honestly think, Monsieur Fouché, that if I knew where the Queen was I would tell those who have killed my husband, my brother, my oldest son?

—We found nothing, chief.

Mordu waits.

—Want me to work the duchess over?

—No, leave her here under guard. She may help us entrap some fellow plotters.

Surrounded by pillows, by dust, by a life that repels him, Fouché grabs a crucifix off the wall and breaks it over his knee.

At its best, religion is revealed ignorance and superstition; at its worst it is fanaticism. That is why the spiritual is counterrevolutionary. Duchess, you think that by dying your Queen will be a Christlike martyr who will sacrifice herself for the redemption of France? Maybe so, but there are two vital differences: Marie-Antoinette is not innocent; Christ was. And she is not God's flesh and blood sent to earth; she is a whore.

Pasquier enters and draws Fouché to the side:

—My men have just come back, citizen. They have interrogated all the names in that hospice visitors' register, examined their alibis, and they all check out. The city is quiet except for a carriage being packed outside Danton's house. He's leaving Paris soon for his house in Arcis.

This offhand throwaway puts Fouché in a spin. Why should Danton be leaving today of all days? Danton is a patriot, but he can be bought. He has substantial debts to pay off. Of course it is him. Who else has the power and stature to pull this off? Who else has been publicly advocating her release?

Fouché, calm down. Control your breathing, be circumspect, try to relax. Danton has a lot of influential supporters. If you do not have Robespierre's full support, if you miscalculate this, Danton can crush you.

Fouché now finds all his hypotheses veering and converging on Danton and his moderates, Indulgents, undecided weaklings who want to sue for peace at any price. Arcis-sur-Aube, Danton's native village, is a day's ride east of Paris, closer to the border with the Austrian Lowlands; is that by chance? From there she could easily escape France. There is too much coincidence tonight, and Fouché has learned that no fact is wholly innocent.

Danton has been ill since the middle of September, but yesterday, Pasquier reports, he applied to the National Assembly for and received permission to go to Arcis and convalesce. Such leaves of absence are almost never given. Yet Danton claims he is worn out, the pressure of work is too great.

It is a lame excuse, Fouché knows, especially for one who is so busy every evening with his many lady friends.

—Pasquier, do not let the sonofabitch slip away. We will go there right away. Goodbye, citoyenne.

The duchess follows him out, fighting not to mention her son. She knows it is too late for that, and anyway pleading would only make things worse.

The squadron awaits on horseback, while Fouché reviews the evening: Marie-Antoinette disappears at 5:05 P.M. in the Duchess of Tours' carriage. No one can identify those who escorted her out of prison. At 8:10 P.M. the carriage is found abandoned at Nurse Guyot's hospice. It is now 9:28 P.M. and the Queen has been gone almost four hours. By coincidence, Danton is about to leave the city, one of the few men in France who has the authority to order any closed city gate in Paris to open.

—Let us go!

Ensconced once more in red damask and bouncing above squeaky springs, Fouché draws his wheel again. This time he tries to think of every suspect he can place on the wheel rim—de Tours, Guyot, de Batz, the Austrians, the Duke of Coburg, and everyone at all connected to the Queen, the Queen's old servants, the Queen's lovers, even Noverre, her old dance teacher sent from Vienna to Paris when she was fourteen to try and give her some grace. He tries to see if there is a link between any of them and that fat pastry-faced ladies' man, bon vivant, and sometime patriot, Danton.

Two Februarys ago, stealing in to France to see you inside the heavily-guarded Tuileries was relatively easy. You could still get mail to me. I knew the guard postings, and I still had the key; the revolutionaries had not changed the lock to your apartments.

I shall always remember that ground-floor corner room of yours facing the Seine. The ceiling moldings, the rich woodwork, the blue and white velvet on the walls. I hid for two days and one night with you there. But in eighteen months how all that has changed!

Now the Committee of Public Safety uses your old bedroom in the Tuileries for its private audiences. And the big oval table in the green dining room next door is where the committee sits and works through the night, often fifteen-, eighteen-hour days. They say Saint-Just and Barère have beds in there.

Pay no attention. I am just muttering.

Danton

Some bastards buy false certificates saying they took part in the attack on the Bastille. The certificate even states whether you were the first, second, or third over the drawbridge on July fourteenth. My brother-in-law works at the Luxembourg prison, and he said, *Mordu, you can make real money there if you close your eyes to certain goings-on, especially the night before an execution.* Prisoners who want to say goodbye or kiss their wives pay in gold. He's put aside a real packet. Money is not what I'm about, mind you. There's no future in being a prison guard. I mean, one half of France can't kill the other half forever, can it?

Finally, I came clean with Fouché. I told him, *Chief, that certificate I showed you that said I was the second over the drawbridge at the Bastille was a fake.* And he said, *I assumed as much. That's why I hired you, for your ability to lie and get false certificates.* That's Fouché for you. Just when you think you have screwed up royally, he turns around and congratulates you.

Unfortunately, building a new world is not too remunerative. I mean, when I see how my brother-in-law's doing, I think the rich may deserve death, but even in prison they know how to tip handsomely. There were 40,000 aristos before the revolution, and now, with natural attrition, illness, old age, the guillotine, and those who've escaped abroad, it doesn't leave many behind. And once the rich have all disappeared, who will be left to give tips then?

Sometimes I receive a few cuts of beef or the odd bottle from patriots come to denounce a traitor. If he notices, the boss tells me, *Go give it back!* As if I could possibly remember who gave me what. Informers would think me mad if I tried that. To them a bribe isn't a bribe, it's a form of politeness.

Now in front of Danton's house at 20 passage du Cour-du-Commerce, there is a huge berline, weighted down with trunks, baskets, and a cask of wine, and the boss tells me, *Take the two foot-men protecting the carriage into custody.* Then he has us roll the carriage to the corner of the street where we can search it out of sight.

—Mordu, for Chrissakes, after you finish put everything back. I do not want to see a garter or silk handkerchief hanging out. Danton must suspect nothing.

—Yes, chief.

—And send riders to Arcis-sur-Aube and alert garrisons along the way.

—Right away.

The chief has a lot on this bastard. He's been collecting it for the Incorruptible One because it's too hot to entrust to anyone else. We have even intercepted his coded messages.

—Mordu, would one of the most important men in Paris up and leave for his country house at a time like this, just to be with his new wife?

—That's what the son of a bitch is doing, chief.

—You find this hasty exit the night before the Queen's trial suspicious?

I shrug.

—I don't know, chief. I can think of a lot of reasons for getting out of Paris right now. And Danton was born in Arcis. The region has excellent champagne. He has nine siblings there.

—No, Danton is posing as a patriot trying to stop a losing war, but in fact he is hedging his bets in case the royalists win. Mordu, by saving the Queen's head, he could save his own. That is why he would help her escape.

—Or maybe there is too much graft swirling around just now, chief, and the big fat lard is so deeply implicated in a dozen different plots that he can't keep them straight himself and needs a breather.

—Yes, he has never been too fastidious about the company he keeps.

I help the men open up a second trunk. Danton has a lot of supporters, including Robespierre, so the chief is being more careful than usual. He's like a cat circling a wounded rat, not knowing how wounded it is. But just when we have slid the second trunk off the berline and opened it, I see him. It's too late to hide in the shadows or run. Danton comes out of the house, and there is no mistaking him. He has a head like a lion, and white hair swept back in a thick mane. The small upturned nose could be a pig snout. His eyes are small and shoved deep under a heavy forehead, like an ape, with lots of red marks around his mouth from the smallpox he had as a boy.

—Rifling through my carriage, Fouché, is that how a priest acts?

The chief backs away, mumbling.

—Citizen, you of all people must understand the need for public security.

—Security?

Danton keeps advancing undeterred. His roar stops our men cold.

—Fouché, if you are out to get me, you are not going about it with much subtlety.

The man has cognac on his breath—a lot of it, I would say.

He was born just five months after Fouché and also educated by Oratorian priests, but, unlike the boss, Danton has a gift for getting along with people. His ugliness doesn't stop him from charming the ladies; on the contrary, they seem to like his bluntness. Three months after the death of his first wife, Gabrielle Charpentier, he married fifteen-year-old Louise Gély, the nanny of his children. It raised eyebrows because Louise insisted on a religious ceremony with a nonabjuring priest. I know, because their wedding party drank all night at the Procope.

Several faces peer down from his windows—Danton has the whole mezzanine floor, seven rooms of number 20 Cour-du-Commerce.

—Citizen, we were not rifling through your things. The horses took fright, startled, and a trunk accidentally fell and opened.

—Yes, and you accidentally took my two footmen into custody, I see.

The chief doesn't look or sound too confident. His soft voice is even thinner and reedier tonight than usual. We are deep in merde now. This is exactly what he did not want to happen. But when Danton has you dead to rights, he is magnanimous. It's curious about him; he could send us all packing, but he is not vindictive. He seems to want to toy with us; nothing scares him.

—Our interest is only to protect you, citizen.

—Fouché, I hear friends of yours want to gut me like a fat turbot. Well, tell whoever tries that I will eat his brains and shit in his skull. Be sure to pass that along, will you?

How many confrontations has Danton won just by the sheer power of his baritone voice? Even his bull head and wide face have a strength all their own.

—Come, policeman, you'd only break in after I leave, so I will do the honors.

He hooks an arm through the boss's arm and drags him into his house. Fouché is like a delicate flower carried in a bear's paw.

I order the men to keep searching the carriage, because that is what the chief's last look meant.

Inside, Danton presents his dining room.

—Drink and eat, Fouché, you must be starving!

On the table is a magnificent *poularde roulée aux crêtes,* but also *potage d'asperges, cochon de lait à la lyonnaise,* wild rabbit pâté (now that hunting is no longer the preserve of the aristocracy, a lot of wildlife is being killed and brought to market), *côtelettes de veau au petit lard, moules en beignets, oeufs en mâtelote, petits pois à la bourgeoise, oie à la moutarde.* The table is covered in bottles and serving dishes.

There is enough for a regiment, and Danton picks and chooses from all the plates.

—You don't drink, Fouché? Aaah, I hate men who are slaves to their willpower. What the hell is Virtue anyway?

Danton laughs that big throaty free laugh of his.

—Virtue is what I give my wife, Louise, every night.

The boss backtracks. Coarse cynicism is not to his taste, and he's embarrassed. It's funny; next to Danton's white mane, Fouché's thin dark hair plastered against his skull looks listless and sick.

It's a beautiful spacious apartment: two salons, a lobby, three bedrooms, a dining room. The wallpaper represents allegorical paintings with rose-colored ribbon connecting one set of figures to the other. The cream-colored settees and chairs are brand new. Danton pulls Fouché into his study, a smaller room where a fire is burning and two deep chairs await them.

When Danton let himself be voted off the Committee of Public Safety on July 10, he said he was tired of the work routine and the continuous criticism. But maybe the dog had better things to do with his evenings? He is busy planting his seed all over this city, and that is why he needs a rest. He is having a right juicy time with the ladies. According to Charlotte Robespierre, his celebrated masculinity does not always work. When Danton met the youngest Duplay girl he kissed her and grabbed her the moment he set eyes on her, assuming he could deflower her, but Elisabeth Duplay ran off and told Robespierre.

The National Convention reelected Danton to the committee on September 6, but he declined. The convention overruled him. So on September 9, Danton reminded them of his oath never to rejoin the committee and forced them to accept his refusal. No one could understand why. The only way to stay alive is to sit on the Committee of Public Safety and hear what they say about you. I think Danton is hoping the committee will be overwhelmed with problems, discredited, and then they will turn to him to save the country. But if so, he is making a big mistake, or he is getting too old and soft and has no stomach for the fight anymore.

In his study, Danton unpacks a crate and finds an expensive Bordeaux. Servants are putting away his papers, carrying trunks and baskets out to the waiting carriage, but he leaves this up to his first valet to oversee.

—Citizen, there is a plot afoot tonight.

Fouché stands by the open fireplace. I have never known the chief to be warm enough, even in summer.

—Plots, plots, plots. Is that all the police can think of these days?

Danton uncorks the bottle and brings the cork up to his nose.

—They've tried to spring the Queen tonight!

—Good for them!

Danton eyes the boss with a smile on his lips. He's such a huge presence that when he approaches the chief just disappears. I'm not used to seeing the chief so small.

—Fouché, the revolution has gone far enough. Any further and we lose everything. Halt the killing, preserve our hard-won gains.

—Citizen, have you heard of anyone planning to save the Queen?

—Yes, just yesterday that crazy American, the deputy from Calais, approached me in the hallways of the National Assembly and tried to get me involved in some fantastic plot to spirit her away to America.

This is so obviously a false lead, it almost sounds plausible. The problem is, Thomas Paine was thrown out of England and he may be spying for Pitt, so we have had our eye on him, his friends, and his writings.

The boss plays for time because he wants us to go through the carriage thoroughly, but also because Danton talks too much, and a crumb of information from his table can be invaluable. The problem is, he's far from stupid.

I run down to see how the search is proceeding. Pasquier's men have opened four of the seven huge trunks, and they are checking under the floorboards. If the Queen escapes Paris again, it won't be like the Varennes attempt, when she went with great pomp. This time she'll be squished behind a pile of fruit or under a laundry basket. When I get back, they are both seated at the study with a small table between them covered in food, and Danton is eating a quail egg *en gelée*.

—You don't like me do you, priest? Tell me why.

If the boss were Saint-Just, he'd answer, *You cavort with whores; you arrive at public meetings late, stinking of women and wine.* But he is not Saint-Just. The chief can be tentative, he can wait people out; he never fights the powerful straight on, he never goes for the jugular unless he knows he can win.

—Priest, when we started the revolution it was full of passion. Now it has been taken over by bores and mean little men. It is no fun anymore; there is nothing but ambition and cupidity on all sides. I keep thinking we are executing men who have sons and fathers. And if I didn't regard myself as indestructible, I'd begin to wonder whether I myself will survive.

Danton stretches his legs toward the fireplace and puts his hands behind his head. The chief stays seated upright like a boy in school, listening intently, eyebrows arched. He never looks comfortable, Fouché, either in his body or in his mind. He always looks like something is bothering him.

Danton's eloquence has often turned the course of a national debate. And even Fouché seems captivated by his mulberry lips. He is not rubbing his knuckles or jotting down any notes, he's like a skinny cat staring at a big dog, not letting a single detail escape him.

Danton has a rapid direct style of talking, avoidance of all abstinence, a loathing of silence, and a disregard for tentative visitors.

—To make Europe free and republican, Desmoulins used to say that all we need is my big mouth. But now that Robespierre has consolidated his power, that has changed, has it not? The Incorruptible One doesn't want panache. He wants people in line, tame and quiet.

Danton leans forward, over his big stomach, and whispers:

—The Incorruptible One wants things to run smoothly. He wants a different age, an age of quiet work and civic duty. No loud talk, no partying.

Like a priest offering absolution, the chief answers softly.

—The guillotine accomplishes what a whole century of reason could not hope to produce.

—Lasting change is slow.

Danton cuts himself some cheese and pours himself a glass of port.

—It is our enemies who are pushing us to these excesses to make us fail. Fouché, you have turned a perfectly normal province like la Nièvre into a hotbed of rebellion. You have bled the Vendée dry, and things are worse than ever there.

—I protect the revolution.

—Fouché, your protection is destroying us. If anyone is in the pay of foreign powers, I would say it is you. What better way to discredit the revolution than to have us killing our own people?

If the chief were a cat, his hair would be standing on end. Instead, it is flat and limp against his head, but everything else about him is bristling. I know he's hungry, but he has not touched a thing.

—The republic has to forgive. We must release those unjustly imprisoned.

I don't bother checking on the carriage; I keep listening. Danton stuffs his mouth with rabbit pâté—little wonder he has that Montgolfier-size belly.

—The rich like to show clemency, says the boss, staring into the fire. It is what they do to give themselves a good conscience.

—The poor need clemency too.

—No, the only thing that works for the poor is brute strength.

Danton empties his glass. Everything about them is different: One is fat, the other thin; one is a talker, the other a listener; one is practical and generous, the other is idealistic and cheap.

—Those who speak of helping humanity have a tendency to kill men.

Danton's handwriting may be illegible, but his speech is crystal-clear. The house is empty now, only the two of them are left in the study, with the fire going down. Danton, his mouth no longer full, suddenly grabs the boss's right hand as if to woo him.

—Don't you see your course is leading the nation to suicide?

—All of nature kills.

The boss's voice is flat and monotone; it's the only way he can compete with Danton.

—Even in a beautiful forest, there is a struggle to the death to see which tree gets the most rain, the most sunshine.

—Just so. Nature is free to decide, not twelve men seated behind a locked door.

His tone becomes more intimate.

—Priest, you were so quiet for the first six months in National Assembly, I thought you were a deaf mute. When you finally spoke, it was obvious you had rehearsed in front of a mirror. And shall I tell you? You are pedantic when you make a speech, Fouché. I don't know what kind of a teacher you were, but nobody likes to be bored.

—It's not enough to have principles, Fouché, you have to show some warmth and humor—the French only trust full-blooded men. Get a lover. And do yourself a favor; gather a fortune while you can.

The chief pulls his hand free, stands, and walks to the window. The berline is out of sight around the corner, but I know he is wondering if Pasquier's men have finished packing the last trunks and putting everything back.

Now the valets return and start packing the roasts and the leftovers into baskets, and for the first time Danton takes an active interest in their work.

Standing at the window, the boss turns and narrows his eyes. His voice is quiet but as precise as claws.

—Between the purchase of your law office in 1787 and its closure in 1791, you were involved in only twenty-two cases. Yet in that period, you paid debts of 9,600 livres; you paid 2,000 livres a year for the running of your home, plus the interest due on your debt. And suddenly, in August of 1789, you incurred an upholsterer's bill for 3,000 livres which you still have not paid off. And in March of 1791, you invested in property in Arcis valued at 56,000 livres, and a house costing another 25,000 livres.

When the boss has all his facts and goes for blood, I have seen grown men tremble and fall to their knees. But not Danton; he seems amused.

—Are you a policeman or an accountant?

—Since it was expropriated church land, you were only required to pay twelve percent down in paper script. But you chose to pay for Arcis, all in gold.

—Why not? I had just sold my law practice.

—But you still have not received payment for that.

—How would you know?

—Even if you had been paid the exaggerated price you claim for your law practice, it still leaves 100,000 livres unaccounted for. I think you would be the first to sell the Queen's life for that amount, Danton.

—Priest, I know you cannot understand this, but we are in a war, and to the victors go the spoils: fine houses, the best food, handsome clothes, the women of one's dreams. Now to hell with you and your interrogation!

He swallows a cream cake and grabs a decanter of red wine.

—Fouché, if you want to run a country, you have to learn to cut corners.

I leap down the stairs to warn Pasquier that they are coming. The berline is ready. It's in place and waiting by the time Danton reaches it.

He climbs in.

—There is not one of you who knows anything about government. If I gave my balls to Robespierre and you my brains, maybe the Committee of Public Safety could last a bit longer.

The boss's breath steams in the cold night air. He stands on the lowest rung of the carriage's stepladder and looks in.

—Danton, I always held you in great esteem. You were the soul of the revolution. You stank, you lied, you bullied, you charmed, and you took us far! I remember when the convention attacked you for taking money from royalists to save the King's life; you counterattacked. You proposed that a commission investigate the conduct of every deputy since the convention first met, and seconded by Marat you worked the deputies to a boiling froth. I remember it like it was yesterday.

Still standing on the step of the carriage, the boss adds:

—But now that I have met you up close, I have nothing but disdain for you.

—Good, it will help you the next time you give a speech. Use your anger!

The carriage begins to pull out. We watch it disappear into the mist, the horses' shoes clicking on the cobblestones.

—Warn all the city gates, Mordu. I want the carriage stopped and checked again before it leaves Paris. Danton is the key to this plot.

I slip the black cape over his shoulders and fasten it.

—Chief, if you catch a cold, you could be in bed for weeks. We can't afford that. Cover yourself.

—And send a man to Saint-Denis to drop in on Thomas Paine. If there is anything suspicious, bring Paine to me for questioning. After all, Danton and the American are close friends.

Danton's departure has left a real silence. Fouché gets into his carriage but I can see he is still mulling over the conversation.

—The revolution will be made not by opportunists like Danton but by hard-working stiffs like you and me. So don't let them take it away from you, Mordu.

I remove his shoes because I know they must be pinching him. He always takes them off when he goes to sleep.

—Take away what, chief?

—Your having been poor.

—Hey, anyone who wants my poverty is welcome to it, chief!

In the carriage, I tuck a blanket over his knees. That's when I realize that Mirabeau, Talleyrand, Danton, and Robespierre were all born *de* something. Only the boss is *de* nothing. He was born in the merde, like me, and his poverty is as tight as a fist in his chest. It's the strongest, hardest thing he has. Now it's me standing on the bottom step looking into the carriage just like Fouché was doing moments ago.

—Shall I tell you what the real problem is with aristocrats, Mordu? They are too interested in having fun and cavorting while we rebuild the world.

—And priests? This just blurted out of me. I'm worried the boss may take it as a veiled attack, but he answers before I can change the subject.

—No, Mordu, priests have another agenda. Priests talk to God every day, they're trained to do it from their tenderest age.

He thinks for a while.

—Morning, noon, and night priests have God inside them, an omnipresent voice, a smell, a feel. Even if they cut him out, reject him, something of him remains. It is hard for one who comes to God as an adult to understand this. But if you come to him young, Mordu, you continue to have him inside you even when you try to kill him over and over. He can't disappear. He's in you.

A woman has stepped out of the shadows, a big stout woman with short white hair and thick arms.

—Citizen, I'm a patriot, elected by the neighborhood committee, and I've been watching Danton all week. Today he received a visit from a man who spoke German. I know it wasn't no French that he spoke, so I reported it to the committee right away.

Fouché, leaning out of the carriage, describes a bald man, short and thin.

The woman nods.

—That's him, yeah.

The boss smiles.

—Where can we find Lindhal at this hour, Mordu?

—Up in the Palais-Égalité, chief, at the café Grotto. If he's in town, he'll be drinking himself to death up there.

I slip the woman a coin.

—Good, let's find our Austrian agent. And fast!

Without you for the last two years, I lost my feelings; I lost interest in life and the ability to laugh.

Without you, the world around me was extinguished.

I made a dozen different plans for your escape, each one more daring, more complicated, more expensive and difficult than the last. Each had a flaw. There were too many unknowns.

I thought I had lost you forever.

Only now that you are with me do I feel I can begin to live again. Now I too long for peace and quiet.

The First Time They Met

Normally the rhythm of the carriage at this time of night would put him to sleep, but there is no question of sleeping tonight. He feels the tension and danger of the evening squeezing his chest and gripping his temples. He closes his eyes, but he can go for two or three days without sleep. If he were to lie down on a bed right now, he would be as rigid as a board. And to think that tonight Nenette was going to give him a bath and rub his back.

He recalls her white skin, her warm smells, her arms, how she sleeps on her back with one arm around him. He misses her hands, her strength, her beautiful face.

Why is Danton fingering Paine? Since March the American pamphleteer has lived in self-imposed exile up in Saint-Denis, ten kilometers north of Paris. Paine never comes to the convention anymore; informers describe him as frozen with fear now that most of his Girondin allies have been arrested. Representatives of his constituency came to Paris this summer to protest that Paine is not up to the job of deputy. He does not attend the assembly anymore but spends his time feeding ducks and pigs in the courtyard of his lodgings. On October 3, in the convention, Deputy Amar read out Paine's name in a list of traitors. No wonder; he has given up politics in favor of playing marbles, hopscotch, battledores, chess, and cribbage.

No, it is not Paine; the American is a marked man with a noose tightening around his neck. This is Danton's doing. My agent closest to Danton is Lindhal. Why has he not made a report yet?

Fouché sends agents to check on Danton's house in Arcis as well as all the roads leading there from Paris. The hunch is so strong it is overwhelming. Danton's financial dealings, his taking bribes to save the King's life, to inflate army contracts, make him the obvious culprit. And dining on truffles and fresh crayfish is not cheap.

The situation is so jeopardized that, without effective police, evil would win the day. My forte is the slow accumulation of detail, much of it apparently useless, which builds over time into a giant web, revealing truth slowly. But tonight the hunt is too rushed, and the problem with doing things in a hurry is that leads get dropped, forgotten, missed. What has happened to Nurse Guyot, for instance?

Fouché has followed the wheel of likely suspects from the Queen's prison cell to the hospice, to the getaway carriage, to the Duchess of Tours, to Danton. Given a month, he could investigate each suspect one at a time and sew the case up tight, but he has only a handful of hours left: nine, to be exact.

Riding in the back of his carriage, he pulls out his order pad and his new pencil, given to him by the engineer Nicolas Conté. Since February 1, when France declared war on Great Britain and all commercial relations between them were interrupted, France has not been able to import any graphite from the Cumberland mines. Now Conté has come up with this ingenious idea of placing either clay or a tiny sliver of graphite in the bored-out center of a stick of cedar. It fits the hand perfectly, it writes well, and the British do not have it. Ah, French ingenuity! The only problem is one keeps needing a knife to sharpen the point of the pencil.

His mind goes back to those nudes on the Duchesse de Tours' walls:

Suddenly I saw you lounging about with stags and shepherds in Elysian fields, at play with satyrs. I could not stand the thought of you, Nenette—all innocence, honesty, simplicity—reclining half naked among goat boys. Humanity deserves better than a show of buttocks and breasts. To think of you among royal hunts, masked balls, and tapestries while citizens as skinny as scarecrows beg bread in the street is torture. Aristocrats fill their lives with dance, operas, dinners, disguise parties—all of them slaves to Madame Whore—but not you, Nenette, not you, I cannot abide it.

Now, between arrest orders, Fouché jots down images, fleeting thoughts, impressions about Nenette, but not in Alexandrins:

> Your smell is on the breeze.
> I have kissed it a thousand times.
> How outrageous,
> how banal too,
> this need for you.
> Even now, the breeze
> brings you to my side
> and I see myself
> kissing your round full lips.
> Nenette, I need to break
> this addiction to you.

He recalls the first time they met.

Nenette, you looked cold. I made Mordu give you his overcoat. I was hoping that if he covered up your goose bumps and your hourglass figure, you would appear more neutral, but the loose blue army coat only accentuated your femininity, like surrounding a flower with rough stones.

—Let me explain something, *you said.* My name is Nenette. They have made a mistake. I am a commoner, not a baroness.

Under normal circumstances, I would have attacked you for betraying your supposed working-class background, and I would have picked your story apart for inconsistencies. I would have confronted you with records from Mondoubleau that proved you were a baroness, but I did not want to argue with you over petty details. I said:

—The moment you entered this jail, citoyenne, there was no hope for you. So do not shout, beg, or throw yourself at my feet. All I can do for you is delay the day of reckoning.

Our eyes locked. It was a stare of such sweetness, I had never known staring could be so sensual. It was like eating a rich warm dessert without using one's hands.

—No one can live without hope, Citizen Fouché. Give me hope.

—I can protect you while you work for me, Nenette. That much I can do.

You removed your shoe and rubbed your foot, and your unveiled ankle was a marvel to behold. I knew then we were talking about us, you and me.

—Citizen, please lie to me; I don't care if you lie. It will help me to live.

We could have been two timid lovers standing naked facing each other for the first time, neither one daring to move in the room. I wanted to touch you, but horrified by this desire I shrank back.

—What work would you have me do, citizen?

—I would use you as a decoy to flush out royalists. Have you a problem with that?

—No.

—You do not mind helping us to hunt down your old friends?

—Not if it will give me hope.

—It will not be pretty work, and it will not be easy. But that is life.

—No, for me life is a book I like to read, or a child I hold in my arms, or the warm sun on my face. Life is going to sleep at night tired and waking up in the morning to the smell of rich hot coffee; that is life.

For the first time ever, you reached up and touched me. You placed four fin-

gers on my chest, held them there—*I remember it exactly, even the pale half-moons of your nails.*

—Nenette, every day I send far prettier women than you to the scaffold. Women with children and heartbreaking stories. Do not think that you are special in any way.

—Then stop playing with me. Just kill me and be done with it.

I marveled at how your face flushed, how quickly you changed, and how effortlessly you regained your composure.

—You think you are doing me such a favor by plucking me out of the line, telling me you want me to betray all my friends, but later you'll kill me? Farmers have a Judas goat, and that goat leads all the others to slaughter, but he never gets killed. The Judas goat is safe forever.

You stared at the place where one is not supposed to stare at an ex-priest.

—If you are going to kill me later, why don't you just kill me now?

—Because I can use you.

You were tired; you looked like a tracked animal. You turned away to the window, and I heard you mutter:

—I should give up.

—Can you be my Judas goat, Nenette?

—Yes, of course. I said it already.

You seemed far away.

—But do not make the mistake of thinking that months from now I will soften.

I hated myself for being so stiff, so Fouché-like. I knew I was losing you.

—Are you cold, Nenette? You are shaking like a lamb that has just learned to walk.

You smiled.

—When the mob broke down the gates at Petit Trianon, I was holding the last of Marie-Antoinette's prize lambs. The poor thing was so nervous, he was running around his stall banging against the walls to get out. I think I was more afraid, more agitated than he was. I took refuge in his little pen, hidden in one of the out buildings. I prayed to God they would not find us. To get him to keep still and not give away our hiding place, I calmed him down, I talked to him, I lied. I whispered that everything would be all right and there was nothing to worry about. I held out my hand. I gave him some fresh grass. I didn't know what else to do. At last he seemed resigned to my presence, and he approached me. He chewed the grass from my hand, but he was trembling all over, and he kept his ears pricked, ready to bolt at the first approach of the horde. What could one of Marie-Antoinette's beloved lambs expect from a mob of illiterate cutthroats? What could I, for that matter? We were both trapped. After a while, it was the lamb calming me down. I prayed they would tire of so much pillaging and just leave. I began to think they might pass us by, but eventually they started in on the barns, and I could hear animals bellowing and screaming, being chased and hacked to death. Sitting in the golden sunlight streaming through the window, I stared at my beautiful scared lamb, all white and trembling, his nostrils shivering, the air full of dust. And I broke down in tears for him and for me and for the world at large. Eventually, the mob found us and slit his throat. When they hung him upside down, I saw that bit of just-chewed green grass still there.

—And you, Nenette, what did they do to you?

—Nothing. The day before I had rolled myself naked in thistles. The sheep did not mind, but the people shrieked when they saw me. I had huge black swollen welts all over my body. I paid a doctor to lie and say I had the plague. It was not difficult to convince the mob to leave me alone after that.

Somehow that story does not affect my image of your innocence. On the contrary, it reinforces everything I think of you.

His carriage now stops on the edge of the Palais-Royal (redubbed Palais-Egalité). It was here that the first look-alike, Nicole le Gay, twenty-three, plied her trade under the name Madame de Signy until the night of August 11, 1784, when she was used to impersonate the Queen in the Affair of the Diamonds. After the scandal broke and the trial established the fraud, Nicole gave birth to a bastard child in the Bastille and died in a convent on June 24, 1789. But what mattered to Fouché was proof that the subterfuge could be done. So this den of harlots has special significance for him.

Through the flow of dressmakers, single mothers, and fallen actresses who live off men, all promenading arm-in-arm, Mordu comes running up.

—Boss, we found Lindhal! He's here!

Fouché always insists on respecting the formality of covers for his spies, but tonight he loathes the ridiculous apparition he sees approaching down the sidewalk.

The Austrian's hair is wispy across his bald pate. He approaches stinking of lavender water and blood sausage, with three young cocottes on his arm and two dandies in tow. Lindhal speaks at the pace of a slow minuet.

—Here are my three muses, Beauty, Truth, and Justice.

—Be in my carriage in ten minutes, Fouché whispers.

Lindhal nods, but his face betrays nothing as the cocottes laugh and drag him away.

Being apart from you for so long was for me a sort of death. My worst nightmare was when I imagined that perhaps you doubted my sincerity, my devotion. This thought nearly drove me out of my mind.

Sleep now, sleep. Shhh.

I suppose I do not really believe this is happening, that you are lying here, my love, in my arms, and that we will soon be free, you and I. It seems so impossible. Will I wake up and find this has all been a dream?

It is so good to feel your slow warm breathing on my arm. Even if the entire rest of the world hounds us and chases us to the ends of the earth, from now on we will always be together.

Hugo Lindhal

In the back of his carriage, parked by the Jardin-Egalité, Fouché
awaits Lindhal. He takes a sip of water from his silver flask and
splashes some on his face to wake up. A commissioner plenipotentiary, he is also a man of letters. This year he has published
three pamphlets, *Reflections on the Judgment of Louis Capet, Reflections on
Public Education,* and *Report on the Draft Law Relating to Colleges.* But what
he cares most for these days is the writing he never shows to anyone, his poetry.

Don't waste anymore time thinking about her, Fouché.

He glances out at the stew of bodies. In front of a tavern,
voices and aromas press and jostle. Past the window, he sees
gentlemen of uncertain quality mixing with fops, pedants, wits,
artists, odd-job men, rough artisans. The crowd here at Palais-
Egalité is not as wild as it used to be, but they still come thick
as lice to see farces, melodramas, marionettes, and child actors.
Some sip lemonade; others visit wigmakers, play chess, applaud
a strolling minstrel, listen to a defrocked priest attack his bishop.
Many ogle the lantern and shadow-light shows. Others play
billiards. Whores and magistrates mingle here. The Terror has
not put a stop to this yet, only increased its tempo and its despair. Philippe d'Orléans recently converted the Palais-Royal,
his family's Paris property, into a popular shopping center. The

cafés, taverns, and arcaded boutiques surrounding the entire perimeter of the garden are full of explosive and excited oratory, a distribution center for thousands of pamphlets and scurrilous libel.

How did Christ spend so much time with the scum of the earth, with whores, tax collectors, and beggars?

Fouché loathes the suggestive stares of night ladies who mistake him for a possible customer; to avoid the possibility of being recognized, he covers his nose with his handkerchief.

A rider appears and reports.

—Commissaire, they have stopped Danton at the Porte de Vincennes. They are searching his carriage again.

—Good, do not let him get away until he has been cleared.

—Chief, take care, says Mordu; Danton has permission to retire in Arcis. It was a vote of the National Convention.

—But he has not permission to sell out his country.

In the carriage, Fouché checks his watch. Why should Danton be quitting Paris the night before the Queen's trial? Does he owe the Austrians a favor? Why should a man who loves women so much leave Paris to hide in Arcis, and why tonight of all nights? No royal escape comes cheap. Who is financing this?

—Mordu, bring me Lindhal. Drag him out of the whorehouse naked, if need be; I can't wait any longer. Fouché places his fingers one against the other so his hands form a little chapel.

So often I have looked at a blank wall and seen a painting, or I have looked at a sky or a sunset and have thought I should capture this moment. And wanting to hold on to the moment, fix it, make it last, I jotted it down. But papers get lost, the moment passes, and I misplace my notes, my insights. Thousands such moments have come and gone in my life. Nenette will be another, another in an endless series of losses. That is why I jot down poems in my arrest-order booklet. I am Marcus Aurelius writing philosophy while defending the empire from the barbarians, and this is a map of my heart.

Fouché opens his order booklet and writes:

Infinity is a label we use
for a number that is
bigger than anything we can name.
Infinity plus one, plus two,
does not exist, or does it?
I shall miss you, my Nenette.
You are the only purity in my life.
You are my infinity.

Fouché, throw your poems into the fire. They are too personal. You fight for the public good, you have no time for the personal.

He jots down: Nenette, what you give me, you give without even knowing you give it.

Breguet time: The Queen escapes, her getaway carriage is found, the Duchess of Tours is in on the plot. So is Danton. The wheel of suspects grows more elaborate on his note pad, more difficult to read.

Hugo Lindhal walks up, stands with his back hunched over as if carrying a heavy load. Without his cocottes, his dark eyes give him the air of a tired street peddler. He has a posture Fouché always wants to straighten when he sees it. There is an old-world uselessness about Lindhal, his sad eyes forever squinting, an air of someone out of breath from running to stay up with the times.

—You go too far, Hugo. I should not put up with your whoring around.

—I have to, citizen, in order to be of use to you and allay suspicion. Otherwise my aristocratic friends would be on to me in a minute.

He is bald, but he carefully combs his long side hairs up over his large bony head. Fouché opens the door of his carriage; this is his rolling office, where conversation can take place without risk of being overheard. Lindhal climbs in, trailing cheap perfume.

—What do you know about Danton's machinations to spring the Queen?

He sits opposite Fouché and takes his time answering. Without ladies to inspire him, Lindhal has a sad little rat face, made smaller by his heavy dark eyebrows and long nose. He was private secretary to the last Austrian ambassador to Paris, Count Mercy-Argenteau. It gave him access to invaluable information, including the fact that since 1791, when Mercy was appointed governor of the Austrian Lowlands, he has continued to advise Marie-Antoinette by secret mail. It is Lindhal who pointed out that the Queen uses the code name Josephine when she writes to Fersen. It is Lindhal who told Fouché of the aborted plan by General Dumouriez to ride on Paris with a small cavalry corps and snatch the Queen away. It is Lindhal who unveiled the plot hatched by von Fersen to hold French deputies, including the French Minister of War, as hostages in exchange for the Queen— a plan that might have succeeded but for the stupidity and inconsistency of the allies, who returned the four without any quid pro quo. So Fouché gives Lindhal, his most reliable Austrian double agent, freedom to cross the border at will.

—There is a plot tonight to spring the Queen. Is Danton behind it?

Lindhal speaks slowly, as if a marble fountain were throwing perfumed water into a scalloped bowl.

—No, the Austrians will make it look like Danton is involved, because they want you to tear each other apart.

Fouché's first hunch is that Lindhal is lying. He has a sudden desire to blow the man's head off.

—Danton is not involved?

—No, for once he is clean.

—Danton claims Tom Paine is involved.

—The American?

Lindhal smiles at various cocottes who advertise themselves in doorways.

—No, Paine does not speak French well enough. He is a friend of Danton's, but he is not corrupt. He has risked his life to destroy the power of monarchy in America, England, and France; Paine is a man of principle. He would never have anything in common with Marie-Antoinette.

It is late, already past 11 P.M., and Fouché cuts off his spy.

—Danton could engineer this last-minute escape from the Conciergerie. Danton could put all the pieces together, the secret funds—

—Yes, he could. He has the safe houses, the mercenaries, the passports. Everything.

—But I have been with him these last two days, says Lindhal, and believe me, he is not involved.

Fouché tries to ignore the smell. On the sidewalk, not far, a woman is stirring a stewpot over a fire. To the half-full pot she has been adding bread, garlic, grated onion, some butter, water. If she were even a little more affluent, she would add cabbage, broad beans, turnips, carrots, and peas, but this permanent cooking pot stews here for days, and no well-brought-up dog of the ancien régime would touch this. Yet here the hungry line up to beg or buy a bowl. He motions for Mordu to advance the carriage out of range of the smell.

—So if not Danton, who would snatch the Queen at this late hour?

—I don't know. That is why I didn't report anything to you yet.

Fouché has no time for business as usual; he leans forward and whispers.

—Last Monday, we took back Lyon from the rebels. On Friday, the National Assembly decreed that the city be destroyed stone by stone. If we can make the second city in France disappear, imagine what we can do to you?

He points his pistol down at Lindhal's crotch. *Go for what they prize most.*

—I am telling you the truth, Fouché. For security, the best-laid plan is arranged so that one knows only a piece of the puzzle. No one person knows the overall plot, so that if he is caught he will not endanger the whole operation.

—So what do you know?

—I need money. Lindhal wipes his forehead, and in doing so his handkerchief fills the carriage with the scent of wildflowers and easy women.

—You are in no position to negotiate for anything.

—But I need money.

—Lindhal, tonight is not a good night to try my patience. You will be without a head by morning if you do not give me a name. Is Danton behind this plot?

Lindhal knows when he can fool around, and he knows how fast Fouché can make a man's tongue dance inside his head, so he speaks quickly now.

—Most likely Deputy Chabot could be involved. Remember, he received thirty thousand livres for spiriting Dillon and Castellane out of prison. And Deputy Delaunay is blackmailing the East India Company.

Fouché stops jotting down these names, and as precisely as a tailor pushing pins into cloth, he says:

—I have no time for hearsay or dubious leads. What I need is a confession.

Lindhal nods.

—This is raw information. That is why I did not come to you sooner. If every time I heard of money passing to corrupt officials I ran and told you, I would never get out of your office. I need more time.

—We have no time. What else do you know?

—Just bits and pieces.

—What else? Tell me.

—Delaunay's mistress is cheating on him with the painter Jacques-Louis David. She is a conduit for Austrian money as well.

One of the investigations that Robespierre asked Fouché to make this past spring was to study the illegal transfer of funds by émigrés and prisoners about to die. His report, delivered in May, described in detail sales to straw men, transfers to wives, signatures on blank wills, placing property in the name of unborn children, and how deputies threatened foreign banks with sequestration of their French assets in order to blackmail them into paying bribes. That is how Fouché uncovered a payment to Chabot of 200,000 livres from the English banker Boyd, which he assumed was an economic bribe to save bank assets. Now, he wonders, Was it a bribe to save a royal neck?

—Who else?

Lindhal purses his lips, checking what effect the name has.

—Hébert.

Fouché's face in the darkened carriage stays impenetrable. But he rubs his left knuckles with his right index. His are soft hands, pale hands, hands that never get calluses from physical labor, but they are never idle.

—Hébert has called for the Queen's death more loudly than anyone else. Why would he want to save her?

—Money. More of it than you can imagine.

Fouché's strength is all in his pauses and silence. He can make people talk just by staring at them. But what Lindhal says makes no sense; it is so preposterous that for this very reason Fouché says nothing. Editor of the newspaper *Le Père Duchesne* and president of the Paris Commune, Hébert keeps accusing Robespierre of being too moderate and delaying the trial to protect the Queen. The greatest of all my joys, he says, will be to see with my own eyes the head of the Austrian bitch separated from her fucking tart's neck. Jacques-René Hébert is so rabid, he has even demanded that each army battalion have its own mobile guillotine to impose summary justice.

Lindhal continues.

—On September 27, Hébert made a speech requesting that Marie-Antoinette be transferred back from the Conciergerie to the Temple so she could be reunited with her children. Why? Why would Hébert push for a royal family reunion? Why would he advocate leniency?

Fouché looks for a way out. Too many on the right want to frame Hébert. Even Robespierre would like nothing better than to exterminate Hébert and his ultra-enragé faction. That leaves the door wide open to manipulation by émigré circles who wish the Jacobins to massacre each other. So is Lindhal feeding him tainted information? Is Lindhal doing the aristocrats' dirty work?

The carriage has gone very still. Fouché can even feel the ticking of his watch. He himself is closely associated with the Hébertistes, so accusing Hébert is like fingering Fouché himself, and Lindhal knows this. The carriage suddenly feels cramped and hot.

Lindhal continues in a whisper.

—The Duchess of Rochechouart passed a million livres to Hébert. Hébert has admitted meeting with her.

Claustrophobic, Fouché steps out into the street. Lindhal follows. In Palais-Egalité, they walk past a string of whores, each standing in her own doorway. This potpourri of sodomites and dissipation, women of few morals and men who gape at them, does not interest him.

Fouché watches a woman scrounge in a pile of garbage for a crust of bread that she wipes before eating. *Instead of saving the Queen, why do not those fancy émigré barons dash in here with their pomp and feathers to save this wretch from starvation?* On all fours, the woman scratches for leftovers. *When will she be saved, and by whom?* Uneasy, he again kerchiefs his nose.

Laughter bursts from a tavern. They walk by pleasure spots that stink of sweat and cheap perfume. Men in a stupor of alcohol try to buy love, marketed here as little more than shared despair between strangers. Fouché's mind keeps going back to Danton. Never overlook the obvious suspect. Some of Danton's straw men and friends run illegal gambling halls here at Palais-Egalité. He sends Mordu in to look for them; then he turns to Lindhal.

—Forget Hébert. For tonight concentrate on Chabot and Delaunay. Here are blank arrest warrants. Fill them out as necessary. I will send a detachment of men to accompany you.

—What do you mean? That is your job, commissaire.

—No, I have no time tonight. They trust you. Wake them up, threaten them. I will send a man with you experienced in interrogation techniques.

—I can't, says Lindhal; I will reveal my cover; I will be finished.

—If you do not find the Queen for me by seven A.M. tomorrow morning, I will make you wish you were never born.

Lindhal grabs Fouché's arm, a liberty his agents almost never take.

—They have actually sprung the Queen? Tonight, she escaped? How? When?

—This may be your last mission, Hugo—Fouché waits for his man to unhand him—so do not use half measures. Failure means death. Pasquier!

Fouché explains Lindhal's mission to Pasquier—to question the two corrupt deputies and search their houses for the Queen or for any proof of an Austrian bribe.

—Pasquier, send five men with Lindhal to interrogate suspects. I want signed denunciations or a confession no later than six A.M.

Once Lindhal has disappeared on his mission, Fouché turns to Mordu.

—Bring in for questioning that second valet who stayed behind in Paris to run errands for Danton.

Enthusiasm is a sacred flame. I cannot let it be eaten away by all the ugliness around me. We follow a higher code. We need not look outside ourselves for moral, political, or spiritual lessons. We are complete, but we must not lose our sense of self-sacrifice. France is the Messiah among nations!

The money that passes through Danton's fingers is staggering. On June 28, the National Convention voted 4 million livres for Danton's secret diplomatic negotiations with France's enemies: England, Prussia, Austria, and Spain. So everyone in his entourage gets tainted, and everything about Danton smells—even his marriage to his first wife. His father-in-law would not consent to the match unless he had some respectable job. So in 1787, Danton bought a law firm, a council advocacy position. He scraped together 5,000 livres, borrowed 15,000 from his future father-in-law, 36,000 from his ex-girlfriend Julie Duhautoir (who also happened to be the seller's mistress), took credit from the seller for 22,000, and finally gave his property at Arcis as security. To compound the dubious nature of the whole transaction, Danton's brother-in-law became the notary public who processed these documents.

Restaurants are a recent development in Palais-Egalité, replacing individual caterers. In front of the Trois Frères Provençaux, Fouché stops and examines the menu: *Brandade de morue*, bouillabaisse, green olives, red mullet. While his carriage waits, he counts the dishes—twelve soups, twenty-four hors d'oeuvres, eighteen entrées of beef and veal, twenty of mutton, twenty of fowl or game, twenty-four dishes of fish, over fifty desserts. Who says Paris is going hungry, that there will be a famine this winter?

To save innocent lives from starvation, last June Fouché and others proposed a month-long fast, a civic duty for all good citizens, so that during August cattle and sheep could fatten, grow, and multiply. Unfortunately, the National Convention did not adopt his measure or any other national fast. Even the ration cards are not applied nationally, but only locally by each city.

Fouché orders an agent to stay on Lindhal's tail and climbs back into his carriage, tired, dirty, desperate. It is not a good sign if Lindhal knows nothing about Danton's involvement. Either Lindhal is lying or they are better organized, more careful. Either way, it is a bad omen. Is Danton leaving to avoid any responsibility for the trial and execution of the Queen?

—Mordu, take me to Danton's old apartment on rue des Mauvaises Paroles.

I am thinking, my love, that between me and death there is only the width and breadth of a single human being. Remove that person, and then for me there is only death.

Midnight

Lying on the narrow bed, facing the damp wall, which carries traces of blue wallpaper, Nenette smiles to herself. The Queen's red and white spaniel must have stayed behind in the Temple prison with the children and their hyper-nervous aunt, Madame Elisabeth. The King's sister is so diminished, so frail and anxious since her brother's execution, she suddenly looks like an aging grandmother. Thinking of the dog reminds Nenette of the pet Fouché gave her, and in her mind she reconstructs the scene with care.

During a night search in what was once named Montmartre, then Mont de Mercure, Mont des Martyrs, and today Mont Marat, Fouché came across an odd sight: At a street corner, a woman was beating a small object, pummeling its face. It was a tiny creature, a sort of midget with its arms twisted behind its back. Fouché stopped to watch. It looked like some inanimate statue, narrow and wooden, which the woman kept punching in the mouth, left-right, left-right. The grimacing immobile creature turned out to be a live monkey, with a chain tied to its waist; a seated man, pinning back the monkey's arms, held the chain wrapped around his wrist like a leash.

From its uniform—a gold-buttoned red jacket and blue pants—Fouché deduced the monkey was used in street performances and immediately stopped the woman in mid-swing. She told him to mind his own business and continued the abuse. So Fouché, who rarely takes direct physical action himself, punched her in the head and kicked her to the ground. Noticing the soldiers, her man did not budge. Fouché yanked the chain out of his hands, lifted the monkey in his arms, and the next day delivered him to Nenette's room above the Procope. What makes her laugh now to herself in the heart of this prison complex, behind three-foot walls, is that Fouché abhors pets but he knew of her longing for one. And the thought of Fouché feeling something for that poor monkey warms her heart. She especially likes the fact that Fouché stepped on the woman's hand and crushed her fingers. To the Monkey Woman he said:

—Citoyenne, take a good look at my face, and do not come within a league of me ever again.

The image lasts only a few seconds in Nenette's mind, but the feelings it generates remain and help her to forget how long the wait has grown. Ouistiti, as she dubbed the monkey, is about the weight of a big cat. He is not used to cold weather—he shivers inside his uniform—and often she has to wrap him in a blanket.

Where are you, Fouché, what is taking so long?

She tries not to think of the worst, but the worst is here like a gaping wound.

The monkey became their child. When Fouché is away, Ouistiti shares her bed. He is forever wrapping his tail around her neck, shivering, clutching at her, begging to be kept warm, warding off any tendency of hers to sadness. And his presence brings out the best side of Fouché, fatherly tenderness and calm.

She hears the two guards talking behind the screen.

Where are you, Joseph? What is taking so long!

She recalls how she tamed and civilized him, the big Ouistiti, not the little one. First she had to slow down his eating habits. Fouché used to eat standing up, shoving food down without tasting it or caring if it was served hot or cold. And at first he lived in the same boots, same pants, whatever the season or the temperature. She had linen shirts tailored for him and a new black cape, one he insisted he did not need, did not want, would never wear, but from which he has become inseparable.

Fouché, I want to hear your footsteps echoing in the hall; I want out. Take me away from all this. It is enough now!

A bath before lovemaking? He did not see the point, insisted it was a waste of time, but eventually he gave in. She smiles. And candlelight during lovemaking—that was not easy. Fouché was embarrassed, he thought it would allow a peeping Tom to gather blackmail material, so he went around the room checking for cracks and spy holes in the walls. But now she has gotten him used to it, and to the sandalwood and oils she rubs on his back. As if he were not worthy of tenderness and did not deserve it, after making love Fouché would say *I am sorry* and get up to prepare lists or give orders. Since he did not drink, she could not use a hangover to keep him in bed next to her. She had to rely on more subtle tricks.

Where are you, Joseph? It is midnight, and my cell is freezing cold. I am bored with this, I have been here for five hours. I want to go home now.

She remembers her childhood river. Not the big Loire with an e at the end, the Loire of Kings where national coffers built huge castles, Chenonceau, Chambord, and Chinon, and where the royal retinue massacred wildlife and cut down entire forests, but just north of there, the little Loir which feeds into the bigger one, where manor houses are smaller and the castles are all on a human scale— nothing for royalty or the court here, but just right for Nenette.

She remembers the birth and death of days on the banks of the Loir.

She recalls where the water lilies accumulated, where a toad lived and what the trees and seasons smelled of. Birds alighting and the wind filling the willows and poplars. From a distance, her valley looked like an open book with the fields being the tilted pages and in the middle, and down where the spine of the book should be, was the quiet river. Nenette collected wheat and dried it out in bouquets with wild flowers, buttercups, bluebells, poppies and lupines, and made garlands of it. And when her grandmother was dying, she led her out to a nearby field where they ate baby corns, hidden by the tall corn stalks, and long after her death that field carried meaning for Nenette, became synonymous with her beloved grandmother, so that each new crop was a secret message from beyond the grave.

But her happiest memory was hiding in the fields of flowering mustard that grew so tall that a man on horseback showed only his head. There, Nenette, would lie down on the warm teeming bug-rich earth and would look up at a universe of yellow as far as the eye could see. The others called out her name and searched for her, but their voices lost themselves in the waving raspy wind, and lying there hidden, completely alone, lost and magical, a child felt singled out and special, close to the heart of the world. Nenette would go back there as a teenager and even as an adult, to crouch down and hide in those yellow fields.

Then there was fall, the great apple pickings, when all the children joined in and every apple had its own special taste, and they dumped buckets of apples into the great wooden presses, and drank the clear clean juice from the first pressing. And then the lonely, evocative mushroom-picking walks up and down the great opened pages of that valley, careful to avoid the cowflops, spying the pink and white toadstools hidden in the grass and straw as the cows watched you. Then the rainy nights when she cast chestnuts to roast in the fireplace, and it was clear that nothing would change, nothing would ever change at all.

It was a valley of big forests, of vineyards, of wild boar and stags, of little villages, full of odors and rivulets forming tributaries, all racing and burbling to the big distant river which alone knew the way to the sea. In her memory, the Loir was the center, the heart of things. And what she would not give now to be back in one of those houses built of glazed narrow brick, with the long slanted roof and no windows on the north side, she who always took the valley for granted, who spent so many years dreaming of leaving it. Now that she has seen Paris, Versailles and the Petit Trianon, she wants to run back to the Loir and lie down on the warm soil as if in her mother's lap, summer-warmed with big yellow mustard flowers filling the sky.

Nenette finds her mind slipping away to various plots to save the Queen. Rumors abound. Fouché has told her which plots have come close to succeeding, and the one she admires the most is the attempt by the Baron de Batz. Unlike other plotters, de Batz went right to the top. He bribed Michionis, an ex-lemonade seller then the Inspector of Prisons and in charge of the Temple prison, as well as of other jails. He also bribed Cortey, the military commander of that section of Paris. Thus, with the help of vast sums of money, de Batz had the military and civilian guardians of the Temple prison under his thumb.

Enrolling as a private under the name of Forguet, de Batz arranged to be posted among the guards of the Temple so he could keep a close watch on his plans. Musket in hand, dressed in the dirty ragged uniform of the National Guard, this rich aristocrat took his turn in doing sentry duty in front of the Queen's cell. At the same time, thanks to Commander Cortey, an ever-larger number of men in the baron's pay were introduced among the sentries. So a few months ago the incredible became reality; in the heart of revolutionary Paris, in the stronghold of the Temple prison, which no one could enter without a permit from the City Commune, the Queen was guarded by a battalion of disguised royalists led by the Baron de Batz.

What the baron wanted to accomplish was nothing less than to steal the Queen and her children out of prison and thereby destroy the revolution. On the night of the planned escape, Cortey marched into the prison yard at the head of his detachment, accompanied by de Batz. He distributed his men so that all the exits were in the hands of the royalists recruited by the baron.

Simultaneously, Michionis, the other official who had been so liberally bribed, was upstairs in the Queen's room and had already provided Marie-Antoinette, the Queen's daughter, and Madame Elisabeth, the King's sister, with uniform cloaks. At the stroke of midnight, the Queen's party, wearing military caps and shouldering muskets, was to march out of the Temple with the bribed National Guard, and the Dauphin in their midst. The plan was simply for Cortey to march the little force under his command out to freedom without arousing the least suspicion. De Batz had posted a few determined royalists in the street, each armed with a brace of pistols, to slow down any pursuit if the escape was detected. He owned a country house under a false name not far away, where the royal family would hide for a few weeks until a favorable opportunity arose to get them across the frontier into the Austrian-occupied Lowlands.

But things did not go their way. A gendarme brought a letter to the Paris Commune betraying de Batz's plan. The town council receives hundreds such denunciations every day, and considering that the Temple was guarded by 280 men under the most trusted officers, this rumor was not taken seriously by anyone in a position of responsibility. Only Antoine Simon, a shoemaker, gave it credence. At 11 P.M., he ran to the Temple and sounded the alarm, thinking that the Queen had already been carried off. Rather than risk a bloodbath, de Batz aborted his plan, saving the conspirators for a later attempt.

The courage, precision, and artfulness of that plot always astounds her.

Nenette continues facing the wall, immobile so as to give the guards nothing to stare at. She imagines a thin haze resting on the Paris rooftops, long shadows of buildings along the river and on the surface of the Seine. There all night, but not there—like Marie-Antoinette—indistinguishable from everything else, a city of shadows and mixing vats, a city of random couplings. A chilly night in the damp gloomy autumn. Everyone is asleep. Her judges are in bed, so too the members of her jury, and the audience who will attend. The Incorruptible One is also asleep. Even bakers have not started up their ovens. She imagines, on the banks of the Seine, a poet sitting with his feet dangling over the embankment, writing love poems to his imprisoned mistress.

What makes Nenette smile is what happened after the failure of de Batz's plot for the Queen's escape. The Paris Commune did not extol Simon for his patriotism and zeal; on the contrary it told him it did not take the conspiracy seriously, and that he was imagining things. But according to Fouché that was a calculated move, and the Committee of Public Safety has directed Fouquier-Tinville, the public prosecutor, not to mention any details of the plot during Marie-Antoinette's trial. They do not want to let the world know how far the poison of corruption had spread among their most trusted followers.

But in order to take no further chances, the authorities decided on July 1 to separate the Dauphin from his mother and to appoint Simon as his tutor. Nenette cannot think of that scene without tears coming to her eyes. It was then that Robespierre made Fouché personally responsible for the Queen's safety.

From long practice, I have gotten good at suffering. Now it is happiness I no longer know how to deal with. Lack of habit, I suppose. That is why I am glad you are asleep. I do not have to make a fool of myself.

What ragged, patchy lives we lead!

II.

23 Vendémiaire, Year II
Monday, October 14, 1793

Happiness is a new idea in Europe.
—Saint-Just in a report to the National Convention

The Deal They Made

Fouché oversees a vain search of Danton's old apartment on rue des Mauvaises Paroles, where he is rumored to forge paper money, or assignats.

He waits for his best agents to return. The one who rode north to Saint-Denis to arrest Tom Paine is not back yet. Neither are the men who went to snatch Danton's valet. The hardest part of a chase is the waiting and doing nothing.

> Neglect no hints in your interrogations, spare no promises, pecuniary or otherwise, let them ask us for the liberty of any prisoner who promises to expose de Batz. Offer a free pardon to his secretary Devaux or to anyone else, even if they have taken part in an attempt to rescue the royals. But find de Batz dead or alive.

That order went out three months ago and so far nothing, so Fouché has no illusions about finding the man tonight. Fouché checks his Breguet: 1:10 A.M. It has been a chaotic, undisciplined hunt. And now it is Monday already, the fourteenth of October. The trial starts at 8 A.M. sharp, and Herman is a punctilious swine. At one minute to eight in the morning he will ring for order in the court, and Fouquier-Tinville will call in the defendant. No chance whatsoever of their being late, bet on that.

The night is pitiless. The horses are snorting, trotting down empty streets. Six hours after the Queen's escape, Danton leaves Paris and travels east toward the border. Why? Fouché eats a piece of bread. The government requires all flour to be gray, aristocratic white mixed with peasant black so there will only be one class of bread throughout the nation. The Bread of Equality, it is called. And, officially, bakers are not allowed to make pastry. Yet national leaders like Danton eat *filets de sole à la rocambole, fricassée de poulets à la crème de mousserons, beignets du Portugal, alouettes en coque, marinade de pigeons joyeux aux citrons, raie à la Sainte-Menehould*. This is what sticks in Fouché's throat, not the dark bread but the flouting of laws.

He recalls the interrogation cell inside the Conciergerie where Nenette and he stood that first day, just the two of them, with no guards. Nenette looked around for a place to sit down but found none. Then she stared at him, her lower lip quivering, on the verge of tears. While she sobbed, he gazed out of the barred prison window into the Cour des Dames. The problems that every day face a representative of the new order are endless, and he takes them one by one like a workman takes up mud and mortar and settles a brick on a wall he is building. But it is exhausting to keep the masses orderly; it is like pushing shit against the tide. And these days even the mildest of men are agitated. Strife and passion fill the air. Who can think when such unquietness rules?

When I finally had you alone, I could sense every mirror in my house awaited your reflection, every parquet slat awaited your footfalls, and every one of my pillows your laughter. But the certainty that I could never possess something so clean, so perfect, so resonant of goodness stopped me. Also the fear of appearing ridiculous.

—Hide me someplace, in one of your safe houses, Fouché. Give me a false identity, I could be your go-between to the émigrés. You could use me as a decoy.

—To make a double agent out of you would take some doing.

—Well, do it then, or are you one of those who likes to toy with helpless prisoners, give them false hope, then watch them die?

—No.

—You are a friend of Robespierre's; you can save me.

Nenette, you moved closer and started to say something in a lower more intimate voice. But, embarrassed, you stopped. Or maybe you thought it would be of no use to say anything because I hated everything you stood for. You were so near me a loose hair touched my face.

While I pretended to jot down a note, you stepped back, undid your hair, bent over so that it touched the ground, and put it up again in a bun, as if I were not in the room. But of course I was in the room, and that was why you did it. I closed my note pad without having been able to write down a single word.

—Citoyenne, you are a courtesan, a mercenary, that is what you are, and all your life you have gotten your way by charming men and having them fall at your feet.

—Well, look where it has gotten me.

I stared at the gloss on your lips, the upturned mouth, the white, waiting teeth. It was like staring at the sun; after a while I could not say why I found you beautiful or if you really were beautiful or ugly. I could not stop looking at you.

—What a seductress you are.

—Oh, not as good as you think, citizen. My mother always begged me to hide my real feelings. She would say, Nenette, be quiet, you are going to get us in trouble. Do not throw out every objectionable opinion you have. You are a girl, and you have to dissemble and say what you mean in a roundabout way. Men cannot take the raw truth about themselves. They do not like the truth thrown in their face.

—I like the truth.

—Yes, a lot of people say they want truth, but only a little bit of it at a time.

—I want the truth and nothing but the truth.

—Men of your rank are usually surrounded by lies.

—Nenette, your honesty is a ploy like any other, a deliberate attempt to get close to me and disarm me. Don't think I do not see through you.

You rubbed your arms with an air of resignation, of giving up the game.

—Before you go, could you have a fire lit in here? I am bone-cold.

The meeting should have ended there. I could have nodded and walked out the door, planning my next move, but I knew that if I did not act now, if I returned to that holding pen tomorrow, or even in an hour, I might never find you again. I had to decide right then. I went to the door and called for a guard to light a fire in the chimney.

—Citoyenne, you think life is worth all the trouble?

—Oh, yes, condemn me to live. I would suffer life gladly.

We stopped talking as the guard entered, and I suddenly felt reduced and deprived. I wanted the guard gone and me alone with you again. I resented the intrusion. I hated the smell of his sweat, the leather of his boots, as he added wood to the open fireplace. I could not stand anyone robbing me of even one second of my privileged moment. When the guard left and the cell door closed, no one in the city could guess the intensity I felt just then, standing again before you, alone with you.

You rubbed your hands and held them up before the new flames, eyes bright.

—I was never a good or attentive child. I always touched things I was not supposed to. I spilled wine, I ate pastries that were not meant for me, I broke earthen pots by leaping on them. I hated doing what I was told to do.

—You will have to follow rules now, citoyenne.

—Yes, I know.

—You still harbor hope?

Facing the flames and only half listening.

—Yes.

The new fire was now roaring. I did not want to risk never seeing you again, still I hesitated as long as I possibly could, as if holding my breath underwater, but holding back was just as difficult as blurting it out.

—I will move you out of prison to a room above my work-place.

—Yes?

—Yes, if you agree.

Nenette, you approached to press my hand or to hug me, but I pulled away and walked out before you could say another word. I forced myself to calm down. I never divulge myself, yet that day I was certain you knew everything there was in my soul. In that first meeting, you were humiliated, weak, suffering, yet I sensed everything about you, your taste for happiness, for laughter, all the contra-dictions between us. But also in that room that day there was one common sen-sibility, one soul, one feeling heart.

The world will never understand what I am feeling right now as I gaze down at you. They think of you as a monster. We must go to the farthest ends of the earth, to some place that has never heard of Versailles or the Petit Trianon or this revolution.

Oh, how I hate the French and all they have done to you!

2:14 A.M.

The Interrogation

How long this night. How tiring. Blackness invades.

Fouché loathes Mordu for yawning and Pasquier for awaiting orders blindly, loathes them all for not being able to find the Queen, loathes the traitors, the informers, the hangers-on, God too. *A life sentence on this evil world. There is no pride to be had tonight. My enemies I would kill for nothing; my friends I would kill for justice.*

Exhausted, he sends a rider to each city gate, demanding immediate reports.

The other side is more desperate. All I need is to make them slip up, somewhere, somehow. I do not need to be a genius tonight, I only need to be lucky and catch their mistakes.

The moon is out. And so are autumn smells. The soil is muddy. A hint of fresh rain from Normandy fills the air. Fouché stares at the black waters under the Pont Neuf. At last, his men bring him Danton's second valet. He has been roughed up, and now with wrists tied behind his back, head down, he is not speaking.

Fouché enters the nearest church—much of his interrogation he does in disused chapels.

He orders Pasquier to bring torches inside. The Sainte-Chapelle is now a legal archive. Fouché moves under Gothic arches that disappear into vast shadows. Sleeping guards lie among piles of documents. The reliquary, once at the center of the apse, covered by a wooden baldachin and reached by twin circular stairs, is gone. The shrine is gone too, melted down to pay for the revolution. At the back, behind the altar, Fouché nods at Mordu to begin.

While the horses drink at the fountain, a pail of water is brought inside. Danton's valet is not talking; he shivers, purple-lipped and yellow-eyed.

It is 2:33 A.M. Mordu dunks the man's head in and holds it there until the bubbles cease, then lifts him and says:

—Where is the Queen?

No answer.

Fouché paces and checks his watch. Mordu is a pro, he knows just how much pain to administer. They wasted too much time at Palais-Egalité, searching out Danton's friends and straw men.

—Talk, and I will make sure you don't suffer.

Mordu is all bones, skinny like his boss but taller, darker, and he has not two thick eyebrows but one, for they meet over the bridge of his nose in one continuous line. His collar is open; his long brown hair flaps like a dirty mop.

—Come on, Mordu, play him, squeeze him. It is late, much too late.

—Talk, man. Make it easy on yourself. Where is the Queen?

Fouché prepares the smelling salts that he keeps handy for whenever any prisoner blacks out. This scent is a grappling hook to bring back the near dead to more interrogation. There is no time for failure.

With one eye swollen shut, the Danton valet shouts, out of his mind, at Fouché:

—Your mother was a heathen viper, may you rot in hell.

Mordu starts to choke him, fingers deep in the neck. The valet gags, his tongue blue and his face wine-colored.

—A little more, Mordu. Scare him, scare the vinegar out of him.

Fouché walks off to leave Mordu to his work. He reads a prayer posted on what was once the altar:

Saint Guillotine, protectress of patriots, pray for us.
Saint Guillotine, terror of the aristocrats, protect us.
Kindly machine, have pity on us.
Admirable machine, have pity on us.
Saint Guillotine, deliver us from our enemies.

Yes, our justice is prompt, severe, inflexible, a shining sword in the service of liberty; it strikes like lightning, it is efficient and hard-working, but our struggle goes to the very heart of what man is. The guillotine cannot obliterate self-interest. That is the enemy here: greed, corruption, human nature, people filling their pockets. How does one change man made in your image? We must first change you, Father who art in heaven, we must alter you who do not exist.

Before returning to the interrogation, Fouché studies the sixteen stained-glass windows, images he knows by heart. Window 1: Genesis, Adam and Eve, Noah, Jacob. Window 2: Exodus, Moses on Mount Sinai. Window 3: Exodus, the Law of Moses. Window 4: Deuteronomy, Joshua, Ruth, and Boaz.

The screams of the valet do not affect Fouché's concentration. He is used to ignoring the sounds of his prisoners, but even in school he had this power to focus on his work.

My presence here, Father, may seem cynical and mercenary, but everything I know I have learned from You.

He recites from II Samuel 4: They beheaded him, and brought the head unto David, and David said unto them, The Lord liveth who hath redeemed my soul out of all adversity. . . . And David commanded his young men, and they slew the enemy, and cut off their hands and their feet, and hanged them up over the pool in Hebron.

The smell of a church, even desecrated and pillaged, brings Fouché back to his days studying with Father Merault de Moissy.

I was a class B priest, I never took my vows, I was free to throw off my cassock and marry, but prayer for me was hygiene of the spirit, generous, strong, sensual. It never left me. I loved the intimacy of your voice, Father. I still do. But now I don't have time for that luxury anymore. Unlike you, my time is limited, I have to act now and act fast!

Professor of logic, itinerant brain with thin voice and round shoulders, Father Fouché kneels. Above him, the tall thin windows depict Samuel, David, Solomon, Saint Helena, the True Cross, and Saint Louis.

The chapel brings him something warm and strong inside. Fouché loathes this feeling. He gets up and tries his best to ignore it.

Father, four days ago in the Nièvre, I issued a famous decree. It shocked the people, but it is having a national impact. I understand it is being copied from the Atlantic to the Austrian border, from northern Picardie to the Basque region: I desacralized all cemeteries, I prescribed purely secular funerals from now on, and I ordered that all cemeteries should bear a sign that reads DEATH IS AN ETER-NAL SLEEP. *Father, de-Christianization is not a war against you, it is against counterrevolution. Do you understand? De-Christianization is inseparable from our effort to construct the new Republican man, an individual purged of slavish vices and the prejudices of the old order. Everyone is morally equal; everyone has a right to understand and follow the new philosophy even if they cannot read or write yet. Liberty, fraternity, and equality requires that people believe in Natural Religion or Reason.*

Father, at first I tried half measures. I tried gentle persuasion, but the passive resistance was terrible, so I had to become hard, I had to become terrible. Look how harmful are practices and beliefs held in your name! In Burgundy, peasants attributed a hailstorm that destroyed two-thirds of their vines to the disappearance of their priests and stone saints. Attempts to remove priests or close churches are a constant source of riot. I understand that a thousand faithful gathered in the fields outside Mortain in the Manche to hear a nocturnal mass recited by a priest believed to be your direct agent. In the Cornouaille region of the Côtes-du-Nord, the virgin has started to appear and announce the end of the world. In Cébazan in the Hérault, Saint Michael has started to warn of your terrible vengeance. In Buxy in the Saône-et-Loire, the faithful have seized churches and are reciting white masses without any priest at all. In my own Nièvre region, it has been worse: Crowds of countrywomen invaded my district headquarters at Corbigny demanding that I hand back their church bells and religious ornaments, as well as the free use of their churches. In the Sancerre region, conscripts marched from village to village forcing municipal officers to restore crucifixes and compelling priests who had resigned to say mass.

So you know exactly what you are doing, Father. You have put them up to it, I know how you go about things. Every adult male of Plessis-Biron in the Oise petitioned the convention for the reopening of its churches. You make things hard for us, the apostles of Liberty! And mind you, I do not kill all your rotten priests, I show incredible restraint and let most of them live. Have you ever considered that?

Disgusted, Fouché gets up off his knees and looks up into the darkness above the Gothic arches.

Tonight may be our last time together, Lord. I know that all human prayers, even the selfless ones, are self-serving, and I know you do not bargain, but this is what I propose. You help me find the Queen, and I let you have my soul back—if I have one.

Down the central nave, he returns to the interrogation.

—Boss, I'm losing him, says Mordu; we want him alive, boss!

Fouché, checking his watch, shakes his head.

—Keep squeezing.

But suddenly the man's head, liver colored, lolls to the side like the head of a broken puppet.

—Enough Mordu, enough! Mordu!

He rips the valet free of Mordu's grip and sends him rolling on the floor. Mordu, breathless, helps Fouché up, wipes dirt from his knees and elbows.

—Goddamn you, Mordu, what are you doing?

—Boss, I told you I was losing him!

A hoarse rattle. They both turn; Fouché shoves smelling salts at the man's nose.

—Mordu, wake him up! Wake him, you have gone too far. Squeeze an informer until he has nothing left to squeeze, but do not be a hothead. This is no time for emotions. It's already two-forty-five A.M.!

Chief, remember, in Moulins, I slammed that priest's head wide open. A man of God, you think he'd be happy to meet his maker. He was bleeding like a stuck pig, but the sonofabitch almost strangles the life out of me. He would not let go. I had to let him have it a second time.

Fouché sprinkles more smelling salts; the valet does not move. He breathes, but just barely. Fouché walks off, tries to calm himself. Maybe Danton really is not involved. Maybe for once in his rotten, mercenary life, Danton is playing it perfectly clean.

—I got carried away.

Mordu is on his knees to Danton's valet.

—I'm sorry; a lot depends on finding the Queen before morning. We can save you; we'll bandage you up.

The man's eyes grow big and black. His mouth opens as if he is going to speak. Fouché's hopes soar—you never know with torture; pain has unpredictable effects. Mordu grips the valet in his arms as if he were going to kiss him. He holds the back of his head as one does a lover.

—What, whispers Mordu; tell me. We can help you.

The man is held by Mordu, like Christ down from the cross held by his mother. The image of the two men, one on the ground, the other bending over him, is clean, powerful, and intense. Fouché has always liked pietàs. He stands over Mordu, bending to hear the truth revealed, and he waits.

The man's eyes roll up into his head, and he dies. And so does Fouché, insofar as tonight is concerned. He orders a search of all recent files in the Passport Commission. He should have done that sooner, but now he starts to make alternate plans; he prepares for the worst.

Happy mortals know nothing of these things. They eat, they sleep, they make love; but the world is made up of disasters. Tutto a te me guida, *everything leads me to you.*

He notices a spider crawling up his arm; he watches it and lets it live.

He gazes out at the city. Curtains are drawn, shutters shut, all good folk are tucked in bed at this hour. It never ceases to surprise Fouché that during the Terror people continue to make babies, chat with neighbors, beat their kids, cook family meals, refuse to die. How do they do it? How do they have the requisite innocence, courage, or blindness to keep on living normal lives? It astounds him—all this normalcy amid counterrevolution, war, and famine.

Nenette, your soul is a virgin. And reason of State is a whore.

Mordu, Pasquier, the men and the horses waiting outside, the chase: all grows faint and distant. Alone, Fouché walks back into the Sainte-Chapelle and gazes up into the darkness at the back of the church. Time stops. Behind a Gothic arch, lit by a single wavering candle, he spies a skinny boy standing very straight as an old priest approaches. The angelic Merault de Moissy takes the boy's warm hands in his and says:

—You are a good student, always first in your class, but you are too rigid, Joseph, too secretive; I shall whip you until you change your ways.

—How do you know I will *ever* give in, Father?

—Do not be insolent. Just for that you will get another ten lashings.

The boy bows his head.

Fouché cannot see the rest of the room, the crucifix on the wall, the books on the shelves, the desk. All he can see is the old priest.

—You are not evil, Joseph, but we cannot afford such secretiveness or reticence among our scholarship boys. Your silence borders on insolence. It is not what you say that worries me, but what you are thinking. If I have to, I will whip the silence out of you and make you like all the other boys.

—What do you want of me, Father?

—I want you to play and run and be happy like other students. Why do you insist on always being by yourself, never having friends or anyone you trust?

Joseph twists his legs as if he needs to pee.

—I never know what you are thinking, Joseph. However, I cannot punish you right now because the archbishop will hand out school prizes this morning, and he has come today to congratulate you for being our best pupil. Do not let it go to your head. You will have to come back here right afterward to receive your lashings. Understand? Now I permit you to ask forgiveness.

The priest holds out his ring for young Fouché to kiss. The older Fouché does not move, just smiles, watching the boy bring the ring up to his lips. His father confessor waits patiently, but the boy does not kiss the ring; instead, he stares at it as if to bite it off.

—All we want is for you to become like other boys, Joseph, says the priest, jerking back his hand to remove temptation; we want you to play, run around, join one of the gangs in the schoolyard, tell stories, laugh, eat. You are far too skinny; a good Frenchman always takes time to eat a proper meal. Do you think you are a saint? Is that what you want to be?

—No.

—Well, even saints cannot be overly secretive, they have to be part of humanity. For instance, what did you eat for lunch today? Do you even know?

Joseph shrugs.

—Your father is away, and your mother is overwhelmed, so it is up to the holy mother church to teach you the refinements of life. First in Latin, first in Greek, first in physics, history, and math;

no wonder the other boys resent you! There is more to a man than his brains, Joseph. Look at you, just skin and bones!

The priest checks the time.

—Now do not keep the archbishop waiting, and do not be silent if he asks you a question, but do not volunteer anything either. Just receive his benediction and keep your eyes down. Oh, and Joseph, I am so busy this morning, I may well forget your lashings. Do you see what I mean?

—No, Father.

—What I mean is, if you choose to forget to come by for your punishment, I will forget it too. It will be our little secret together, all right?

—No. I'll come for my lashings after the archbishop.

The priest slams the desk with the palm of his hand.

—When I give you an easy out, take it like everyone else, Joseph. Now you've gone and made me angry!

—I am sorry, Father, but I don't want an easy out.

—Yes, you do. Everyone wants an out. Even I from time to time need an easy out. Even Christ on the cross said, *O Lord, let this cup pass from my lips.* You must learn to be more human, Joseph, less proud, less stubborn. Now go on, run along.

He watches the boy run off.

Shall I tell you, my love? It was not your fame and beauty that first caught my eye. No, it was the sight of your naked shoulders that first taught me obsession.

That is how I fell in love with you at official ceremonies, when it was impossible for us to talk.

And I knew from the very first time I set eyes on you—even before I went to America, even before there was a friendship between us—that with you I ran the risk of suffering a great deal.

The Dauphin

The person that Nenette pities most in Paris this year is the eight-year-old Dauphin. So many times she watched the precocious boy forming letters in his notebook, carefully crossing out words he misspelled. So many times she played with him, went for walks with him around the Trianon gardens. She always found him enchanting, with a sparkle in his eyes, a quick smile, a penchant for practical jokes, and a fear of big dogs. His solitary confinement breaks her heart. She imagines Fouché going to the Temple prison tonight to make certain the Dauphin has not been switched for a double because the Queen will not leave without him.

Fouché . . . where are you, Fouché?

Nenette dozes off for a few minutes, but she has no desire to sleep. She pulls the cover tightly around herself.

Have you forgotten me and left me to my fate? It is so cold here. Where are you, Joseph? What is keeping you? And what time is it?

She recalls that her father when he was old, and without enough time to read the books in his extensive library anymore, would run his hand down their spines to let them know: *I am still here, I still exist.* That is what Nenette has been doing tonight, running her hands along her memories, recalling the good times.

Who is left from my old days; what old friends are still in the city? Not many, and the few are getting fewer: Noverre, the Queen's old Italian dance teacher, who arrived from Vienna over twenty years ago and who was used as a conduit for Austrian money; the hairdresser Leonard, whom the Queen took along on her escape to Varennes; the Duc de Biron, a roué and member of her circle who became an ardent revolutionary, served as a general in the Vendée and is now in prison awaiting trial; Jeanne Campan and the Countess Geneviève d'Ossun, two of the Queen's ladies-in-waiting (the latter's uncle, the Duc de Choiseul, commanded the dragoons that were supposed to meet up with the royal carriage before Varennes); and Louise de Tourzel, the royal governess, who was locked up in the Abbaye prison last year.

Not a terribly illustrious group. The rump end of the Petit Trianon. They are all like that lamb, the one who, in his small shed behind the Trianon, raced back and forth, knocking his head into the walls, trying to escape the inescapable. I know that none of them will live long.

Tonight has all the trappings of a disaster, a personal one as well as a national one. Evil abounds. I see you, Joseph, losing the Queen, losing your nerve, losing me. I know how things work, and I know I will not see you again, ever.

She recalls young barefoot girls washing their hair in buckets and children running down sunlit paths screaming at butterflies; she sees oak trees with dark green leaves and brilliant late-summer days full of heat and sunlight. She imagines undiscovered lands where deer and tall handsome natives live in harmony with nature, full of love for the waterways, the birds and their fellow man, a world where there is always enough summer and where men grow as tall and straight as cypress trees. She sees a place where when you speak the whole universe understands you, and even unspoken thoughts are respected. She sees a land where every living soul wears a golden halo like the savior. She is mouldering here among the living dead, desperate, yet tonight she sees only what she wants to see, a valley where a radiant fresh faced girl runs free and full sunlight.

Her mind swings back to the Dauphin, the one she took care of so often at the Petit Trianon. She recalls him with his reddish hair long—he always looked quite feminine—round-cheeked, his mouth black from eating berries, with deep circles under the eyes from having stayed up late. How many times she hugged him, played horsie with him, chased him around playing battledores, hopscotch, and blind man's bluff. Nenette recalls the small-scale berline built for the boy. It was pulled by a liveried servant and painted white, with a young pageboy dressed as a coachman standing on the footboard at the back.

Tongues wagged. Little Louis-Charles was born March 25, 1785, exactly nine months after the visit to Versailles of Gustavus III of Sweden, who was accompanied by von Fersen, just back from three years of fighting in America's war of independence. Nenette was not there in May 1784, but the party given that night was described as one of the wildest and most spectacular in the history of Versailles. Lovers were skipping off, she was told, and the greatest freedom reigned; people went this way and that into the woods with whomever they pleased. And of course von Fersen was there. He was the only one who addressed his letters to the Queen by the code name of Josephine.

Most insiders date the start of Marie-Antoinette's affair with von Fersen from this time in 1784. The Queen told Nenette the following year, *At this moment, the cup of my happiness is full.* And once Fersen himself read her a letter he was writing to his beloved sister Sophie in Stockholm: After an ecstatic description of the wonderful *she,* Fersen said: *It is eight o'clock in the evening. I have been at Versailles since yesterday, but do not say I am writing you from here, for all my letters are being dated from Paris.*

Nenette recalls von Fersen as full of self-confidence and polite charm. At thirty-three then, the same age as the Queen—and as Christ—he is a tall and slender Swede with blue-blue eyes. He has a soft mouth and even softer voice, which is further attenuated by his Scandinavian accent and his reserve. But he is an excellent rider and a gallant soldier. His wardrobe is impeccable, his movements graceful, his manner most elegant.

Incognito, the Queen dances with Fersen. They are both masked, but in spite of their anonymity everyone knows who they are.

The Petit Trianon hamlet is sprinkled with 1,232 white china flowerpots from Lorraine marked with the Queen's initials in blue. It is the one place where the Queen reigns supreme. Even the King can only come when invited, yet von Fersen is a permanent guest there. The Queen in white gowns, bare arms, her hair unset and unpowdered, treats him to snacks of honey and fresh milk. When the fancy takes her, she leads him to the farm, the dairy, and the mill but especially to the large two-storied house called her boudoir.

Marie-Antoinette has the reputation for being a superficial, spoiled creature with whom it is impossible to conduct a normal conversation because she constantly changes the subject, forgets what she is saying, and shows no interest in the answer to a question she poses. But Nenette does not find her frivolous or restless at all. Her infatuation for von Fersen has transformed her, and so has her suffering.

Her youngest daughter, Sophie, dies on June 18, 1787, of a putrid fever, barely a year old. To make matters worse, her eldest son, Louis-David, has one leg shorter than the other, his spine is a little twisted, and he suffers from rickets. Grown too weak to stand, he lies on a heap of cushions, and the Queen grieves for him. Some ill tongues try to say the boy is a bastard, but he has the exact same ailment as Louis XVI had as a boy. They said the air of Meudon was good for Louis XVI, so they send his son there. But the boy runs a temperature every day and loses weight. The poor Queen blames his teeth, but he dies at the age of seven of scrofula.

The Queen says: *It is only in adversity that we realize who we are. Dear Nenette, is it unhappiness that allows us a glimpse of real happiness?*

Nenette tries to think of something more cheerful: The Queen had a strong potential for sensuality and radiance. And although many young courtiers would have liked to console her—Versailles was a graveyard full of panting suitors—only one man could. Nenette knew whenever the Queen met von Fersen because that is when she had to be a decoy, either at Versailles or at some other public outing.

And when the revolution hardened, von Fersen did not leave France with all the other aristocrats but stayed on, despite numerous appeals from his father and others to leave the country. He stayed and tried to save the royal family, he risked his own life and all his personal fortune for this, not because he loved the monarchy, not because he had fathered a royal bastard, but because he loved the Queen. He understood her, adored her. And in return, the Queen always carried a gold watch close to her heart; the watch is engraved with the initials *AF*, Axel Fersen.

One night Fouché made a thorough search through every article of clothing in the Queen's prison cell, and he returned to Nenette having found only this:

1. A red leather portfolio containing a few addresses of no consequence
2. A pencil holder without a pencil
3. A stick of sealing wax
4. Two miniatures of her children
5. An old hat that belonged to Louis XVI
6. And the words, unsigned, *Never doubt that I love you.*

Asked to identify the handwriting, Nenette pleaded ignorance, but of course she knew who it was from; love is an energy that happens so deep inside you that you change totally forever, and Nenette saw it happen with the Queen. How alive she became at the mention of von Fersen, how excited!

Do you still feel that way, Queen? The way I feel now?

Nenette recalls the Dauphin's birthday reception after the death of his older brother. The chimney sweeps' guild carried a chimney, on top of which were seated little chimney sweeps singing. The sedan-chair men provided a fancy gilded chair. The shoe-makers' guild bore boy's shoes. The tailors' guild provided a miniature uniform of the regiment he would one day command. The blacksmiths brought an anvil that would hammer a musical rhythm. And the locksmiths made a metal key, fashioned as a tiny dauphin. Fersen that day claimed the boy was his reason for living.

Will the boy now become a ward of the state? Will they kill him? It is against the law to execute minors, but that is no guarantee of anything. Nenette worries about him in the Temple prison without his mother, as pale as if he had no blood in his veins at all. Nenette has heard terrible stories about his tutors, Antoine Simon, a member of the Paris Commune who cannot even spell or multiply, and his wife, Marie-Jeanne. Antoine is a tall brute with wide eyes, a short pug nose, and a red liberty bonnet glued on his head. The royal tutor is paid to institute republican morals.

Nenette feels guilty because she has not done more for him. She tells herself she should have insisted that a proper doctor be sent for.

She forces herself to think of something else. She uses as an exercise the findings of the Weights and Measures Commission. Since August 1, the standard length in France is a meter, exactly ten millionths of the great circle passing around the earth at sea level through the poles.

Fouché, you want your work to be as precise and exact as the new measures! You want everything to fit into a pattern, a system; rationalism will save us. Perhaps that is why Lagrange, father of metrism, has not been imprisoned like so many other scientists. His commission decreed that a gram is the weight of distilled water at zero temperature centigrade, occupying a cube each side of which measures one centimeter, or one hundredth of a meter.

Lagrange, fifty-nine, is living with the sixteen-year-old grand-daughter of the astronomer Lemonnier, and the two plan to marry.

Nenette likes to dwell on that image—two unlikely creatures snatching their happiness at a time like this.

Are you never coming back, Fouché? I must have less than four hours left now.

Nenette feels a nervous exhaustion. She tries to visualize the complex conversion table showing the old months and days side by side with the new ones just announced—Pluviôse, Ventôse, Messidor, Thermidor—but soon she abandons this. Instead of four Sundays a month, now we only have three decadies off a month—is that progress, one day of rest every ten days? This new ridiculous calendar, that will make it impossible to trade with any other country in the world, was voted only last Monday, so no one is really familiar with it yet.

We surrender individual rights to the greater good, Fouché said. We cannot think only of our narrow petty interests. We are building a new and better world.

But of all the ideas Fouché has voiced, the one that most impresses her is the notion of time theft: If anyone stole your money the way they take your time, says Fouché, you would scream highway robbery, chase them down, and prosecute immediately. Money we can replace, but not time. Like fools, we allow ourselves to be robbed of this most precious, most unique commodity, and we do nothing about it.

What if I cannot do this? Joseph, what if I am just not up to it?

⌒

Nenette recalls another escape attempt by General Jarjayes, whose wife was one of the Queen's ladies-in-waiting. Right after the King's execution, Jarjayes left the safety of Coblenz, and on February 2, 1793, he managed to get a message to the Queen that he was ready to make any sacrifice on her behalf.

One of the Queen's guards at the Temple prison, Toulan, considered absolutely incorruptible (he wore a medal for having been one of the first to storm the palace of the Tuileries the previous year), had become her secret admirer. He risked his life for the Queen, not out of greed but out of respect and newly won devotion. Nenette smiles, recalling the escape attempt that Toulan and Jarjayes concocted.

Every evening a lamplighter came into the yard of the Temple prison so the place could be brightly lit and thus foil any escape. Toulan convinced this man that he had a friend who wanted to see the inside of the prison just for fun. Handsomely paid, the lamplighter agreed to hand over his clothes and equipment for one evening. Thanks to this subterfuge, Jarjayes met the Queen and agreed that she and her sister-in-law, Madame Elisabeth, would escape posing in the uniforms of municipal councilors, as officials on an inspection tour.

As for the two children, the real lamplighter was often accompanied by his children. So it was agreed that after lighting all twenty lamps in the courtyard, Jarjayes would lead out the Dauphin and his sister, dressed in rags to fit the part. Unfortunately the plot failed because Jarjayes did not have sufficient funds to get the four captives simultaneously out of the Temple, and the Queen did not want to leave without the Dauphin. She wrote to the plotters:

My son's interest is my sole guide, and however great the happiness I might feel at getting away from here, I cannot possibly consent to part from him. . . . I am well aware that the chance we are now letting slip may never return, but I should have no joy left if I were to forsake my children.

Recalling this, it seems to Nenette that for all the failed attempts, the Queen has had far more opportunities than anyone would have imagined possible. Nenette only wishes she had such selfless and devoted admirers risking their lives for her.

Love and Terror

Where are you, my Toulans, my Jarjayes, my von Fersens? Joseph, what time is it? What is holding you up? I do not carry a watch, I prefer to be free and timeless, but tonight I hear the guards talking. And their work is regulated by time. It is late now. Are you ever coming back? Was I a total fool to believe in you?

You are so weak, so thin. It's no wonder. For the last two months you have been confined to a tiny cell without being allowed outside even once, with nothing but a coarse prison blanket to keep you warm, no air, and bad food. But never fear, my love, I am taking care of you from now on.

Keep sleeping. We will make you stronger.

You and I have never had the demon of Habit, the daily numbing ritual that destroys so many love affairs, but how I long now for some everyday boredom with you.

Dr. Pressavin

Fouché walks on dead leaves. Pigeons coo under the roofs, and threads of smoke rise from chimneys. Paris is still closed for the night. But now bakers have started their work. Lit by the orange glow of ovens, one can make out bread baking in long thin shapes, yeast rising, browning, becoming full and crisp. Other storefronts are still shut tight. Men are sleeping huddled in doorways, and street children lie as if dead. Hungry paws prowl and pick at garbage. Usually this is Fouché's favorite time, but soon it will be dawn, and soon the judges and jurors will awaken, shave, put on their robes of office, have breakfast, say goodbye to their wives, and rush to the revolutionary court for the trial of the proud Queen.

Has Rosalie Lamorlière gone in to check on you yet, Nenette? Will Fouquier-Tinville or Herman supersede my orders and enter your cell? When they go to fetch you at 8 A.M., they will assume I engineered the escape. Then it will be done with me. All except for the execution. . . . Oh, still night where I draw breath, you are monstrous and putrescent, you are my night on the Mount of Olives, and the thought of morning is unbearable to me. O Father who art in heaven, is there any end to the darkness I am facing?

A sense of panic overcomes Fouché. Time is running out. Fouché, so alone, so isolated, wants an exit. He needs time to think, to see how things will improve, how he and his loved ones can stay alive in a place, where survival is a likely option. In desperation, he stops his carriage in front of Albertine Marat's house. She is a good friend of Danton's; she might know something about him. The house on rue Marat (once rue des Cordeliers) feels like a church full of holy relics or a necropolis. Marat's effigy is everywhere, and symbols of his immortal soul fill each room: the crown of oak leaves he wore on his deathbed, the bath in which he was assassinated, the box desk on which he was writing, his inkwell, his paper.

One sign on the front door reads:

> Marat is not dead!
> His soul, released from its earthly casing,
> glides around to harass our enemies
> and to spy on tyrants.

Another reads:

> O sacred Marat, long may your spirit live!
> Like Jesus you loved the people ardently.
> Like Jesus you detested priests and scoundrels.
> Like Jesus you led a poor and frugal life.
> But their Jesus was a false prophet
> and you, Marat, you are a God!

—Chief, come on, what do we do now?

Mordu, Pasquier, and the men surrounding the house await the order to enter and search, but Fouché does not move.

I have no time for mistakes. My margin is down to nothing, I must know what I am doing, and I must do it well, without any false moves. And to search Albertine's house is a waste of time!

The pain in his entire being is unlike any other he has ever felt before. He needs to spend time with Nenette; he needs to be with her, eat with her, laugh, forget, explain, talk this out. The urge to throw up his hands and give up is not there; rather, anger, aggression, and the urge to kill someone sweeps through him.

I have to take this evening to its logical conclusion.

—Chief, you all right?

—Fine.

He feels the tension of the evening in his temples and in his locked jaw muscles. Aristocratic women have no shame; in prison, they will do anything to get pregnant so they can avoid the guillotine.

I have heard of a countess begging a guard to mount her and put her with child. Also a duchess. Maybe Nenette is doing just that, but it is not likely, no, not likely at all.

Fouché looks up at Albertine Marat's windows. He recalls the living room hung with paintings of Marat that ignore the man's scabs and flakes, the ugly flattened Sardinian nose, the bulging eyes but, rather, give him a Christlike glow. He recalls the martyr's early inventions kept there, the factitious antipulmonic water, and his sister dieting on oranges to keep her skin pale. There is no use in questioning her. Enough of this wild-goose chase. Time is passing and Fouché knows what he has to do; now he has no choice. It is 4:07 A.M., and there are no options left.

—Mordu, take us to that apothecary, Pressavin.

He sinks into the back of his carriage and tries to sleep. His temples are pounding, his mouth is dry. He is chilled to the bone, and his eyes are sore. They gallop past where the Bastille once stood. That huge fortress has been removed stone by stone and the rubble has been cleared, leaving a big empty space. On one side, they have erected a fountain of Regeneration. The plaster statue of the Egyptian goddess Isis, whose breasts spout water or, on ceremonial occasions, the milk of Liberty. At the Festival of Unity, leaders drank this republican libation using a custom-made silver goblet. When his turn came, Joseph Fouché sipped milk for the first time since he was a baby. No one cheered.

The carriage turns down rue de la Lanterne, rue de la Vieille Draperie. Past the old leper cemetery.

O France, it is I, Fouché, your faithful son, who has fought for you on every front in every guise in every season. If it were possible to amass all the blood and tears I have bequeathed to your welfare, it would form a pyramid climbing up to heaven. I have given you so much, why do you ask more of me?

A cold sweat cuts through him and a shortness of breath, brought on by too much concentration on one small specific fact: The Queen could not have fled far. She would not leave her son behind. She has no physical strength left, no will to fight for her life. That is all logical, but is that in fact so?

The coachman does as he is told and stops the carriage. After a moment's hesitation, Fouché gets out and stands in front of the apothecary at rue Quincampoix, number 7. There is a light on at the back. Fouché knocks.

Through the window, he sees blue-tinted vials on the shelf and all manner of drugs: spiderweb, unicorn horn, virgin's milk, theriac, crab's eyes, wood lice, viper fang, pearls, and mummies' bones. Bottles of opium paregoric, of ipecac, tartar emetic, spirit of sal volatile, valerian, sweet spirit of niter, balsam tincture, arnica, sasswood, sarsaparilla, cascarilla, magnesia, tincture of opium, castor oil, arsenic, colchicum for gout, and foxglove for dropsy.

—Mordu, keep Pasquier's men away. I must have privacy.

Fouché knocks again. This time he sees a shadow move and pick up a candelabra. Slowly the man's shadow moves along the wall to the front of the store.

Lord, the stray lamb is the one you go after, not those who stay put. You need me, Lord, I am the one you say you need most in the world.

The door opens. The doctor's white hair is combed back, his skin pale; he is of medium build and gentle manner:

—Citizen Fouché, come in.

Dr. Pressavin holds out his hands.

—Come in, don't mind the mess. Just watch where you step.

Fouché enters the apothecary and moves past magnetic tubs filled with copper and hydrogen sulfide. On one shelf: Mesmer's *Memoir on the Discovery of Animal Magnetism*. On the walls, diagrams show how disease, old age, and gout can be cured by touching copper poles and feeling the igneous liquid of electricity. Dr. Pressavin communes with the deities of the Nile and the Euphrates; he boasts that he is a thousand years old, although he is in fact sixty-three. He claims he was born in Medina, raised in Mecca, and acquired his art while traveling in the Levant. He alleges he can cure diseases by stroking the affected parts with magnets.

One needs impostors, madmen, and quacks. They are the most likely to help when the wind of madness is blowing in all directions, and intelligence and good sense have disappeared.

—How are the tests that I ordered coming along, doctor?

—Well, come and see for yourself.

The doctor moves toward a separate room. He opens a small closet.

Fouché follows him into the closet, leans over, and glances into several buckets, each full of dead rats and the smell of putrefaction. He covers his mouth and nose.

The doctor smiles.

—The gas acts twice as fast as the one we tested last week. Nine seconds to death. Now I shall have to test it on higher species, of course.

Fouché tumbles backward, sits, and asks for a glass of water.

—What we need, doctor, is an effective and cheap terminator that can be administered impersonally to those who have ceased being members of the human race.

—Yes, I am well aware of your requirements.

—But you must speed up your experiments. We have a heavy workload ahead of us. We have tried several guillotines working at once, and also one machine with a multiple number of windows and blades. In the Bicêtre hospital, we tested a five-blade, a nine-blade, and a thirteen-blade machine, but none performed well. We need something more foolproof, more practical.

—Surely, citizen, this is not why you have come here at this hour?

—No, it isn't.

Fouché stops, uneasy. He feels the werewolves howling. It is a wicked night. Dr. Guillotin, a philosopher and national deputy of no talent, came up with the idea of benefiting mankind, but he was not the guillotine's real inventor. The real inventor, the permanent secretary of the Academy of Surgery, Dr. Louis, rectified Guillotin's design flaws, such as making the blade diagonal instead of convex so that it could sever the neck cleanly. Some tried to dub the machine a Louison-et-Louisette, but as luck would have it Dr. Louis avoided that indignity. Fouché wonders if one day there will be a gas known as the Fouché which causes rapid and clean mass executions.

—I have heard that Guillotin is handing out suicide potions to his friends who want to avoid the guillotine. Is this true?

Dr. Pressavin shrugs.

—Speak plainly, citizen. What is it you need?

They are sitting in Pressavin's Temple of Health, a round room with ceiling mirrors that guarantees newlyweds beautiful children. Above the bed, these words are written in gold: WHAT WILL SURVIVE OF US IS LOVE.

Nenette, sand is slipping through the hourglass. At eight you place your throat in the mouth of the wolf. This is not a time to be pusillanimous. I must prepare my exit, yours too. You will not be strong enough, but I can help you.

—What I need, doctor, is flexibility: a potion that if taken in a small dose will paralyze temporarily, but if taken in a larger dose will terminate life.

—Something that would act on the muscles and the central nervous system?

—Yes, exactly.

The doctor gives him a long look, then pulls down various colored bottles with names on them like belladonna, valerian, arnica, and tincture of opium.

—I must know the person's weight. If it is a child, my dosage will be less.

—It is for an adult, a woman prisoner.

He watches Pressavin mix a potion.

The doctor approaches, holds up a vial, looks through it at the moon.

—Citizen commissaire, the active ingredient of belladonna is atropine, an alkaloid from the deadly nightshade plant.

—Bella donna, meaning beautiful woman?

—Yes, Italian ladies used it to make rouge. That is how it got its name.

The doctor shows how much of the potion should be administered.

—Belladonna, repeats Fouché, staring at the vial.

He offers to pay. But Pressavin, far too clever to accept, merely bows.

—I am always at your service.

He stops Fouché at the door and adds:

—You know what my favorite word is in the German language? *Schadenfreude.* It means pain-joy, pleasure in another's ruin.

Fouché waits for more, but there is no more. The doctor's kindly eyes and general manner invite him to speak, but Fouché nods and pushes his way out.

How tired I am of it all.

These past few months have sapped my strength. I have seen too many terrible things, I am tired of people. Tired and disgusted.

All I want to do is watch over your sleep. And repeat the five words that dominate the way we have led our lives since I returned from America.

Tutto a te me guida.

The Belladonna

The Conciergerie is the antechamber of death. Here twelve hundred men and women are held for a few days, waiting their turn to be tried. Fouché hurries toward it. It has four big towers, two less than the Bastille, but the effect is the same. Farthest downriver, the Tour Bonbec—good beak—so-called because it houses the torture chamber and the interrogation rooms. Then comes the bridge of Charles the Bald; the Tour d'Argent, which contained the royal treasure; and the Tour César's, where Fouquier-Tinville now has his private apartments. Farther upriver is the clock tower, which, since 1370, has housed the city's first public clock, but this year its silver bell was melted down to pay for the army. A clock that chimed the hours of the monarchy has no role to play in the republic.

—The Queen did not escape, Mordu. My hunch is she is still here.

—Be careful, chief.

They enter by the Cour du Mai. The gimpy-legged registrar stops them at the gate and makes Fouché sign the visitors' book. It may seem disrespectful, but the rule is applied to everyone. Fouché checks the prisoners' main gallery. This is the busiest part of the building. It has a constant air of urgency, like a stagecoach station, with people coming and going all night: prisoners arriving, officials leaving, lawyers, guards. Fouché examines every cell he can, leaving none unchecked. Up the spiral staircase to one of the turrets, through a door on the right, into the gallery that gives onto the council room. Then down another spiral staircase; he checks the antechamber to the men's yard.

—Boss, this place has more cells than there are holes in a Swiss cheese. You can spend a lifetime searching for her in here.

Fouché checks the cell where the prisoners are given their last haircut. Here the tumbrel will await Nenette. Here sit rebellious writers, black marketeers, corrupters of public opinion, bluebloods, forgers, and priests. One proclaims he wants to run to Robespierre's house and eat his heart out.

—Give it up, chief.

Mordu tries to stop Fouché, who pushes him off and stalks away, grunting and half mad, through the humid, cold dank smells. Mordu runs after him.

—If they want to hide the Queen, chief, they can bury her so deep in the darkest dungeon, not even God himself would find her.

Mordu catches up with Fouché, and this time pins him down.

—Boss! He manages to hold his arms pressed against the stone wall.

—It is no use, chief!

For a minute, Fouché glares at Mordu. He knows his man is right, but only when he has calmed down does Mordu let go of his arms.

—Here, chief, you will be needing this. Mordu hands him the vial of belladonna. Fouché nods and takes it in silence.

Just then, Concierge Bault's second-in-command rushes up. He beams with pride.

—Commissaire, the widow Capet has not uttered a word all night. She has slept, do not worry, we are in control here.

Fouché, on mission for the Incorruptible One and the Committee of Public Safety, makes his way to the royal cell with Mordu breathless on his heels. A guard lets out a rasping cough. In the women's courtyard, he crosses a pathetic patch of grass where grows a lonely tree surrounded by an open gutter. During the day, female prisoners are allowed out here, but not the Queen. In the southeast angle of the courtyard, just beyond where the twelve selected daily for the guillotine say their farewells, he can see Nenette's darkened window.

Fouché looks in through the spy hole in the door and sees Nenette on her cot, lying almost in the exact same position she was in when he left her. He signals for the guards to open the royal cell and stand aside. They defer to his commissioner's sash and his deputy's rank.

It is a tiny room, two meters by three and a half meters, with torn dark-blue wallpaper printed with small golden fleurs-de-lys. The cell has no chimney and no changing alcove, only a narrow bed, a chair, and a single barred window on the left at the foot of the bed. The other wall is a metal screen that divides the room from a space where guards watch her night and day. The Queen has been here for two months and eleven days, deprived of her children, sister-in-law, and servants, not allowed out in the court-yard, not even allowed a private toilet.

Nenette has a woolen blanket pulled over herself, and her face is turned to the wall. The most closely guarded prisoner in France is shivering. He motions for the guards on the other side of the screen to leave them alone. When they have done so, Fouché walks to her and stares down, waiting for her to sit up or signal that she is not sleeping. The seconds tick by.

—You should not have come, she whispers, facing the wall.

—I am having some trouble, Nenette.

—Yes, I figured. She speaks without moving her head or limbs or giving any outward sign of their barely audible conversation.

—I want to give you something in case I cannot find the Queen in time.

He studies the angle of her cheek, her eyebrow, a wisp of blond hair.

—Nenette, I brought something that can make things painless. If you take a quarter of this potion, you will be incapacitated for a time, and no one will be able to make you talk.

He notices her index finger tracing shapes on the wall. He can just make out that she has changed into one of the Queen's two black mourning dresses.

—If I take the whole thing?

—Death will ensue in a few minutes.

He does not touch her. He listens for her breathing but cannot hear any.

—We think so much alike, you and I.

—Forgive me, Nenette.

From the movement of her eyelashes, he can tell she has closed her eyes.

—There is nothing to forgive, Joseph. This is what I expected all along.

—I am going to try and delay the trial.

—All night I have been thinking about what I wanted to say to you, Joseph, so you do not have to answer. It is better if you don't. Later on, after I am done speaking, you will have time to think about what I said. This is my turn to talk; this is for me, not for you.

He pulls the chair close to her turned back and listens.

—Joseph, I grew up in a village called Mondoubleau in the Loir valley. My father worked for the Baron of Mondoubleau. He was the chief cook, an ineffectual man who let his wife become the baron's mistress. She had six children by the baron, five girls and a boy, the youngest. I was the third girl. We grew up not in the nice part of the castle but off in the servants' quarters.

No need for the belladonna, thinks Fouché; she is babbling already.

—My mother said I was too rough, but I could not accept boys taking advantage of us. I defended my sisters. I warned boys once, and if it happened a second time I smacked them. *Why are you not shy like the other girls?* my mother used to say. I helped with the milking and haying in the fields, and every day neighbors complained: *She is too rough, she hurt our boy.*

Fouché knows her father, the baron, was caught when he disguised himself as a peasant but, having no idea how real people live, he ordered an omelet with five eggs. Three eggs would have hanged him too. But he does not interrupt; he lets her tell the story she has told over the years.

—My father recognized me when I was eighteen, but the promised stipend never came. My future husband, a captain, was unfaithful to me, and I left town the day I found him in bed with another girl. I went to Chartres and worked for a rich merchant. There two courtiers were struck by my resemblance to the Queen, though I am ten years younger than she. Deciding to use me as a surprise royal birthday present, they dressed me up, gave me a phony title, and took me to a costume ball at Versailles. Even the King was fooled and mistook me for his wife.

—Nenette, we do not have time for this.

—Of course we do. Joseph, if I am to die, I want you to know what is in my heart. I have seen all the last letters you promised your victims that you would send to their families, so I will not make you lie to me. My last letter to my loved one is this conversation.

It is not cold, but Fouché wraps his cape around himself.

—Marie-Antoinette took a liking to me and hired me as one of her ladies-in-waiting at the Trianon. She was the real power behind the throne, not the ministers, certainly not the King. She used me as a decoy whenever she had private meetings with von Fersen. And when she was tired and in no mood to provide marital services, she would send me up to the King's bedchamber, and

I did manage to get his nose out of locksmithing. The King never let on he knew who I was and never complained. I was so excited, I thought all my prayers were being answered, but beware of answered prayers, Joseph.

Fouché knows all about the King's love life, his too-tight foreskin, and how starting on his wedding day, May 16, 1770, he would enter his wife but could not ejaculate. For seven years the marriage was not consummated, and the Queen had to endure all types of public calumny and accusations of lesbianism for not getting pregnant. But in August 1777, an operation, a snip of the foreskin, liberated the royal member, and the King finally used it with marked success, making four babies in a row.

—I joined the Queen the same day *The Barber of Seville* opened at the Trianon, August 19, 1785. I was just twenty-one, and later I was able to get positions for my sisters and a small pension for my mother. Only my brother stayed in Mondoubleau. I used to send him money and worry about him, but today he is the only safe one.

If you were born a baroness, Nenette, you are a filthy blueblood from birth. But if you were born, as you say, to a cook, then you have betrayed your class. And that is worse.

—When the mob broke into the Trianon, I found broken furniture and glass everywhere. I thought at first it was blood on the walls but it turned out to be preserves; they had pulled down a commode, and the jars of jelly had smashed so that cherry and strawberry jam was sticking to the wall in big gobs and slipping down ever so slowly. I cried like a baby, but all this we are going through tonight, Joseph, you and me, all this could have been avoided if I had remained in Mondoubleau and remained to marry my unfaithful soldier. No?

Fouché does not answer. Not answering is not indifference; on the contrary, it can be a way of reinforcing what has just been said.

—It is completely unreal, isn't it, Joseph?

He leaves the vial on the prisoner's pillow.

—And your poems,—why did you never show them to me when I asked to see them?

Her skin is alabaster white. He never expected her to be so resigned, so calm. Fouché cannot bring himself to say anything more. He leaves the room, gives orders to Pasquier, checks the guards' logbook, checks the prison registrar's admissions book. He wants to stay and he wants to go. He wants to rush out and question his spies, and he wants to stay put and protect Nenette. He stops three times at the prison exit.

He hears the sergeant submitting his hourly report to Louis Larivière on what the widow Capet has done and not done. Seeing her in the hands of this scum sickens him. He cannot stand so much ugliness surrounding her.

A fit of coughing erupts next door, oaths, spitting, a call for silence. Wind and wet leaves blow outside.

Fouché returns to Nenette's side, and this time he unfolds a sheet of paper as if to write down her answers. The guards understand police work.

—Joseph, I want you to put me to death.

—No, I am going to get you out of this.

—I would rather you cut my throat than they. Joseph, don't let them torture me. Her whisper is almost inaudible now.

—The vial is right by your hand, Nenette.

—You could cut my neck here in the back of the cell and be clear away before anyone finds out. It would be a blessing, Joseph.

He can see windows lit and guards smoking in the courtyard, washing their faces at the fountain, getting ready. All so innocuous and normal.

—You are a survivor, Nenette. You have made it so far.

As he speaks, he imagines heads in a basket, the people voting not with ballots but with heads, and a horrible lifelessness steals over Nenette's cheeks, negating all possibility of who she is.

—Everyone gets caught sooner or later. That is what you always said, Joseph. Even at our first meeting you told me it would end like this. I am surprised we have had it so good for so long.

Roof tiles glisten, chimneys release threads of smoke, and leaves flutter in the rain gutter. He looks around to see if the soldiers are getting suspicious.

—You want to know the first time I fell in love with you, Joseph? When I realized that you actually cared about this revolution, that you were exactly what you seemed to be—a lonely official, unloved, bitter, with ugly wife and a sickly child—and that all you ever cared about was not your country, not your family, not even yourself, but social justice. Then I began to feel sorry for you. I thought to myself, poor man, he will never be happy in this life.

—This is not the social justice I had in mind, Nenette.

He can hear cows being led into the courtyard, tied four by four, roped—the prison needs meat, and they have come bearing themselves.

—I always knew how much disillusionment awaited you, and I pitied you. I thought, He wants to get rid of inequality in the world, get rid of hunger and profit takers. If that is what he wants, he will go through hell.

—One does not fall in love due to a sentiment of pity.

—Oh, yes, I did.

She stares at the wall. So does Fouché, but a few feet above her.

—I fell in love with the little boy I saw caught inside you, Joseph Fouché. The boy who could betray all those you love, including me one day, yet still remain true to his hard little choirboy self.

Fouché clears his throat. Eyes are watching. He must leave.

—Do you remember the first day when you came up to me, so shy that at first you did not dare look at me? I thought, It will never work; he is too skittish, too nervous. I will never get to this man. I could see you were trying not to show anything beyond objective professional interest. Before you signed the official receipt taking me into custody, I pricked my finger and rubbed some blood onto my cheeks so you would find me pink and pretty. If you had not approached me, I would have come to you. And when you said, citoyenne, I can protect you and help you, I knew right then and there, from your first words, that it would work out. And you have given me life, Joseph, the greatest gift you can give to another human being. So I have used you too; we are even.

—Nothing is played out yet.

—Yes it is, it always has been.

Silence. Nenette has not moved, she is still lying on the bed, facing the wall.

—Are you crying, Joseph?

—No.

—There are times when it is best to be dead, don't you think? No answer.

—Another lady-in-waiting might welcome the chance to give her life for her Queen, but not I, Joseph. Marie-Antoinette had her children, her millions, her hour in the sun. If I could grab her with my bare hands and put her in this cell, I would.

Fouché checks the time, 5.35 A.M., and the whole futile night comes rushing back to him: Louis Larivière breathless, Nurse Guyot, the poissardes, the Duchess of Tours, Danton, the circle of suspects, and then the death vial.

Nenette is silent, but her index finger slowly traces the wall. She closes her hand on the vial and squeezes it.

—One quarter will put me to sleep?

—Yes.

—And all of it will put me out of their reach?

—Yes. The whisper is inaudible even to himself.

—You better go now.

—Where will you hide it?

—The vial? I shall leave it in plain view with the Queen's tooth-brush and soap. I'll decide at 8 A.M. before they come to get me.

—If I am not back, you will decide then?

—Yes.

Neither of them moves. While the guards in the hallway ex-change words, Fouché recites quietly from memory a passage from the Song of Solomon:

> Behold, thou art fair, my love; behold, thou art fair; thou hast doves' eyes; thy hair is as a flock of goats; thy teeth are like a flock of sheep that are even shorn, which came up from the washing. . . . Thy lips are like a thread of scarlet . . . thy temples are like a piece of a pomegranate within thy locks. . . . Thy two breasts are like two young roes. Until the day break, and the shadows flee away, I will get me to the mountain of myrrh, and to the hill of frankincense. Thou art all fair, my love; there is no spot in thee.

—King Solomon, he adds, after a silence.

—No, you, she says.

Staring down at her, he ties his black cloak up to the neck. Only his nose, eyes, and mouth show. He cannot stay here any longer.

A key sounds in the lock behind him.

—I am with you, Nenette, always.

She turns to look at him for the first time in this meeting. The door opens.

—Citizen, you asked me to fetch you after fifteen minutes.

Fouché walks out of the cell and says nothing to the gimp-leg registrar, or to Bault, or to Larivière. He leaves the prison, mis-sion accomplished.

He says nothing to Mordu, who is shining his sword hilt, or to the coachman. Mordu knows to keep quiet when the boss is in one of his moods, and to stay out of his way, polish something, anything at hand, even something that needs no polishing.

In the courtyard, Fouché climbs into his carriage and slams the door. Darkness.

Pasquier, whose men fall in behind, rides up and asks for a moment of the proconsul's time.

—Citizen, our agent is back from Saint Denis, and Paine has not spent the night in his lodgings. No one knows where he is. Shall we send a search party out for him?

Fouché does not answer.

—Citizen, should we?

Fouché does not look up.

—Yes, find him for me.

Pasquier waits a few moments, then leaves.

I wanted to be your coachman as in the Varennes escape, but since that attempt I am well-known in police circles. It would be too dangerous for you. But a friend whom I trust completely will take you in a simple lightweight coach to Bordeaux. He will have a passport for you to get out of Paris and to travel through France. In Bordeaux, I will meet you and we will take a ship to America.

Trust me.

We shall start a new life in the New World, under assumed names. But I am afraid of your reaction when you find out we must leave the Dauphin behind.

Life has us in its grip, and there is only so much we can do.

White's Hotel

It is long after closing time at 7 rue des Petits Pères, Place des Victoires, opposite the Eglise Sainte-Victoire. In the darkened tavern of White's Hotel, the curtains are drawn, the glasses and mugs are washed and put away, the floor scrubbed, the dishes stacked, but at one corner table a candle is still burning and two men are whispering. One is the American writer Thomas Paine, and the other is his close friend and translator, Joel Barlow.

—I thought you were just hungry and wanted some leftovers, says Barlow, looking around, but I see your bag is packed. Are you really leaving us?

—Go back to bed, Joel.

—I have been up all night, wondering if you would really go through with your plan.

Barlow pulls up a chair. He sits opposite Paine and leans forward into the candle.

—What you want to do is utter madness, Tom.

—Sshhhh, I am expecting someone important, and I don't want you scaring them away. Paine's voice is uncharacteristically soft, almost like a cat's purr.

—Who are you expecting?

—You will see.

At fifty-six, Paine's long narrow furrowed face and high fore-head look tired. He has a defensive, almost haunted look. His gray unpowdered hair is combed back in a well-groomed ponytail, but his prominent nose and cheeks are a blazing red, with purple splotches that attest to the amount of drink he has consumed over the recent months. The eyes may be alive and gleaming, but his teeth are dark with wine, and his clothes are rumpled and stained. His whole appearance tonight is slapdash, but not his mind.

—Go back to your wife, Joel. Ruthy will be worried.

—I am not going to let you do this, Tom.

Barlow, seventeen years his junior, has gray hair, and he is far handsomer than Paine. With his square jaw and short nose, Barlow is an aristocrat, a Yankee version of Thomas Jefferson. A poet, a radical, a leading member of the Connecticut Wits, and a Fran-cophile, he came to Paris in 1788 and managed to convince a com-pany of French immigrants to form and settle Gallipolis, Ohio. He has recently written pamphlets against the leisured class in England. Last December he was made an honorary French citizen and even ran for election as a deputy from the Savoie.

—Will you not at least discuss this with me, Tom?

—It is none of your business, Joel. Go to bed.

—You were going to leave in the middle of the night without bidding any of us goodbye?

Paine motions for his friend to lower his voice; he too leans into the candle.

—I cannot leave without the passports. They are supposed to be delivered tonight. I don't know what is taking so long; in a few hours it will be too late. Now you know everything.

Thomas Paine, the best-selling author of *Common Sense,* the pamphlet that turned the tide of the American revolution, and of *The Rights of Man,* a book that last year sold more than any other and nearly tore England in half, is a deputy in the National Con-vention, and tonight he wears the tricolor sash around his waist, as well as the tricolor cockade in his lapel. Last fall, Paine arrived from Dover to a hero's welcome: banquets in his honor, welcoming speeches, kisses, honorary French citizenship bestowed upon him, election to the convention from four different constituencies. He finally accepted to represent the Pas de Calais, the place where he landed on September 13, 1792, so he also represents Robespierre's hometown of Arras.

But tonight the adulated hero acts more like a criminal. He goes to the window and peeks out from behind a blind, and again scans the night.

—Tom, you loathe monarchy!

Paine pours from a bottle of wine and drinks down his glass in several gulps, then wipes his mouth with the back of his sleeve. There are several empty bottles on the floor by his chair.

—The Queen is nothing to you, Tom. Why try to save her?

Both are men of words. Barlow, who started the influential magazine of ideas, *The American Mercury*, is famous for his nine-volume tome, *The Vision of Columbus*, a poetic paean to America. Yet Tom Paine is more than famous, he is a legend in his own time; along with Benjamin Franklin and George Washington, he is one of three Americans whom the French revere as the guiding spirits of their revolution. It is the reason why a younger writer like Barlow is content to act as Paine's amanuensis, translator, and aide. Paine is fearless, inexhaustible, relentless, and self-obsessed, but this is a minor defect in a soul as great as his.

After the fall of the Bastille, Paine received a package from Lafayette, a present to the American people, containing the key to the Bastille and a drawing showing a crowd demolishing the old prison. Barlow recently ran across a draft of the May 1, 1790, letter which Paine addressed to President Washington along with the artifact.

Here is a trophy of the spoils of despotism, and the first ripe fruit of American principles transplanted to Europe. . . .

I have not the least doubt of the final and complete success of the French revolution. Little ebbings and flowings for and against, the natural companions of revolution, sometimes appear, but the full current of it is, in my opinion, as fixed as the Gulf Stream.

How hollow these words sound tonight to Barlow, when a *little ebbing* has become the Reign of Terror.

—How much have you been drinking, Tom.

—I am not doing this to save the Queen but to save the revolution. The Queen is nothing; she is a selfish half-witted little spendthrift, but the salvation of freedom hinges on her survival. I do this for France.

—Oh, Jesus, Mary, and Joseph.

—And for the world!

Barlow cringes and keeps looking at the door. Paine's talk is full of conviction, the way he writes, and although tired he welcomes the discussion.

—Tyranny, like hell, is not easily conquered, Joel.

—Tom, the only thing you will achieve by this plan is your premature death.

—The charges against Marie-Antoinette are trumped up. The jury, judges, and lawyers are all scared for their own skin. Her execution will only be legalized murder.

Paine starts uncorking a bottle of white, a Suresnes '88.

—Robespierre is always going on about morality. To be an executioner destroys a man's humanity, but Joel, if a republic becomes an executioner, it too looses its humanity and its reason for being. That is why we must take special care of deposed tyrants.

—Let the French handle this. It is their problem, not yours.

—We cannot condone abomination merely because it happens to our neighbor Joel. We are all citizens of one world. Where would the American revolution be without the help of France?

She bankrupted herself sending guns, uniforms, and men to help us. Want a glass?

Barlow waves the bottle away, but Paine pours anyway.

—The Queen is ignorant, narrow-minded, and as shallow as a butterfly, like all her kind. Killing her is beneath the dignity of this great nation.

—Yes, maybe it is. But, Tom, you are not the republic of France.

Paine turns the glass under his long, carbuncular, carmine nose. He is not, as the American ambassador Gouverneur Morris reported to George Washington, a drunk, but he has been drinking especially heavily these past few months.

—Joel, you and I have been made French citizens, and I am a deputy of the convention, but what I propose to do now is merely carry out the duty of any good citizen of the world.

The candle in the room has burned down and is nothing but a bit of tallow and liquid wax in the bottom of the brass candlestick holder. Paine fetches another candle, lights it, and presses it down into the hot liquid of its predecessor until it sticks there and stands upright.

—Listen, you are not alone, Tom! Clio Rickman, William, Choppin, and William Johnson are sleeping upstairs. You have twenty or thirty supporters in this city; you want them all to go to the guillotine?

An antique grandfather clock in the corner of the tavern gets ready to strike and, as it does, it winds up all its springs. The coil tightens, groans, stiffens, and strikes: 5:30 A.M.

—Mary Wollstonecraft, John Hurford Stone, Captain Imlay, me—you put us all at risk. We will all be tarred with your treason.

—I know, I have thought about that. But you can all leave. I have gotten Choppin and Johnson passports as well.

Paine has saved many Englishmen, republicans and anti-revolutionaries alike, from the guillotine. Back in February, a young

Englishman by the name of Captain John Grimstone argued with Paine and struck him in the face for betraying England, and he was due to be executed because striking a delegate of the National Convention is considered an attack on the entire French nation. Paine had Grimstone released from prison with the help of Foreign Minister, Barere. He got him a passport, had him escorted out of France and even paid the cost of his transportation back to England. Paine went into prisons and did the same for George Munro, a British spy, for Zachariah Wilkes, for the pro-revolutionary English banker Robert Smyth and his wife, and just about anyone who called on him for help. His generosity and humanity are legion, but now his power and influence are far diminished.

—I will not translate for you on this, Tom.

—Of course not. Joel, you have a wife. I understand you cannot get involved. So as far as I am concerned we never had this conversation; you know nothing about this. Now go back upstairs to bed.

Taverns all over Paris are losing business to fashionable cafés that sell homemade liqueurs with foreign spices and exotic aromas, but Paine disdains all such novelties. As he says, *I have a penchant for the pressed grape, which even the Bible seems to bless.*

—I am going to denounce you to the police, Tom.

Paine gags and coughs up the wine he was in the process of swallowing.

—You would not do that!

—It is the only way I can stop you.

—The authorities would assume you were in on the plot and they would kill you. If you are scared, Joel, just head for the countryside now. You and Ruthy speak French; you can melt away easily. And take the others upstairs.

White's Hotel is Paine's home away from home. So many supporters, friends, and visitors came to see him when he lived here that Paine had to institute a system of written requests and limited visits to only two mornings a week, or he would have had no time to work. But this March, when his political friends and allies started getting arrested and it became increasingly dangerous to be heard speaking a foreign language in Paris, he moved out of the city, to Saint-Denis, and from that place of semi-exile he comes into Paris only seldom. But when he does he stays at White's Hotel overnight. This is one such time.

—Tom, have you any idea how mad Parisians have gone? Just now there is a motion in the convention to make all foreigners wear an armband stating the country they are from and, below it, the word, HOSPITALITÉ.

—Well, yes, hospitality; why not?

—It will be used to tell us apart from the general population and to round us up when the time comes. We are trapped! They refer to you as an Englishman, and as France is now at war with England, that makes you a traitor. Robespierre has called for a purifying scrutiny to drive out all foreign spies. There is no place anymore for your cosmopolitanism and friendship among citizens of the world. If word gets out that the Queen has been spirited away by an American, anyone in France who speaks English will be rounded up and impaled on a pike.

—That is enough, Joel! Disgusted, Paine throws the dregs of his glass of white wine on the floor and opens another bottle of red.

—Last Wednesday, the Committee of Public Safety ordered the arrest of all British citizens.

—I know. Paine waves this away.

—They arrested about 250 Brits, some say 400, mostly nuns and clergymen and took them in closed carriages to the Luxembourg prison. They took Helen Williams, her sister, and mother around midnight. They even arrested me, until I convinced them I was an American. Mary Wollstonecraft escaped only because Imlay had the foresight to get her American papers.

—They took me at dawn on Thursday, with proofs of *The Age of Reason* in my pockets.

—So you obviously know that you are in no position to help anyone, Tom. You are a marked man.

—Maybe so. But a revolution cannot be made by sunshine patriots or the faint of heart. It cannot be made with rosewater either.

There is a knock at the door. Barlow freezes and looks for a place to hide; he moves behind the bar.

A muffled voice:

—Citoyen Paine, it is me. The French pronunciation makes his name sound like *peine,* meaning sadness in French.

—Joel, it is okay. This is the man I have been waiting for.

Paine goes to the door and opens it a crack. The visitor explains in French.

—It was Sunday yesterday, Citizen Paine, the Lord's day, but since the new calendar went into effect last Saturday a week ago, the day of official rest has been shifted to the decadie, every tenth day. This has not been greeted by the staff, by their families, or by the general public, I may add, with any sense of great joy. And as yesterday was unfortunately the first working Sunday, so when you reached the foreign office to pick up your travel permits, only a skeleton number of workers had showed up for duty. Please forgive us. The staff was so ill-tempered and difficult with you, but with me also, and I am their superior. But I could do nothing to remedy the situation. Still, I came as quickly as I could. I hope this delay will not have importuned you too much.

Paine follows only the roughest of outlines of this speech in French. For a man who remembers faces, stories, and anecdotes and can keep a dinner enthralled for hours, it amazes Barlow that Paine has never made any effort to learn French. He acts as if he were still living in New Rochelle, New York, and when someone does not understand him, Paine just repeats his words in English twice as loud, treating the French as if they are all deaf.

But now he whispers with a heavy accent—*Merci, merci beaucoup*—and hands over a purse. While the man counts the gold coins, Paine checks the papers, but he is far from the candle and has trouble seeing anything.

Barlow wonders where this money comes from. Paine has always been as poor as a churchmouse. The architect of American independence had to petition the U.S. Congress, as well as the New York and Pennsylvania legislatures for a stipend to live on.

The Frenchman continues.

—I believe this new calendar will not be enforced with vigor by the Bureau of Longitudes, so Sundays will continue to be days of rest and will continue side by side with the new official feast days.

—*Merci,* says Paine. The men shake hands, and the door closes.

Back at the table, he opens the red leather satchel and holds the various documents up, one by one, to the candle.

—Good, good, says Paine; it is all here. My passport and one for a thirty-eight-year-old woman servant. And these are for Johnson and Choppin to make their way to Switzerland. Joel, give these to them in the morning with my best wishes, will you?

Most writers are intellectuals, incompetent with practical matters of day-to-day living, but not so Paine. Watching him, Barlow sees not a wordsmith but the son of a staymaker, a man who publishes firebrand rhetoric and yet who came to Europe to sell a new type of wrought-iron bridge he had designed. Paine is practical. Barlow knows that, even drunk, Paine can mastermind this escape and maybe even get away with it.

Watching him read his passports and permits, something else strikes him: Paine is not afraid. Once in the Tuileries gardens when Paine had left behind his tricolored cockade and sash, a mob suddenly surrounded him and a man called him a royalist. In spite of Barlow's best efforts to explain that this was the great Thomas Paine himself, defender of the weak, of the oppressed, of the disenfranchised, descended from Olympus to aid France, they began beating and kicking him. Then someone shouted, *Aristocrate, à la lanterne!* and a burly man put a noose around his neck and the crowd began hauling Paine toward the nearest lamppost. His English accent only made things worse. He was saved by a stranger who stepped out of the crowd and displayed a symbol of his office, and this calmed the crowd. Had this happened to Barlow, Barlow would have fled France immediately, but Paine just laughed off the incident, saying, Thank God for government spies and police tailing me.

So warning Paine of the dangers of the mission will not convince him to give it up; on the contrary. Paine now stands up, with the satchel under one arm, and downs one last glass of wine.

—Goodbye, friend. Thank you. I know you speak out of deep loyalty, and I have always valued your help and advice—even now I see your wisdom—but sometimes the rash and the foolish gesture is best.

Paine shakes Barlow's hand, but Barlow does not let go. In addition, he does not move aside to let Paine pass to the door.

—Let me out, Joel, they will be waiting for me.

—The Queen will not thank you for this.

—Of course not. I do not expect or want her gratitude. Chopping off her pretty head will not do a thing for democracy. A single drop of blood spilled wrongly in a revolution soon forms rivers and torrents that wash away liberty. Look at what good it did to kill the King! But saving her can save democracy.

Barlow still bars his way.

—Your enemies will say that you are at heart a royalist, that you have abandoned all your principles. Why do it?

The two men are about the same height, but Paine looks as if he could be his father or grandfather. He puts a hand on his friend's shoulder and smiles. They are nose to nose—Barlow's is small, perfectly shaped and clean. Paine's is too long, too red, and a mess, but neither take any notice of this.

—The laws of this new republic, Joel, are imbued with love for mankind. They affirm that all human life is sacred. But with this trial, the revolution will leap from humanity to barbarity. The new constitution is generous and merciful. I am moved to tears just reading the Rights of Man in the new constitution. It would never condone human sacrifice! But the ink will not be dry on that document before it is replaced by calls for murder. I tell you, the moment the Queen dies, so do our finest dreams and hopes. The only way that Liberty and Freedom can ever be established on a durable basis, my friend, is by saving Marie-Antoinette.

—You sound like the enragés, only in reverse. They say that for the revolution to live, the Queen must die.

—Yes, they are right. Their kind of revolution needs her death. Now I do not like the Queen anymore than they do, but I say punish by instruction rather than by revenge.

Paine turns around and looks at the grandfather clock.

—They open the gates of the city at six A.M. Come on, Joel, we must stanch the bloodletting and get deadly enemies to forgive each other and reconcile with each other. We have to do the impossible. If not me, who? If not now, when?

—You have absolutely no fear, do you?

—I am scared witless.

—No, you're not. You are oblivious to danger; you are like a machine.

—Joel, why do you think that for the last four months I have been playing chess and dominoes up in Saint-Denis with the chickens and the ducks? I cannot sleep, I cannot eat. Paris has become a cat's cradle of suspicion, lies, fanatics, and policemen on all sides. Death is everywhere. Even if I do nothing at all, I know my days are numbered. On my last visit to the convention on June 2nd, Danton stopped me as I was about to walk in and said, *Ten more steps will cost you your life.* Thank God Danton speaks English. He saved my life. The assembly were debating which Girondins to execute, so I hightailed it back to Saint-Denis as fast as I could. Sometimes at my desk I meditate as if I were already in prison, already awaiting execution. Often I imagine I am sleeping on my deathbed. This morning I dreamt I was standing naked before my maker.

Barlow goes to the door of the tavern, locks it, and pockets the key. The two things Paine cannot resist are a good argument and a good bottle, and Barlow knows that for Paine the French revolution far surpasses in importance the American one, for this one is not just political, it is also a revolution in sentiments, manners, morals, and general opinion. For a year now, the two of them have greeted each announcement of a spark of rebellion from Santo Domingo to Prague as proof of a revolutionary tide sweeping the world. *In spring when a bud blooms, it is madness to assume that only one tree will bloom,* Paine keeps saying. *Sooner or later democracy will erupt in every part of the globe.* Paine means to enjoy the spectacle.

—Joel, give me the key now. You are going to ruin everything.

Barlow uncorks a bottle of Montparnasse '80, which surprises Paine.

—To secure our own liberty, we must guard even the enemy from oppression. Marie-Antoinette is the enemy; that is why we must save her.

Paine laughs.

—You listen well, you memorized my ditherings. You are a good man, Barlow; I do not think I have ever thanked you properly. I take you for granted, sometimes I even forget you are translating, you are so effective and self-effacing. But it is almost six A.M. I have to go now.

—If we kill her, we kill everyone of us, continues Barlow, pouring him a glass; if she commits suicide or dies in prison, our revolution will be remembered first and foremost as a killer of defenseless mothers.

—Joel, I know you are trying to get me drunk, and I thank you for it.

Paine examines his glass.

—It is rare that people tell me to drink more.

Barlow holds the bottle in his arms like a child.

—No one will understand the subtlety of your argument, Tom. This is not a time for subtlety. There is nothing subtle out there. There are only blades falling, that is all. *Zing, zing, chop, chop.* They will not hear anything you say. They will only see a queen escaping the judgment of her people. Back in January you fought against those moderates who wanted to save the King's life by putting his fate to a vote of the people. A popular vote would almost certainly have spared his life.

—Yes, but I thought it was more important to underline the principle of representative government. It was vital to have elected deputies vote and thereby play their role as people's representatives.

—You ensured the King's death.

—Yes, in retrospect. But I never expected it to go that way. During the debate and the vote, I thought I could save the day, yet they shouted me down.

Paine rifles through Barlow's pockets without success.

—No, Joel, France is now in a situation to be the orator of Europe. She must speak for all those shackled people who cannot speak for themselves; she must put thoughts in their minds, arguments on their tongues. What we are living here is of fundamental importance!

During the trial of the King in the National Convention, Paine's outspoken role changed the course of his life. His proposal, made on January 7 last, that the King should be exiled to America struck Robespierre and other Jacobins as outright treason. Marat shouted that Paine's translator (not Barlow that day, but Deputy Bancal, the philosopher) must be lying. After Paine interceded and verified the truth of his motion for leniency, Marat shouted that Paine being born a Quaker opposed capital punishment and should be ignored on this matter. There was pandemonium at the speaker's podium. Yet still Paine managed to sway many deputies. One of them explained his vote this way:

> By the example of Thomas Paine, whose vote is not suspect, by the example of that illustrious stranger, friend of the people, enemy of kings and royalty, and zealous defender of republican liberty, I vote for imprisonment during the war and banishment after peace.

Others said merely, *I follow Thomas Paine, the most deadly enemy of kings and royalty.* In spite of this, Louis XVI was condemned to death by just one vote out of 700 cast. In the following ten days, Paine addressed the National Convention three more times, beseeching them in vain to *spare the man who had helped America, the land I love, to burst her fetters.*

On January 21, the day of the King's execution, Paine told Joel Barlow, *I will leave, I will not abide among such sanguinary men.*

The problem is if he returns to England, he will be imprisoned for life or executed for seditious libel. Even returning to America he runs the risk of being stopped on the high seas by a British man-of-war. All those who voted to spare the King's life are today deemed traitors and one by one have been eliminated. Twenty-nine of Paine's allies in the National Convention were removed from the convention by the sans-culottes mob in June. Their trial is set for Tuesday October 15, but Paine is not taking up their defense.

I cannot endure the doleful spectacle of the triumph of imbecility and inhumanity over talent and virtue, he confided in Barlow. *Anarchy is even more cruel than despotism.* Now, by sitting on his hands and doing nothing, some accuse him of indifference. In the convention, Jacobins attack him as an enemy and a foreign spy.

—You insisted the King be tried; why not let the Queen be tried? Paine smiles at his now-empty glass and at Barlow.

—If as you say they will not listen to me, what chance is there that they would listen to a foolish queen who does not have a thought in her head except her next dress, her next diamond broach?

—You know what I think, Tom. I think you are a most pugnacious man. Because of your enforced inactivity and silence recently, you are spoiling for a fight, and if you look for one you will get one.

—Just give me the keys. It is almost six A.M. I have to go pick up my passenger. I do not want to make the lady wait.

When Paine is imbued with a cause, he becomes a carrier of fire. George Washington was so impressed with his writing that he ordered his *American Crisis* to be read out to all his troops at Valley Forge. Without food, clothing, or money, all America had to boost its army's morale was Paine's syntax.

Barlow pours him more wine.

—Joel, you skunk, you think I cannot function drunk? Paine burps.

—You need sleep, Tom.

—I could drink this entire bar and still keep my appointment.

He quotes from his proposal for a new constitution that calls for universal suffrage. He keeps pushing for the vote to be given to servants, cobblers, fishermen, laborers, dairymen, and, to Robespierre's horror, even women. His other losing argument has been for an independent judiciary:

> The rule of law requires impersonality. It cannot be left in the hands of the constantly altering legislatures and men vying for power. Unchecked legislatures are potentially as despotic as unchecked monarchs.

—It is von Fersen, isn't it?

Paine slips a bottle in one deep pocket and another bottle in his other pocket, he winks and smiles. Barlow continues:

—Yes, von Fersen is an old friend. He fought for American independence for three years. You met him at Yorktown when he translated for Rochambeau. Von Fersen distinguished himself so much that he earned the Order of Cincinnatus from George Washington himself.

—I'll be back, my bladder calls.

While Paine goes to the toilet out in the courtyard, Barlow unlocks the door and climbs the stairs. He wakes Clio Rickman and William Johnson, Paine's other close friends, and quickly explains that Paine has had too much to drink and that if he goes out now the police will arrest him for they are scouring the roads for moderates to add to the Girondins' trial on Tuesday.

Rickman gets up and rushes down to help. In his nightshirt, yawning and scratching, he waits for Paine to return. Barlow stashes Paine's red leather satchel and his traveling bag away. Johnson picks out a piece of beef from the cold remains of last night's dinner, *Laitance de carpe* in one dish and *pot-au-feu* in the other.

When Paine returns, ready to go directly to his waiting lightweight coach, he finds his three determined friends all waiting for him and unwilling to listen. The struggle is not long. They carry him upstairs and lock him in his room.

Afterward, the two Englishmen ask for details. Barlow explains in an urgent whisper that, being a conscientious interpreter, he sifted through Paine's disordered correspondence and drafts on his desk and discovered the following:

On September 4, just over a month ago, Paine was in Paris on one of his infrequent visits and bumped into Barère, the French Foreign Secretary and a member of the Committee of Public Safety, who begged Paine to help France buy at least fifty or a hundred boatloads of wheat from America to help stave off the looming winter famine. That gave Paine an idea. Why not use the forty-five American ships that France impounded, to prevent them from falling into British hands, and had been holding ever since in the port of Bordeaux. The plan was that Paine should go back to America with the boats, load them, and return to France. On the way, the French navy would protect them from British gun-boats as far as the Bay of Biscay.

Rickman nods and waits for more explanation.

Paine wrote to President Washington and to Thomas Jefferson about this. They and the French Foreign Ministry agreed to the plan.

Rickman shrugs.

—Why not? Paine has not been back in almost seven years. His house in New Rochelle has burned down. He should go back and get himself to safety. What is the matter with that?

—Because he intended to go all the way with an escaped roy-alist widow who is wanted for high treason.

There is a silence.

—Is he mad?

—Maybe. But tonight we saved his life, and tomorrow we shall have to convince him of that, or we lose a friend.

Shhh, shhh.

I have so few friends left in Paris. They are all either in prison or dead, have emigrated, or been sent to the front.

This American does not speak French. Do not be frightened by his mean appearance, he is an excellent man, the best. Now we must dress you as his house servant. I am sorry, Madame, I wish I could have given you silk sheets and a bed instead of hay on the bare floor and a woolen blanket, but I did not want to attract attention. You leave at the crack of dawn. Wake up my love, wake up. And don't worry about the Dauphin. I will find a way to get him out. But it is far too dangerous for you two to travel together. It would be suicide.

The lesson of Varennes is that the fewer the people who travel together, the easier it is to escape. Remember, your brother-in-law Artois slipped across the border in a simple carriage unnoticed the same day you were caught at Varennes. We shall not make that mistake again.

Now be strong, have faith, my love. The city gates open in half an hour.

315 Rue Saint-Honoré

From where she lies now, staring at the dirty wall in her cell on the ground floor of the Conciergerie facing west into the Cour des Dames, it is hard to imagine that the peasant cottages at the Petit Trianon were equipped inside with every possible convenience—billiard tables, couches, mirrors, stoves—all clean and in perfect order. It helps Nenette to recall this. It helps her to say, This is not me you have imprisoned, not me at all, I am far away, I am back at the Petit Trianon.

One of Nenette's sisters was gang-raped, and she retreated so deep inside herself she did not talk for months. When she finally spoke, she told Nenette, *Where I went they could not touch me; it was only my body they had, not me.* That is how Nenette feels now. She makes no excuses for her past. On the contrary, she basks in its glow. The river of memory is endless.

Every year the Queen redecorated her Trianon palace. One of her caprices was to create a primitive innocent garden and live close to nature. She ordered French, Indian, and African trees, Dutch tulips, magnolias from Italy, a lake, a river, Greek temples, a windmill. The volcano spouting fire and the Chinese pagoda were too costly, but she insisted on having a brook murmuring gently through the meadow. So the Seine was brought in pipes all the way from Marly. It formed an artificial pond with its own artificial island. The layout of this pastoral scene was studied in countless watercolor paintings and worked out in twenty plaster models.

Of course, Marie-Antoinette liked to have fun, and Nenette is glad of it. The Petit Trianon love grotto had loopholes so that a pair in amorous dalliance could glimpse any approaching intruder. The Queen needed a temple of love and a Cupid. In order to make nature more natural, she hired real peasants, real milkmaids with real cows, real calves, real pigs, rabbits, and sheep. She hired scythe men and reapers, shepherds and hunters, laundresses and cheese makers. To imitate poverty and decay in the village she had built, the plaster on the dwellings was romantically chipped away in patches; rifts were made in the walls; here and there, shingles were ripped off. Decorators painted cracks in the woodwork, and the chimneys were carefully smoked.

Nenette recalls this with real enchantment, with dazzlement and delight. Suffering has made the Queen wiser and calmer; now she reads books and can make decisions of state, but Nenette prefers to remember her on a swing, twirling a parasol, causing puritans to raise their eyebrows and whisper behind their fans. The Queen bought three hundred dresses a year, and her jeweler had perpetually to find her new trinkets. When bored, Marie-Antoinette played peasant with her ladies-in-waiting. With Nenette, she collected fresh farm eggs and even boiled them herself. One day she took Nenette to make butter—but nothing could soil the pristine royal fingers, so before her visit the stable floors were scrubbed by unseen hands. Blanchette and Brunette were curried and combed so much that one looked like alabaster and the other mahogany. The warm foaming milk was received in a porcelain vase carrying the Queen's monogram.

That is how Nenette likes to remember the Queen—frolicking with an admirer, giggling with her hired washerwomen down by the rippling brook, playing hide-and-seek with her girlfriends among the cottages and in the shady paths, or sneaking off in disguise to

Paris to attend a theater or a masked ball. What is so wrong, she wonders, about a queen fishing, culling flowers, watching the good peasants at work? Nenette sees the two of them, Marie-Antoinette and her look-alike, dancing a minuet upon the flower-bespangled turf. She extends her hand and they begin—one step, three steps, *demi-coupé échappé*, then three more steps—as a flight of wild blackbirds wheels and dives over a nearby field. Then a gavotte. It is not proper etiquette, certainly not in the middle of the day, for two women to dance by themselves—the King's somber aunts will scowl—but the Queen has ordered musicians to play, and from the vantage point of where Nenette is now, on a narrow metal cot in a prison cell, awaiting death, she wishes they had danced longer that day. She wishes she and the Queen had danced all year long and to hell with propriety. But that day the music was cut short by a contest. The Queen's Italian and French theater companies vied to see which one could make the ladies laugh louder.

Tonight, Nenette longs for it all back, the laughter, the softness, the rashness, the overblown mad excess. They call the style of the day Louis XVI, but it should be called Marie-Antoinette style, for she set the tone. She personified all the curves, curlicues, and twists of this end of the century, not her husband; that oafish lout had no taste for refinement or culture, only for deer and boar hunting.

At a time when the rest of the country starved and begged by the side of the road, the Queen spent a fortune on her Petit Trianon, the Little Schönbrunn at Versailles. A report of August 31, 1791, to the National Assembly put its cost at 1,649,529 livres, but in point of fact it was over 2 million. A drop in the royal sieve. But if you have to go, thinks Nenette, go in style, before the deluge.

⁘

Riding home in his carriage, Fouché's nerves twist and his bowels boil and amplify with gas. Fear. There are just two hours left.

Dawn will come soon. Fouché rechecks the time. Wounded in the deepest part of his soul, wounded on behalf of all France, he finds it unimaginable that the Queen will escape justice. This is what they deserve for having been so lenient up until now.

Understanding a traitor is tantamount to pardon. There can be no pity! He who does not seek revenge becomes an accomplice in treason.

Where is Lindhal? Why has he not returned with information about the bribery trail, the deputies on the take, and who is paying for this escape? Fouché snaps shut his gold watch. This night is a nightmare—Fouché haggard, Fouché red-eyed, Fouché cold, feet tired, mouth pasty. His loathing for the Queen and all she represents has amplified into self-loathing.

France carries within her, like a foreign body, scoundrels who made her suffer and will continue to do so. Men of treason and injustice. Our response must be prompt and pitiless. We do not want a nation of traitors and mediocrities, we want a France that is pure and regenerated and has clean hands.

Time has melted away, vanished, and every minute that passes makes success less likely. Fouché's carriage enters the courtyard of 315 rue Saint-Honoré, where he lives, and he sits for a moment, waiting for Mordu to open the door, but Mordu does not come. It is too late to stand on ceremony, Fouché gets out and finds his man asleep on the box, the coachman tending to the horses.

—Mordu! Hey, Mordu, wake up!

Mordu curls up in the fetal position and Fouché shakes him.

—While I wash up, make the rounds, have Lindhal report to me by seven A.M.

Fouché grabs and shakes his man, but Mordu cannot be raised.

—Mordu, don't let me down. Not now. I need you.

—Sorry, boss. Just an hour's sleep is all I need.

Mordu talks with his eyes closed.

—Boss, you could do with a half hour's rest yourself.

Fouché gives up on him and crosses the courtyard to his first officer.

Pasquier, get your three best men, give them fresh mounts, have them go to our best informers, and I want Lindhal brought to me immediately.

Fouché recalls the King's pathetic last letter, giving Breteuil powers to do anything necessary to change the course of events; Fouché saved it as an example of utter ignominy, but now the shoe is on the other foot, and the commissioner plenipotentiary, minister without portfolio, is just as powerless as Louis was. Sending green boys out with just a few hours to question contacts they have never met is as impotent as the King's never-used letter.

—Mordu, bring me my usual mint, verbena, and honey; then you may retire.

No answer from Mordu. Fouché tells the coachman to drape a blanket over his servant. He cannot afford to have Mordu sick and in bed tomorrow.

It is my own incapacity that will kill you, Nenette, not the revolution but me. This night of impotence and dead ends is the sum of my failure. My mind is a blank. I don't know what to think anymore. I feel jackals devouring me with silent stares.

He enters the building and climbs to the second floor, where he kicks off his boots. Everything hurts. At thirty-four, he sighs like an ancient mariner, sips a glass of mint water. There is nothing more to be done; the dice are cast. He wants to lie down for five minutes. His temples throb, and even sitting down hurts, but he does not trust himself to wake up. The air in the bedroom is heavy. It seems to him the smell of Nenette is all around him, in his clothes, on his sheets, on the walls. It is 6:20 A.M.

Are my enemies on to Nenette? How could they have found out; from Mordu, from some spy who wants to be Robespierre's police chief in my place?

Usually Mordu shaves him, but that rascal is snoring on the floor of the carriage and Fouché, who has sent so many to eternal sleep, feels betrayed whenever Mordu sleeps; he sees it as a personal attack against him.

Sleep is the ultimate betrayal. The imitation of death.

He splashes water on his face, rubs pork bristles onto soap and water, and lathers up. Then he removes the straight razor from its carrying case and sharpens it on the leather thong with quick strokes, back and forth. He covers his cheeks, mouth, and throat with white and creamy lather.

His left hand holds his right ear, and the razor glides down his cheek. He shaves one clean swath of skin, another swath; he tugs at the edges of his face, pulls the blade along, the seraping noise takes shape in his ear, he relathers; after the white is removed, the skin pinkens. *I must be perfect today.* In the mirror, two sunken eyes stare back at him. He shaves the other cheek, his upper lip, his chin, his throat—a nick. Even before the strawberry appears on the cream, he feels the cut. He works his way down to the Adam's apple, under the ears, one wrong movement would speed events, assure peace of mind, stop anxiety, end shortness of breath, just one unsteady gesture would replace the guillotine and the entire instrument of state too. To stem the bleeding, Fouché presses down on the cut and splashes it with water. A clean white face emerges under the white towel.

Quickly, he washes his neck and underarms over the sink, sprinkles on cologne, then urinates. Now he squeezes homeopathic paste for the teeth and checks his breath. Back at the closet, he unfolds a clean white shirt and ties a new tricolor sash at the waist. Then he pulls on his shiniest riding boots.

Not one of my spies or anyone in my network of agents, no purveyor of deceit and innuendo, will step forward to help me because a paymaster on his way out is worth nothing. On the contrary, when they find out that I am down, they will give the knife an extra turn; they will jab it in to save their own skins.

It is time to go.

The hour has come, my love; this is important. Last night we did not have your travel papers. Now all is ready, but we have to move fast. They may come back and search this place again. You must get out of town as soon as the city gates open.

You will be traveling with an American. He does not speak French, so you will have to address him in English. I have to go out now to see what is delaying him and the carriage that will take you. He should have been here by now with your passports. Do not open the door to anyone.

I am only going a few blocks away, to rue des Petits Pères in front of the Eglise de la Trinité. Never fear, I will be back soon.

I won't abandon you. Never.

The Incorruptible One

Fouché rushes down the stairs three at a time. What to say, how to put it? What not to say? Number One sees enemies everywhere. And it will be difficult to get an audience without an appointment, or without sounding desperate.

Unable to rouse Mordu, he leaves him sprawled out and snoring like a drunk. Why do we expect perfection from our servants, when we do not expect it from our peers? He wakes his stable boy.

—Saddle up a horse, quickly.

He checks his watch; it is now or never. Robespierre lives only 150 meters away, with the Duplays, at 398 rue Saint-Honoré. Fouché could walk, but he is in a hurry and Robespierre would deem a carriage too luxurious. His stomach is in knots, he knows he should issue orders to Pasquier, but he has no time and does not know what to say. There are no orders left to be given, no spies left to be sent out or heard.

This is the end. I have come to where I did not ever want to be.

He mounts his horse and rides down the street. The morning is fresh and vigorous on his face, just what he needs to wake up and look alert. The sky is a faint blue, clean and cloudless. This will be a perfect day, dry, sunny, lean, and quiet. *Oh, but how I loathe this day, this place, this life!* Shutters are opening. A woman in a blue bathrobe and clogs is rushing down to the basement for coal. An eiderdown is being shaken from an upper balcony. Fouché loves the early morning smell of roasted coffee beans brewing. Men are coughing and looking wearily up at the sky.

The Incorruptible One will be up, dictating correspondence, reviewing laws, answering questions from the deputies. *I need something hot with plenty of sugar to wake me up.* He walks as if both his legs drag a ball and chain.

In La Martanière, Fouché's father, Joseph senior, had old olive trees, and once a year when he came back from the sea he would cut them back almost to the trunk. After his father went down with his ship, no one pruned the trees, and they became not just wild but completely mad; trunks, branches, and roots grew in all directions. One could hardly tell the top of the trees from the bottom. It is what Fouché remembers most after his father's death, the olive trees revolting and becoming unnatural and defiant. Even his mother did not know what she was looking at when she stopped on the road and gazed up at them. They were not trees anymore.

Police investigations are like olive trees. You have to keep them under tight control, and prune everything right down to the bone, down to the essence, cutting away all that is unnecessary or tangential.

Guards in the courtyard of the Duplay house at 398 rue Saint-Honoré bar the way.

—Proconsul Fouché desires an audience.

—Please wait, citizen.

—I must see him right away.

—I said, Wait.

—This cannot wait.

—You will have to wait.

It is an ordinary house, narrow and cream-colored, nothing special, but the kind of house that no leader of France has ever lived in while ruling, or ever will live in. Robespierre is a guest here of Mr. and Mrs. Duplay and their four marriageable daughters. The fact that he has moved in with the family of an ordinary shoemaker makes his power all the more extraordinary and terrifying.

—You may enter, citizen commissaire.

It is Charlotte Robespierre, already dressed at this hour, surprised to see him but smiling shyly. Here at the Duplay house she is not herself, she is in no-man's-land, foreign territory. Madame Duplay allows her to stay only because her brother has been ill. But it is a permanent tug of war between Charlotte and Madame Duplay. Charlotte occupies the street-front building with her younger brother, Augustin. Robespierre lives in a small narrow building on the left, connecting the front building to the Duplay house in the back of the courtyard.

Charlotte Robespierre has a clear complexion, a pointy chin, and her dark eyes always on the brink of smiling betray a vivacious spirit. Dressed in black with a white scarf, a simple tricolor ribbon on her chest and her hair in an untidy bun cascading down all sides, she is quite pretty.

Her hands smell of dishwashing and ironing; they are good hands, strong hands for housework with no rings on any fingers. She would make a loyal wife, and she does not want to remain a spinster, yet long ago she turned down her best offer of marriage because at the time Joseph Fouché was a nobody, an undecided priest who could not support her.

They have remade themselves: Her brother, who once resigned a judgeship in Arras rather than have to hand down a death sentence, is now the Incorruptible One. Fouché, who early on helped Robespierre overcome his slight speech impediment by training him before a mirror, is now proconsul. Only Charlotte is still the same caring sister, home-fire ally she always was. And now that he is someone, Fouché is still one of her closest allies, the one she calls on to write a pamphlet defending her honor when a libel attacks her.

—Mon ami, how are you? Charlotte studies Fouché's face to guess his purpose.

—May I see him? I have important news.

—Yes, his fever is down. But don't distress him.

Their sister Henriette Robespierre died of pneumonia at eighteen, and Fouché knows how deeply the siblings felt that loss; it was like becoming orphans for the second time. Now, as a parental substitute, Charlotte is careful that nothing should affect Robespierre's sensitive constitution.

The day is bright, but the staircase into which she leads him on the left of the courtyard is small and cramped. He follows her rustling hems, enters a narrow hallway, and comes to a corridor where a framed engraving shows Benjamin Franklin holding a lightning bolt in his right hand, George Washington carrying an American flag, and an eagle spreading the Declaration of Independence between its talons.

The residence is like the man, not showy, not fashionable or ornate, but correct and in simple good taste. Walls perfectly white and sober, nothing luxurious. Everything here is in frames of polished wood, clean and neat amid enormous quietude.

I need more time to think, is there no other way? I need to buy time.

When they reach the second-floor landing, only the scratching of quill on paper is audible. Then a voice:

How can we create a government powerful enough to force everyone to conform to the national interest without usurping power? The answer must lie in the people. They have escaped the multiple corruptions of the ancien régime. The people know neither flabbiness nor ambition, the two most fertile sources of all vice. They are nearer to nature and less depraved.

Robespierre is seated facing the window. At this early hour, he is dressed in white knee socks, gray britches, gold waistcoat. His white lace-cuffed shirt à la Valencienne and his Florentine taffeta coat are from Vanzut et Dosogne, the top men's haberdasher in Paris, but he wears no jabot, no watch fob. Gold does not interest him. Neither does idle chatter. Whenever his siblings played cards or spoke of insignificant things at home, he leaned back in an armchair and lost himself in thought. To Charlotte's constant *What do you want to eat?* He always answers, *I don't care.* He is so absent-minded, one day he served himself a ladle of soup without noticing there was no bowl in front of him.

In a mirror, Fouché glances at his own face.

I am not of the sturdy hero breed, that is for certain. I am more the poete manqué, *knobby face, narrow jaw, rusty-black hair, eyes with that oblique slit of pupil like jack-o'-lanterns of death. This is not the face of a man who often speaks the truth, but this morning it has to be that.*

The Duplays have hung portraits of Robespierre on every wall and placed statuettes of him on almost every shelf. Suddenly, the voice stops reading out loud.

If I tremble or smell of weakness, I shall give the appearance of having something personal at stake. Even looking red-eyed or tired will be interpreted as a bad sign. Wait out the silence. The Incorruptible One always takes some time to descend from his internal heights to the mundane world. Respect his silence.

Robespierre nods and smiles, but he is still wrapped up in his thoughts, and his smile hangs in midair as if he has not changed or moved in the week since Fouché last saw him. It is not a smile at all, but a rubber band pulled taut and tight, waiting to snap back into place. He is thirty-five, one year older than Fouché, but he looks far younger. His body is small, compact, but the head is big and the nostrils flared. Without his wig, the receding hairline gives his skull a pointy appearance. Seated at his desk, he does not look like a powerful leader but more like a society dandy.

—You wanted to see me, my friend?

—Yes, citizen.

—Enter, enter.

Fouché steps into the room and stands on the Persian carpet amid a freezing silence and cleanliness. This room is always perfectly dusted and neat, as if no one lived here, as if Robespierre, fastidious to a fault, floated a meter above the floor and barely breathed at all. He has accumulated no assets to speak of; all he owns are fifty books, some clothes, and his sense of order. Charlotte cleans the room for him. She is the only one allowed to enter when he is out. She says there is nothing to clean, but she does it anyway to make certain the Duplay girls do not go in and snoop around.

—So Fouché, you are back from la Nièvre?

—Yes, citizen.

They call each other *citizen,* but this code word, an imprimatur of the great task of creating a public citizenship, also reinforces their closeness over the years.

—I have heard most disturbing accounts about you, Joseph.

—How so?

—Well, that you are killing priests and monks, that you deny there is a God.

Fouché waits. *I do not want to waste any friendship or political capital discussing the de-Christianization campaign. But neither can I let my actions go undefended; that would only make Robespierre suspicious.*

—Joseph, we cannot fight on all at fronts at once. Ninety-nine percent of France is Catholic. We cannot change that overnight.

—The church organizes and exploits superstition, citizen. They are at their heart antirevolutionary fanatics; even abjuring priests cannot be trusted!

—Of course, you are right. But is not atheism immodest and aristocratic too in pretending that man can know the unknowable?

—Citizen, you have been misinformed. I want to annihilate fanaticism, but that does not mean that I wish to set up the reign of atheism.

If the Supreme One were other, he would offer me coffee and a piece of chocolate. If he were other, I could ask him for a coffee without his concluding that I am weak and desperate.

—My friend, focus your energies on what matters. Our war must be against hoarders and speculators and for free universal primary education, the abolition of slavery, state pensions and sickness benefits, national health, medical aid for the poor, relief for the old, increased food production. Your forced redistribution of émigré landholdings and property to the have-nots, that revolutionary tax, was an excellent initiative.

—Thank you.

—But to achieve all this, we cannot set every Catholic against us; the church helps prevent constant upheavals.

—I will take your words to heart, citizen.

This dandy scrivener from Arras still has not reimbursed me my loan. I paid his way to Paris back in '89, but I have never had the courage to ask him for it and, knowing him, he probably does not have money to repay me.

—So you wanted to see me, Fouché?

—Yes, citizen. It is essential that we delay the widow Capet's trial by a day.

Charlotte has been standing at the door all this time, like an old mother hen making sure that everything goes right, that Robespierre does not need anything. Robespierre waves her away. She nods silently, closes the door, and goes downstairs to prepare his breakfast, but does she creep back up?

The old house has its own creaks and groans, but I do not trust any of them; it could be Charlotte returning to listen at the keyhole.

—Delay the trial? Whatever for, Fouché?

—To give us more time, citizen. I do not want to waste your patience on police matters, but there is a new treasonous plot afoot concerning the Queen.

—You know full well that revolutionary justice is up to the Court and out of my hands. Bring this up with Fouquier-Tinville or his assessor, Herman.

—I cannot, citizen.

—Why not?

—Because the plot may involve those very men detaining her in prison.

Robespierre puts down his quill. He has no time for this but he cannot resist, and the wings of his nostrils flare.

—Speak freely, man.

—Something unthinkable happened yesterday.

—What?

—I cannot be everywhere at the same time.

Coming here is a mistake—the messenger becomes the message and gets blamed for it. Always let someone else bring bad news. It would be better if Louis Larivière, keeper of the keys at the Conciergerie, announced the escape, but there was no time to seek Larivière, and anyway he might sing another tune today, might finger someone else. And just as important as the message is how I pass it. In this hurried hour, I cannot sound rushed. Let him be the one who starts to panic, not me.

Fouché advances and presents the forged order with the false signatures of Saint-Just, Fouquier-Tinville, and the others.

—Where is Marie-Antoinette now?

—I need more time, one more day to find her. My spies are everywhere. We will find her, we only need time.

The Incorruptible One studies the document. The scrupulous politeness of his manner freezes; his eyes fix on Fouché's boots, shined on their upper part but muddy at the heels. The Incorruptible One abhors dirt, for him cleanliness is next to Godliness.

—There is evidence of a plot financed by Austrian funds and no doubt involving Danton. But I need more time to expose him.

—This is grotesque! snaps Robespierre.

—Exactly, citizen. After the foiled Red Carnation escape attempt, security was quintupled. And then just three weeks ago a guard walked her as far as the front desk and then got cold feet, so I instituted a daily rotation of guards to prevent any possibility of friendship developing. They have managed the impossible, unless of course she has not escaped at all. Unless she has been hidden by your enemies to embarrass you.

The Incorruptible One walks around his desk, twirling a quill in his clean fingers.

How like a bantam rooster he struts about. Pettifogging lawyer, he would not have been first in any class I taught, not last either, probably just in the middling middle.

—I do not want it said around Paris that you have misplaced the most guarded prisoner in all of France.

—Citizen, we have a look-alike of the Queen that Citizen Saint-Just passed on to me. I have placed her in the cell.

—Excellent, use her.

—Leave her there while we continue the hunt?

—No. Guillotine the look-alike.

Fouché waits. *Anything I say will be misconstrued. Let this play itself out.*

—Execute the double so appearances are preserved.

Robespierre's blue-gray eyes catch his.

—And we will take our enemies one by one, as they come, Fouché, even our closest allies. Your job is to find the traitors, root them all out of their nests. I want a full report on this in three days. Prepare the case carefully.

—But if the Queen surfaces in another capital? She will surely become a rallying cry, a focal point for royalist resistance.

Robespierre stares out at the rooftops of the city where dawn is breaking.

—Who will believe some old Austrian crackpot claiming to be Queen of France? We will say she is a fake. Everyone will have seen the real one guillotined. Anyway, once abroad, émigrés automatically become enemies of France and traitors.

—Citizen, just one day's delay and we could get Marie-Antoinette back.

I have gone too far. I have shown my hand. And the words Robespierre now says are not as important as the way he looks at me.

—You would put me in an impossible position, Fouché. Only we know she is a look-alike. What are you afraid of?

—Citizen, what will the double say at the trial? I would have to drug her, and drugged she will not be a credible witness. Undrugged she will not cooperate; after all, it is her head on the block.

—All right, just tell the president of the court not to let her speak.

—If I can capture the widow Capet before her trial starts, that would prevent any attempt to blackmail the government later.

Robespierre checks the clock on the mantelpiece.

No one sees him like this, like I do, with his receding hairline, high forehead, thin black locks down to the shoulders. He only appears in public in a powdered gray wig.

—This is a government of laws, not of whims, Fouché. I am not going to impede republican justice merely because of police incompetence. I made you responsible for her security until her execution. It is five after seven. You have fifty-five minutes before the trial starts. If you find her in time, fine. If you find her too late, dispose of her privately. What nancy-pants out there on Place de la Révolution, when the drums begin to roll, will imagine it is a double? An approximation will do!

He taps his fingernails on the desk, which is as shiny and spotless as the man himself.

—Impure blood must flow so that the people may live. The nation needs this execution. I am against it, I tried to delay it as long as I could, but to delay more will only strengthen our enemies. Weakness puts at risk our national resolve for renewal.

Nod and wait. I cannot compromise myself further than I already have. Seneca warned, Talk only to him who is ready to listen.

Robespierre turns to his papers.

—We have a head. Cut it off, and do not waste my time with this anymore. Speed the execution!

Fouché bows and retreats toward the door, as the scratch of the quill on paper resumes. On his way down, the parquet slats creak in the staircase, but he tries not to give the impression of hurrying or of having any personal feelings at all.

I have failed, and in the worst way possible. Now he knows or suspects every-thing. Should I poison Nenette to make certain of the dose? Could I, if I tried?

The day is filled with loathing—self-loathing and world loath-ing. From this moment on Fouché knows he will be shadowed day and night, so even if he finds the Queen, they will report on his every gesture, and it will be impossible for him to hide Nenette. Robespierre will police his own private police chief.

Can I place my own small personal interest above that of the state? Nenette, you are not a blameless virgin, not a white lamb of God, you are a royal cour-tesan, a paid layabout, a hank-of-hair, a molly, a skirt, a trollop, a round-heel.

Should he administer the potion himself? It would be safer to let her do it.

Back home at 315 rue Saint-Honoré, Pasquier comes running.

—Your agents are all here waiting for you, citizen, all those we could find.

He recalls Robespierre's speech concerning the importance of ridding the nation of the monsters responsible for its ills, and inducing a state of sanctity by making possible a sacred republic:

The real sacrifice is not the King's. The real sacrifice is the one that I must make. To accept his execution I must banish the feelings of compassion which under normal circumstances would be a virtue. I sacrifice my pity for him because it is essen-tial for the survival of the Republic. We must all sacrifice our natural human feelings for the greater good.

Today, the real sacrifice is that I must banish not only the feelings of compassion I have for Nenette but all that I am. I must sacrifice everything I feel for the greater good.

Fouché follows Pasquier to the stables. As he goes, he dips his hand in his pocket, pulls out the gold ring he snatched from de Tours, and reads the motto. *Tutto a te me guida.*

There are such excellent forgers of script in Brussels. The problem is that here fewer and fewer accept paper assignats as payment anymore. I could not bring as much gold as I wanted. So my means are limited. If Paine fails me, I have no backup. A million things could go wrong. The biggest mistake was not to try and leave yesterday, but how far could you have gotten without passports?

The Widow Capet

His agents are waiting for him there: stalwart Jacobins, thieves, double and triple agents, ne'er-do-wells, war wounded, turncoat aristocrats, twenty or so of the least honorable men in the city. But his eyes fall on Lindhal. The Austrian spy has a squished bald head, big sad dog-like eyes, and a face that only a mother could love. He reports on his night search and how difficult it is to get any straight information. Fouché is only half listening: *Tutto a te me guida.* He loves that motto, and to calm his nerves he plays with the gold escutcheon on the ring. If he still had time, he would present it to Nenette. *Everything leads me to you.*

—Where did you get that? says Lindhal, peering at the signet ring.

—Why?

—This is his coat of arms.

In the center of the signet ring is a fish with bird wings on it; in the upper left-hand and lower right-hand corners of the family shield are crossed weapons; in the opposite corners are rearing dragons.

—The flying fish is von Fersen's family crest, says Lindhal.

When he was private secretary to the Austrian ambassador, Lindhal had countless meetings with von Fersen, sometimes on a daily basis. In exile, both men continued to meet.

—Where did you find it?

—I took it off the old Duchess of Tours.

—It could only mean one thing.

Fouché searches the squished face of his best agent.

—What?

—Von Fersen uses the crest of that signet ring stamped in wax to identify the bearer as a person of confidence. I know, because I carried a letter last year to Mercy bearing that wax seal. So if anyone wore that ring into the prison yesterday, that would immediately let the Queen know, without a word passing, that they were acting for Fersen.

Fouché stares into the sad Austrian eyes,

—We searched de Tours' place, tore it apart from floor to ceiling.

—One of her wine cellars has an underground tunnel; it leads to the river.

—How do you know that?

—You pay me to know a lot of things.

Lindhal's long prominent nose and his patches of dark hair around the bald crown of his head have something pathetic about them. His eyes are bloodshot. Fouché checks his watch: forty minutes left. He sniffs the air.

—How much will you pay me to show you the passageway?

—Mordu! Fouché calls out, assessing his chances; he dons his bicorne and rushes to the gate.

—Lindhal, you get anything you want, just name your price.

—I want to see the money first.

Fouché grabs Mordu's leather pouch containing the walk-around money and pulls out a similar one that he carries stuffed inside his shirt.

—You get the other half when we find the Queen.

Fouché leaps on Pasquier's horse. Lindhal follows on another horse. Out of the courtyard they gallop, fingers in the mane, their heels pounding the belly of their beasts. Steel-shod hooves slam the cobblestones as they careen down rue Saint-Honoré. Mordu is not far behind. They ride straight for rue des Cinq Frères. Horse-mad, they race against the fall of the blade, against the motion of time, back to the old Duchess of Tours.

All the pieces are falling into place. *Tutto a te me guida.* This escape has nothing to do with politics or bribery. There is no grand design, no grand Austrian plot. This is only one desperate man on a suicide mission. Who else would risk such impossible odds? It makes perfect sense to Fouché. None of the usual conduits were used. This is the work of a man ravaged by guilt who has been torturing himself in Austrian-occupied Brussels for two years for having organized the ill-fated flight to Varennes, having driven the royal family halfway to freedom and then having obeyed the King's orders to abandon them.

Tutto a te me guida.

Commerce and food wagons are starting to fill the early morning streets. Merchants are raising their stalls, setting out their produce, writing out their prices in chalk on tiny slates, arguing. A child screams and runs away from her mother.

They enter number 1 rue des Cinq Frères at a gallop. The three municipal guards left here last night stand to receive new orders.

I should have been more thorough; what was I thinking of? Von Fersen is desperate, but I too am a desperate man on a suicide mission. That makes two of us. How can I be so messy? Under strain, in crises, I am always so rational.

Lindhal breaks open a door, and Fouché rushes after him.

—Nothing down that passageway, citizen! shouts a soldier. Fouché grabs a torch and orders the soldier to stand aside.

—Mordu, make certain no one follows us down here.

Fouché follows Lindhal into a maze of old wine cellars and underground storage rooms. They push through dust and cobwebs. Lindhal tries opening a locked door with his shoulder but manages only to bruise himself. A battering ram is needed.

Fouché begins to shout—Morr—but stops in mid-scream.

The Duchess of Tours is standing like a ghost not more than an arm's length away, smiling in the darkness.

—I left orders that no one was to follow me. Who let you down here?

Tears rim her weary eyes. He cannot stand the way this ancient wreck of a duchess looks at him, white hair hanging loose, a vulnerable intimate silence in the air. She has the wry smile of a child caught with her hand in the cookie jar.

He pulls out a pistol to shoot the lock off the door, but the duchess is already holding out a key which glints in the torchlight.

The key fits, and the bolt slides back. He enters the dirty dark wine cellar, holds up the torch, and a frightened bat flies out. Or something else, black and bold. There are barrels of flour and wheat stored down here, also bales of flax fibers, hemp, cotton—Fouché detests hoarding. And that is all there is in France these days, selfish greedy onanists who think only of themselves. He finds a woman lying among clean warm bedding and pillows on the ground, with the leftovers of an evening meal on a tray. Unable to see who it is, Fouché raises her. Her lips are dry and cracked. He removes her servant's bonnet slowly, and tresses of white hair cascade down. She looks too old to be the Queen, but it is she. For a moment he forgets the press of time and just gazes at the lines of the face, examines her as a lover would examine his prize possession, his older look-alike for Nenette. She has driftwood skin and buffed nails, but she is not nearly as beautiful as Nenette. She is pathetic, really. He tries to wake her. The royal lids barely open.

Fouché hears a scrambling of shoes in the hallway.

—Mordu, bring me some water fast.

Then, to the duchess, he says:

—Is von Fersen the father of the Dauphin? Is that why he has come back?

—Your majesty, forgive me, says the duchess, ignoring Fouché; we wanted to get you out of town and away as fast as possible. But at the last minute, our plans went awry. Poor Queen, look at you now!

Fouché takes the pitcher of water that Mordu hands him and brings it to the Queen's lips. She drinks slowly.

—Mordu, get rid of the pestilential crone. I do not want to smell de Tours standing here one more second.

Fouché turns his head so as not to see the blood. It is 7:29 A.M. by his watch. Mordu's gun echoes through the basement gallery, and the duchess slumps to the floor, a pool of blood spreading around her.

—Now run, fly, Mordu. Hold off Bault and Larivière until I get there.

—How, chief? They won't let me into the Queen's cell.

—Just stand guard outside. Use Pasquier's men. Order him to fire if he needs to, anything, but prevent them from entering until I get there with this prisoner. Now run, damn you!

Mordu's shoes slam the steps, and he disappears up into the light.

Joseph Fouché, commissioner plenipotentiary, deputy of the National Convention, removes his black cape and drapes it over the Queen. She is his ticket, his one chance, to grow old on this earth and aspire to happiness.

—Monsieur, I demand to see my children. The Queen's voice is flat and dry like a beached fish. No social demarcation here, just an old tired woman.

—Quiet, citoyenne.

—Monsieur, I am grateful you want to save me, but I cannot live without—

Fouché searches for a blunt instrument. The smell of chalk dust fills his nostrils and the royal bleat continues.

—Monsieur, I refuse to go into exile without my son. It would not be—

He balls up his handkerchief and stuffs it into her mouth. The Queen's eyes bulge, and her jaw stretches. He scoops hay from the floor and wipes the duchess's blood on the Queen's cheeks, lips, and face. *The last thing I want is anyone recognizing her before I get her back inside the prison.*

He lifts her by the arms, and Lindhal takes her legs. Municipals come to lend a hand, as they carry her up to the courtyard. Two neighbors walk over, but Fouché barks them away. They retreat, assuming the police interrogation has gone too far. Under the black cape, the Queen simpers into her gag. Fouché slings the body over Pasquier's horse and climbs up behind. He orders the detachment of municipal guards to follow. Lindhal climbs on his horse and follows as well.

The streets are becoming crowded. Fouché calls out.

—Let me pass, let me through, you dogs!

Sans-culottes press around: 7.36 A.M. Fouché shouts again:

—Let me pass!

Behind him, Lindhal's foreign accent only confuses the crowd, fans their suspicions.

Fouché's horse rears; he keeps digging his boots into its flanks. He has too small a guard, and only himself and the Austrian on horseback to open a path. One man tries to sell him a gazette called *The Patriotic Tailor,* with the headline, REPORT ON ARISTOCRATS TO BE SUITED OUT FOR THE LATEST NECKWEAR. Another wants to examine the body slung over the horse. Fouché uses the barrel of his pistol to knock him back, but the crowd turns on him.

—Citizen, what is your hurry?

—Out of my way! Fouché puts his gun to the man's head.

From behind, the crowd pushes, turns ugly and confrontational. Fouché and Lindhal are the only ones on horseback in the melee, so they are natural targets. He calls for the Municipals to close ranks around him. There are shouts of *Hang all the aristocrats to lampposts!*

A gun goes off, and Fouché's horse buckles, shot in the chest. There is blood flowing everywhere.

Fouché is done for, pinned under his horse. Lindhal manages somehow to pull the Queen clear. She has stopped moaning, perhaps she has fainted, but he keeps the cape over her. Municipals come to the rescue. They arrest the man with the gun, a patriot with a walrus mustache and a huge tricolored cockade on his chest who claims the gun fired by mistake. A police sergeant manages to hold back the crowd.

—Find me a cart or a carriage! shouts Fouché, desperate. It is 7:41 A.M.

The Queen must have fainted because as they carry her, Lindhal at the feet, a Municipal at the shoulders, her body sags like a sack of potatoes. There is no carriage to be commandeered. The sergeant returns with a wheelbarrow.

—This is the best I could find, commissaire.

They dump the widow in, rear first, and Fouché covers the wheelbarrow with his black cape, thanking Pascal for his genius in inventing this single-wheeled vehicle in 1615. Escorted by a double row of Municipals, he heads down the Montagne Sainte-Geneviève, then rue de la Harpe, onto rue de la Boucherie. He lets a soldier push the wheelbarrow but he runs alongside it.

Mercifully, it is all downhill. He can see it, smell it. The Conciergerie prison is in the distance. Ile de la Cité is in sight, through the leafless trees: 7:45 A.M.

All of Paris is up and about. Drunks are sitting on the sidewalk, dogs are sniffing at the base of trees and at garbage. Children, washed behind the ears, are going to school.

They cross the quay and cross the bridge, Pont Saint-Michel. Then take rue de la Calandre, back to rue de la Barillerie and the sole entrance into the Conciergerie, through the Cour du Mai. Fouché enters under the first arcade on the right where Federals are milling about and members of the public are pressing to get into the trial. The hallways are full of activity: jailers, guards, secretaries, archivists, and lawyers. Citizens Tronson Ducoudray and Chauveau-Lagarde are there, whispering together. Every person having any sort of business at the court is arriving early to find a seat. All want to see and hear the Queen testify.

Keeper of the Keys Louis Larivière is talking to his superiors.

—I say imprison the soldier who brought the widow Capet a glass of water.

Fouquier-Tinville nods and mutters:

—Yes, aiding a traitor, sympathizing with an enemy of the people.

Mordu arrives, all asweat.

—Chief, we are waiting for you. It's been a rough standoff to keep them out of the cell. Nenette is safe for now. But I don't know how long we can protect her.

I must slow down, catch my breath before entering.

Fouché orders the Municipals to form a flying wedge around him. They are not as good as revolutionary guards, but Pasquier and his men are inside, and he has to get to them. *Tutto a te me guida.*

Court officials who recognize Fouché salute, guards too, but he pushes through the crowd of officials without stopping or acknowledging anyone.

He dares not remove either the gag from the Queen's mouth, or his cloak from her body. Her chest is full of phlegm and coughing, but it is better that she choke to death than that he give away her identity before they are inside her cell. Now comes the trickiest part.

He pushes the wheelbarrow into the registrar's office. Joseph Fouché, proconsul of the National Assembly, police commissioner plenipotentiary responsible to the Incorruptible One, deputy from the Loire-Inférieure, gains entry without needing to register because the man on duty recognizes him and waves him past.

But the chief registrar follows him in, staring at the body slumped in the wheelbarrow.

—Who do you have there, commissaire?

—I want to confront the Austrian whore with what crimes are committed every day in her name.

Three guards stand at attention.

The registrar touches the foot dangling from the wheelbarrow, but before he can lift up the cape and check the face, Fouché yells:

—I want all those responsible for the widow Capet in here right now! Tell Larivière and Bault that I need them on the double.

When he reaches the hallway leading to the Cour des Dames, Fouché whispers to Pasquier.

—Arrest Lindhal and keep a close watch over him.

He knows the best way to avoid attention is to create a loud and obstreperous diversion. Suddenly, Larivière arrives, then Prison Governor Bault.

—What is all this about? What is going on? The trial starts in five minutes, and we have no time for nonsense. Who is this? They stare at the figure in the wheelbarrow.

—A suspect we have just interrogated, says Mordu.

—Is she dead?

—No, not yet. Come inside quickly, all of you, orders Fouché, and close the door. Mordu, do not let anyone else in.

Concierge Bault, Keeper of the Keys Larivière, the gimp-leg greffier, the sergeant, and the captain of the guards, they all crowd into the registrar's office. The wheelbarrow with the bloody female is left behind Fouché and behind Mordu, and for now no one pays attention to it. Hands behind his back, lips thin, hair pearled with sweat, Fouché addresses them.

—By your lack of vigilance you betray France. You betray our women, our children, our soldiers fighting on the front. You let outsiders visit the widow Capet. Any person can enter here at any time of the day or night.

—Citizen commissaire, the order yesterday was signed by—

—Quiet, Bault. Death is too good for those who fail in their duty. I want the guard doubled, vigilance tripled. It is not just France but all of history that is watching you and will judge you.

—But, says Bault, we monitor her every breath.

—During today's trial, I want every item in the widow Capet's possession, the entire cell from stone floor to ceiling, examined thoroughly. Anyone trying to gain access to her or have any communication with her at all will be suspect. And no one is above the law, not even us, understand?

There is a loud knocking. Fouquier-Tinville shouts through the locked door.

—What is going on here? Open up!

Fouché can imagine the public prosecutor standing in the hallway, long nose like a hawk's beak, heavy eyebrows, black hair combed straight back from a hairline that forms a sharp V at the forehead. He often holds his head to the side as if it broke off and were stuck back on wrong. His hands are bony with blue veins, and he is clutching heavy files. Until recently, he was an unknown small-time lawyer, but now he shouts through the locked door.

—Fouché, you are way out of line. You have no right to enter the widow Capet's chamber.

Fouché does not deign to respond. He gathers the authority of his priestly studies, the stature of his work for the Committee of Public Safety, stares knives into those in the room, pushes past Mordu, and waits behind Larivière while the latter unlocks for Fouquier-Tinville, the public prosecutor.

Fouquier does not enter, but stares down his long nose at Fouché. His hawk eye frozen with disdain, he says:

—Explain yourself at once.

Fouché stands tall in black cloak and tricolor sash.

—Your spies will have told you by now that I saw Robespierre this morning. This is a matter of gravest concern. I must now confront the widow for two minutes.

—You have no mandate to interfere with or delay revolutionary justice.

—I shall have my man shoot in the head anyone who attempts to interfere with my business, and you will have to answer eventually to your own court. Mordu, cover the public prosecutor.

Mordu, his neck disappearing into his shoulders, raises his gun.

—Are you threatening me, commissaire? says Fouquier.

—It is not a threat, it is a promise. Lieutenant Pasquier, quick!

Bault and Larivière retreat. No one wants to be singled out for the displeasure of either of these two commissioners. Humiliation and abuse are usually a prologue to killing. First you dehumanize an enemy, make him a nonentity; then you eliminate him. Lieutenant Pasquier rushes up.

—Pasquier, set your men here at the door and arrest anyone who tries to interfere while I interrogate the widow Capet and confront her with an informer.

This is the usefulness of having your own detachment of National Guards who are loyal beyond all else. The prison guards at the cell door hesitate.

Fouquier-Tinville checks his watch.

—The audience room is full. The jurors are waiting, witnesses also. I order the Queen out of her—

Fouché advances so close he can smell Fouquier. He whispers:

—You are an efficient bureaucrat, but you are not as clean as you pretend to be. You have received two hundred gold Louis in the Ecluse affair, three thousand livres in the Linville affair, eleven thousand livres for Dillon's and Castellane's escape, thirty thousand livres to save the life of the Countess of Boufflers. Since you sign the execution orders and have seven children to pay for, you are a perfect target for bribes, citizen. Now shall I give my evidence to the Committee of Public Safety?

Fouquier-Tinville is red in the face.

Information is far more useful when stored and not acted upon, when accumulated close to the vest and used only sparingly, as and when needed.

—Are you going to check your watch, or shall you try mine?

The prosecutor ignores the Breguet dangling before him.

—If we do not have the widow Capet in exactly five minutes, I shall arrest you for delaying court proceedings. Your police work be damned.

Larivière nods to his guards, and they stand aside. Mordu and Pasquier lift up the bloody suspect from the wheelbarrow and carry the body inside the cell.

With Pasquier and his men standing guard in the hallway, Fouché enters the royal cell too, holding his loaded gun at the ready. Nenette is there. Her voice leaps up.

—Joseph!

She helps Mordu to remove the bloody servant's dress, revealing the Queen's skin ivory pale from long absence of sunlight, muscles flaccid. A drop of sweat rolls down Fouché's armpit. All his moves have been calibrated and refined throughout the detours of this endless night, so he moves now without hesitation.

In the hallway, Fouquier-Tinville is all ears. Mercifully the Incorruptible One is not here; neither is Saint-Just—they would be the only ones with sufficient authority to force entry into the cell against Fouché's orders. He hears Hébert scream.

—I have promised the sans-culottes the head of Antoinette, and I will cut it off myself if there is any more delay!

In the cell, Fouché removes the Queen's gag. She is stretched out on the narrow bed. Mordu is in front of her and Nenette behind her; their hands work quickly like giant bees mulcting a flower.

Fouché is at the door, impatient; he stands atop the excrement bucket with a cramp on his twisted face like some Old Testament prophet keeping his eyes peeled on the promised land. His nerves are lightning rods. *Who is the prisoner and who is the victim now?*

Fouché stares out through the Judas hole into the hall and meets all those who glance in with his pistol at the ready. In the distance, he can make out the groans of the sick and the sound of iron bars scraping shut.

Nenette crouches and dons the Queen's bloodstained dress. Mordu washes the Queen's face. She is now once again dressed all in black, in her mourning dress. Fouché moves smelling salts under her nose.

—Come on, come on, these salts can bring back the dead.

She coughs a hacking cough and opens her eyes: Pale as if varnished, yet clean, and solid they are. They stand her up, and Nenette combs her hair. Mordu moistens a rag with the small bottle of water for the Queen's teeth and wipes her cheeks, nose, chin, and forehead clean. Then Nenette holds up Rosalie Lamorlière's little red pocket mirror, so the Queen can see herself.

Fouché admires her.

—Citoyenne, you are fine now.

The Queen walks, wobbly, helped by four hands, then two, then alone.

—Shall we proceed to your trial, citoyenne?

She smiles wanly at Nenette, not recognizing her, or not daring to say anything lest she incriminate an old friend. Nenette embraces her and whispers:

—May God bless you and keep you, ma belle.

Herman, assessor and, today, president of the revolutionary court, arrives at the top of the staircase above the hallway.

All eyes are on the widow Capet's cell. She emerges white-faced, impassive, expressionless, wearing her most stoic resigned appearance.

Fouquier-Tinville turns and leads the way up the stairs into the large courtroom. The widow follows, surrounded on all sides by Municipals. Fouché should see her to the dock, but he stands back waiting at the registrar's door. Everyone follows the Queen. They whisper: *She looks so old, all white-haired. What happened, is she ill? Is she hemorrhaging again?*

Herman, president of the court, calls for silence. The other three judges waiting there are Foucault, Donzé-Verteuil, and Lane. The jurors enter the room and take their seat: Ganney, Martin Nicolas, Chatelet, Grenier Trey, Souberbielle, Trinchard, Jourdeuil, Gêmon, Devez, and Suard. The court secretary, Joseph Fabricius, now prepares to read the act of accusation.

Fouché's work is done, at least for now. It has been a night in hell, a night he will not want to experience again as long as he lives.

They think I am cruel and inhuman, but someone has to take out the garbage. That is what I do, throw out the trash. Thanks to me, France is purified, cleansed, and made benevolent.

Proconsul Fouché moves through the crowd. Next to him, Mordu pushes the wheelbarrow carrying the bloody suspect. All three surrounded by Pasquier's men reach the Cour du Mai and move into a patch of morning sunlight. None of the prison guards stop them. Mordu has sent one of Pasquier's men to bring Fouché's carriage, and it is there waiting for them on rue de la Barillerie. Mordu opens the door, and he and Fouché help Nenette into the carriage.

—I want every single available agent to hunt down von Fersen. He will be disguised, Mordu, but give them a description of his appearance, size and weight. And round up any of his friends still in Paris. Any of his old Royal Suédois mercenaries. When they were disbanded, some of the men must have stayed behind, certainly those who were French and did not emigrate, or those foreigners who married here or joined the National Guard.

—Boss, we found Thomas Paine sleeping over at White's Hotel.

—Good, have an agent follow his every move, I shall pay him a visit tomorrow. It is enough excitement for one day.

The carriage pulls away. Nenette, resting her head on his shoulders, whispers.

—Joseph, I think I would like that hot bath now.

Fouché draws the blinds down but does not answer. She is breathing deeply and the carriage is taking them home, and he slowly closes his eyes.

—Joseph, you don't always have to wear such shiny shoes and dress so spotlessly for me. You can be scruffy, and I would love you just the same.

Where are you? No Paine. No carriage. And now, no you! I run like a lunatic. I run until neighborhood police and surveillance committee people start to notice me running. But I do not care.

One hour ago I had you in my arms, and everything seemed possible—but soon it will be one day, one week, one year, then a century. I want time to stop. My body and soul you once caressed are already rotting; I feel them turning to abomination and dust.

Then I see the street incident from afar: The Parisian crowd surging around and the overpowered proconsul trying to hold them at bay. His horse is shot from under him. The situation comes under control, and the Municipals lift you inert into a wheelbarrow and cart you away. I recognize you by your shoes.

My first reaction is to chase after you, fight them off, and die with you in my arms. That would be better than to live. So I race after you. They are running, and I follow you at a gallop, but I am too late. I see them wheel you into the Conciergerie, and the gates close behind you. I think nothing; I do nothing. I stand outside the gates of the Cour du Mai, a blank, without any desire to save myself.

My life is over.

The Trial

Back on the third floor of 315 rue Saint-Honoré, Fouché's house, the curtains are drawn. Zebra stripes of light stream in pale through the shutters, but the rooms are hushed and shadowy. The furniture is covered in bedsheets. No glib rococo here; all is tasteful and sedate. A muted grandfather clock rings the hour. Some distant street noises reach the living room and dining room, but the master bedroom faces the inner courtyard, where only the odd chirping or cooing disturbs the eaves. The commissioner is not receiving today. He sleeps the sleep of the righteously fatigued.

Mordu knocks on the bedroom door and waits discreetly. Fouché hears it as if from the next faubourg.

Is he kidding? Has Mordu waited thirty seconds to come and bother me? The Queen is on trial in the revolutionary tribunal, and I do not want to be disturbed under any circumstance by anyone, not even the Incorruptible One! Today I am staying in bed.

More knocking. Fouché slips on a bathrobe and goes to open the door.

—Mordu?

—You said you wanted news every hour about the trial, boss, but I let two hours go by because I thought you needed sleep.

He is annoyed at Mordu's familiarity.

—Yes. So how is it going?

—Witnesses are proceeding, boss. The Queen has not said a word so far. She seems completely imperturbable, almost indifferent. She is just sitting there, on her hard chair in the middle of the courtroom, her fingers drumming the armrest as if she were playing the clavichord, but otherwise she shows no emotion.

—Good. Go back and keep an eye on the proceedings.

Mordu checks that he has Fouché's *laissez-passer*, bows, and slips away. Fouché now orders Pasquier to go to the hôtel de Vauban and bring a victory meal: foie gras, veal sweetbreads in an un-churned butter sauce, a fine pullet, a vegetable dish of broad beans and turnips, and, though he is not a drinker, some cold champagne for Nenette's sake. Robespierre, who cannot even sip champagne at a wedding, calls it the Poison of Liberty, but of course he is not invited today. To stay any remaining pangs of hunger there must be a dessert: apples, cherries, and pears bathed in Malaga wine, and of course white and black chocolate truffles.

Every warrior rests after battle. And what I like about Pasquier is that he is the supreme professional, never an ironic look, never a raised eyebrow or a comment out of turn, but meticulous attention to detail.

—Will that be all, citizen? Pasquier reviews the list.

—Yes, rush and tell them I want it by noon and to put it on my bill.

The cook at the hôtel de Vauban knew Nenette when she was one of the Queen's intimates. He is now writing a book called *The Physiology of Taste.*

Fouché orders well water to be heated for a bath and tells the guard at the door that no one is to enter under any circumstances. Barely glancing at the most recent gazettes, he leaves them on the sideboard with the rest of his mail and lies back in bed, touches her just-washed locks—perfumed, satiny, and golden. Nenette is asleep on her stomach; her face, turned to the side, carries a look of such peace, eyelids pale with mauve overtones, mouth drooping sideways with the tilt of the pillow that he stares at her for a minute.

They say desire grows and matures over time, but I felt this attraction from the moment we met: Saul thrown from his horse, blinded by the light. In that prison lineup when I first approached you, it was not your beauty but your truth which struck me. I knew you at once, recognized you like Saul the soldier on his knees, squinting up into the essence of goodness.

At each breath, her nostrils flare slightly. Nenette sleeps so deeply he can feel her exhaustion. A drop of saliva forms at the corner of her mouth; her lips, dry with cracks, need cream or ointment. From under the sheets now rises a smell left from their lovemaking like a warm and heavy sea.

Tonight I found a needle in a haystack. Being a bloodhound is my job. But you, Nenette, are a master at something far more important, the workings of the human heart. Tonight you played a role that would have destroyed a lesser being.

He cups a hand over her buttocks. *What political system can deny this and long survive?* He smells her warm skin, kisses her.

I always wanted a strong woman with big bones, thick ankles, wide feet, someone who could drag my skinny frame to safety when the shooting starts. And in spite of the royal likeness, Nenette, you have something of the peasant in you, something that never left your village in the Perche, a drag-me-to-your-cave directness.

He feels the moles on her back and strong shoulders.

You lied about being an illegitimate child and being raised as a servant. I know that was the story you invented to save yourself, and you probably believe it by now. Your father, the Baron of Mondoubleau, was a ridiculous figure. His castle collapsed not from any mob assault but from poor foundations, and the family never had sufficient funds to rebuild it.

Nenette curls in to him, hand on his erection. There are no traces left on her skin, but he tries to imagine her leaping naked into stinging nettles to save herself from the mob.

I am in awe of the iron willpower beneath this softest of skins. Why do I not have the courage to show you my damn poems?

Half asleep, she turns on her back, and he lies down on top of her white warm enveloping body.

Poet of hunger, ex-priest, barbarian, father, family man, pillar of the new order, teetotaler, ideologue, I harbor doubts, but you, Nenette, have no doubts, no contradictions; that is what I admire in you most.

Nenette calms him, whispers:

—Shhhhh, shhhhh, slow down, Joseph. Take your time. This is not a chariot race. You will get there. Don't worry. Ssshhhh.

He stares at her closed eyelids, holds her hands down on the pillow, clamps them there like prisoners, feels the pulse parting her pale lips. She slides her ankles along the back of his calves. Fouché faster now holds her spine, her haunches, a wild noise struggles and sinks in his muscles. A drop of sweat falls from his armpit, and her teeth open as if in pain. Her nails dig his back, oh God she says, and bringing him to a boil, she raises her croup with knees up and receives him as deep as he will go. Fouché, hero of the revolution, hollers deaf into her ear. And she takes him, holds him, and drowns him.

Fouché gasps and slumps on her chest, wet with love.

Nenette, full of energy, gazes at the ceiling moldings, but her Fouché too soon dozes off like a baby. Usually she insists on talking after making love, but it is not fair after the night he has been through.

Joseph, I think no one has watched you sleep like I have, with your head on my shoulder.

After a while, they both sleep.

⌒

There is a knock on the door, an insistent knock that will not go away. Fouché awakens, held by soft white hands. He gets up, fumbles for his slippers, ties his robe, and goes to the door.

—What is it, Mordu?

—Hébert has taken the stand, chief. He has accused Marie-Antoinette of having incestuous relations with her son. He has even produced a written confession from the Dauphin. Everyone was appalled; not even Herman or any of the other judges, give it any credence. It has handed the Queen a huge moral advantage. How can anyone be so stupid? We may not get a guilty verdict after this.

Angry, Fouché eyes the mass of catered food that Pasquier's men are placing on the dining room table. The grandfather clock says 1 P.M.

—Thank you, Mordu. Report back if there is anything else.

When Mordu's footsteps fade, Fouché places foie gras and consommé on a tray and takes it to the bedroom. Sitting on the edge of the bed, he spoon-feeds Nenette. With her eyes closed, she spills some on her breast.

—I must go, Nenette.

—But you said you were going to spend the whole day in bed!

—I have to go. He kisses her.

—Joseph, you have to eat first and get some rest. Tell them you are not feeling well. A hard-working proconsul can afford to be ill once in a while, it is only human. Look at Danton.

He lets her massage his temples and his face. Then she feeds him a slice of foie gras. His wife, in Nevers with the baby, has never treated him like this. He slumps on the bed; her fingers massage his back, his butt, his calves, his ankles, his belly, the part he never allows her to touch. A precursor to a cycle of mouth and fingertips.

Later, she brings another tray to bed and feeds him sweetbreads, his favorite dish. It is so decadent, Fouché does not dare glance in his mirror. The champagne and the food make her hungry for love. She places the tray on the floor and sits astride him.

—Open your eyes, she whispers, when you make love to me, Joseph; open your eyes, chéri. You are missing the best part, trust me.

Fouché does as he is told, and, laughing, she leans down and licks his ear.

—No, no, please, Nenette.

When you scream I want to cover your mouth, but I let you scream even though all the servants will hear, and the neighbors too. I like your rhythms, your hands on my chest that urge me on. I have never been this way before.

She grimaces as if she is in pain.

—Am I hurting you?

—No.

Fouché places his hands on her breasts and flattens them, grabs them and looks down at where their bodies meet at the belly. He watches himself, the dark barbarian, entering the cream-white queen. He watches the spectacle, repetitive, unimaginative, yet totally engrossing. Gasping for breath, he grows, becomes airborne yet more rooted inside her.

He lies breathing hard, exhausted, speechless, enveloped in her wet arms and thunderous heartbeats.

—*Merci, cherie,* he says.

From the kitchen, there is the muffled sound of plates breaking and a chain jerking. Ouistiti, her monkey, must have found some scraps to eat.

⁀

The clock chimes and Fouché awakes with a start. The master bedroom is quiet as he gets up and pads barefoot on the parquet floor. The cold air tingles his skin. He slips on a white cotton shirt and urinates in the chamber pot against the side of the porcelain, so as not to wake her. Seldom has he felt so happy to be at home. The day is now two-thirds gone. He slips into his dark blue bathrobe and slippers and enters vast empty rooms, one after another.

—Mordu, my bath! My clothes!

No answer.

—Mordu, are you here or what?

—He is still at the trial, citizen, says the cook; he will be back in an hour.

—And my bath?

—I will get it ready, citizen, right away.

As he moves to the vestibule, Fouché discovers aches and sores from his long night of the soul. In the half-light, he picks through the day's mail. Nothing here but denunciations, accusations, edicts of the National Convention, plus reminders and notes from various deputies and informers, as well as hand-carried petitions.

Go back to Nenette, stay in bed, fool. Fouché glances through the official communications, then moves toward the bath.

It stands on four lion's paws. The water is as hot as you can get it, with steam curling up, just the way he likes it. To the right of the tub is a small traveling desk with an inkstand, quill, and sheets of monogrammed paper awaiting his orders. He gets in the tub, reclines, and closes his eyes. The best part of the day is sitting here, soaking. Usually he bathes before dinner, in the languid *cinq-à-sept* in Nenette's apartment over the Procope, but he brought her here to have her close by all day. A hot bath is how he rewards himself. It is his only acknowledged sin.

David's painting of Marat dead in his bath has just been completed, and it shows almost exactly the same scene: tub, writing board, quill, ink, drying sand.

He smells Nenette in his hair and in his underarms. He writes a list of all the elements he still needs to close this case and draft his report to Number One. His goose quill scratches and darkens a page.

A wild grunting noise interrupts Fouché. He looks up. Sansculottes are parading two heads on the end of long pikes. *Hang all the aristocrats from a lamppost,* they sing without harmony, hard voices pounding repetitive rhythms. He returns to his work. The quill catches, and a drop of ink spreads. He sprinkles drying sand, raises the page to his lips, and blows the sand off.

Mordu, back from the trial, stands in the penurious light and reports.

—Chief, they broke for lunch finally at 4 P.M. The Queen had some broth in a room off the court but spoke with no one.

Mordu glances down at the signet ring that Fouché has on his small portable desk next to the ink.

—So it was von Fersen acting all alone, huh, boss?

—Yes, von Fersen rode in from Brussels alone. He speaks perfect French and knows the city well, having lived here for almost a decade. He lent his ring to Nurse Guyot to wear when she entered the prison. No words were spoken in the cell during the Queen's medical checkup because no words needed to be spoken; all she needed to see to understand was his ring. *Tutto a te me guida.* Then von Fersen borrowed de Tours' carriage to enter the Cour du Mai, a slow berline he intended to ditch at the first opportunity. He did not pay off Bault or Larivière; it was too risky to try and bribe them. The allies refused to move on Paris, and the failure of the flight to Varennes taught him not to trust any émigrés, so he divulged his plans to no one.

—He forged the release order himself?

—No, he had it done in Brussels. A lot of Parisians escaped there with orders signed by our officials. The best plots are often the most improbable ones.

—And he had money to pay for all this?

—His father is one of the richest men in Sweden. That is how von Fersen could afford to fight for American independence for two years, then come back and outfit his own private battalion to serve at Versailles.

—Chief, we rounded up all of Fersen's ex-Royal Suédois we could find.

—Good.

—One is a baker's assistant, one is a major in the National Guard, and another is an invalid.

—He needed men of absolute confidence, men he could buy on a moment's notice, with whom he had worked before, and who would not turn him in if they decided not to help him. Mordu, take your time, squeeze everything out of them.

—I will, chief.

—Once von Fersen had the Queen, he drove her to Guyot's hospice. Why they did not take a lightweight faster carriage and leave Paris immediately is not clear. Something must have gone wrong. They took the tunnel from the river (on the embankment in front of the hospice) to de Tours' cellar, which explains why de Tours' committee neighbors did not report seeing anyone suspicious or any unfamiliar carriage arriving back in the late afternoon. Mordu, were any departure permits given in the past week?

—Yes, chief. Two passports were issued yesterday evening by the foreign office for Thomas Paine and a servant woman of his.

—Find me those permits and I want to see Thomas Paine tomorrow.

—Chief, Danton also got passports for friends of his from the Passport Commission. I think he bribed them.

—Of course he did. Mordu, tell Pasquier I want all travel permits issued within the last week, and have him investigate all those who applied for passports. Then check on the trial and report back to me.

—Right away, boss. Mordu leaves.

Fouché can smell Nenette sleeping next door, he tastes her on his breath, meek and milky. She sleeps to forget and wash away the smell of jail. Through the closed shutters, the horizontal gray darkens—*a little obscurity here and there throws into clarity all the rest. I can now see Nenette's importance as never before.*

Fouché lights a candle at his portable desk, closes his eyes, and for a moment dozes in the tub. Hot water gives life, Dionysian lethargy, Arcadian end of strife.

I see you, Nenette, seated at a fountain, dressed like a courtesan: Your shoes are too showy, lipstick too red, arms too bare, teeth too bright. I try to ignore you. I ignore you with all my might, but you are watching dandies stroll by, and I can tell your ignorance of me is a sham, so I watch you, not wanting to let you know that I am watching you, your legs, the way you sit. I will not let anyone say you are too provincial or brash, too bold or upstartish, too sexy, but that is what you are. Boats leave in the fog, foghorns blare, but you stay, controlling me by ignoring me. Impulsive and wordly, you stare at your nails, at the night, at men passing by. Your bare legs are twisted under the chair because you are a whore, a whore, a whore. I loathe you, and I am a traitor for placing you on a pedestal and elevating you. But that is your price. And I would not have you any other way.

Footsteps approach.

The cook enters with another basin of boiling water. He helps Fouché move his writing equipment and his writing board to the floor. The new hot water lifts his spirits. Fouché soaps his feet, groin, arms, penis, rectum. He wants to wake Nenette and drag her here to scrub his back, but he is happy she is sleeping, happy he can avoid her charm, her demand for affection. For he is late, and now at last he rushes to avoid her softness and goodness.

Nenette, you chatterbox, you can sleep for days on end, a quality I loathe, as well as your love of display: I feel like a thief, working quietly, racing to finish before you wake up. I am so restless.

Fouché washes his hair, then rings the silver bell again.

—Coming. Coming, citizen.

The cook appears with a tray of food left over from lunch and three red candles in a candelabra.

—Is Madame not eating?

—No, she will ring for you when she wakes up.

He points for the cook to try a bite. Usually Mordu is his chief taster, but the cook now takes a forkful and chews.

—Thank you, says Fouché, not meaning to thank him at all. The cook adjusts the tray on his writing desk, astride the bath.

—Will that be all, citizen commissioner?

—Yes.

He makes a slight bow and retreats.

Fouché attacks the food, bites into the foie gras, but keeps jotting down a note, then picks at the pullet.

My one defense against easy living and the natural aristocratic tendencies of those who govern is to avoid extravagant meals. I keep inequality and privilege at bay by eating on the run. So I shove in the food and pee in the bath like a barbarian.

Yet today I could be the Count of Artois in the role of Figaro and Nenette could be the Queen playing the merry roguish maiden, Rosine. To any Jacobin entering my house now, we would appear universally guilty of seeking pleasure.

Just then Mordu returns, hair flopping behind him.

—Chief, the prosecution is still calling witnesses. No one suspects anything about an escape from the Conciergerie. It's only the usual old rumors, nothing new.

Fouché steps out of the bath onto the cold parquet. Mordu holds up the towel so the commissioner can cover his whiteness. Once Fouché is dry, Mordu sprinkles talcum powder on his back and feet and legs and helps him to dress. He has no need to shave again today.

Fouché enters the bedroom, kneels on the bed, and kisses Nenette, who is just beginning to open her eyes.

I love to watch you sleep. My life has been a story of failure, loss, and redemption.

She smells good and, smiling, she touches the new tricolored silk cockade he has slipped into his lapel buttonhole.

—I shall be back in a few hours, he whispers; Mordu and Pasquier's men are here to protect you.

Nenette nods, eyelids heavy and mauve.

—Lock the door after I leave, and open only if you hear my code. He blows her a kiss.

Outside, he says to the guard at the door:

—I am counting on you to protect her. Let no one in under any circumstances.

III.

24 Vendémiaire, Year II
Tuesday, October 15, 1793

Intrigue is as necessary to him as food . . . He has a mania to always want to touch everything and to always want to put his feet in other people's slippers.

—Napoleon, about Joseph Fouché

At the Center of His Web

Nine A.M.: Fouché leaves his house and heads for his usual session at the Procope. It is the same weather, overcast, windy, leaves swirling down in marmalade colors. Soapy water, lacy and white, flows across the curb as a waiter mops down the sidewalk. Informers have lined up in the passage du Cour-du-Commerce, where a handful of Nationals keep order, and one by one the informers enter and face his same table in the back. The ballet of whispers and counter-whispers continues; the old routine is stale after the events of the night before last.

Fouché hears the usual denunciations: a priest is hiding, an aristocrat is hoarding salt. The Master of Complications dismisses his informers before they are finished. Spies bore him, their intrigues are so contemptible.

Marie-Antoinette is still in court. Fouché sits hunched over his table, hands held up to the fireplace so he can get warm. Questions persist. Did von Fersen momentarily leave the Queen to go fetch his carriage; is that why she was found alone? To make certain that von Fersen does not become like de Batz, one of those plotters who comes and goes with impunity and is never caught, Fouché sends an agent to Brussels to confirm that von Fersen is there and, if so, to cause him problems. The ex-Royal Suédois are still under interrogation.

Fouché is a spider. His web spreads out across all of France, and all the threads he has so meticulously knotted have their center at this table in plain view of all in the Procope. No movement is necessary; the successful spy stays put for days.

Every hour, more unremarkable news filters in from the Queen's trial. Dozens of witnesses have appeared so far. And, pell-mell, they confuse one bribery scheme with another decades earlier, or with embezzlement and waste, mixing innuendo and rumor with fact. The Queen has taken her own defense. She has been oddly eloquent for a battered old hen; some in the audience even imagine she will get off. She has shown strength and been steadfast in her answers, dignified in her demeanor, while her accusers have appeared shrill, ridiculous, and often out of control.

—Pasquier, let me know thirty minutes before the trial ends. I must ensure her security to the end. I cannot leave this up to anyone else.

It has been a rough few days, and Fouché is worried that his usual meticulous choice of venue and timing is off stride. Was it a mistake to leave Nenette at home and not bring her back to her own quarters here above the Procope, close at hand? He wanted to let her sleep, but is she safe there with Mordu and Pasquier's men to watch over her?

I am too conscientious, too duty-bound. Any other man would have stayed with you, taken another day off.

While Mordu watches over Nenette's sleep back home, his replacement, La Grenaille, lets in Tobias Schmidt. The German, red-faced and in a hurry, slams an official letter on the table beneath Fouché's nose.

Paris, October 1, 1793
Dear Citizen Schmidt,
Humanity is repelled by your request to be granted a patent for an invention of this kind. We have not sunk to such a barbarous level. Since

your discovery can only serve for executions, the patent should be offered to
the government, for the guillotine's true nature is as a machine of state. . . .

Fouché slides the letter back toward its recipient. He now understands this is why Schmidt has been trying to get to him for days now, and Fouché gives the man total freezing silence. He sniffs, for he still smells Nenette on his shirt.

—Proconsul, what am I to do? I have a monopoly on construction, but without a patent how can I protect my rights?

Fouché half closes his eyes like a basking snake. This fool Schmidt does not realize that the very success of the machine is hurting its future. Fouché has recommended that the guillotine be transported to the outskirts of town because residents close to the place of execution complain it is unhygienic. The quantity of blood spilled cannot get absorbed by the soil, so it remains on the public squares for the dogs to lick. It smells, and it could start an epidemic. Executioners have to be paid extra because their clothes are drenched with blood and cannot be reused. Superstitious locals fear that hundreds of headless ghosts will haunt the place of execution. And there is no room to bury the bodies, so they are popping up out of shallow graves. When Fouché reported this to the Ministry of the Interior, all they did was issue more quicklime. The worst problem of all is that the regularity of the spectacle is eliminating the shock element. Executions are too constant; they are dulling the people's fear just as too much strong liquor blunts the palate. That is why he wants Dr. Bossavin's tests of the new deadly gas to be speeded up because demand for the guillotine has outstripped supply.

Schmidt is drunk, but not too drunk to sense that this is not the right time. He retrieves the letter, bows, makes his excuses, and leaves through the back door.

The Procope is filling up with thirsty citizens.

Fouché stands and stretches:

—La Grenaille, what news from those ex-Royal Suédois?

—Their alibis do not check out. But they have not cracked under pressure.

—Good. Turn up the heat and keep at it.

Fouché sits back down and sips his Populo.

—Three more informers; then I will call it a day.

⁔

Back in Fouché's apartment at 315 rue Saint-Honoré, Nenette wakes with a start. In the master bedroom, the bed faces three tall windows. The curtain and shutters have been left partially open, so with her head up from the pillow she can see the half-denuded trees standing like balding men in the courtyard. The room is full of muted light. The dressing screen is in the near corner, to the immediate left of the bed. In the far left corner by the window is a chair and writing desk, which she uses as a makeup table. Opposite the desk, on the right, is a walk-in closet.

They rendezvous usually at her place above the café, but when Fouché wants her around the clock, he prefers to have her at his house. Nenette has slept here many times before, but now something feels wrong, something she cannot describe. There are traces of chocolate on her fingertips, and the remains of yesterday's gastronomic feast on the bedside tables, but that is not it. There is someone in the house.

To her immediate right, the bedroom door opens.

She pulls up the sheet to cover herself.

The Incorruptible One enters, with small yellow-tinted wire-rimmed oval glasses to protect his delicate eyes. He wears cotton leggings, a sky-blue coat, and a powdered wig, and he walks self-consciously and rather stiffly, as if he were watching himself in a full-length mirror.

—Forgive me, citoyenne, I did not mean to frighten you. I only wanted to make sure who is on trial today, and who we are sending to the guillotine tomorrow.

Where is Joseph? Where is Mordu? Nenette is too scared to call their names, but she expects them to enter at any second now.

—We are quite alone, you can relax citoyenne.

With one hand behind his back, Robespierre examines the books on the bedside table and the couch to his right.

—Fouché keeps you well hidden, he says, circling the bed.

Nenette does not dare answer. Her heart is beating triple time.

—You are Nenette, the royal look-alike?

She nods, not knowing how many more minutes she has left to live. The Incorruptible One places his hands above the back of a chair, not daring to dirty his fingers.

—What can Joseph Fouché possibly see in you?

If she is going to die, Nenette wants it to be on her own terms, dressed in her best outfit, not a flimsy negligee. She gets out of bed. Catching a glimpse of her bare legs, Robespierre turns violently to the window and closes his eyes.

—What are you doing?

At the closet, she selects a white muslin dress and combs her hair. Why did Robespierre not send one of his henchmen, Saint-Just or Couthon or even some lowly spy? Why did the most impeccable, most inexorable, most irreproachable man in France come in person? Has she always expected this end? Is that why it comes as no surprise? Has she lived with fear so long it has become a part of who she is?

The Incorruptible One stares out the window and speaks to the courtyard.

—I am not a prude, but I smell hedonism and immorality here.

Behind the dressing screen, Nenette removes her nightgown and proceeds to dress. Her movements are quick and efficient. The screen has three sections and it is painted gold with wooden cherubs carved here and there, and in each of the three large oval picture frames, there is a painting of a romantic rural setting, cows, sheep, and trees. Nenette is especially fond of this screen because it is one of the few pieces of furniture Fouché has not gotten rid of in favor of drab republican modernism.

She stares at Robespierre over the screen, daring him to gaze in her direction, but he doesn't. Yet she notices his back muscles tensing up.

—I plan to ride to the tumbrel in style. That is what you have come for, isn't it, to exterminate me?

She steps into a gown, but Robespierre still faces the courtyard.

—You may look now, says Nenette.

Moving to the window, she stands at his side.

—Can you button me up?

The Incorruptible One makes certain the shade is properly drawn and then begins to button her dress in the back. This is a slow process because it is the first time any woman has asked him to do this, and the many buttons are small. Nenette can smell the man's contradictions, his impotence, certainly his anxiety, his paranoia.

—It is not you, madame, that I would kill; it is the tyranny you served.

He has left his soldiers outside, so it seems to her self-evident that he wants to talk.

—You had something important to say to me, Incorruptible One?

—No, not at all. Private lives like yours are of no importance to me.

He has stopped buttoning but stands close to her neck, as if staring at her skin or discreetly sniffing. Nenette, on her toes, turns to see what is going on. He catches himself and after she turns back, he continues buttoning her.

—My mistress is an idea, citoyenne. A world where no one will go hungry, no one will be without a house or clothes or shoes. Can you understand that?

—You wanted justice, but you have ended up organizing a secret police.

Robespierre walks over to the bed and glances at the sheets, holding his breath. With his upper lip curled, he whispers.

—The price one pays for hedonism is death.

—Death, death, death, is that all you know?

She sits down at the desk to put a gold chain around her neck, a broach, and the gold signet ring that Fouché just gave her, *Tutto a te me guida*. It is too big, a man's size, so she slips it on her thumb. If this is the end, at least she will speak her mind.

—Terror is not revolution.

—True, but it is a means to an end, a shortcut to virtue.

She pulls up a chair for him, but Robespierre keeps pacing the room.

—Laughter and sunlight, these are also means to an end, she says.

—Our monarchs laughed for five hundred years; look where it has gotten us.

She pours cold water from the porcelain pitcher into the hand basin, splashes her face and neck. When she has washed and dried her face, she squirts on cologne. This may be the last time she can do it. This may be her swan song.

—I came because I wanted to make sure my police chief was trustworthy. Citoyenne, you have put one of my best men in grave danger.

Robespierre stares from the window down at his guards in the courtyard.

—Before you, Fouché loved only virtue.

—I call virtue human kindness.

—No, proper virtue is love of country and of its laws. And Fouché was the surest man I had. I could always trust him with the toughest missions, the missions no one else wanted or could handle. Like the Vendée, the Mayenne, Lyon.

She pours him a glass of mint water, which he waves away.

—You soil France, corrupt her, weaken her, and I will not allow it. You put the whole revolution in danger.

—How can a single little woman do all that?

He opens the door that gives out onto the landing and motions to his men in the staircase. Soldiers rush inside, cover the windows, break open closets. The Incorruptible One uses the small mirror on her make-up table to retie his cravat and check his wig and his shirt cuffs, as if primping for a dinner party. He removes his small glasses, breathes on them, and wipes them with his white handkerchief.

—Now you will die.

She shrugs.

—Go ahead. What are you waiting for?

Robespierre disinterestedly checks the papers piled on one corner of the desk.

—I will let Fouché do it. That will test whether he is a public or a private man.

—My death will not clothe a single orphan. It will not in any way help one widow or hungry person in all of France.

—If this revolution does not go all the way, if we do not kill all our enemies, what we have done so far is all for naught.

Aware of the sudden silence, Robespierre checks his fob watch, bows slightly, and leaves, followed by the soldiers.

Saint-Denis

Atel von Fersen met his beloved regiment of 1,000 infantrymen and 300 hussars while fighting in America with Lafayette. Their commander, the Duc de Lauzun, told him, *I buy men, I don't sell them,* and so von Fersen acquired the Royal Suédois in 1784 in exchange for nothing but his word of honor that he would take good care of the men, and this he did until 1791, when he disbanded the regiment.

After interrogating one veteran, Fouché rides north to Saint-Denis. The house, which once belonged to the King's mistress, Madame de Pompadour, looks a great deal like any old country mansion. It is closed off from the street by a high wall and an arched gateway. The courtyard is more like a farmyard, stocked with ducks, turkeys, and geese, which for amusement the lodgers feed out of the parlor window on the ground floor. There are some hutches for rabbits and a sty with two pigs. Out back, a garden of more than an acre is stocked with excellent fruit trees. Tom Paine claims its apples, pears, and greengage plums are the best he has ever tasted.

Fouché examines Paine's rooms. The first is for wood, water, and necessities; the second is his bedroom; and the third is a sitting room that overlooks a garden and has a glass door leading to a small railed-in balcony. There, a flight of narrow stairs almost hidden by thick vines allows one to descend into the garden without going through the house.

—The place reminds me of my childhood in England, says Paine.

The great writer reads and writes little these days, seems upset by the interruption on his privacy, but all this may be a ploy to avoid suspicion, for Fouché understands he is finishing a long work on religion. Paine plays chess, dominoes, and drafts and takes a long nap after lunch. Fouché searches his desk and confiscates a letter about to be mailed to Secretary of State Thomas Jefferson, which Barlow translates for him:

> The United States should send a delegation to negotiate a truce in Europe so that the civilizing influence of the New World can reduce the pressures on the Jacobins, reduce their fears of counterrevolution.

The letter puts Paine in the Indulgent camp, with those who want peace at any price. Under certain circumstances, it could constitute treason, and Fouché pockets it for future use.

He does not think much of Paine's fellow lodgers; most of them are traveling crackpots, militants, and foreign-born radicals who are planning uprisings and revolutions around the world. On January 5, they formed a club and called it the Friends of the Rights of Man Associated at Paris. Its most prominent member is the Venezuelan general Francisco de Miranda, who is trying to raise funds to attack Spanish Florida in order to begin the liberation of the entire southern hemisphere of the Americas. Miranda, the victor of Valmy last year, was exonerated by a court in May of having betrayed the French armies.

There is also a vegetarian Scot, John Oswald, who has published a pamphlet called *The Cry of Nature,* and a group of Irish freedom fighters: Henry Redhead, known as Yorke; the Reverend William

Jackson; Robert Madgett, who translates for the Committee of Public Safety and whom Fouché does not trust at all; and followers of Lord Edward Fitzgerald, who wants France to fund a volunteer army of 40,000 men to liberate Ireland from Britain.

Here Fouché also meets friends of Edmond-Charles Genet, an ardent supporter of Robespierre and the younger brother of Madame Campan, the Queen's chief lady-in-waiting. Named France's ambassador to the United States last year, he visited with Paine to learn as much as he could about the American political scene, but now he refuses to return to France for fear of being guillotined. He also meets cosmopolitans, deists, Americanists, leading figures in the Society des Amis des Noirs, and a Prussian nobleman who calls himself *the orator of the human race* and wants to offer representation in the National Convention to New York, China, and Arabia.

These good folks have collected 1,000 livres to buy shoes for French soldiers. At dinner, they sing revolutionary songs like *Ça Ira, La Marseillaise,* and *La Carmagnole* and give thirteen toasts to symbolize the thirteen freed states of America, but they speak only English among themselves. And what little Fouché understands— such as the mad plan of building a united democratic Britain, Belgium, and France—does not sit well with him.

The only halfway trustworthy member of the group is the writer, poet, and businessman from Connecticut, Joel Barlow. Paine fomented revolution in England, and Fouché heard it said that English gentry inscribed the initials TP on the hobnails on the souls of their boots so that when they walked they could crush his name. Witch hunts and riots throughout England against the arch-traitor Paine sponsored by the government only increased since his conviction last December 18. But the sheer excess of these reports causes Fouché to question whether the government of William Pitt does not have something to gain by sending him to France.

—So your plan for feeding us this winter is going well? Fouché attempts a smile.

Paine eyes him in silence, making the deep lines of his long face look deeper.

—I heard you were going to America to bring back fifty ships full of wheat.

—Yes, I have President Washington's accord, and it is proceeding, but I do not need to go with the fleet. I am staying right here. Paine glances at Barlow.

—Good, good, we need foreign friends willing to help our country.

Fouché believes only what he can see and feel and know with his own senses. In the convention, Paine sat next to Danton, another point against him. Today Paine is scrubbed and clean, and his long hair is gathered in its customary ponytail. But he speaks no French, and Fouché is tired of waiting for the translation of his words through Barlow into English and then back into French.

So each time Barlow tries to transmit his words for Paine, Fouché cuts him off.

—Barlow, now you explain something to me about your friend Thomas.

—What is there to explain, citizen?

—Well, under torture, various suspects keep giving his name as part of a failed plan to spirit the Queen out of France. What do you make of it?

Barlow looks away into the distance and shrugs.

—Why should an ex-Royal Suédois, about to die, spill the name of Thomas Paine? Deathbed confessions are usually trustworthy.

I don't know, commissaire. Many people invoke Paine's name for a host of ideas and actions that have nothing to do with him.

—No, I shall tell you why, because Paine's plan to buy wheat from America was a ruse to smuggle aristocrats out of France, including the Queen.

—No, it is the Foreign Ministry that approached Paine for help on the wheat purchase, not the other way around.

—I am having all his bank dealings examined.

—You won't find anything, citizen. Paine has never cared about money.

Fouché sniffs the air.

—Ask anyone, continues Barlow; Paine sells millions of books on both sides of the Atlantic, but whenever possible he takes no royalties so that he can reduce the price per book and so make available his opinions to the poor, who can't otherwise afford books. That is what so terrified the Brits. He reduced the price of *The Rights of Man* from three shillings to sixpence.

Fouché knows Paine has had a difficult time of late. Even if he is playing a double game and working for Pitt, last year in England he was shadowed by government agents, shadowed everywhere he went. His *Rights of Man,* an instant best-seller, sold 10,000 copies in just three days, 400,000 overall, making it, except for the Bible, the most widely read book of all time in the United Kingdom. One reader in ten bought a copy. Because the book defended the French revolution, William Pitt viewed it as wicked and seditious writing that threatened a revolution in England if it were read by the lower classes. The British government organized anti-Paine propaganda; they burned his effigy and his books all over the country. Booksellers who sold his pamphlets were arrested and sentenced to up to seven years in jail. The fire-breathing three-headed monster Tom Stitch, Mad Tom, MacSerpent, a seller of Humbug, and a Correspondent of Satan, as they called him, did not help his case by calling King George III His Madjesty.

Finally, his friend the poet William Blake, convinced that Paine would be killed by angry mobs, urged him to leave for France, which he did on September 13, 1792. But in his absence, he was found guilty of propagating seditious libel and declared an outlaw. If he ever sets foot in England again he could be executed.

—Paine does not get paid for his writing?

—No, he is as poor as a churchmouse. The only payment he wants is—

—Barlow, I belong to the Society of Friends of the Constitution. We voted Paine our honorary chairman, so I know of his many qualities. But Paine's friends are all traitors—Lafayette, La Rochefoucauld, Brissot.

—That is because they speak English or fought in the American revolution, not because he agrees with them.

—He should be among the Girondins who went on trial today.

—No, Paine is a firebrand. The book he is working on now is the most scathing attack imaginable on organized religion. Just listen to this passage:

> The Christian mythologists have erected a fable which for absurdity and extravagance is not to be exceeded by anything that is to be found in the mythology of the ancients. . . . The story of Christ, so far as it relates to the supernatural, has every mark of fraud and imposition stamped upon the face of it. It is in vain to attempt to palliate or disguise this matter.

Barlow hands him the French translation of a few pages of *The Age of Reason*. Fouché flips through the manuscript, and the direct and powerful message puts him in a good mood; he pronounces it excellent.

The French can identify originality in other foreigners, thinks Fouché. And surely it is easier to be original in America; in France, you have to fly away from Descartes, Pascal (who was terrified of universal emptiness) and all the other heavy gravitational pull, which is why Robespierre still wears a powdered, and why he still holds to the idea that the state can rest on one individual, one colossus.

For his part, Paine is playing chess by the fireplace. The man may tap into the power of the inevitable and may spew out declarative sentences, but he is far too self-involved to be dangerous, it seems to Fouché. He takes Barlow out for a walk through the fruit trees out back, where no one can overhear them.

—Barlow, you have a great career ahead of you. You could return one day as America's ambassador to Paris. Don't throw this all away.

Barlow gazes at him, not understanding.

—Provide me with information from time to time as to what Paine is doing.

—I cannot rat on a friend!

—Well, now, let us think together. I do not trust your friend Thomas at all. Neither does Robespierre. This means that without your intercession we would throw him in prison immediately. But with your reports and your guidance, I can leave him in freedom. By cooperating with us, you would be protecting his life; you would be a sort of guarantor, if you like.

—You put me in an impossible situation. Barlow flushes.

—Yes, I do. But such is life.

—How much time do I have to think about it?

—If I don't receive a detailed report on Paine's activities by next week, I shall consider him dangerous and eliminate him.

Barlow shakes his head.

—I can't be everywhere at the same time, I must rely on informers. But if he is one of us, Barlow, then you have nothing to fear. Do you?

Fouché then reads him a quote from ex-deputy Manuel, who at the trial of Marie-Antoinette today said, *I trusted in the morality of Thomas Paine, master of republicanism. I aspired like him to see the reign of liberty and equality established on a durable basis. My intentions were pure.* Barlow nods.

—Nothing wrong with that.

—No, but intentions are not enough. Manuel will be tried and executed shortly. Citizen Paine should pick his friends with greater care. Understand?

—Yes. Perfectly.

—Barlow, did someone warn you I was coming?

—No, why?

—Because you are so level-headed. Usually when I interrogate people for the first time, they are visibly shaken. Are you telling me the truth?

—I stopped lying the day I saw my first execution.

—Good, to be reliable an informant must have self-respect.

Fouché then approaches Paine's landlord and invites him for a ride in his carriage. And he makes much the same succinct request, with the difference that he promises to take all of his lodgers into custody and confiscate their wealth, so the landlord will fall on extremely tough times if he does not cooperate.

Pleased with a good day's work and the addition of two new informers, Fouché returns to Paris.

The End of the Trial

She does not mention Robespierre's visit and pretends that everything is normal about this evening.

Moonlight brightens building cornices and cupolas, and the night moves from table to bed. *Love is a sure thing, and this we know.* It seems to Fouché their bodies move with more closeness, more honesty, as they scramble together, eager to be saved, to be lifted up, to be redeemed. Their limbs fit more tightly, the embrace is more lasting, more real. Tonight he keeps his eyes open and glued on her because he wants to see her, but also because he wants to pay homage and to atone for the night he almost lost her. Her legs rise on either side of him like wings. *You are too beautiful, Nenette, too beautiful for me. I do not deserve you.*

Nenette has brought delicious Tortoni chocolates to bed, and she eats as if she will never eat again, her fingers runny with fresh cream and laughter. It is so decadent, it is downright outré, and she knows her gluttony will shock Fouché, but she does not want to hold back, certainly not tonight. *Fear makes me hungry and thirsty.*

He pretends to go downstairs to give orders but returns on tiptoe and checks on Nenette through the crack between door and doorjamb. Fouché sees her crouching, taking the belladonna vial, putting some on her finger, then on the monkey's tongue. Beautiful woman: *bella donna*. Is she trying out a sleeping potion to get the monkey to calm down?

When he returns, Nenette is so happy she lies in bed, peeling an orange. With sweet juicy pulp dripping from her fingers, she feeds a slice of orange to Fouché, then licks the juice from her index finger.

—What is that tune you are singing, ma belle?

—The overture to Handel's *Theodora*. It tells the story of a slave woman who falls in love with a pharaoh. It ends badly, but it is so beautiful.

—Humming foreign operas could land you in jail fast, Nenette.

—But you are not so small-minded, Joseph, are you?

—No, just be careful.

Rather than listen, Fouché emphasizes his detachment from the aesthetic fashion of the day by taking this time to adjust the grandfather clock. Nenette brushes her hair and Fouché watches the long soft gold in her hands. It happens on a mission, in the middle of the worst human degradation, that he will find a hair of hers on his clothes, and, overwhelmed by longing, he will place it carefully in the back of his arrest book, as if collecting a slice of sunshine, and glance at it whenever he wants to recall her.

—What we imagine is always worse than the reality, Joseph. Do you know that for this whole past year, waiting for your knock on my door, I lived like a scared rat, jumping at every footstep, every creak, barely seeing the light of day? But in the Queen's cell yesterday morning, awaiting death was not so bad. After so much uncertainty, I was glad the waiting was over!

Fouché checks his watch: *Tutto a te me guida.*

It was a mistake to remind Robespierre of Nenette's existence. The flames from the fire make his face hot. *Had I not tipped my hand to Robespierre at 6 A.M., the existence of this look-alike might have been swept under the rug and forgotten. With Saint-Just off at the front, the Incorruptible One would have forgotten all about her.*

—I want to ask you something, Nenette, but you must answer me truthfully. When I saved you from those sans-culottes in the Conciergerie, is that what put you in my camp?

Fouché does not explain that, after he first took her into custody, he directed ruffians to enter her cell and manhandle her. When he saved her from them it put her even more in his debt, cemented the relationship, and gave him more reason to move her close to him, right above the Procope. *Now, in retrospect, it seems puerile and even shameful, but I have never had the courage to tell you.*

—Are you asking me why I am with you? Nenette guffaws.

—Yes.

—I told you in the Conciergerie, remember?

—Tell me again.

—I fell in love with you because I found you so unloved: so unlovable, really. I took pity on you because I saw that deep down you really were as hard and uncompromising as you pretended to be, and I felt sorry for you. I could see the little schoolboy in you always striving to be first in class. I could see you beaten down by the system.

Fouché studies her beautiful throat. He recalls the report of Dr. Guillotin:

> If we consider the structure of the neck, the center of which is the spinal column, we note that it is composed of several bones that overlap at their junctures, so that there is no joint to be found. It is not therefore possible to guarantee immediate and complete separation without a device sufficiently strong and heavy enough to act efficiently in the manner of a drop hammer driving piles. It is well known that the force increases with the height from which it falls.

Nenette continues.

—The night before last I thought the end had come, and I told you the truth. I can see inside you, Joseph, a purity and an innocence you cannot see.

Fouché shakes his head. He cannot say why, but he feels a black widow spider growing, an octopus of doubt with tentacles of loathing and fear that reach right into the center of his being.

At twenty minutes past midnight, Mordu knocks on the master bedroom door.

—Sorry, boss, you asked to be awoken when the trial was about to end.

Fouché gets up and dresses slowly, meticulously.

I am too thin, I feel like a coat hung upon invisible wires. In the mirror, I see a hunchbacked scarecrow figure, black-cloaked in dusty light. May the curse of hell liven up my nights; this weary official, thin hair splayed in all directions seems too tired to frighten anyone. Only a red, white, and blue sash for a belt and a cockade at the collar gives me any color. I squirt cologne to chase away the end of this damned day. How I wish I could sink back in between the sheets.

—Chief, let me go back to the court, I don't mind.

—No, I want to be there at the end of the trial.

Fouché ties a white silk handkerchief around his neck.

—I have to make certain we do not have another slipup, not after what we have been through.

—Forty-one witnesses have come and gone, boss. Now there is nothing more but final statements and the verdict.

—Are they using a special jury?

—No, it is a usual everyday jury. Twelve nobodies: an ex-priest, a wigmaker, a surgeon, a lemonade seller. A sometime marquis named Pierre d'Antonelle is the foreman.

Fouché holds up his hand for silence, listens intently to check whether the woman in his bed is getting up, but hears nothing.

—Mordu, you have done enough for tonight. You stay here and cover the door. We shall leave Paris tomorrow during the execution.

The little green monkey lies on his back, snoring.

Outside, Fouché can hear carnival sounds, laughing and street dancing: *Hang all the aristocrats!* With his ornate sword at the side, he kisses Nenette on her sleeping forehead. *A judas kiss, a kiss of remorse more than of leave-taking. A kiss because there is nothing else I can think of doing, a kiss because every time I leave you, I know I may never see you again.*

—What are you looking at, Mordu?

—Nothing, chief.

—Why are you so quiet?

—Boss, if I speak, it gets on your nerves. If I don't, it also gets on your nerves.

—You want a raise, Mordu, is that it?

—No.

—So what is it?

—Nothing.

So much in this business can earn you a smack up the side of the head, thinks Mordu, waiting in the living room. Once the chief beat me for just burping. It takes a thick skin to be a good Mordu.

—Is my horse ready?

They walk out of the courtyard.

—How long have I had you now, Mordu?

—Almost four years, chief. You were the principal at the Oratorian College in Nantes back when I hired on.

Fouché nods. Once in a while, a Mordu can help you defy the laws of nature, defy fate; that is why you keep him. One day of particularly violent reprisals in the Vendée, Fouché slumped his head on Mordu's shoulder, and it scared the piss out of Mordu, as well it should.

—Why do you not ever say what you are really thinking, Mordu?

—Well, I am your chief earlobe. That is what you said you wanted.

—But I do want you to voice an independent opinion once in a while.

—Boss, you pay the piper.

—And do not call me boss or chief or master, call me citizen. Have you never heard of Liberty, Equality, and Fraternity?

—Sure. But it is a bit unequal between us, isn't it? I mean, it is totally unequal.

—Why do you stay with me?

—Because, sir, nine times out of ten I would say you know exactly what to do. But just that one time, you need me because I can see things you don't. I can make out the trees from the forest, and you are too busy. No, I found the right boss at the right time, when he was just rising. I was lucky.

Fouché stares at his man, half priest, half judge.

—I am prepared to live on bread and water for the rest of my life, Mordu that is the biggest difference between us.

Mordu is up at 5 A.M. because I am up. He would sleep days on end if he got a chance. But I am up at five because I cannot sleep.

—Stay and guard Nenette.

Mordu nods, smiling, and brushes Fouché's lapels and the collar of his cape, then hands him his bicorne. Fouché checks his Breguet. It is already 1 A.M., Wednesday, October 16, and he leaves for the revolutionary tribunal on the first floor of the Conciergerie.

I know when I get there that eyes will not settle in their heads. Exhausted court officials, jurors, witnesses will get nervous at my very presence. They will whisper, Look, spectral Fouché is back. Lightning finds its way. The Horseman of the Apocalypse has come to separate the quick from the dead.

As he rides, he knows that Fouquier-Tinvile will request the death penalty. His assessor, Herman, acting as chief judge, will get the three other judges and the jurors to convict and pass sentence. Fouché will then make certain the Queen is escorted back to her cell. Job done. The nation comes first.

Then, past 4 A.M., Fouché will finally turn to private matters, ride straight back to Nenette, and find her still asleep on her back, pale lips barely parted, waiting for him.

IV.

25 Vendémiaire, Year II
Wednesday, October 16, 1793
(Feast of Saint Amaryllis)

Love and do what you will.
—St. Augustine

The Last Meal

It is execution morning, and a huge crowd has gathered on Place de la Révolution. Today people are lined up all along the winding three-kilometer path that the tumbrel will take, from Ile de la Cité north to the Quais and then west down the rue Saint-Honoré. It is the same route the tumbrel takes every day, so the weakhearted may keep away. Concerning a public spectacle, a report by Fouché states:

> Varying the route to the scaffold allows aristocrats to move the public to pity and sympathy for the men and women who are to be executed. Some say the spectacle renders children who see it violent and cruel, that pregnant women faint and will bear progeny marked at the neck or motionless as statues. Such lies cause citizens to doubt our humanity and to have feelings quite contrary to those that we want to instill in our people.

Some argued that in this case the widow Capet should travel farther so that all of Paris could have a chance to see the evil harpy getting her just reward, but in the end it was decided that a foreign-born traitor deserved no honors. Her route follows that of all the others.

Usually the procession is made up of two or three red-painted tumbrels, each drawn by two horses escorted by five or six gendarmes, and they move at a walking pace through the crowd. The purpose is to display the victim to the public. And at the sound of the wheels on the cobblestones, everyone rushes to the windows: fathers, mothers, children.

Today, thousands have gone early to get a good seat to bid adieu to the fallen Queen. Loaded cannon guard all the bridges, regiments of infantry with fixed bayonets line the streets, columns of cavalry are on high alert: all await the she-wolf of the Petit Trianon who, herself, wishes for nothing but the end.

In the Conciergerie behind the registrar's office, it is another sleepless night. They are dressing her, chopping off her hair to ensure it does not interfere with the blade, offering her the last rites from a priest who has sworn loyalty to the revolution.

Meanwhile, at Fouché's house, the cook enters with a tray of fresh bread, butter, jam, coffee. He tiptoes into the master bedroom, sets the tray down on the table, and leaves. Mordu follows, opens the heavy dark bedroom curtains, opens the shutters, leaves the gauzy inner curtain in place to mute the morning light, then sets down a pile of the latest gazettes.

Fouché yawns; his whole head throbs and his body aches. It has been another too-short night, and Fouché needs sleep the way an old man needs death. Nenette pulls the covers over her head and continues sleeping.

Mordu tastes the coffee, the jam, rips one end of the baguette.

—So what happened last night at the trial, chief?

—The verdict came in at four A.M. Execution is set for ten this morning, but knowing how slow they are, they probably will not get to her until noon.

Mordu is smiling broadly.

—May I permit myself a personal comment?

—Go ahead.

Mordu's eyes light up his face, and he smiles under his thick mop of curly hair.

—The bastards had 1793 years at the trough stuffing their faces, lording it over us, eating quail, growing fat and lazy; well, now it will be the little man's turn to be on top.

—You think so, Mordu? You think the little man will prevail?

—Yes, look what we have done in just two years!

Fouché is in no mood for such a conversation before coffee, but he lets him talk because right now it is easier than making him stop.

—Chief, today we release the energies of France, clean out tired old blue blood, make way for vigorous youth. You said yourself: What is immoral is impolitic, and what is corrupt is counterrevolutionary.

—I said that?

Nenette, her eyes still puffy from sleep, lifts her head from under a pillow.

—Would you two like to know how liberty works in actual practice?

Fouché and Mordu wait for her to go on.

—Our priest in Mondoubleau avoided the scaffold by marrying his seventy-year-old ex-nanny. His church was changed into a temple of reason and the sans-culottes dressed the town whore up as the Goddess of Reason and sat her atop the altar. The poor girl just sat there like a crowned goose, while her ex-clients filed by and worshiped her dirty feet.

Mordu wonders why the chief lets her go on in this vein.

—And to celebrate your heroic July fourteenth, the town council ordered a papier-mâché and wood model of the Bastille that the good villagers would storm. The thing fell down due to a strong wind. Half the village had to hold it up, while the other half of the village tore it down. What a glorious revolution, huh? She drops her head back on the pillow.

—Will you be needing anything else, chief? says Mordu.

—Pack everything; we leave this morning for Nevers.

There is the sound of a chain dragging along the floor, then little feet and the crash of a vase.

—Aah, he is alive, perfect. Nenette smiles. I was worried.

Ouistiti appears, running on all fours. Mordu screams *Oh la, oh la!*, grabs a fire poker and chases after the monkey to the other end of the apartment.

Fouché checks and finds that his Breguet is not running. He pushes down the *pendant,* the button at the top of the watch, but hears no ringing. When it works, it gives a short *ding* for each hour and a longer *ding-dong* for each quarter hour. But now it is silent. He removes the small key, opens the back, and rewinds the watch, but in vain. He wonders if it might have gotten wet while bathing Nenette. *Why must things always break down at the worst possible moment? I must get it fixed.*

There is a loud angry knock at the front door. Fouché glances down into the courtyard and sees horsemen there dressed in black; they outnumber Pasquier's guards two to one. He considers escaping to the attic, but, leaving Nenette in bed, he goes down to the front door and opens it slowly. A thug pushes a tricolored badge in his face which says THE LAW and grunts.

—Are you Fouché?

Fouché's hair is sticking up in the back, and he pushes it down, taking his time to answer.

—Who wants him?

—A message for you.

Fouché knows the handwriting. He takes care to read it with his back turned so that no one inside the house can see his face.

Fouché:
Terminate the look-alike by 3 P.M. today. I love you more than ever, and unto death.

    R

Fouché's thin white fingers close the message, fold it in half, carefully crease it, and fold it in quarters. *I love you unto death? Robespierre has the gall to say that? I am the enforcer, the one who makes things happen. He may control the Committee of Public Safety, but not the streets, not the countryside or the provinces; they belong to me. Without all the information I give him, he is deaf and blind and stupid. Without me, he is nothing.*

—What is it? says Nenette, her voice sleepy from the bedroom.

—Nothing.

—Some neighbor who objects to my Ouistiti?

—No, there has been an unfortunate misunderstanding somewhere.

He enters the room to check on her. Nenette is up on one elbow.

—Are they changing the rules of the game, Joseph?

She takes a bite from an apple, then drops her head back on the pillow. Fouché feeds the letter to the flames in the fireplace.

Robespierre claims to love equality and fraternity also, but in fact the man is jealous of anyone with an ounce of intelligence, anyone superior. Robespierre needs the rest of humanity down at his small-town-lawyer level. That is what he wants, my public abasement.

—Come, Joseph, come back to sleep and stop worrying so much. When did you get to bed finally last night? I did not hear you come in.

He stands and stares at the fire, full of loathing.

They have me in a vice, a wine press, and they are turning the screw. I want to kill someone.

—It is cold, Joseph. Get under the blanket and put your arms around me. What is a man for if he can't keep his woman warm?

He sits down next to her. How did Robespierre know she was here? *Accumulating secrets is only one part of my job; then I have to deny them to anyone else.* He caresses her back absentmindedly. After a while, he leaves the bedroom, moves to the other wing of the house, and confronts the cook.

—Has anyone come here while I was away?

The cook stands by the kitchen table, his white tunic buttoned to the collar, a kitchen rag tight in the hand, face red. He catches his breath, waits, wipes his mouth like a schoolboy who does not know where to begin.

—Now speak, man. Who knows Nenette is here?

—I was frozen in the kitchen; I didn't move, says the cook.

—What are you talking about?

—The Incorruptible One. He came here when you were out.

—When?

—Yesterday. It was almost like he knew exactly the moment you'd leave before he made his appearance.

—Where were the guards I put around the house?

—You could have put two battalions on your front door, and Robespierre's men would have swept them aside like a cobweb.

—Yes, of course. But why would a man so busy waste one minute on Nenette?

The cook shrugs.

Her superficial chatter is of no interest to him, but the loyalty of his secret police chief is!

Fouché can imagine the small fop with his ruffled collar moving through his private rooms, but he makes the cook tell him every cough, every gesture: How soldiers forced the front door, how the dandy in a gray wig entered surrounded by silence, how this elegant bantam cock inspected his vestibule.

The cook's delivery is slow, and, like all amateurs, it trails off, leaves holes, so Fouché prods him when he forgets or when the retelling deviates too much from what he knows, but this is how Fouché works and makes information his own. He even has the cook act out certain scenes so he can visualize things better. Sometimes the cook is Nenette, sometimes he is Robespierre, sometimes he is both and gets confused.

Love and Terror

Being a policeman means being at the heart of the action, indispensable, in the thick of things, and that is where my informers place me.

He sees Nenette, her blond hair spread out over the pillow. Innocence revealed, innocence unmasked. Robespierre comes closer and closer until he is almost directly above her—it is not the cook who describes this for he was next door in the pantry shining silverware and could not see; it is Fouché who places Robespierre thus—like a satyr, a hoofed goat with a man's head studying a sleeping nymph, her face, arms, legs, skin follicles, underarms.

Fouché tries to stay calm, but his hands shake. The cook's testimony and the written order just received from Robespierre are too raw. He needs to refine and distill them, examine them from all angles, find a solution, take control over his agenda and his life.

I should have kept her better hidden. Paris is too small. It is not Nenette that interests Number One, but proof of loyalty; that is what he wants. Robespierre leaves nothing to chance. I should not have lowered my guard.

Fouché rushes out of the kitchen and calls down the stairwell. Mordu! The written order confirms everything the cook said. There is no need, and especially no time, for further investigation. Fouché waits in his study.

—You wanted to see me, chief?

—Enter and close the door.

Mordu, who has been packing, does as he is told.

Fouché carefully locks the door.

—So you allowed Robespierre into my house yesterday. Why did you not inform me of this immediately?

—I don't know anything about it, chief. I swear.

—Mordu, are you going soft on me? Is that why you hid the truth?

He smacks him on the head, a hard cuff. Like a schoolboy caught cheating, Mordu remains silent, his eyes riveted on the floor and his shoes.

—Mordu, are you trying to sink me? Are you on the take? Do not lie to me!

—I don't know what you are talking about, chief! In his hand, Mordu holds the monkey chain and collar he has been fashioning.

—Mordu, you heap of dung, your only task was to make sure no one entered this house. You should have said that there was typhoid here or bubonic plague. The Incorruptible One loathes disease; he cannot stand even a bit of dust. You could have started a smoky fire in the other end of the apartment, and that would have been enough to drive him away. Have you lost your mind, letting Robespierre into my house, into my bedroom; are you mad?

—Chief, I was asleep.

—You thought it might help me, didn't you?

—No.

—Yes you did. You thought that the Incorruptible One coming here in person was a mark of great honor, I know you, Mordu.

Fouché walks around his servant.

—I should terminate your measly existence right now. After all these years you betray me like this. You are on the take, aren't you?

—No, chief. I was in court all night, I was exhausted. You can ask the cook. I was asleep and I didn't hear them coming. Once they were in the staircase, it was too late.

Fouché, always restrained, always in control and thin-lipped, kicks Mordu out the door—*Out, traitor! Out, Judas!*—and smashes a wall-hung Delft plate over his head, flings another down the stairwell. Mordu clatters as fast as he can down the steps. Fouché leans over the banister.

—You are lucky I do not take your head!

Fouché returns to the living room, breathless, searching for some solution, some way out. What to do with Nenette and the deadline?

In my early days I would have finished off Mordu, murdered him. I am too soft, too kind. The same with Nenette. Finish the look-alike by 3 P.M.

How to make Robespierre believe that I have eliminated Nenette? I must get a head somewhere. With Robespierre's squeamishness, any head will do. I could deposit a burlap bag on his desk, let the blood seep out onto his papers, and the Incorruptible One would never open it and look inside. But the more proof I present, the more he will doubt me. All I can control is the rumor mill; yes, that I can do. I can make certain not a soul breathes a word about a look-alike.

Fouché's anger is running wild, and the river of fiction is boiling over. He keeps turning known facts around, refashioning escapes for Nenette, altering the situation's givens in various ways.

I must kill Robespierre before he kills me; that is the solution. That is clear. The problem is how and when? Robespierre's direct-action boys, his thugs, will be here long before the deadline. They will be here at noon to make sure I follow orders.

Fouché knows how they work. He checks his broken watch.

Nenette is a liability and must be eliminated, but only when, how, and if I so decide. Not a minute sooner. And if I should choose to keep her, to use her again in the future, what story will I tell Robespierre? Nenette is there, warm in my sheets, waiting for me. What started as lust has built up into something far different. I was so sure I could push her aside at any time, just forget her and get on with my work, like changing horses. It was only a question of when. She was nothing to me. But now she has burned into me. To get rid of her now will be a form of suicide—I am lost!

Departure

Fouché enters his master bedroom.

The room is all in pale shadows and softness. Nenette's eyes are closed. She is asleep again. Fouché stands over her and stares at her round full face. Her nose turned up at the end, her lips pale and cracked, the skin dark and mauve just around the eyes, she looks so peaceful. It is a face that has suffered, and having her sleep here gives to his house a layer of meaning, an innocence and a depth it never usually has. He feels something strange and waits for it to pass, but it gets worse. Is this sentimentality? Not even under the influence of opium can he imagine such a powerful feeling. He sits on the edge of the chair and tries to fight it off.

I never knew this depth of feeling. Why is that? Why, when it was staring me in the face all along, did I repeat that you were nothing, that you were a means to an end, Nenette, an aristocrat like any other? Maybe truth needs a moment of decision when the choice is stark and unequivocal. Maybe I have grown weak. I have never felt what I feel right now, sitting on the edge of this bed, watching you sleep, this richness like watching my baby being born. I wish we could be like this forever, I watching over you and no one else around.

The soft sound of sheets moving creases the silence.

—Joseph? I was dreaming of you. And we were far, far away, both of us, on an island.

Fouché moves to the bed and puts his face in her neck, smells her warm clean skin, her soft morning breath. She is a woman oddly immune to the times, as if in falling she falls upward, not down. Fouché dares not speak.

Child, this is my wish, I give you the sun and the moon. I give you a kingdom of unicorns and sirens. I will protect you from all suffering, all pain.

He touches her long thin neck. But he is tentative, for his fingers feel dirty and ugly, as if he has maneuvered a pubescent girl into an alleyway. His hands are too big and too dark on her skin. He wants to say something appropriate, something loving, but mushrooms are growing inside his mouth, mulch-rotting soil as well. One day Death enters into a contract with us all. Master seeks virgin.

A grain of sand goes *crunch* between his teeth. *Nenette, you are a knife I carry in my heart.* He wants to stand up and look down and be angry, but he stays seated.

—Why did you not tell me he was here?

She closes her eyes and pulls the blanket up to sleep longer.

—Did you think I would not find out?

—No, I knew you would find out.

Her voice is flat and passive, her eyes still closed. Fouché feels the world closing in, the sky darkening, becoming hostile, survival receding, and normal life once again falling into the stewpot.

The steaming coffee and toast are going cold on the tray.

—You should have told me, Nenette, we could have left Paris last night.

She pulls her knees up to her chest and clasps his hand.

—Nenette, what did he say?

She does not answer, but kisses his hand and gives his fingers a long bite like a puppy gnawing on a bone. He wonders what she is up to. He has never seen her so distracted.

—Robespierre—what did he tell you? He pulls his hand away and shakes her.

—That I am making you weak and impure. It seems you are Incorruptible Two.

She opens her red eyes and stares at him.

—As long as I am with you, Joseph, you are in danger. So I should leave you and disappear, that is exactly what I should do, you know it and I know it.

—Where would you go?

—Anywhere. The world is a large place.

—He has asked me to kill you.

Her pupils widen.

—Yes. I just received the order this morning.

It is a terrible moment. A moment of betrayal, of hurting. But today truth is more important than feelings, and he waits for her reaction. He imagines she will say something unexpected, laugh or get angry. Nenette's way is always to surprise him. But she says nothing; she moves to be closer to him, closer still. She kisses his arm. He notices her eyes are full of water. She is shaking, and her soft skin feels hard, suddenly covered in goosebumps.

—Sshh, sshh, he says, it'll be all right.

—I don't want them to touch me, cut my hair, drag me through the streets like a whore, spit on me, tie me to that board. I couldn't stand it, I wouldn't.

—They won't touch you. I give you my word.

Tears stream down her face, she pulls herself into a tight ball.

—Sshh, sshh.

—I am cold, cold all over.

He tries to warm her, to be her strength. But he smells the overwhelming futility that washes over her this morning and keeps her sobbing and shaking in bed. This is not fear or anxiety, this is terror. He has never tasted such terror in her before, perhaps because now for the first time defeat comes from his own lips.

—How unfair life is, Joseph, how unfair and short. Just when I thought it was finally safe to step out from the shadows and be happy with you.

She looks around the bedroom, eyelids wet, her voice full of despair.

—I am twenty-eight, I am an ant, an ant one steps on.

She says it with such pathos, such density.

Giving up changes who she is and how Fouché perceives her: Nenette is naked, Nenette is alone, Nenette is undone. He does not know what to say or what she needs to hear, so he touches her, brushes away a blond hair that is caught on her lips. The love sheets smell sour, and the pillow has left lines on her pale cheeks.

We need to give ourselves time and things will improve. The important thing is to stay alive, and then anything is possible.

—If you have to do it, Joseph, do it, but do not talk about it.

—I am not going to kill you, don't be ridiculous.

—You will kill me. That is exactly what you will do.

—Why do you say that?

—Because you have to, Robespierre has ordered it. And it is what you always said you would do from the very beginning.

She pushes hair out of her eyes.

—Nenette, I am a priest, a teacher, a national deputy, my friends tell me I can be elected president of the Jacobins, so I have resources and connections.

—Yes, and you always get your own way in the end.

—No, not always.

He presses his lips to her warm palm, smells her cologne. He tastes the salt of her tears. She feels so vulnerable, so weak and alone, trembling with a fear she cannot control, a fear and a condition he loathes. Out of the corner of his eye he sees movement. He looks up, and in the wall mirror he sees himself bending to kiss her. For a split moment, that couple in the mirror looks perfect; the man seated on the edge of the bed carries his role without blemish.

I have at last grown into myself. I was always nervous and uneasy with members of the opposite sex, ungainly, a scarecrow, but now finally I look and act like a man of means, like a man who knows what he is doing with a woman, a man in control of his world and his loved ones.

—You will kill me, Joseph, because the revolution is your highest duty. Your highest calling.

Fouché feels a dryness, tastes her saltiness in his mouth; maybe it is blood. He touches her hand. He did not cry at his mother's funeral, or at his father's. He did not cry for his best friend. *For some reason, I never cry.*

—I am not the revolution, Nenette. I am merely its instrument, I am the stick in the blind man's hand. But the revolution can get things wrong. It has a crowded agenda, so it makes mistakes. It can overlook or forget many small details.

—I am one of those details.

—Yes, and I can take care of you. I have seen the revolution take a wrong turn and stumble on blind. No one is perfect. Some days I question every single edict the National Assembly passes. At times I even question my own actions.

—But not really, not in your guts you don't.

—Nenette, let us go right now, you and me, let us escape while there is still time.

—Where would we go?

—To the south, the west, the east, anywhere, but let us go before the executioners arrive. Robespierre said three P.M., that means they will be here by noon. We have to leave right now, this instant. Get dressed. Hurry. Later it will be too late.

—It will not work, Fouché. Disobeying will only get us both killed.

—No, we will find a safe hideout.

—Alone I can melt into a crowd, but with you it is impossible. You cannot hide, Joseph, your every move is watched, and I will only endanger you.

—But this bunch in power will not last forever. Even Robespierre is doomed!

—You are his right hand. He needs you and counts on you.

When his time is up, so will yours be, Joseph. When the Queen dies today, my time is up too.

—Who told you that?

—It is common sense, darling.

She wipes her eyes dry.

—Our only chance is to separate and lie low until the Terror passes.

Fouché wants words that will strike deep into the heart, cut a swath and cling there. But he does not know which those are. And he needs to get Mordu back.

—We all have our time, Joseph.

—No, no, we do not. The Republic has even changed the hours and the minutes. We have created new years, new months, new days, new everything. I can handle this.

—You are Master of Complications; that is your job. Nothing in police work is impossible for you, I know that. But Joseph, this is your *life*, and that is different. We are all amateurs when it comes to ourselves.

—Pack nothing. Just get dressed.

—Joseph, you cannot be serious.

—Yes, I am. Come on.

He checks the grandfather clock; it is 9:35. The Paris rooftops are full of morning sunlight, clouds are high, the fall air is fresh, the cold parquet floor tingles his bare feet.

—Our usefulness to each other is finished, Joseph. You are just saying these things to clear your conscience.

—Nothing is finished! he shouts.

In the silence that follows, the house's ancient wood beams shift uneasily, and distant footsteps stop. Ears that overhear know they should not and move on. There is the smell of burning coal and wood stoves in the air.

—Nothing is done with!

He grabs her by both arms and shakes her.

—Nenette, at the last minute I once granted a condemned man a reprieve simply because I liked the look on his face. At the last second, I have seen the blade not descend, and the twenty-three kilos of steel just get stuck and not slip down the wooden grooves. I have also seen the blade descend on the wrong head. So never give up. There is always hope.

Fouché lets go of her. His fingers leave deep red marks on her soft white skin.

Nenette says nothing but takes a step back, settling her white cotton nightdress in place, wondering whether he feels slightly ridiculous shouting at her when he knows deep down that she is right.

—Robespierre told me yesterday he would give you this order.

—You knew and said nothing?

He smiles and shakes his head in disbelief. Has everyone around here gone mad? He leaves the room.

—Mordu, Mordu! Goddamn it, where are you now that I need you? He opens all the doors in the house, shouting Mordu's name.

I should not have dismissed him so quickly. He knows too much, knows where all the bodies are buried. That bonehead has tricks up his sleeve. But he will come back, yes, Mordu needs me.

Fouché runs to the staircase. His guards stand at attention.

—Mordu! he shouts down the stairwell.

There is silence. Pieces of Delft porcelain plates lie smashed on the stairs.

—Mordu, you cow plop! You worse than horse dung, you half-Catholic brown-nosing lying lazy xenophobic small-minded bony-arsed dull-witted shit, get up here immediately. I know you are hiding down there, you snake. Come up!

Fouché waits, breathless, peers down, listens intently. His fingers twist on the banister. He sees nothing, just the shiny parquet steps and, at the bottom of the stairwell, the distant tiles, too white.
—Mordu!

I was a fool to fire Mordu. It serves me right; this is what I get for losing my temper. To outsmart the bastards, one must remain forever calm and fast like a machine.

Shoes scamper up the stairs.

—Mordu?

Fouché cranes but cannot see who is coming up.

Mordu arrives uncombed, out of breath, on the second-floor landing, more soiled than usual: shoes muddy, fingers stained with tobacco.

—Chief? He follows Fouché into his book-lined study

—Mordu, I have marriage plans for you. Immediate ones.

—But citizen, I have a wife in Cahors.

—Yes, so you say. But she need never know. I will double your salary, Mordu. And this will introduce you into police work in a more formal way.

From the master bedroom:

—Joseph, now you are being odious, odious and mad. I cannot believe you are serious.

—Be quiet, Nenette. This is only for show.

Mordu, eyes wide, points to himself and then to the bedroom. Fouché nods.

—Yes, I shall marry you off to Nenette. That way I will keep you both under my wing, protected and close to me, and no one will know a thing.

Nenette from next door again:

—It is not funny, Joseph. No one is laughing.

—Is the carriage ready, Mordu?

—Yes, boss . . . but about—

—Are the horses fresh?

—Yes.

—Trunks packed?

—Yes, since last night.

—Money?

—All I could get, chief, for the trip back. And white bread too. Fouché smiles and pulls his servant's left ear.

—Good man, Mordu.

—Chief, I always try my best.

—And Ouistiti, do not forget him, shouts Nenette from the bedroom; he goes wherever I go!

—Make haste, Nenette, get dressed; we have no time to spare.

—He is the most ill-mannered monkey you can imagine. Mordu gives the chief a meaningful look.

—Did his business all over and ruined the lamb chops.

—That is because he does not get enough love! shouts Nenette through the door.

—Chief, we cannot take that animal with us!

Fouché checks his dead Breguet.

—Mordu, I want to avoid delay and arguments. Fetch the beast quickly, and let me have your watch.

Fouché pockets Mordu's watch and returns to the master bedroom. Nenette is pinning up her hair and donning her long black cape.

—Joseph, your wife will make certain that Robespierre finds out about us.

—Do not worry about Jeanne. She will do what I tell her.

—You will not be able to keep me, Joseph. I will be a ball and chain for you.

—I am telling you a thief can steal heaven if he believes in himself enough. And is this not what you have wanted all these months, that I take you away from Paris?

Mordu waves the fire poker and the small fire broom at the cornered monkey. The cook backs him by pounding a broomstick on the tiled kitchen floor.

—Don't hurt my poor baby, screams Nenette; come here, my little Ouistiti.

She pulls on the chain, which the animal has been dragging behind him. The monkey bares his teeth, tries to untie his harness, to loosen the long chain, but Nenette reels him in, and the monkey slides along the tiles toward her waiting arms.

—Come, maman is not going to hurt you.

Fouché, Mordu, and the cook watch the beast as it is taken into a pair of white arms, kissed, hugged, and pressed to the breasts with the low-cut lace trim.

—Joseph, why don't we love humans the way I love animals?

—Let's go, he whispers.

—Mordu, do you still have those two passports we confiscated from Thomas Paine, for him and a would-be servant woman?

—Chief, we can always get new passports if we need them.

—There is no time, Mordu. And I don't want any trace of my having asked for passports. Do you understand? Those documents are perfect for us. And the American ships are in Bordeaux, ready to leave. We head for them immediately.

Fouché nods to Mordu and opens the front door. They are ready. The guards, a mix of Federals and Municipals, join on the landing fore and aft, a contingent of twenty-four men.

The Execution

The courtyard of 315 rue Saint-Honoré is still half in the shadows, but its neoclassical facade of clean pale sandstone is bright with morning sun. The cook and a soldier carry the monkey and chain him to the carriage so he will not run away.

Nenette, hooded, black-cloaked, and high-heeled, descends holding the commissioner's hand. She steps inside the coach and is swallowed up in shadow. Behind Fouché, Mordu folds up the carriage stairs, closes the door, and pays the national guardsmen one gold piece each—extra for out-of-town duty, extra for silence too.

Guards open the courtyard gates. Municipals run out to clear a path in the street. Pasquier's cavalry squadron forms a flying wedge, and soldiers scatter the plebes. Mordu climbs up next to the driver, and they move out onto rue Saint-Honoré and follow the crowd streaming west toward Place de la Révolution. It is a crisp autumn day. Trees are etched in cold sunlight, and the clouds few and high in the sky.

This morning's bloody sacrifice of Marie-Antoinette is a redemptive act for the Republic. Today on the feast of Saint Amaryllis, we immolate the past so that France may enter a new age of justice and virtue. All childbirths are painful, including that of a new era. But what do I do with Nenette? What do I do now? I will let her go. How? Will I arrange for Mordu to let her escape so it cannot be said I have forsaken my zeal or love for the revolution?

Fouché stands and leans out of the carriage window, talks to Mordu, who puts his ear to Fouché's mouth.

—No matter what happens, what counterorders anyone gives you or what Nenette says, you have only one duty. Understand?

—Yes, chief.

—What is your duty?

—I don't know. Marry her?

—No. If Nenette is abducted, taken prisoner, or escapes, you follow her, hide her, and protect her for me. Whatever happens, you do not let any harm come to her, understand? You have failed me once already. Do not let it happen again.

A nod.

—You betray me on this, Mordu, and you can race to the ends of the earth, bury yourself in a vault, and I will still find you and kill you. Understand?

—Yes, chief.

Fouché sits back in the carriage, feeling better, as if he has just created a safety net or a backup that can circumvent any later indecision or weakness on his part.

Now I will open my hand and the bird will fly free.

—Nenette, I will find a corpse and make it look as if I had you killed. If anyone manages to trace you somehow, I will say that clemency has its uses, and every spy has an afterlife.

—No. I have to be eliminated. Robespierre thinks I am a whore, a liar, a sleep-around, but even if I were the most virtuous woman in the world, in his eyes I would still have to die for the greater good of the revolution and of France.

Fouché stares at the city passing by. He barely sees the crowd going to the execution, is almost not aware that it slows the carriage down to a walk.

—If you let me live, Fouché, you will sink into cynicism and become like everyone else. You will raise the personal above the principle. You will lose your ideals and become as bad as the system that went before—corrupt, self-serving, pleasure-seeking.

—Enough, Nenette, it is not funny!

She has learned well, but being right is not always right.

In the silence that follows, Nenette reaches out to hold his hand. Babies born on this Wednesday morning will have a Saint Amaryllis medal slipped secretly into their swaddling clothes. Fouché cannot stand such superstition.

—Joseph, why do you love me?

There is a tone of urgency in her voice, knowing full well he is not likely to answer this question. She makes him look into her eyes.

—Maybe people are not what they seem, he says, paying no attention to the news shouted by gazette vendors: *Le siège de Maubeuge s'aggrave!*

The Duke of York, the Dutch generals, and the Duke of Coburg, commander of the Allied armies, are tightening the siege of Maubeuge and are trying to punch a hole in the French defenses in order to march on the capital. Generals Carnot and Jourdan seem overpowered.

—I think I would much have preferred to spend my life as a cat yawning in warm sunlight, says Nenette.

—You? Never.

—Yes, or a dog sleeping by the hearth before a warm fire.

He watches the news vendors.

—Tell me about your youth, Joseph.

Nenette speaks as if she is far away, thinking about another place and time.

—I never had much time to be young. I was always studying.

She nods and peeks out at the street. Lines have already formed in front of the milkman, the baker, the butcher, the fishmonger. The word *queue* has become a new verb. All over Paris, people are queuing for food; even to see the Queen's execution, they are queuing.

—Joseph, you are so restless, always up in the middle of the night, making lists, pacing. Why do you worry so much?

—I don't know, maybe to survive.

—The night in Marie-Antoinette's cell, awaiting trial in the Conciergerie, was the longest night of my life, and when you came in at five a.m., I felt it was the first conversation we had where we actually understood each other, you and me, both in the things we said and in what we did not say.

She smiles.

—What if I were to tell you I was pregnant?

Fouché looks at her with raised eyebrows.

—Are you?

The monkey, fastened on a long chain to the seat facing them, stares. His eyes go back and forth, back and forth, first her, then him, then her, then him.

—Would that make you happy, Joseph?

—You know I love children.

—Yes, I know you want to populate France with new citizens, but what would it mean for you personally?

Usually the carriage is a fine and private place, but with so many sans-culottes crowding on all sides, they have little privacy. He latches shut the windows, pulls down the blinds, but it is not much protection.

—My beloved little Nièvre is sickly, and the prospects for her are not good. A child by you would be the greatest gift you could present to me.

She examines his soft white hands.

—Joseph, I was not going to tell you, but then I thought it would be too dishonest of me.

He places his hand on her flat belly and smiles.

—Even if this baby were for you just a form of insurance, a stay of execution like so many aristocratic female prisoners want, I would be glad of it.

The light streaming in at the edges of the blinds cuts white slashes on the red interior. They can hear voices outside, songs, muted laughter.

—If they separate us, the baby will be a part of you, Joseph, that they cannot take away from me ever, even if they kill me.

—They will not separate us, Nenette.

—Of course they will. We will be stopped at the first barricade. And that will be the end, I will never see you again.

She tries to smile, but tears have appeared, tears which Fouché touches with the knuckle of his index finger.

—I have travel documents, Nenette.

—Your documents have probably been revoked by now. We are dealing with the Incorruptible One, not a bon vivant like Danton.

Uneven cobblestones and bad road repair cause the carriage wheels to rise and fall. The springs squeak hard. A dog goes by barking and voices are raised in song. They are reaching the Place de la Révolution, and the crowd slows them down further.

—You will be arrested.

Her voice is soft, resigned. His is raw like a crow's.

—Do not talk like that.

—Joseph, I do not want to live hounded forever, and if they catch me they will torture me. When the word gets out that you let me go, they will kill you.

—Shhhh, shhhh.

He caresses her cheek.

—In trying to save me, you will lose yourself, and you will never forgive me for it. How can you even hesitate? I deserve to be killed a hundred times over; do it! Follow the enlightened path of an enlightened revolution, Joseph.

—That is enough. Be quiet now!

—Reason must rule over emotion. You are angry, Joseph, because you know I am right. Experience must rule over sentiment, head over heart. You are a rationalist, not a——.

He covers her mouth with his hand.

She hugs him and presses her warm face against his shoulder, breathing in the dry woolen smell of his cape, she gives him her desperate mouth.

It is 11 A.M. and Nenette opens the blind on her side of the carriage. There is a chill in the air, but the sky to the west is bright blue and cloudless. The last leaves fall from trees in the Tuileries; the gardens are usually empty on a Wednesday morning at this hour, but today they are full of people making their way to the execution. Schmidt's finest piece of carpentry is waiting on the scaffold. Windows overlooking the square are renting for fancy prices. Many have come arrayed for a feast day.

Place de la Révolution is thick with onlookers. Tricolored bunting hangs old and soggy from yesterday's rain, but also soggy from something darker and redder than rain. The whole square smells of old blood. Local merchants are demanding that the guillotine be removed to Vincennes or Passy, anywhere but here.

—They say the nation will be happier and freer when the Queen is dead. What do you think is the likelihood of that, Joseph?

Out of habit, Fouché checks his watch, the one she inscribed *To the Master of Complications*, and the fact that it has stopped working bodes ill.

—The death of Christ was also supposed to usher in a better world, he mutters, and no one is suggesting Marie-Antoinette resembles Christ, are they?

I must get it fixed at once. In La Martanière when someone died, they would stop all the clocks in the dead man's house until he was buried.

—I want to see the execution, Joseph.

—No, we cannot, we have to get out of town fast.

—Please, it is important to me.

—Nenette, this is no time for jokes or divertissements. Robespierre's men will be looking for you even now.

—Marie-Antoinette is a friend, a part of who I was and where I come from. And she will pass right by here.

Nenette looks out over the crowd.

—But why do you need to see the actual execution? Nenette, she has crossed over, she has reached that place from where no one can bring her back. Whether you like it or not, it is too late. We have to move fast and get out to safety. He said three P.M., but our deadline is right now.

—I want to see her, says Nenette, gripping the hand rest; I owe it to her, Joseph!

—If we stay, we have no chance, no chance at all!

Fouché hates yet admires her impudence, her courage, her independence, her hard-headedness, her lack of restraint. He stares knives into her. She refuses to return his stare but scans the street to her right, where the tumbrel will come.

—For a policeman who is constantly listening to informers, I wonder if you have ever heard me, Joseph, or listened to *me*. No wonder women are smarter than men; we listen! The Queen was my close friend. You put that out of your mind; you never wanted to believe it. You wanted her to be a monster, but she was a whole chapter of my life, and I owe it to her to be there. You have no intimate friends, so you would not understand what I am saying. She had her faults, but even with her faults I loved her. Now go, Joseph. Go without me, leave me, I do not need you.

Fouché checks Mordu's watch.

—Even if the Queen does not know I am there today, *I* need to know it. I cannot run away.

—All right, you want to see the execution, we will stay in the carriage. You can bid adieu to your friend from a safe distance.

Fouché gives a new order to Mordu, the carriage stops, and Pasquier's men surround it in a protective wedge. Only Ouistiti seems excited; he stares out the window, and now and then he tugs at his chains, hops off Nenette's knees, and then back on. The city waits, fanions flying; mounted regiments wait; people in windows wait. Soldiers and ne'er-do-wells to pass the time share secrets, tell jokes. A horse rears. The crowd keeps swelling. A farm tumbrel is coming, one like any other, which creaks and bumps along. In the crowd, they jeer, hoot. Hooligans sing songs, dance the *Carmagnole,* and drink wine.

—Goodbye, Austrian dinge! Eat brioche!

—Marie-Antoinette? Where?

—There.

—That's not her! That gray-haired old crone? That can't be her!

—That's a gargoyle.

—A witch.

—A hag.

—Look at the whore, how bold and impudent she sits!

—Harlot from hell.

An old woman with stringy white hair shorn at the neck, a creature with no smile and exhausted eyes, rides alone in the first tumbrel. Marie-Antoinette stares straight ahead, looking old but dignified. She sits rigid on the wooden plank, hands tied behind her back, and makes no movement whatsoever, except for the slight swaying that the farm cart imparts to her. She goes with honor.

People rush to see the millionairess who bid them eat cake. Some view her in silence, others with a vindictive joy, a sort of madness. Later, Nenette will learn that close to the Oratoire church, a mother held up a child of the same age as the Dauphin so he could blow a kiss to the Queen. And on the square in front of Saint-Roch church a man screamed, *Dieu t'aidera, Marie!* But from the carriage where she sits, Nenette sees nothing so respectful. This long procession triggers intense drama, with everyone getting to participate in the death. One citizen throws a chamber pot of dirty water at the tumbrel. One waves goodbye. Others call her a monster, but most say nothing at all, just watch in silence.

This is your real death. Later on at the machine, it will be more like a deliverance, Marie. There everything will happen so fast, it will not have time to gather meaning. The suffering is here where the living see you and talk to you

One sans-culottes shouts *Vive la République!* Another declaims:

The Autri-Chienne goes to her end like a butcher's pig. Incredibly calm, she goes to the Scat Fold. She doesn't flinch, she looks down on us with contempt. I can't wait until your head is taken off your long scraggy neck, you insolent bitch.

But Marie-Antoinette is not a person anymore; she is a monument, and the living cannot reach her. She is a legend; that her frozen silence confirms. She rides high, and all around, elbows shove and the crowd of mere mortals pushes. Ruffians squeeze through to get a better view. Some young children ride on their fathers' shoulders.

Nenette holds up the blind, stares at a slow, sloping curve of blue where city roofs meet the sky. This is the last sky the Queen will see.

Fouché checks his fingernails and avoids gazing out. *Maybe Danton is right. Maybe this execution is a mistake, but we had no choice.*

The crone passes. The wheels go slow and crunch on the cobblestones.

Fouché does not glance up. That job is done, and he is on to the next one. Robespierre has a problem in Lyon; the second largest city in France needs disciplining, and wherever things are difficult, Fouché knows he will be sent. He files his nails. *Why do I never have time for a good manicure?* Index finger, middle finger, fourth finger. He notices that none of the usual officials are here: Fouquier-Tinville, Hébert, Le Bon, Couthon, Robespierre, they are all squeamish cowards.

Some executions proceed so vigorously that the head leaps right off the scaffold.

They must cross the entire square, cross the Seine, and ride south, and Fouché worries about how this festive crowd will slow them down when they have to make their getaway. To the right sits Liberty, an oversized plaster cast of the goddess with a bow in her right hand and her left hand resting on an orbis. She is brand new, but already cracks have appeared in her toga, and she looks tired and more frail than the statue of Louis XV that preceded her.

—Know what is unfair?

Nenette breaks their silence.

—The king rode to his execution in his gold carriage with all the honors due a monarch. Marie-Antoinette has to ride in a farm cart like a poor peasant.

An accordion begins to play, it leaps and sways. A girl sings, *Give me a heart less mangled, less torn,* and a man barks at his own shadow. Another sings a foul lampoon, listing thirty-four dukes, actors, and lackeys, including the King's brothers, with whom the Queen had debauched relations. She inflamed the erotic fantasy of the gutter, yet today the Austrian hardly looks like the most lascivious or most depraved woman in France. She looks like a tired old washerwoman.

Fouché is bored.

The plebeian curiosity for the mechanics of death sickens me. The grisly issue of whether the head continues to live after being severed, or whether the head can be sewed back on and the body brought back to life, is of no interest to me. It titillates them to hear that when the executioner held up Charlotte Corday's head and slapped her face to teach her a lesson, she actually blushed.

Two hundred and seventy days after her husband, the Queen climbs the scaffold. It is the exact same spot, with the Champs-Elysées on one side, the Tuileries gardens on the other, and the same goddess of Liberty seated; only the blade has changed to replace the old one dulled from overuse. The Queen stands, and the executioner holds her by a rope tied to her hands as if he had a dog on a leash. She is strapped down.

—She did all the harm, says one citizen, they should have executed her first and spared the king.

—They should have exchanged her against our brothers and husbands, the 5,000 French prisoners the Austrians will surely massacre when they hear about this.

Some citizens say nothing at all, but remove their hats in a sign of respect.

When the blade drops and her neck spits into the basket, the gush is like any other, but at the foot of the scaffold they rush to soak their newspapers or handkerchiefs in the royal blood, to grab a memento, a piece of her dress. The executioner holds her head up by its short white hair and lifts it for the crowd, just as he does with commoners, and now many in the crowd clap.

One citizen holds out his hand and shouts, *Five livres for a lock of her hair!* A man pays ten livres. Some dip the tips of their sabers or swords in the bloody bucket, in a sort of inverted baptismal right. A sacrifice that can be shared by all. An executioner's assistant sitting on the boards of the scaffold sells little packets of hair bound in a ribbon. Nenette sees schoolchildren elbowing each other out of the way to dip their fingers in the blood. She hears one exclaim, *How salty she tastes!* But others ignore all this and chat merrily, laugh, walk away arm-in-arm. The body reminds Nenette of a pale decapitated statue as they push it onto a cart. Other prisoners arrive in the next tumbrel and await their turn. It will not take long; the executioner prides himself on his speed; he even boasts he can dispatch twenty heads in twenty-two minutes.

—Seen enough?

Nenette does not answer. Her face is quiet, fingers knotted, a sickness fills her soul.

Fouché knocks on the carriage wall, and the coachman undoes the hand break.

As they move, Nenette stares back at the scaffold; she cannot help herself. The cobblestones around the statue of Liberty are covered in red footprints. Thousands of bloody clogs and boot-heels redden the walkways. She watches a yellow leaf roll on the ground and join the tired soggy ones in the gutter. In the distance, on the scaffold, an official reads words out loud that do not reach this far. Nenette, pensive and quiet, lets the blind drop down, and the carriage reaches the edge of the square. Fouché slips his fingers through hers.

How could Robespierre write such a sentence: I love you more than ever, and unto the death? *How dare he? The man will have my neck. When he cannot use me anymore, he will want me in the next tumbrel, receiving the next insults.*

I touch your hand, Nenette. There is no contradiction here—revolutionaries must live and also love. I too harbor a thirst for purity, for perfection, for cleanliness (Versailles courtiers had lice in their wigs); I need to keep you, Nenette.

So what now?

The Escape

The carriage now crosses a bridge over the Seine, where the sunlight sparkles. It is one of those days that almost never happens in Paris in the fall. The gray drizzle and overcast that hung over this city for weeks has gone, and a crisp fresh light glows in the air. The buildings look clean and new. The river is full of reflections, and Paris has never looked better. Flags fly, and from a distance the streets are so clean and bright you can almost imagine there is no Terror at all. Nenette is filled with sadness and nostalgia for her life, for the Queen, of course, but also for Fouché, for this city she is leaving, for everything she is losing and cannot take with her.

—Take nothing for granted; enjoy it while you have it, Nenette mutters to herself.

She leans forward and opens the picnic basket.

—Do you mind if I get drunk, Joseph?

She pulls a cold bottle of champagne from the picnic basket that she had the cook pack as they were rushing to leave.

—And please, no speeches about the evils of liquor! Consider this a medicinal cure, not a vice. Anyway, I may not get a chance later.

Fouché is not in a celebratory mood. Robespierre's police must be following, must be closing in even now. His temples throb, his heart thumps heavy and hard in his chest, and his entire torso feels as tight as a fist. He finds it hard to breathe. He does not like champagne, and if the sans-culottes get a whiff of this, they will tear the carriage apart. But Fouché does not want to appear petty, not at this hour. Her hour. You ape your betters before you butcher them, thinks Fouché.

—Funny, isn't it? This is the moment I have always wanted— you and me leaving together, Joseph. Somehow I never saw it quite like this. I saw it as a beginning, not an end. I thought everything was going to be possible for us once we finally left Paris.

She pours a glass, and as it foams up and up, right to the brim, Ouistiti reaches out, grabs the glass, and spills it onto Fouché's black cape and down his lap.

Fouché reaches over to hit the pest.

—Bad monkey, bad!

Nenette pulls his hand away.

—Forget it, it's for good luck. To us, Joseph.

—To you, Nenette.

—No, to us.

—Ma belle, I don't think I have told you my escape plan.

Nenette nods without paying much attention, and smiling she kisses him.

Her mouth tastes foreign, as if a lie has crept in. Perhaps that is the price of so much fear, thinks Fouché.

—To our future together.

It is the biggest lie of all, the one that sickens him, but it is inevitable, for one must live with hope. He closes his eyes.

Nenette pours herself another glass of champagne.

Things are spinning out of control, Nenette, and I have no time to waste or dither. This is my destiny. Right or wrong, I am ordered to execute you. I dominate everyone; I manipulate everyone, even my enemies, but I cannot escape this order. It is the dark struggle of the soul: truth versus justice, good versus evil. As a priest I know the answer is not as important as how the question is posed. And when all is said and done, I wrestle not with Robespierre but with the angel of the Lord.

—This was supposed to be a new age of reason and of logic, Joseph.

Fouché, chief garbage collector of the soul of France, professor of logic, dean of reasoning, principal, Master of Complications, nods at Nenette and kisses her hand.

—But who says logic is the highest of all human virtues, Joseph? This monkey can reason but he cannot laugh.

She takes a sip.

—Even a mouse can reason and make love, but has a mouse ever laughed?

While kissing him, she passes champagne from her mouth to his. At first, he struggles against it, gags, for he does not like the taste and is not expecting it. But it reminds him of a mother bird feeding its chick, and he likes the exotic feel of her warm mouth feeding him cold liquid.

I have nerves of steel. I can piss ice water, Nenette; you are nothing to me, a nobody, a parvenu. Why should we both die? Yet I cannot do what I must do. I am weak; I do not want to lose you. I think we can get away with this. The risk-taking and the will to do it are everything.

—I do not feel well, says Fouché suddenly.

He grabs the window ledge of the carriage and slips to the side.

—My head, he mutters.

Nenette holds him and sets him upright.

—I have drugged you.

—What do you mean?

Fouché searches for his handkerchief. Her face appears to him now, but dangerously out of focus.

—I gave you some of the belladonna.

Fouché, his red-rimmed eyes big and his mouth aslant, tries to hold on to the strap on the side of the carriage.

—When did you do this?

—In that kiss.

She says it matter-of-factly, even smiles, and shows him the vial that he got from Dr. Pressavin. It is still three-quarters full.

—Forgive me, but it was for your own good.

Fouché grabs his neck, his wrists. It feels like wooly mammoths moving inside his head.

—Nenette, what could you possibly be thinking? Are you mad?

She kisses him.

—No, calm down. I tested it on Ouistiti and gave you just enough to put you to sleep.

—Sleep?

He tries to say something more but smiles instead. *Only Nenette has ever been capable of hoodwinking me like this and taking control.*

—I love you, Joseph.

—We could both make it; we had a real chance, you and me! Now you have gone and ruined everything! He calls out *Mordu!* and tries to stand, but falls back.

—Joseph, do not let your heart run away with your head. They would have caught us. Why should we both die, for what?

Fouché tries to speak, tries to sit up, but slips back.

—Joseph, shh, shh, I am taking matters into my own hands. I have never been so certain of anything.

She places a small seat cushion under his head. Fouché breathes with difficulty, his eyes grow shiny.

—What is your game, Nenette, what are you up to?

—If I did not love you, I would have given you the whole vial and finished you off with this.

She pulls a razor out of her boot.

—But I am saving your life. This is my repayment for your saving me and my family, and because I love you.

He stares at her and whispers:

—I do not want to be paid back. I want to make a life with you.

—Yes, you were going to do something stupid, stand up to

Robespierre and lie to him, which would get you killed and accomplish nothing for me. No one lies to Number One for long, you know that. Now I am setting you free.

Again he tries to sit up but falls back on one elbow.

—Do not be ridiculous. In the provinces I rule supreme; we could have made a new life there.

—You always told me my mistake was that I fell in love with you. It seems, Joseph, you did not take your own advice.

Shaking his head and squinting at her:

—What are you doing, Nenette, come to your senses! Give me an antidote and let us forget all about this well-meaning mistake.

—Joseph, listen to me; we can't waste time. When they come and question you, say you poisoned me and give them this as proof.

Nenette takes a small pair of scissors from the picnic basket, cuts a lock of her hair, removes one of her rings, and empties the rest of the contents of the vial into an old locket around her neck.

—I may still need this.

She holds his face in her hands and speaks to him as if to a baby.

—I love you, Joseph. Do you understand that?

Looking up into her face makes him feel part of a pietà, at the heart of Christian iconography.

—Where will you go?

—I will dye my hair, dress as a farm girl, and disappear.

—Do not leave me, Nenette.

She pushes her hair out of his face and kisses him on the lips.

—We have had a good run for our money. My father the baron, who gambled and lost everything, always said you have to know when to leave the table, and the best time to leave is when you are ahead. Never doubt that I love you, and that I always will.

—It is not your style to give up, Nenette.

—Oh, I am not giving up. A year ago I was too terrified to run. Now I have seen so much death, I am quite numb to it. But you

Jacobins are not the only ones building a new world. I have our child to consider.

She looks at the chained monkey, who has been intently following the conversation.

—What are you looking at?

Fouché has fallen backward, face up to the roof of the carriage, eyes open. Nenette kneels and puts her mouth right at his ear, arms around him and whispers.

—Joseph, what cowards men are. You could have done it in this carriage. You could have slit my throat in the dark after we made love, and I would not have struggled. I would have thanked you. You could do anything to me, I told you that when you put me inside Marie-Antoinette's cell.

—I am cold, Nenette, cold all over.

—It will pass, my darling. Just promise me one thing.

She rubs his hands and blows on them.

—If they catch me, Joseph, do not let them parade my head around the streets or drag my body naked over the cobblestones. I could not stand that. Bury me in my churchyard, down at the château de Mondoubleau next to my father. You can do that for me, can't you, my little ex-Oratorian?

Fouché, sweating, tries to open his eyes wide; he reaches for the window strap, clutches her, turns red.

—Nenette, hold me!

His whole body seizes up, shakes violently.

The carriage jolts to the side, and Fouché suddenly goes limp. Nenette looks out the window and waits for the carriage to move forward again; then she checks his pulse, lifts one of his eyelids, lets it drop.

—Joseph, you were always better at organization and details than I was.

She crosses his arms, brushes back his hair, centers his collar. Thoughtful, she says slowly, breaking each word off:

—You will never know how much I felt for you, Joseph. Never. Maybe it is better that way. You would have panicked and run away if you had known it.

Nenette takes a last swig of champagne.

Now she moves like a cat, and it is obvious from her movements that her actions have been rehearsed a dozen times in her head. She puts back the small pair of silver scissors into the picnic basket. She places the lock of her hair, the ring he gave her, and the empty vial of belladonna in his handkerchief, folds it, and returns it to the breast pocket of his vest where he usually keeps his handkerchief. Then she rifles through the deep pockets of his black cape and finds what she was looking for, the love poems he has never showed her.

She tucks them away in the bosom of her dress and looks out at the street and at the military escort. She checks that the belladonna is still in the locket around her neck and looks for a crossroads where the carriage will slow down. Then she whispers:

—Joseph, you know what I was thinking when Robespierre was in our bedroom? I was thinking how absurd that he wears a wig and knee britches and uses the *vous* form. I remembered you introduced a bill in the convention to make the *tutoiement* obligatory even in official correspondence, and I was so proud of you!

Kissing her fingers, she touches them to Fouché's sweaty forehead. Then she unchains the monkey, hugs him to her chest, and unlocks the carriage door as carefully and quietly as she can. At the next crossroads, she steps out.

～

Mordu, turning, sees a glimpse of skirt and has a split second in which to decide. Without checking with Fouché, for there is no time, Mordu yells at La Grenaille, *Keep going, I will catch up!* and with that he leaps to the ground and races after Nenette.

1:30 P.M.

Le Club de Rosati

Fouché, lying on the back seat of his carriage, paralyzed, sees violent men with swords. They are all young: he is thirty-four, Danton thirty-two, Robespierre thirty-five, Saint-Just twenty-five. But now he sees an earlier age in Arras when he and Robespierre's sister Charlotte would gather wildflowers, and then they would order the best coffee and fruit that their meager savings could buy. The simple pleasures of life.

He sees Charlotte mending a pair of her brother's striped stockings. Fouché has arrived with comments on a disquisition that Robespierre plans to give at the club de Rosati that evening. He sees Robespierre, who, with froth oozing from his lips while tooth cleaning, claps him on the back. In spite of this camaraderie, Fouché is careful not to displease him by using the familiar *tu*.

Rosati's outside Arras is a social club where local gallants meet on weekends to celebrate poetry, wine, and women and to tease and entertain each other. Robespierre, defender of widows and orphans, was elected to the Rosati in June 1787, and Fouché a year later. Its fifteen members are freethinkers, but politics strains their friendship. One shoves his fist into Fouché's nose and calls him a godless liberal; in the little world of allegiances and enmities of Arras, this becomes a major incident.

That evening, the first rhymed couplets and witticisms concern the national debt. Then there is a dull speech that praises Necker, the finance minister, and then another member plays the piano between recitations of Corneille and Molière.

The two of them, Fouché and Robespierre, are tight, they are almost like family, they do things that are fun. They are accessible, ordinary men, and at Rosati's they dance the Farandole all night sometimes.

How they cheer Robespierre when he stands to speak. He is dressed in perfect pale colors, a sky-blue coat and striped knee stockings, and he stands ramrod-straight, with his hands on his lapels. His body is compact, but the ladies there, especially Mademoiselle Deshorties, seem charmed by his youthful voice, the blue of his eyes—or are they grayish? Some call their color *metallic reflections*. What is certain is that they are not brown. Robespierre does not speak about the rights of bastard children or arbitrary royal power, no, he speaks in favor of breastfeeding championed by Rousseau: If mothers breast-fed, family bonds would be tightened, mothers would be more attached to their duties, and our mother's milk would teach us our patriotic duty, thus preserving and maintaining our national wisdom.

When it comes to Fouché's turn to address the members, he speaks in favor of their campaign to raise money for the poor. Some members oppose this because they do not want to subsidize the poor to do nothing. Let them work then, says Fouché. Let them re-landscape the city gardens and clean public buildings.

It is June 18, 1788. He remembers it because the members of the club de Rosati bow their heads to commemorate the Queen's daughter Sophie, aged less than a year, who dies on that day of a putrid fever.

These are the best months of our lives, he thinks. And if the poor are hungry, let them eat the rich.

I write in this diary, but I do not know what to do with myself. I am numb. I would be much happier to have died with you on the scaffold. But the thought that your son needs me is always on my mind. He is the last and only interest left to me in France. I understand from Madame de Tourzel that your *chou d'amour* is still very handsome, but I fear the worst.

I must go to Vienna to seek repayment of the million pounds that creditors lent me to finance the flight, because that was your wish. But I have no courage for this. I know the Emperor will not honor the order to pay that you signed. He will not even let me use your own jewelry that you smuggled out through his Ambassador Mercy for this purpose. And I do not have the heart to beg. I would prefer to pay it out of my own pocket than to have to remind those cowards of how they betrayed you. The swine.

I am sick of affairs of state. I have wasted too many years thinking and talking of it, and now I do not care anymore.

At the Last Gate
Porte de Versailles

—Where is she?

—Huh?

—Have you let her go?

—What?

The Incorruptible One himself, in person, is staring into the carriage. He has one foot on the bottom step and stands in the doorway. He shoves his black eyes deep into the darkness, and only the back of his cloak remains in the sunlight.

—Are you sick, Fouché? Answer me, where is she?

Fouché's eyes take time to focus. He sits up straight. Reaches for the hand rest. Swallows. His mouth tastes of cotton, and for a man who never drinks, he swoons as if under the influence. His heart is racing, and his head feels heavy; the neck muscles are barely strong enough to keep his head upright.

—Fouché, I was led to understand you were helping an aristocrat to flee. Is that possible? Would you betray France? Speak! What is wrong with you?

—Citizen! His speech is slurred.

Robespierre examines his appearance, examines the small picnic basket, the half-empty champagne bottle, the white bread. He waits for Fouché to explain.

—Have I ever let down the Committee of Public Safety in any way, my friend?

Robespierre glances back into the street. Federal, Municipal, and Republican guards—a menagerie of uniforms surround the carriage.

—I am wasting time with nonsense that does not rise to the level of my office or my real concerns.

The Incorruptible One enters the carriage and sits down next to Fouché.

—Take me to the Chamber of Deputies immediately.

Fouché nods to the coachman, who is waiting for orders. The man folds up the steps and closes the door. The carriage turns and heads back the way they came.

—So, Fouché, what have you done with this damn look-alike?

—I followed your orders to the letter, citizen.

—But where is she?

Fouché scrambles for an answer, fetches his handkerchief to wipe his mouth, and, as he does so, the empty vial appears in the handkerchief. The Supreme Being notices it too; he lifts it and sniffs it.

—Is this the poison you administered to her?

—Yes.

—Was it effective?

Fouché's voice slips over the consonants, unable to grab the words as they slide by. He nods; then:

—Yes, it knocked her out in a few seconds.

He lifts a lock of blond hair and rolls it between his fingers.

—Her hair? Robespierre clears his throat.

—Yes, citizen, and her gold ring. I knew you would want proof.

—Where did you dispose of the body?

—I had it dismembered and buried under buckets of quick-lime so no one could trace it, but I did keep the head in case you wanted to see it.

—Excellent, excellent.

—Shall I bring you the head?

—No, I want this entire episode forgotten and put behind us as quickly as possible.

Fouché closes his hand on the little mementos. He feels them pressing into his skin, her golden ring, the empty vial; her texture is there, her smell too. It was stupid of him to say he kept Nenette's head. Robespierre can call his bluff at any time, but now it is too late to take it back. Fouché wishes he had the courage to confront Robespierre, deprive him right here and now of his life, his air of sanctimonious superiority, his so-called virtue.

Pontius Pilate did not care about the truth as much as getting difficult decisions behind him. What is truth anyway? The heart has reasons which reason cannot know, and some lies are truer than truth itself.

—How is it possible, citizen, that you would waste your valuable time tracking me down? You could have sent a factotum. Is it not preposterous to waste your day on such empty rumors?

—Yes, it is, but I have to be certain of my private police chief. Without absolute trust, we can achieve nothing.

The horses pound the pavement. The carriage harness creaks. Robespierre stares out the window, seemingly indifferent to the day. Handbills are being posted concerning the strict new maximum prices allowed: bread, milk, and meat prices. But on every street corner people are waiting on food lines.

Suddenly, Robespierre grabs Fouché's hand, the one holding the hair, ring, and vial, and pushes it out the window and shakes it free as if to rid it of evil.

—You did the right thing, forget her.

Fouché folds his handkerchief back in his pocket.

—I did what had to be done.

Neither speaks now. Horse hooves sound muted through the thick red upholstery. Fouché sits straight, his mouth pasty, his eyes and limbs heavy. Robespierre is careful not to sit too close.

—You are like me, Fouché, we both hate corruption, weakness, social parasites, we hate all that is rotten and left over from the previous society. We need to clean house from top to bottom and bring back a new social responsibility to man. Fouché, you and I have a will and an ability to do this.

Fouché has not been paying attention, but he says:

—I heard confessions for ten years; now I force them. I know what is in the soul of man is usually bad. I know that silence hides dissembling and lies.

Robespierre, a little taken aback by this comment, says only:

—Quite.

How did Nenette know what amount of belladonna to give me? She could not have measured it. Fouché clears his throat, feels his tongue, tastes a granule crunching between his teeth and he recalls her last kiss, the sly one.

He sits up, checks his pockets; the love poems he never gave her are gone.

—What is it, citizen?

—Nothing. He smiles, for after all these months they have been delivered. He is glad she has them finally, only wishes he could have presented them to her in some more intimate way.

—I would have been sad to lose you, Fouché.

—There was never any chance of your losing me, First Citizen.

—No, I see that now. But there were so many rumors. And you more than any other of my acolytes must have only one mistress—France. . . . So the Queen was dispatched at noon today?

—Yes, everything went smoothly. Thirty thousand attended.

—And the plotters?

—Danton received bribes to save her life, but it turns out he was not behind this one. It was all thought up by von Fersen, one of the Queen's lovers, the most harebrained scheme I have ever heard of, but he came close to succeeding. We have signed confessions from some of the ex-Royal Suédois men that von Fersen enlisted to help him. And deputy Tom Paine, the one who always sits next to Danton in the convention, had no small role in the plot. He may have arranged for the travel papers and was planning to take her to New York disguised as his servant. Because of Paine's notoriety, I wanted your guidance first before putting anything in my report or arresting him.

—You did well. We will vote to remove the legislative immunity of our foreign deputies, so we can execute Paine as a spy without unveiling this whole sorry tale. I do not want our enemies using this plot to show how disunited we are. But you are a model of precision and effectiveness, Fouché. I underestimate your many qualities. Keep up the good work.

—No, I am lazy, citizen. Yesterday, I spent much of the day in bed doing nothing!

—We all need more discipline, even I, but I will mention your good work at the National Convention this afternoon.

—Thank you, citizen, but I would be glad enough if you were to support my motion to proscribe the use of *vous*, so that from now on, everyone will be required to use *tu*, even in official documents.

—Yes, yes, of course.

From the Porte de Versailles, they take rue de Sèvres, turn east behind the Ecole Militaire, past the Invalides, and across the new bridge, the old Pont Louis XVI that was just completed in time to have its name changed to Pont de la Révolution.

—Fouché, you bring a special measure of brilliance to your work which is never sufficiently appreciated by those who do not know a tenth of the difficulties you face and surmount each day, each hour.

—Thank you, citizen.

This bean counter, this parvenu, wants to feed me to the slicer. He is most dangerous when he compliments you; that is when your days are numbered. It is only because he needs me to entrap Danton—and clean up Lyon—that he keeps me. Saint-Just is the only one whom Robespierre trusts fully, but Saint-Just is now in command of the army of the Rhine.

—Fouché, the other morning when you told me of Danton's treachery, I thought all is lost, we have no resources, no one can save us. Even our closest allies are traitors, slanderers, assassins, agents of foreign powers. But is it possible that in those accusations Danton is being framed by Hébertistes and enragé extremists?

—The letter I found at his old apartment, on rue des Mauvaises Paroles, is written on paper whose watermark shows Britannia in a circle surmounted by a crown. It has an authentic look about it, but it is surprising that anyone keeps documents so incriminating. It may well have been planted.

Robespierre nods and, squinting, puts on his yellow-tinted sunglasses.

—The government is not paranoid. We are sometimes wrong, but corruption is everywhere, and we cannot have deputies for sale. What else have you found on Danton? What about this rash of stock market speculations?

—Last Thursday, October 10, his good friend Delaunay made a speech in the convention against all financial institutions, but especially aimed at the East India Company. As a result of that speech, everyone now expects the company to be shut down, so share prices have plummeted. Now he, Danton, and various straw men in this conspiracy have bought up shares of the East India Company for next to nothing. Danton is drafting a Decree of Clemency that will pardon the company, push the market price of the shares back up, and result in a huge benefit to him. The risk-takers in effect take no risk; they will collect millions.

—I am, says Robespierre grimacing as if in physical pain, not surprised, but offended in the deepest part of my soul. What you say sickens me profoundly. No wonder Danton wants clemency!

Robespierre breathes on his spectacles and wipes away the condensation with his white silk handkerchief and says:

—Danton is a patriot, but he loves the good life and fame. He has made his pile of money, so he wants to stop the revolution and get off. Naturally the wealthy who are frightened of the sans-culottes see him as an ally.

—Most of the fake script is made in London, some in Coblenz, some in Holland. But I have information, citizen, that, in London, Danton visited the Comte de Puisage. The count has hired seventy-eight French workmen, including some priests, and he manufactures about 100 million livres a day.

—Fouché, Danton has made political misjudgments like many of us. But his real crime—Robespierre pulls a speck of dust from his left eye—is his blatant nature. Virtue is not what he demonstrates to his wife every night. No, the man would not know virtue if he stepped in it. Triple your surveillance of Danton.

—Yes, citizen. Two of Danton's brothers were in England recently, buying weaving machines for their silk business in Lyon, and I have uncovered that Danton went with them secretly. While there, he met with bankers of the Prince of Wales.

—So much of humanity is made up of greed, self-interest, and vice, says Robespierre, sniffing the air.

Fouché opens his handkerchief and closes it immediately, for it has traces of face powder, and Robespierre, egomaniacal little sleuth, will have smelled Nenette's perfume in the back of the carriage. The strutting cock does not mind sending friends to the scaffold, but he cannot accept a sip of champagne with a woman.

The Incorruptible One has never understood that his rigidity is not a sign of strength but the contrary. I should kill him before he kills me.

—Fouché, about the churches they say you desecrate.

—Citizen, I desecrate only the number necessary to establish the republican rule of law.

—That is not what I am hearing.

—Citizen, you do not need to listen to hearsay; I report on all my activities.

—All the same, burn less. We must protect private property. The church and even the Third Estate consider me a moderating force in the Committee of Public Safety. Fine, let them back me.

—The wheat we buy from America must be paid for in gold, citizen. So in that sense, the church gold that I confiscate and send to Paris is saving French lives.

—Yes, I understand. Later we may do away with private ownership altogether as well as the tyranny of capital and speculation in company shares, but for now we must slow down. The people need churches.

The carriage has arrived at the National Assembly.

Robespierre touches Fouché's hand. His fingers are ice-cold. Freezing. For a moment, Fouché wonders if it is a hand at all, a claw, or a prosthetic device.

The Incorruptible One wants me to go lighter on priests yet not be soft! Has he any idea what it takes in the real world to be obeyed, respected, and followed? Who does he think is in control here?

—Fouché, to my closest associates, I am giving one of these each.

He holds up a simple gold watch with a white enamel dial and a crystal cover, but what is strange about it is that it has only one hand and ten hours on its face.

—It is the first decimal Republican watch ever made.

Robespierre gives a thin smile as Fouché takes it.

Fouché silently thanks God that the convention delayed the obligation to use the new clock for one transitional year. But last week it was voted that the days would now have ten hours, each hour 100 minutes, each minute 100 seconds. (Deputy Viallon proposed dividing the day into 20 hours, but it was considered too traditional.)

—Thank you, citizen, from the bottom of my heart. Taking control of time will permanently transform how New Man will live.

—Yes, the Gregorian calendar is full of irrational and evil symbols. The time of kings and oppressors cannot serve men of liberty. It is not enough to feed citizens, we must free their imagination, give them new images, new pictures. And you, Fouché, have always understood this. You are in the vanguard of the new thinking.

Fouché nods, but for all that he still loves his old watch: the inscription on the back, the blue hands, the tip of each arrow in the shape of an apple, the simple Arabic numerals.

In the street, he sees an old handbill showing Philosophy wearing a liberty bonnet, trampling the old Gregorian calendar and reading the Great Book of Nature to find principle for the new republican calendar.

The Incorruptible One has his hand on the door, ready to exit.

—Burn fewer churches, is that understood?

—Yes, citizen.

—These days, one cannot count on anyone except one's friends. Can I count on you, Fouché? Can I rely on you to continue to be a primary pillar of the new France?

—Of course, citizen. You have my deepest esteem and sincerest affection.

He watches the Maximum One walk up the steps into the National Assembly.

Pontius Pilate and I are both officers of the state, both public figures asked to put an innocent to death. Pilate had a problem on his hands. He could see that the accused was a harmless barefoot bearded man, and there was no need or reason to kill him; Pilate just wanted to settle matters and get on with his life and his work. I am the same. I want to get on with other matters. The revolution will never find the ultimate truth; it needs to get on with the day-to-day.

After dropping off Robespierre, Fouché's carriage turns and stops at the western tip of Ile de la Cité. He sends for a coffee and orders three men to find Mordu. He waits exhausted in the back of the carriage, then sips his coffee in tiny sips as his military escort waits.

—Citizen, we cannot find Mordu anywhere.

—Keep searching the whole city, Pasquier.

Christians pray to a cross and press it to their lips. Even if no savior hangs there, they love a vile instrument of torture, so is it so unthinkable that one day free men everywhere will wear little pendants of the guillotine around their necks?

Fouché worries about Robespierre. What if the Incorruptible One changes his mind, and wakes up in a cold sweat demanding to see Nenette's head? Then what?

He glances at passersby, then sits back in the carriage and yawns. He could sleep for a week.

Jacob wrestled with the angel of the Lord in the land of Gilead. His night-long battle left him defeated, marked for life. If God is everything that exceeds me, that gets the better of me, then what are you, Nenette? We all need an absolute as raw as revolution, as potent as sex. Man will never be saved by sentimentality. My long night of lies, my search for the Queen, was a pursuit of the absolute.

The revolution does have some good attributes. For centuries France measured and weighed according to systems that varied from province to province, town to town. The *aune* was divisible by 2 or 3, the *toise* by 6 or 12, the *setier* by 2, 3, 12, or 13. An *acre* of land in Normandie could be the double or half of what an *acre* was in another province. The *muid* in Paris weighed 12 setiers for grain and salt but only 10 setiers for coal. Now the metric and decimal system has been established uniformly throughout the country and in every colony around the world, thanks to the revolution.

Waiting in his carriage, Fouché hears the sounds of the street: Vegetable sellers, newspaper boys, carpenters hammering caskets. But also he hears the sounds of complacency, of deal-making, of self-interest, and back-scratching. He feels—somewhere he cannot describe, somewhere close—whisperings, compromises, money being passed from hand to hand. The nobles will return under the guise of capitalism, he sees this clearly. Birth and rank will be replaced by gold and cash. He even sees Marie-Antoinettism making a comeback. He sees all the society ladies wearing her style of hat and her style of slippers, and shopkeepers whispering that she should not have been killed.

There is no right answer only various degrees of self-betrayal.

Fouché's escort of riders gets ready to leave for Nevers; the feed bags are stowed away, saddles girthed, tails and manes curried, bridles checked, weapons also. Pasquier reports that all is in order.

Suddenly Mordu runs up, out of breath, red-faced, hair sweaty. He ducks into the carriage, after making certain no one is following him.

—I found her, chief, I found Nenette!

—Where is she? Bring her back to me immediately.

—Chief, let me catch my breath.

—You were to protect her. Remember what I ordered? You were supposed to stay with her no matter what happened to her.

—Yes, yes, but—

—Is she safe? Mordu, be honest, did they kill her?

—No, chief, she is fine for now. She will be all right.

—Where is she? Tell me.

—She did not see me at first. She was alone, standing on the Pont Neuf staring down at the river, off in her own world, and you will never believe what I saw her do.

Pasquier reports the men are ready to ride and asks for orders.

Fouché sits staring at his hands as if he has forgotten anyone else's existence.

—Have they caught her? he says, clearing his throat.

Mordu waves Pasquier away and closes the window blind.

—Tell me everything from the beginning, Mordu. Do not be scared, I will not punish you; just tell me the truth exactly as it happened.

—I was watching her from a distance, and I saw her just as plain as day take her Ouistiti and throw him into the Seine.

—Why?

—I don't know. Maybe the monkey was too difficult to care for, or the little bastard was too easy to identify and would give her away. Maybe she didn't know why she did it, maybe out of rage and fear. Or because he reminded her of you. I did not ask her. I should have, but I didn't. There was too much going on. I mean, she loved that monkey, but who can live with such an animal? He is a menace to himself and to anyone around him, if you know what I mean.

Fouché raises his handkerchief to his nose to block the smell of a fly-buzzed cart of refuse passing and collecting garbage.

—Her reaction surprised me. Nenette screamed when Ouistiti hit the river, and she screamed again when his little body disappeared underwater. She stood there and waited for the poor monkey to resurface, but he didn't. I went up to her. I didn't know what else to do.

Fouché does not want to hear this, yet he is all ears.

—*Get away from me*, she said. So because she was crying and I wanted to gain her confidence, I pulled out all the walk-around money I had on me, and I said it was a gift from you to her.

He waits for a reaction but gets not a word from Fouché.

—She kept crying that she had killed the poor monkey. But then we saw the creature dog-paddling over to the nearest quay. She ran down to the embankment, arms outstretched, calling for her Ouistiti. I followed because I knew you would have wanted me to give her the money.

—I gave you orders to protect her, Mordu. And to make sure she was all right.

—Wait. Then she hugged Ouistiti and put a leash on him. After she had dried him off, she pulled out what looked like some notes or a bundle of letters from you and read them.

Fouché nods.

—I did not interrupt her until she had finished, folded them up, and put them back in a pocket.

I told her you had a plan to leave the country with her, and that I was driving you two to some boats moored in the harbor of Bordeaux.

—What did she say? Did she not believe you?

—She said *Joseph, Joseph,* then started to laugh and shook her head. I tried to get her to come back, but she said it was too late, that you were not thinking straight. *He is out of his mind if he thinks his plan can work,* she said.

—Fouché motions for him to continue.

After I gave her the money, she didn't say anything; she just nodded and ran off. Mordu shrugs. And I came back here to you.

—Why did you not follow her?

—She told me not to.

—Since when do you take orders from her?

—She told me, *I am running away because it is the best thing for Fouché.*

—She said that? Fouché blows his nose.

—You crying, chief?

—No, no, continue.

—Well, it was an act of love. She escaped out of love for you. You told me not to let her go, but can you see now that it is just as well?

Fouché looks at his man and nods long and hard; then he says:

—We will need a stand-in for the stand-in. Find me the body of a young woman. We will bury the double's double in Nenette's family grave.

—Why, chief?

—I told Robespierre that I had cut her body up and buried the pieces in a lime pit. But I know him; he is so suspicious that he will not relax until a secret report informs him that I buried Nenette's body in her hometown sepulcher. I may even prepare the anonymous report myself to make certain of its contents.

—Won't he order it dug up?

—I don't think so. But even if he does, the body will be headless.

Mordu steps out of the carriage and climbs up to the coachman's seat. He gives the new orders. The cavalry escort follows.

The hospice d'Humanité (ex-Hôtel-Dieu) is next door to the Conciergerie, a huge complex. First built in 660, it has walls as thick as a fortress. Followed by his men, Fouché barges in and rushes down long dark hallways, as attendants come running.

—What is it? What is going on here?

—Where are your dead?

Patients sit up in bed and cry out. Some beg for food, others howl their mental health, sob that they are perfectly sane and were placed here by vindictive relatives. Pasquier and his men hold off the nurses and personnel, while Fouché checks under every mess of bloody sheets and goes from ward to ward, from cell to cell.

In one room, the smell of burnt almonds mixes with that of opium, camphor, and belladonna. He enters the hall of melancholia, a place of deathly silence where the patients are subjected to bleedings, enemas, mustard plasters on the head, and douches of cold water. Here the victims are quieter: One patient in a nightcap whispers, *They recommended marriage as a cure, but the cure was worse than the disease.*

Fouché enters a menagerie of lunatics where madcaps are tied by chain and iron collar to the wall. The sick and the dying sleep two to a bed. These patients are used to being on public view because society ladies and dandies often pay a fee to come and gaze, so Fouché's break-in is not a surprise. New sightseers have entered the fools' tower.

A tall official arrives, with a gold medal clanging around his neck.

—I am Pinel, commissioner for the reform of care to the insane. I protest this unscheduled search.

I know you, dandy fop. You were one of those who watched us test Tobias Schmidt's first guillotine in the Bicêtre hospital last year and pronounced it an excellent machine. You are for removing patients' chains, releasing them from their cells, giving them fresh air, sunlight, and exercise. You are an ass.

Pinel hollers at the soldiers:

—I cannot have petty bureaucrats forever on my back, questioning what I do here.

—Muzzle the son of a bitch, says Fouché.

Guards grab Pinel, hold him against the wall.

—Citizen commissaire, says Pinel defiantly, read my *Medico-Philosophical Treatise on Mental Alienation;* it covers men like you.

—You want to live, Pinel?

A slap across the face gives him pause to think.

—If I had time, I would issue you a personal lesson. I would sculpt you all in red with this sword.

Fouché has no time for officials and morons; he rushes down to the mortuary. Mordu gives Pinel a parting shot: He walks up to him and draws a swift crude forefinger beneath the chin. Fear is a useful ally, and this gesture means Pinel will not sleep in his bed for the next few months but will go from house to house begging hospitality from his dwindling number of friends.

Mordu races to catch up with his boss. He finds Fouché standing before the corpse of a woman, blond and naked, which from a distance could be Nenette, except of course that it is not.

—Why do we have to do this, chief? You told Robespierre that you had dismembered her and buried her in a lime pit?

—Because the Incorruptible One suspects everyone. Even if he does believe me, his other secret police would like nothing better than to expose me. So for Nenette's sake, I must bury her look-alike.

And now everyone has died who was supposed to die: those who thought one thing, and those who thought the opposite. There were wrong turns, mistakes that could not be avoided, but in the end everyone followed their fate.

My report to Robespierre will detail everything. But with respect to Nenette, I will be economical with the truth. I will describe how one little spark, who thought nothing at all, was caught up in events and got trampled. I will not say the spark wanted to show us an exit, a way out of darkness, I will not say that for now and until the end of my days I will watch and wish for the return of that spark.

Fouché sits in the back of the carriage, seeing nothing. His eyes are open, but he takes no interest in the landscape on this trip south; he sits hunched over like a sick man and does not notice the villages they pass. He carries pain in his belly, corrosive and bilious, and in his throat the melancholy salty taste of a mortally wounded beast.

In the Loire valley, the leaves are marmalade-colored and the empty fields a dark chocolate brown. Old men are walking in the forests picking chanterelles and *trompes de la mort* mushrooms, the black ones with a characteristic deep and striated hollow stem. Families are collecting apples, berries, and quince. Chestnuts are roasting in open fireplaces.

Fouché orders a grave to be dug in the church cemetery of Mondoubleau, behind the castle that has fallen down. He does not even glance at the pale white headless body he buries. He trusts the worms and the lime to do their work loyally. He decides there must be witnesses, so he sends Mordu out to round up anyone who might have known her. Mordu returns with her brother and with the doctor who announced to the mob who had come to kill her that she had the plague. Fouché does not shake their hands or speak to them.

He notices a boy with sores on his lips and snot at one nostril peering into the carriage at him and holding his hand out. The boy must have climbed up on the top step, but Fouché is weary and does not open the window.

—A piece of bread please, citizen, the boy mouths.

One of Pasquier's men walks over, picks the boy up kicking and screaming, and carries him away. His mother scolds him:

—Don't you see that official has important matters on his mind, and you are disturbing public order?

Fouché removes a baguette from the picnic basket and opens the door.

The barefoot boy runs between two soldiers, snatches the bread, and eats it in big chunks standing at the side of the carriage, looking up at Fouché, who waves the soldiers away. The boy eats ravenously, covering his dirty torn sweater with bread crumbs. He stares at Fouché's sword, tricolored sash, bicorne and cockade and suddenly says:

—I want to be just like you, citizen.

—Why?

The boy keeps eating:

—I want to fight for liberty, equality, and fraternity.

His mother calls to him.

—Get away from there; you disturb the good citizen.

—Can I shine your boots?

—You want to?

—Yes, it would be an honor.

The boy bends at the door of the carriage and uses his hands and shirttail to buff the black leather. Fouché can smell the boy's greasy matted black hair.

—Chief, I could be your house-servant.

—Yes, says Fouché, gazing at the boy's soft hands on his boots, and not listening to him.

—I wouldn't take up much room, I wouldn't make any demands.

—Boy do you know that we have gotten rid of God's representative on earth, and of his wife. What will survive now is justice, liberty, humanity. It will be the end of tyranny, the end of slavery, the end of prostitution, the end of night. This is the dawn of harmony and of the sublime.

—Yeah, yeah!

The boy spits on the boots and laughs; they are so shiny he can see his face in them! After a silence he asks:

—And so, what will happen now?

—Nothing, says Fouché, nothing at all will happen. Just more of the same.

—I want to come with you.

The boy looks up with an expectant smile.

—Can I ride along as your servant? Please, please?

—No. Go back to your mother.

Fouché hands him a coin and shuts the door of the carriage.

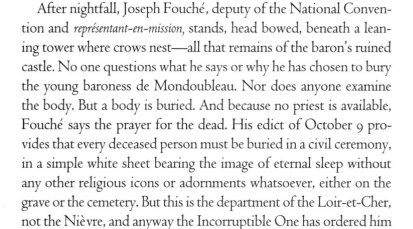

After nightfall, Joseph Fouché, deputy of the National Convention and *représentant-en-mission*, stands, head bowed, beneath a leaning tower where crows nest—all that remains of the baron's ruined castle. No one questions what he says or why he has chosen to bury the young baroness de Mondoubleau. Nor does anyone examine the body. But a body is buried. And because no priest is available, Fouché says the prayer for the dead. His edict of October 9 provides that every deceased person must be buried in a civil ceremony, in a simple white sheet bearing the image of eternal sleep without any other religious icons or adornments whatsoever, either on the grave or the cemetery. But this is the department of the Loir-et-Cher, not the Nièvre, and anyway the Incorruptible One has ordered him to be more lenient with the church and church property. So on the wooden cross he has Mordu inscribe:

Here lies Antoinette,
Baronne de Mondoubleau,
may she rest in peace.

The handful of friends and family of Nenette who have gathered around Fouché stay well away from him and do not dare speak to him. Everyone knows to steer clear, for, in the provinces, Proconsul Fouché is all-powerful. A god, of sorts.

And now for me begins the long and difficult part. Living without seeing you or talking to you. Nenette, I think you are the only person who understood me. I look around me lost in thought, I take small notes, and I forget what I am doing here standing bareheaded in the torchlight on this October night. I am lame, I am done-in.

You still fill my world, and when I escape into my memory I find you there waiting as if nothing at all has changed between us. It is the first time we meet (January 1774), and we are both nineteen years old, at the peak of our physical health. The world is our private garden, and we have no inkling how vulnerable is the whole edifice of our lives.

The masked ball at the Paris Opéra is lit by hundreds of candles and attended by everyone of note. You are wearing a gray velvet mask under the hood of a loose-fitting silk domino, not unlike a monk's cowl. And your arrival sends a stir through the hall for, although incognito, you are escorted by security agents who make little effort to hide their identity. I pretend not to recognize you. And again we talk endlessly about all the things we have done, about what others said and what we said, except that now all the events of our eighteen years together are thrown together. You tell me I am elegant and impeccable, that my eyes are indescribably blue and sparkling, that I am tall and slender with an easy manner. I tell you I have never been so charmed by any soul on earth, and may I see you again.

Dandies and courtesans, bishops and piquet players, sweating beneath pomade and white-face, all want to be who they are not. You want to be a shepherdess and every young courtier wants to be your dance partner. The loveless crave love. The objects of love feign indifference. The King is chatting with the royal locksmith.

A minuet starts. I extend my hand for a one step, three steps, *demi-coupé échappé,* then three more steps. I know you love to surprise foreign visitors, who are the least likely to recognize you, so I feign not to recognize your accent and your throaty laugh. We speak all evening, until you reveal your identity, and then everyone rushes to your side and I lose you.

To avoid the relentless social whirl, the next day we retreat to a manicured lawn at the Petit Trianon, where our horses are tied up, and the sunshine is bright. There is no revolution, no guillotine, no war, no scurrilous libels, no pornographic attacks on your honor, no hunger, no death, no imprisonment; there is only the two of us and the buzzing of industrious happy bees so laden with pollen they have trouble flying.

Sadness tinged with despair has become a way of life for me, and I am really at home only in my memory. But your enthusiasm, affection, overflow of delicacy, solicitude, and tenderness sustain me and give me courage to go on.

The five Italian words on my signet ring, that I once gave you, continue to blaze in my heart and never diminish:

Tutto a te me guida.

Epilogue

For those who take umbrage at perceived flights of fancy on my part and want to know what is real and what is invented, here are a few details for your files.

The Escape Attempt: No evidence has survived that there was any royal escape attempt the night before the trial of Marie Antoinette or that Fouché ever had responsibility for the Queen's safety. Indeed, history places Fouché not in Paris during these fateful days but in the Nièvre. Although little is known about his role as policeman for Robespierre, it *is* known that Robespierre relied heavily on a personal secret police and that Fouché, a close friend and ally, often visited his home and carried out difficult jobs for him that others could not handle.

Joseph Fouché: After the Queen's execution, Robespierre sent Fouché to Lyon on October 30, 1793, to punish so-called Federalists in that city who had rebelled against the authority of Paris. There, Fouché quickly proved his effectiveness: Since the guillotine was too slow, inhabitants were tied up in batches of a hundred and clubbed, bayoneted, or shot at point-blank range by cannon—in total, about 1,900 people. This earned him the sobriquet of *Le Mitrailleur de Lyon*, which would stay with him for the rest of his days.

Fouché also paid the unemployed to tear down the houses of the leaders of the federalist insurrection and concentrated his venom on church property. His atrocities were so extreme that even the local Jacobin Club complained to headquarters, and he was recalled in April in disgrace by the National Convention.

At first Robespierre protected him from some of the worst of the accusations, but even as Fouché was begging Robespierre for support and swearing undying loyalty, he was busy trying to build a coalition against him. By playing rival factions against each other, Fouché managed to get himself elected on June 25, 1794 (a compromise candidate), as president of Robespierre's Jacobin Club, the sole political party allowed in France at the time.

Robespierre responded on July 14, 1794, in a speech to the club in which he said, *Fouché is an impostor, vile and detestable. His hands are full of blood. Fouché is the head of the conspiracy which we Jacobins must eliminate.* He then had Fouché impeached as president and expelled from the Jacobin Club. Diary notes of Robespierre called for his execution. In theory, Fouché was finished, but he fought back by going underground.

Disguising himself to avoid arrest, Fouché now visited his fellow deputies at night and did his best to inflame their fears, telling them, *You are on Robespierre's next list; you are in tomorrow's batch of victims.* On July 26, sensing that Robespierre was about to call for a huge purge of his enemies, Fouché told his fellow conspirators, *Tomorrow we must strike!*

After Robespierre's death, Fouché fell on extremely hard times. Most of his allies were executed, and he himself was imprisoned in 1795. But by playing up his differences with Robespierre, he managed to avoid execution and was let out in the general amnesty of 1796. Poverty-stricken and with children to feed, Fouché took up pig farming in Paris. By betraying his friends and ferreting out secret plots, he made himself useful to Paul Barras, one of the three leaders of the government, and from 1797 to 1799 he became France's Deputy Minister of Police and then Minister. Professing great loyalty to the Directoire government and in charge of preventing a possible plot by General Napoleon, he also secretly aided Napoleon's coup d'état.

Fouché served as Napoleon's Minister of Police twice, from 1799 to 1802 and from 1804 to 1810. Napoleon made him a count in 1804, and then Duc d'Otrante in 1809, but dismissed him as disloyal and traitorous for conspiring with his enemies. During the one hundred days of 1815, Napoleon turned to him again and made him his Minister of the Interior. Shortly before the battle of Waterloo, Napoleon told him, *You sold yourself to the enemy. I should execute you; others will take care of this act of justice. In the meantime I will prove that you do not weigh even one hair in the balance of my destiny.*

After Waterloo, the French Chamber of Deputies named a provisional government made up of five members, including Fouché. On June 23, 1815, Fouché attained his lifelong ambition when the provisional government elected him its president. Napoleon demanded to stay on in Paris at the head of the army, but Fouché ordered him out and sent General Becker to escort him to a boat for America. Later Fouché claimed, with some justification, that he saved Paris from a disastrous battle with the invaders.

On July 3, Paris capitulated and the foreign invaders entered on July 6. Fouché thus lasted thirteen days as head of France, the position he had always wanted so badly.

In exile, Napoleon told his secretary, *If I had only hanged two men, Talleyrand and Fouché, I would still be on the throne today.*

Louis XVIII named Fouché his Minister of Police. In August 1815, Fouché remarried, this time the twenty-one-year-old and quite beautiful Alphonsine-Gabrielle de Castellane, daughter of an impoverished aristocratic family. He still had national ambitions, and her name and royalist connections helped him considerably. Yet in spite of his manifest abilities for survival, he could not circumvent the law of 1816, which banished all those who had voted for the King's death. For a short while, he was named ambassador to the Principality of Dresden, but being a regicide he was not allowed to return to France.

So ended the career of France's top police chief. Fouché served at least seven different French governments, collecting information both to protect them and topple them. His lasting contribution to France, *Les Renseignements Généraux*, is an institution that continues to this day, relied upon by governments of all political tendencies. What Fouché devised is simple: Every workday in every prefecture, the top appointed national officials of France still receive a confidential dossier on their desk, containing information prepared by the secret service on disparate segments of society, professions and individuals.

From Dresden, Fouché moved to Prague in 1816. He became an Austrian citizen in 1818 and lived out his exile in Trieste. Though an atheist, he had assented to the religious education of his children and, suffering from pleurisy, he received the last rites of the Holy Roman Catholic Church on Christmas day, 1820. His last words, spoken to his wife, were, *Now you can return to France.* He died at 5 A.M. on December 26, aged sixty-one, with a fortune estimated at 14 million francs. He was so bent over by arthritis that they buried him in a sitting position. His remains were interred in the Cathedral of Trieste, but in 1875 his family moved his bones to the cemetery du Père-Lachaise in Paris, where they now rest.

His posthumous memoirs, published in 1824, are a web of self-justification and half-truths. For instance, he claims that the outbreak of the French revolution found him teaching in Nantes, but in fact in 1789 he was still teaching in Arras and a close friend of the Robespierres there, a fact that he was eager not to advertise.

Nenette: Nenette is a fictional character, not mentioned in any history book, but her struggle for survival was lived by many aristocrats who were unable to escape France. History is not just made by the ten or twelve people whose names we know but by thousands of tiny characters whose names we don't know, and I would argue that the fictional Nenette is just as real as the historical Fouché.

Mordu, the Duchess of Tours, Hugo Von Lindahl, Dr. Pressavin: These are fictional characters, stand-ins for the thousands whom the sieve of history did not keep track of.

Jeanne Coiqueaud Fouché: Joseph Fouché's first wife had seven children by him, three of whom died as infants. She followed him everywhere, seems to have been happy as a house mother, and several times begged Napoleon to save her husband's life. She died on October 9, 1812. Of their four surviving children, the two oldest, Joseph-Liberté and Armand, died without progeny. Their only daughter, Josephine, married the Count de Thermes. The third son, Athanase d'Otrardi, was named chamberlain to King Oskar I of Sweden, and his descendants still live in Sweden today.

Nièvre Fouché: When Joseph's beloved eldest child, Nièvre, was dying of consumption in July of 1794, he was so terrified of being arrested and executed that he did not dare visit her in daytime. Yet, despairing, Fouché carried her in his arms to the hospital. In Paris, four days before Robespierre's death, he was seen walking behind the hearse bearing her body, his red-rimmed eyes half closed.

Robespierre: On July 26, 1794, Robespierre told the National Assembly that he would call for the arrest and trial of Fouché and other extremists, but on July 27, he and his supporters were heckled by the deputies, prevented from speaking, arrested, and marched off to prison. Liberated an hour later by troops loyal to him,

Robespierre took shelter in the Paris city hall. By nightfall, troops of the National Convention stormed the building, and in the process Robespierre was shot in the jaw.

Unable to speak, he could not defend himself, and he spent the last night of his life stretched out on the oval table in the same office of the Committee of Public Safety over which he had presided for almost two years, and which Marie-Antoinette had used before him. Robespierre lay there fully dressed, with newspaper pressed to his jaw to stanch the bleeding. On July 28, the procession bearing him to the scaffold stopped in front of the Duplay house at 398 rue Saint-Honoré, and there was public dancing around the tumbrel while long brooms dipped in oxblood were used to splatter the front walls of his office. At the scaffold, the executioner ripped off the bandage from Robespierre's jaw, and he was guillotined on July 28 without a trial, along with twenty-seven followers, including his brother Augustin, Saint-Just, and Couthon.

After his death, most of his old allies reviled him as a monster responsible for the worst excesses of the Terror. Fouché was one of the very few who did not attack Robespierre's policies. Yet the only ones who spoke out in Robespierre's defense were some of his victims. For instance, Aimée de Coigny, Duchess of Fleury, a spy for the British Secret Services whom Robespierre sent to prison and almost executed, said that

> if I am not so bitter about his memory it is because it seems to me that people heap on his name all the horrors committed by those who preceded, surrounded, betrayed, and killed him. . . . In the memory of men, the defeated always occupy a bad position. At least I gladly give Monsieur de Robespierre the beautiful name of Incorruptible One.

History has not been kind to Robespierre; there are only two statues to him in all of France. In his hometown, a white stone bust done in 1929 is exposed in a small ground-floor room of the city hall of Arras. The traditional red light district of Saint-Denis, north of Paris, also erected a small statue of him in a square close to the cathedral where all the kings of France were buried. In the wake of the student uprisings of 1968, a lycée in Arras was renamed after him. A metro station on the eastern outskirts of Paris also bears his name.

Attempts by certain historians, such as Olivier Blanc, to show that Robespierre was hostile to many of the excesses of the Terror and a force of moderation against extremists such as Fouché, have gone largely unheeded by the general public.

Marie-Antoinette: *The surgical removal of this queenly excrescence from the body of the Nation,* as Hébert called her execution, was almost not noticed in the wave of bloodletting that swept Paris during the Terror, but since then it has become the most famous of all the executions, eclipsing by far that of those who condemned her.

In the nineteenth century, Marie-Antoinette was depicted in books, paintings, and statues as a saintly martyr, a good mother, and an ever-loyal and loving queen. Her last prison cell, the one described in this story, was unfortunately turned into a gaudy ornate chapel to her memory. However, the floor plan of the Conciergerie had by then changed, and today one can still visit where one half of the original cell stood.

In the twentieth century, Marie-Antoinette's star continued to soar, in spite of the fact that the crime of treason has been proved, thanks to documents found in the Austrian national archives which were not available to the court that convicted her.

At the bicentennial of the revolution in 1989, a popular play was staged in Paris titled *Marie-Antoinette,* at which every member of the audience was asked to vote on her fate via remote-control switches, and every night they voted overwhelmingly for her acquittal and for the condemnation of her accusers. In 1993, an accurate feature-length movie of her trial was distributed. Fascination with the Queen is international. In 1997, all the memorabilia concerning her at the Musée Carnavalet, the Louvre, and Versailles were shipped to Japan for a Marie-Antoinette retrospective in Tokyo.

Louis XVII: Inside the Temple prison, the execution of the Queen did not alter the fate of her eight-year-old son. The Dauphin continued to be cared for by his tutor, Antoine Simon. But on January 19, 1794, after petitioning the Commune of Paris, Simon turned the boy over to prison guards, who certified he was in good health. The boy was then locked in isolation, with no light and no air, seen only by the guard who slipped his food through a small opening in the door every day. Six months later, on July 28, the day of Robespierre's death, his cell was opened and he was found covered in vermin and lying on a pile of human waste.

The boy never spoke after that, and in spite of a doctor's being appointed to care for him, his health deteriorated. In March of 1795 his knees and wrists were found to be swollen with tumors. On May 6, the head surgeon of the Grand Hospice of Humanity found his condition so alarming that he had him moved to a more airy room and visited him every day for three weeks. Still, the boy's disease only worsened. His doctor died suddenly on June 1, 1795, and the Dauphin a week later on June 8, having never once been allowed to see his sister.

The Queen's only surviving child, Marie-Thérèse-Charlotte, or Madame Royale, as she was called, was allowed to go to Vienna to live with her relatives, the imperial family of Austria, in 1795. Madame Royale lived a sad life in exile in Germany and England and died in Italy in 1851.

Rosalie Lamorlière: Even before Marie-Antoinette's execution, the prison servant who helped her in her final hours had become a revered go-between, carrying messages to and from the Queen.

After the execution, it was she who passed along to the prisoners such relics as a black woolen shoe that Marie-Antoinette had worn in prison, as well as a small piece of cambric preserved from one of her dresses. Imprisoned aristocrats and priests in the Conciergerie covered both objects in reverent kisses.

Rosalie survived the revolution, and Madame Royale gave her a pension of 200 francs for services rendered and got her admitted to the Hospice for Incurables. She finished her days basking in the aura of martyred sainthood that surrounded Marie-Antoinette. All those who came to call upon her when she was in her sixties found her still beautiful and imposing, with a noble bearing, as if she had somehow inherited the Queen's mantle.

In 1837, when she was almost seventy, illiterate Rosalie dictated a short account of the last days of Marie-Antoinette to the Abbot Laffont d'Aussone. There she describes the red lacquered hand mirror she bought on the quays for 25 sous, which she lent the Queen.

Concierge Bault: In 1817, the wife of Concierge Bault also wrote a memoir. This was part of the cottage industry that grew up under the last Bourbon kings romanticizing the Queen and explained what the Baults had done to help the Queen in prison, but Madame Bault did not gain any of the positive attention that Rosalie captured, and Madame Royale refused to meet with her or grant her any favors.

Axel Von Fersen: Fersen's private diary indicates that he was in Brussels all during the events of this story; yet if he were on a secret mission in Paris, he might have reason to falsify his own secret records. On October 16, the day of her death, he wrote:

> Though I was prepared for this, and ever since her removal to the Conciergerie have expected it, still the certainty overcame me; I had no strength to feel anything.

Love and Terror

On October 21, he wrote:

> I can think only of my loss. . . . It is horrible. Monsters of hell!—No, without vengeance my heart can never be content.

Soon after, von Fersen lost his beloved father, mother, sister, and best friend, but he stayed on in Brussels until he learned of the Dauphin's death. Then he wrote in his diary:

> This event affected me deeply because it was the only and the last interest I had left in France. Now I have nothing left there, and everything I was attached to is gone. . . . I do not care very much for madame (Madame Royale, the Dauphin's sister).

Still when he visited her in Vienna in 1796, his eyes filled with tears and he almost fainted, but not once did they exchange words.

In 1801, Von Ferson was made Grand Marshal of Sweden and, in 1802, Lieutenant general. He never married, never had children, and spent the rest of his life blaming himself for not having done more to save his beloved Marie-Antoinette. He became fixated on this and every year marked in his diary the anniversary of her death and of the failed Varennes escape attempt, blaming himself for both.

In the popular discontent that swept Sweden in 1810, he was falsely accused of murdering the Swedish crown prince. Warned not to go to the funeral because supporters of the dead prince had vowed his death, von Fersen decided that, being a Marshal of the Realm, he had to attend. As soon as his carriage got out in the street, the old man was confronted by a mob and pulled from his carriage. He sought refuge in a nearby house. Officials came to give him protection and offered to lead him to the city hall, but as soon as he appeared at the doorstep he was hit by umbrellas and canes and his hair was pulled out. Von Fersen did not beg for mercy and did not fight back. As he lay bleeding in the gutter and half conscious, a sailor leapt upon his chest and killed him. He died on June 20, 1810, exactly nineteen years after the unsuccessful flight to Varennes that he had planned, paid for, and led. Thus in death he finally joined his beloved Marie-Antoinette.

Thomas Paine: There is no evidence that Paine tried to save the Queen but much evidence that he tried to save the King. Paine lingered in the Luxembourg Prison for ten months. The proroyalist U.S. ambassador to France, Gouverneur Morris, hated Paine not only because of his radical politics but because years earlier Paine had attacked Morris for his role in a notorious embezzlement scheme. So instead of trying to get Paine released from prison, which would have been relatively easy for him to do, as the United States was then one of France's few allies, Morris told the French authorities he was an English subject (he lied about this to George Washington).

Paine became so ill and delirious, with a high fever and a bleeding stomach ailment, that during the day the door to his cell was left wide open, flat against the prison wall. He avoided the guillotine only because the chalk mark that sealed his fate was made on the open door, and at night the door was closed so that the chalk mark faced into the cell and the executioner did not see it in the morning.

In prison, Paine wrote part two of *The Age of Reason.* On November 4, 1794, he recovered his freedom with the help of James Monroe, the new U.S. ambassador to France, and completed his term of office as a French National Deputy. But he never recovered his full health and never forgave George Washington, who he thought was responsible for letting him languish so long in prison.

Paine returned to America in 1802 and died in 1809, poverty-stricken and abandoned by many of his friends, at the age of seventy-two. He died in Manhattan but was buried in New Rochelle, where he had lived for many years.

Joel Barlow: Barlow was named U.S. ambassador to France in 1811 and tried to mediate a peace among all the warring nations of Europe. In this effort, he went all the way to Moscow to talk to Napoleon but was caught up in the precipitous French winter retreat. He died in 1812 of pneumonia and frostbite in Poland, near Cracow.

Danton: Danton was tried by the same revolutionary court that tried Marie-Antoinette. On the scaffold on March 27, 1794, he said to the executioner, *Do not forget to show my head to the people, it is worth seeing,* a remark all French schoolchildren still memorize today.

Fouquier-Tinville: This public accuser signed the death warrants of Marie-Antoinette, Hébert, Danton, and Robespierre and said, *Things will never go well as long as we don't guillotine a hundred a day.* But when he learned that he would suffer the same fate, he wrote a lachrymose letter to his family in which he proclaimed his innocence and argued that he had only been following orders.

Baron de Batz: In spite of his many attempts to save the royal family and the use of his fortune to bribe delegates to the National Convention, de Batz was never caught. On April 22, 1794, the Committee of General Security ordered Fouquier-Tinville to spare no effort to catch Batz. In May of 1794, the Committee of Public Safety issued similar orders and sent spies into the prisons to speak to so-called sheep and uncover his whereabouts; all they learned is that he had once hidden in a castle near Le Havre.

Tobias Schmidt: The guillotine maker died of alcoholism, after spending most of his profits on his young mistress.

Charlotte Robespierre: In her posthumous memoir, a hymn of praise to her older brother, Charlotte describes how she lived through his downfall:

> The next day, the tenth of Thermidor, I run into the streets, my head full of anxiety, my heart full of despair. I look for my brothers. I learn that they have been taken to the Conciergerie. I run there, ask to see them, plead with folded hands, get down on my knees in front of the soldiers. They push me away, laugh at my tears, insult me, strike me. Several people moved by pity drag me away. . . . When I came to I was in prison.

Charlotte remained a fervent republican all her life, but Fouché interceded to get her a pension, from Napoleon and thereafter from Louis XVIII. She never married and died in 1834 at the age of seventy-four. Like other female survivors of the Terror, she had the last word, thanks to her memoirs.

The guillotine: During the Terror, the daily regularity of the guillotine began to undermine its effect, and the often-repeated spectacle lost much of its power to shock, but only very slowly was it gotten rid of.

In 1832, the public procession to the guillotine was made as short as possible. In 1851, it was decided that the scaffold was to be set up directly at the gates of the prison. In 1872, the scaffold was done away with entirely and the guillotine was placed on the ground, where only the front row of spectators could see it. In 1899, a campaign was begun in favor of all executions taking place inside the prison walls, to avoid the unwholesome curiosity of the spectators. In 1939, the Ministry of Justice finally decided to exclude the public entirely from executions. But the guillotine continued to be used until 1981, when a law passed on October 10 of that year finally got rid of the death penalty in France.

One of the few guillotines still remaining from the time of the revolution is on display at the Musée Carnavalet in Paris, and one original blade can be seen at the Musée de la Conciergerie.

Veracity: I approached this novel with much trepidation. The execution of Marie-Antoinette is still an emotionally charged subject in France, and the French know their history well. But as my research progressed, I found there was precious little evidence that would negate the possibility of the foregoing story actually happening, so I took the risk with all due respect. Fiction being the dream of fact, my initial fears have now been replaced by a quiet feeling that something like this possibly did happen.

Not all of history is what is written, and one cannot believe everything that one reads. History is a qualitative filter, and events recorded for posterity are a pitiful fraction of the ones that actually take place. When the filter of history sifts out significant events along with more trivial ones, it is up to the novelist to go scraping the bottom of the sieve.

Paris and Stockholm, 1998

Acknowledgments

Nobody who helped me with this novel is responsible for any possible failings, errors, or omissions.

Yet I want to thank the following:

My brother James gave me his early version of this story, and provided immeasurable support and advice whenever I got stuck or despaired of this book.

Jean-Pierre Juplet, Archivist of the Museum of Arras, and a scholar in his own right, gave me a most informative private tour of Robespierre's native city and shared with me his deep knowledge of the Robespierre family history.

Gilles Grandjean, the Directeur d'Exploitation of the Restaurant Le Procope, himself passionately interested in this period, provided a wealth of information about the history of the Procope and its patrons.

The closest living family relatives of Axel von Fersen, Hans and Fabian Edelstam, showed me their collection of Fersen's private possessions and memorabilia in Stockholm. Also, Herman Lindqvist, a Swedish author and specialist on Marie-Antoinette, confirmed the view that Fersen could well have been the Dauphin's father.

Emmanuel Breguet allowed me to leaf through the original documents for the sale and repair of the Breguet watch owned by the Queen (etched with the initials AF), for Fouché's Breguet watch number 434 which he wore all through the revolution, as well as for the repair of Thomas Paine's Stevens watch.

Catherine Rolland, Directeur de la Communication Interne for the City of Lyon, gave me access to unpublished research papers on Fouché located in the city hall archives of Lyon.

But above all, I want to thank my editor, Joan Bingham, for her deep wisdom and constant support on this project, as well as my agent, Rosalie Siegel, for her unceasing devotion, and my first readers, the poet Christopher Storey and the filmmaker Carol Polakoff.

And finally, I want to sing the praise of my beloved Cilla, Jake, and Jeremy for putting up with me for the past three years.

⌐

Stockholm, March 5, 1998